Readers love
ZAHRA OWENS

Cleary Palit

"In only 72 pages, Owens had me completely pulling for this couple to make it."

—Prism Book Alliance

"…a comforting friends to lovers tale."

—Joyfully Jay

Moon and Stars

"A nicely written story with great characters… "

—Love Bytes

"I believe Zahra Owens has hit this one out of the park and I can't wait to see what happens next."

—The Novel Approach

"The story is well written with a plot that flows smoothly… you'll find a relationship driven tale with lots of people, and plenty of love, pain, fear, uncertainty and hope for the future. Enjoy."

—Literary Nymphs Reviews

By ZAHRA OWENS

Balance
Charity Starts at Home
Cleary Palit
Diplomacy
Façade
Fine Line
For As Long As We Both Shall Live
Grand Adventures (Dreamspinner Anthology)
The Hand-me-down
Happiness for Beginners
I Can See Right Through You
With Stuart Wakefield: Isali Dreams
Postman Always Rings Thrice
Riding Double (Dreamspinner Anthology)
Santa's Littlest Helper
A Thousand Goodbyes
You Can't Choose Your Family • You Can Choose Your Friends

CLOUDS AND RAIN STORIES
Clouds and Rain
Earth and Sky
Floods and Drought
Moon and Stars

Published by DREAMSPINNER PRESS
http://www.dreamspinnerpress.com

CONFLICT
OF
INTEREST

ZAHRA OWENS

DREAMSPINNER
PRESS

Published by
DREAMSPINNER PRESS

5032 Capital Circle SW, Suite 2, PMB# 279, Tallahassee, FL 32305-7886 USA
http://www.dreamspinnerpress.com/

Conflict of Interest
© 2015 Zahra Owens.

Cover Art
© 2015 Anne Cain.
annecain.art@gmail.com
Cover content is for illustrative purposes only and any person depicted on the cover is a model.

ISBN: 978-1-63216-915-0
Digital ISBN: 978-1-63216-916-7
Library of Congress Control Number: 2014959931
First Edition April 2015

Printed in the United States of America
∞
This paper meets the requirements of
ANSI/NISO Z39.48-1992 (Permanence of Paper).

Acknowledgments

I'd like to thank Clare London and Sue Brown for helping me make several characters born and bred in London actually sound like they belong there (and one Northern character too). I wouldn't have been able to do it without them. Any remaining mistakes are my own.

Chapter One

TOMMY

THE SUSPECT was in custody. Tommy just needed confirmation of what they could charge him with. Stevie was doing the paperwork, which she hated almost as much as Tommy did. To compensate, she'd be running it by their detective inspector, something they both liked to do because it felt a little like showing off, and their chief was good with compliments whenever they wrapped a case up well. Tommy, however, gladly let Stevie take the bouquet if it meant he could chase down the Crown Prosecutor for input. Especially if the CP he had to chase was Finn DeHavilland. It was always a plus if he could go to the Old Bailey and see the man in his own habitat.

Senior Crown Prosecutor Finn DeHavilland looked like a million quid in his robes and wig. In fact Tommy felt he was the only one who could really make the old-fashioned sheepskin rug work. Of course it wasn't just any old wig. Finn had invested in a smart one, and that showed as well, but Tommy liked going to court for more than that. Even if the case Finn was pleading wasn't one Tommy had worked on, even if Tommy didn't need Finn for advice on what to charge a suspect with, Tommy still liked going there after he'd finished work, just to listen to him and maybe steal a look as well.

Tommy had a thing for Finn in robes. Wearing them made him stand up even straighter. They made him look regal and important. They made people take notice of him. Tommy loved the way Finn's voice took on a commanding tone inside the courtroom. Finn had limited room to maneuver, could do no more than sit behind his bench and stand up when it was his turn to speak, and the robes hid most of the physique Tommy had seen Finn possessed whenever he wore ordinary clothes, but he still liked Finn all dressed up for court. Tonight the cherry on the cake was that he actually needed to talk to Finn, so after the trial day was over, he waited for him outside the robing rooms.

Tommy tried to look casual, hands in his pockets and leaning against one of the marble columns as Finn walked out, wig safely tucked away in his locker and his usually pristine starched collar loose. Tommy knew the case wasn't over yet, so Finn was still all business and serious looks.

"Evenin'."

"Tommy," Finn greeted him, his voice lilting slightly, making Tommy's hopes rise that Finn was actually happy to see him. The smile, always absent in court, was present now, and even if Finn had never given any indication of being interested in Tommy—or even that he liked men in general—Tommy would do somersaults to see that smile directed at him. Not that he would ever admit that to anyone other than himself.

"What can I do you for?"

Tommy smiled back, throwing him a questioning look while he digested the innuendo, but when no reaction came, he realized Finn had simply asked an innocent opening question.

"Advice," Tommy answered.

"Tell me about the case."

Tommy tried not to be disappointed. It wasn't a complicated case, but with any luck he'd get to spend a little time alone with Finn. "Can I follow you to your offices?"

Finn smiled "By all means."

FINN

HE WAS tired. The case he was pleading was yet another one dealing with child abuse, and with every one of these it was becoming harder to stay unaffected. He couldn't afford to let his emotions shine through. Court cases were won on facts, and although prosecutors liked to play with a jury's feelings, the prosecutor himself had to remain stoic. It was the only way he could get through these, or any heartbreaking case for that matter.

Tommy coming by this evening was a godsend. Tommy wasn't part of the Child Abuse Investigation Command, so it was unlikely he'd come to talk to him about yet another youngster in danger. He worked Serious Crimes, which covered anything from common assault to murder, but the occasional sideline into abuse cases meant that sometimes Tommy and his partner were the lead investigators on some of Finn's cases. More often than not the advice Tommy needed was for a case that would never end up on Finn's desk, but he didn't mind. Finn did, however, enjoy sharing a beer with the sergeant, talking about something completely unrelated to his current case, and bouncing ideas around. Tommy was a lot smarter than he gave himself credit for, and Finn enjoyed their occasional exchanges, even if they were unlikely to venture much beyond the purely professional.

Inside his office at the CPS, Finn took his robe off and put it on a hanger in his cupboard. "Beer?" he asked Tommy as he bent down to the small fridge under his desk. Besides a few beers he'd bought specifically because he knew Tommy liked them, there was only Diet Coke, courtesy of his right-hand man, Armen. He opened one bottle and handed it to Tommy, then took one for himself.

"Cheers," he said, saluting Tommy with his bottle. "So tell me about this case of yours."

"Pub brawl," Tommy simply said, taking a sip.

Sometimes Finn hated Tommy's economy with words when it came to work. On the few occasions they ended up at the pub on a Friday night, Tommy would be the entertainment. He never stopped talking, and Finn, usually not the biggest fan of men who enjoyed being the center of attention, could never take his eyes off Tommy, even if he tried.

"One of the men almost lost an eye," Tommy continued. "But during questioning we found out he'd been hit on the same eye earlier in the day. The doc corroborates both injuries but can't tell us which injury was the worst or caused the most damage. It's quite possible that the brawl only gave him a nick to the eye and the damage was already done."

"So book him for ABH and we can decide later. It might just end up as common assault if the doc can't give us anything conclusive."

"Better to get a conviction on a lesser charge than not to get a conviction at all."

"If you think the pub brawl was worthy of a conviction."

"Won't be the bloke's first. He's got priors. One of them for slapping his ex-wife around."

"Then by all mean make it Actual Bodily Harm, not Grievous Bodily Harm. We don't need a jury. A judge will know what to do with him on his own," Finn said with a smile, until he noticed Tommy staring at him a certain way. The look didn't last very long. Tommy resumed scanning the office he'd been to at least two dozen times. "So how are your other cases going?" Surely Tommy hadn't come around to ask him something he already knew the answer to.

"Nothing much going on, I'm afraid. We might have another witness for you in that Covent Garden murder case."

"Always helpful." Finn took another swig. It was clear to him Tommy hadn't come over to talk about work, so he decided to give him an opening. "So what are you doing this weekend?"

"Mum's birthday. My sisters are cooking her dinner, and I need to show up with dessert. I'm making Pavlova."

Finn smiled. "With everything you've told me about your cooking skills, you're going to have to demonstrate them to me one day."

Tommy smiled, making his cheeks dimple. "Be careful what you wish for. I just might take you up on that!"

TOMMY

WALKING TO the Underground station from Finn's office, Tommy inhaled the sharp smell of the Thames's water. It was Friday, and he didn't have anywhere to go. He could walk on and get to a club where he might pick up a guy and get laid. That was one option, but not one he fancied. Not after just spending an hour with the man he'd had an unrequited crush on for the last year or so. Ever since Finn had spoken for him during an internal investigation, a seed had been planted in Tommy's brain that was hard to get rid of.

More than a year ago, Tommy had been singled out by his then Detective Superintendent Frank Marchand because the man had seen Tommy kiss another man outside a club. Tommy wasn't closeted, but he knew better than to talk about his sexual orientation at work, with good reason it seemed. A piece of mislaid evidence had been planted on Tommy's desk, and he'd been discredited on the stand by his own boss because of it during one of Finn's cases. In the end the man had tried to get him dismissed. If it hadn't been for Finn coming forward during the subsequent internal investigation to testify to Tommy's professional conduct, he would have been too. Although Finn hadn't given any indication during the investigation why he'd stuck his head out like that, Tommy had a feeling it was Finn's way of saying that he was okay with Tommy being gay.

Tommy knew deducing that Finn was gay as well—or that he had a soft spot for him—was one step too far, but he couldn't help it anyway. Ever since that day, Tommy always found excuses to meet with Finn alone. And invariably he walked away with a spring in his step.

It was that same infatuation that made him go to court the following Wednesday as well. He'd had to wait until after work, so he made it inside just as the final interrogation was picking up the pace. Finn was standing behind his lectern, facing the witness in the witness box.

FINN

"AND WHAT happened after your son came home that day, Mrs. Pierce?"

"He ran upstairs, to his room."

It was like pulling teeth. Slow and painful. "And what did he do to his room?"

"Nothin'."

Nothing? "Did he not, in fact, punch a hole in his bedroom wall? Did he not rip wallpaper off his walls?"

"No."

Finn took a deep breath. Why was this woman changing her statement? "Mrs. Pierce," Finn said, trying to keep his voice level and calm. Finn's starched white collar felt uncomfortable, his proper wool suit prickled, and his robes felt uncharacteristically warm. "Please recall the day that your son's school suspended him. Are you telling me now, contrary to your original statement, that nothing happened after your son came home early from school?"

She shrugged. "Don't remember."

Finn looked at the defendant in the dock. Charlie Everett had a smug smile on his face. Somehow the man had gotten to his ex-girlfriend. Finn had no idea how, but that was the only explanation. He had to change his line of questioning. Entrap her into admitting a few things that were only faintly covered in her statement.

"Did the defendant have contact with your son the night before the incident?"

"Could 'ave."

"Mrs. Pierce, he was your boyfriend at the time, right?"

"He came 'round the house from time to time. Usually after Alfie was asleep so he wouldn't see."

"So he came to see you?"

"'Course."

"What did he do when he was at your house?"

"Drink beer and watch TV."

Pulling teeth. Ever so slowly.

"And you always joined him?"

"Yeah."

"Were you together at all times when he was at your house?"

"He'd go out for a smoke."

"And do you smoke?"

"No."

So she doesn't keep an eye on him all the time. That's opportunity. Let's hope the jury understands.

"So you don't join him when he goes outside for a smoke?"

"No."

Mark Davies, Everett's defense attorney, stood up and addressed the judge. "My Lord, I don't see the relevance of whether or not Mrs. Pierce smokes."

Thank you, my learned colleague. "My Lord, I'm trying to establish that Mr. Everett had access to Alfie without Mrs. Pierce noticing."

"Very well, I'll allow it. But tread carefully, Mr. DeHavilland."

"Yes, My Lord." Finn turned back to his witness. "Did Mr. Everett ever look after Alfie when you were not at home?"

"No."

"In your statement to the police, you said you often work late. Who takes care of Alfie then?"

"My neighbor."

"Does Alfie go to her house when you work late?"

"No, he's at home, but she keeps an eye on him."

"Does Alfie let Mr. Everett inside when you're not home?" From the corner of his eye, Finn saw the smug look on Everett's face disappear. *Bingo.*

"He's no' allowed to. He knows that." Judging by the woman's accent slipping, she was getting nervous too, looking at Everett in the dock. Finn could smell success.

"But he could get to Alfie, right, Mrs. Pierce?"

"He never touched him. I swear. You got it all wrong, Mister!"

"Your statement to the police said you knew he had the chance to be with Alfie without your supervision."

"I never said nothin' like that! He'd never do anything to Alfie!"

She was getting very emotional, almost crying. The expert doctor had testified that Alfie had indeed been molested. Repeatedly. The child psychologist had said the same. He'd presented all that evidence to the jury, but there was no DNA. Finn knew from her witness statement that the mother suspected her ex. It didn't look good to the jury for the prosecuting counsel to make the witness cry, but Finn knew that tying Everett to the crime stood and fell with her evidence. It looked good on paper, but if she didn't corroborate that on the stand, the jury might not believe the statement alone. He looked at the public gallery, and his eyes met briefly with Tommy Drummond's. Finn thought he looked a little sad. Bill Carlton, his boss, sitting not too far from Tommy, didn't look hopeful either. Finn knew he had to go for broke.

"How afraid are you of Mr. Everett?"

"I'm not." She seemed to recover somewhat.

"Did you not end up in A&E with bruises on your arms and face twice after a visit from Mr. Everett?"

"That had nothin' to do with him." She was looking at Everett again.

"Mrs. Pierce!" Finn almost startled at the power of his own voice, so he tried to sound more subdued. "Are you worried that repeating here what you said at the police station will be met with violence at Mr. Everett's hand?"

"No." Her voice didn't sound as sure as before.

"Wouldn't it be better to make sure Mr. Everett is put behind bars, both for your sake and for Alfie's?"

"I love him."

"Yet you threw Mr. Everett out of the house. Why did you do that?"

"We had a fight."

"So it wasn't because you caught him with his trousers around his ankles in your son's room?"

"Mr. DeHavilland!"

Finn looked in the direction of the judge and then at where he now stood. Finn had vacated his designated spot behind his lectern and was standing in front of his witness. He knew it wasn't done in court to leave your space, but the damage was done.

"Answer the question, dammit!" He grabbed her hand, and she started crying.

"Mr. DeHavilland. You will be removed from this court."

Finn stared at her, but she didn't speak. She just sat there trembling.

TOMMY

HE'D STOOD up when he saw Finn push through the little partition that separated the prosecutor's bench from the rest of the court. It had taken Finn only two paces to reach the witness box, and Tommy couldn't believe what he was seeing. This was something out of an American TV series, not something he'd ever seen happen in a London court. The judge was turning red, trying to restrain Finn with his voice. He too would never leave his perch. The ushers were standing by but waiting for the judge to order them to intervene, and the clerk simply sat there stunned. Tommy didn't know what to do at seeing Finn lose control like this. He looked sideways to where Carlton, Finn's boss, was sitting, and the man was shaking his head. He looked at Finn again, who was gripping the witness's hand so tightly his knuckles were white.

Tommy knew someone had to help Finn out, but nobody was moving.

He jumped across the low partition and into the main court area. What he was doing wasn't done either, but everyone seemed to be stuck to their place in the courtroom, and nobody wanted to take action. It didn't take much to reach Finn, and he gripped him by the shoulders to pull him away, but Finn tried to shrug him off.

"Finn, let go," Tommy said softly, trying to stay as calm as possible.

"She needs to answer the question!" Finn repeated in his stern prosecutor's voice. "She's the only one who knows the truth, the only person who can save her own son!"

Tommy looked up at the judge and saw the restrained anger in his face. As soon as the judge noticed Tommy was looking up at him, he nodded, and Tommy pulled harder, managing to get Finn away from the witness box and the frightened woman inside it.

Tommy wanted to pull Finn to the exit, but he saw an usher hold a side door open, so he dragged Finn in there. Finn was still fighting him. Once they were inside and the usher had closed the door, Finn stopped struggling, and Tommy realized he had pulled Finn to his chest.

"It's over. Calm down," he said in his most soothing voice, running his hand over the smooth fabric of the robe covering Finn's back.

When he looked at Finn's face, there were pearls of sweat on his forehead, and his wig was a little askew. His collar had become dislodged as well. Tommy turned them around and pushed Finn to sit down on the bench before crouching in front of him.

"She lied."

"I know," Tommy replied calmly. "Some witnesses do that."

"She was afraid of Everett."

"You tried to get her to admit to that. And you tried to make the jury see her lies too."

"You could tell?"

Tommy smiled, more at the feeling of tension being released than at anything remotely funny. "You were good out there. Only, you let your control slip. What happened today, Finn?"

"I don't know."

Finn grabbed the wig off his head and pulled it down. "Carlton was there, wasn't he?"

Tommy nodded.

"Not that he wouldn't know the minute it happened. He'd have to. He probably has to clean up the mess I left."

Tommy continued to smile. "He's got more experience than anyone."

"He's going to walk free, Tommy."

"Everett?"

Finn nodded.

"And he's going to do it again."

"So we'll catch him then."

"After he's molested another boy? How will I explain that to his mother?"

"With any luck she'll care as little as Mrs. Pierce."

Finn chuckled, and Tommy felt his heart lift. "Are you saying that to make me feel better?"

"Anything for your smile, Mr. DeHavilland."

Tommy jumped up as he heard the door behind him open. Two ambulance men walked in. "Mr. DeHavilland?"

Finn stood up. "I am he."

"Please come with us."

"I'm fine. You should see to Mrs. Pierce."

Carlton appeared behind him. "Judge Faulkner ordered you be assessed. I could only comply, Finn. Cooperate with them, please?"

Finn looked at Tommy for what felt like a long time before walking in the direction of the ambulance men.

Chapter Two

FINN

HE WOKE with a start, instantly sitting upright. He stopped struggling against the sheets and blankets wrapped around his limbs when he realized where he was and wiped his hand over his face to clear his thoughts—4:00 a.m.

Only 4:00 a.m.

The little red dot next to the time, indicating his alarm was on, wasn't there, and then he remembered that it might be a weekday but he wasn't expected at the office. In fact he was respectfully asked not to show up that day. Or the rest of the week, for that matter.

If it had been up to his boss, he wouldn't even be sleeping in his own bed.

He let himself drop to the mattress again and then felt how cold and wet it was, so he got out of bed altogether. He pulled off the sweat-soaked pajama top that was clinging to his skin and replaced it with a clean one from his dresser before walking toward the lavatory. By then his heart rate had recovered from the nightmare that had woken him. It wasn't like this was an unusual feat, but the nightmares had become worse with every disturbing case he'd had to tackle.

Until the night before, he hadn't acknowledged how much the seemingly endless succession of child abuse and rape cases had affected him. He was Finn DeHavilland, for heaven's sake, Senior Crown Prosecutor of Her Majesty's Crown Court and the fear of every junior defender in Greater London. Over the years he'd commanded respect from the more seasoned barristers as well, although they more than kept him on his toes.

Just past midnight he'd reluctantly admitted to the psychiatric consultant at Westminster hospital A&E that he'd lost it, in court no less, after a clear-as-day case was at risk of being dismissed because of one witness statement. They'd had to let a repeat offender walk free to rape another minor, and all Finn remembered before he saw red was the disappointment on the faces of Tommy Drummond, the DS who had arrested the suspect, and Bill Carlton, his superior. He'd worked closely with them on the case, and all three of them felt it had been watertight, until the mother of the young victim had changed her story on the stand.

Finn looked at himself in the cold light of his bathroom mirror. Over the last months he'd gained a few wrinkles in his already less than perfect skin, and his sandy blond locks now had a few more gray hairs as well, but the clearest indication of how hard the last months had been was in the dark circles below his eyes. He rubbed them in the hope of making them look a little less pronounced, but it was to no avail. He felt and certainly looked older than his forty-two years. Too many interrupted nights did that to a man.

Finn walked into his kitchen and made himself a cup of tea. He couldn't help going over the previous days' occurrences and felt the anxiety rise again. Maybe his boss was right and he needed to talk to the psychiatrist the Crown Prosecution Service had on staff to assess a suspect's mental capacity to stand trial. It wasn't that he didn't trust Ayse Kartal. In fact he'd often sung her praise to the other prosecutors and, because of the nature of his work, had worked with her on more cases than he cared to remember. His reluctance to see her had nothing to do with her brilliance and everything to do with the professional distance he kept from everyone at the office. As far as his colleagues were concerned, he had no private life, and that's how Finn wanted to keep it. Not that there was anything for them to know. He was sure the fact that he lived alone in a spacious flat in Kensington and rode his bike to work every day was of little interest to them. He was a typical city dweller who walked everywhere he needed to go when he was alone and took a cab when he was in the company of his boss or Armen Nagocyan, who'd been his right hand for the past two years. His offices were just across the bridge from the Old Bailey where he spent at least half his time, and more often than not, he walked there as well.

As he finished his cup of tea, he checked the messages on his phone. Two of them were from Armen and from his boss. He didn't want their sympathy, so he skipped to the third one. It was an invitation for lunch from Ayse. He couldn't believe his boss had called her in the early hours of the morning, just after he'd agreed to see her so they'd let him go home instead of keep him in for observation. He texted her back to say he'd meet her and then realized the time stamp would betray how little he'd slept. After washing out his cup and putting it back in its rightful place, he decided to go back to bed in the hope of sleeping some more, so he'd at least look less haggard than he felt. He crawled into the other side of the bed, hoping for a dry spot, and tossed and turned for what felt like hours before finally dozing off, only to wake up at six, his usual hour to get up for work.

DRESSED IN his casual knee-length tan coat over brown trousers, a scarf wrapped around his neck and neatly tucked into the coat, Finn walked into the busy café and surveyed his surroundings. Located just around the corner from the Old Bailey, it was filled to the brink with barristers, litigators, and court clerks, and Finn's entrance made heads turn. Most of them looked concerned or outright curious. Finn knew the news of his meltdown would be on everyone's lips this morning, but he hadn't expected it to be this bad.

"Let's get out of here."

He turned in the direction of Ayse's voice and encountered her concerned expression. A crease marked her forehead over her pretty mahogany eyes as she wrapped a hand around Finn's arm and practically dragged him outside.

"I'm sorry I suggested this, but it was two o'clock in the morning when Carlton called me, and I was barely awake then. Let's walk," she ordered more than suggested as she dragged him down the street and paced determinedly in the direction away from the busy cafés. Finn was almost a head taller than she was and had no problem keeping up with her, but he was surprised at the pace he needed to keep.

"It's nice of you to see me at such short notice, Ayse. Let me buy lunch. It's the least I can do." He smiled at her as she stopped abruptly in the middle of the pavement and turned to him, the crease in her forehead now seemingly a permanent fixture.

"All the lunch places are packed, and I think we need privacy to talk," she said, the sternness in her features fading to concern as she cocked her head slightly. "I suppose we can get takeaway from Pret or something. Do you feel like sushi?"

He nodded, making sure he didn't stop smiling, since this seemed to mellow her a bit.

"Bring me a chicken Caesar and a packet of sweet chili crisps, and I'll call around and see if we can use a colleague's cabinet for an hour or two."

Finn grabbed her arm the way she'd grabbed his at the café. "We can walk to the courtyard behind my office. We might not be entirely alone at this hour, but I often go there over lunch for a breath of fresh air, and it's relatively private."

Her eyebrows sought each other out as the crease in her forehead deepened again. "Don't think for a moment that talking to me for twenty minutes over lunch is going to make this all go away, Finn. You're suspended until further notice. Carlton asked me to assess when you'd be ready to come to work again, but he has no intention of letting you step into the Old Bailey until he's assured you won't attack innocent witnesses again."

"She's not innocent! She's the reason the man who raped her son walked free yesterday, and there is not a single doubt in my mind he'll do it again!" Finn knew he was shouting and people walking past them were looking at him, but he felt the rage building in him again. The same rage that had made him lash out at the boy's mother.

Finn had more self-restraint now, so he stopped shouting and simply looked at the passersby until they stopped staring.

"I'll get the food. You go to the courtyard and find us a bench to sit on, okay?" Ayse told him.

Finn knew she was concerned about him. He also knew he trusted her. He could tell her a little bit about how he'd felt the day before and give her a glimpse into his mind, just enough so she'd tell Carlton he was no longer a threat to his witnesses.

"I like the sushi rolls with the rice but not the ones with all the raw fish on top, okay?"

"Straight sushi, not sashimi. Got it," Ayse replied. For the first time she was smiling, and Finn was glad. "Drinks?"

Finn smiled back at her. "Oh, what the hell. I can't work today anyway. They don't need me tomorrow either. Are they expecting you to be back at work today?"

She shook her head. "I cleared my schedule. Carlton's orders. He said he'd call the Home Secretary if I didn't."

"Guess I should be flattered," he sneered. "Why don't you bring us a bottle of wine, then?"

"Why, Mister DeHavilland, I never expected it would be this easy for you to let your hair down."

"Don't push it, Ayse."

She turned and walked a few paces away from him before turning around to face him again. "At least you're smiling."

"I smile."

"Never at the office."

"There isn't a lot to smile about there."

FINN SAT on a worn wooden bench in the secluded area between half a dozen office buildings. The courtyard was one of those small inner city treasures very few people knew about, and that's why Finn liked it. Where he was sitting, in the sunshine, it was warm enough to eat outside, although he was glad for his wool coat and the fact it reached almost to his knees. Some of the calm that always came over him when he was sitting there returned then as well, although he also felt a little nervous about what Ayse would want to talk to him about. He knew if he ever wanted to return to his job, he needed to go through the motions. He just hoped Ayse would make it as painless as possible for him.

He looked up when he heard the sound of footsteps on the slab floor of the courtyard entrance and saw her carefully navigate the uneven floor under her four-inch heels, red paper bag dangling from one hand and her attaché case in the other. Although he wasn't particularly attracted to her, he easily saw her objective beauty, from her dark skin tone and pitch black wavy hair, her almond-shaped eyes and curvy figure, to her lusciously plump lips. She turned many a man's eye wherever she entered. Luckily she was spoken for, although her physician husband was away on army duty more often than not.

"So," she announced as she sat down next to him and started unpacking her purchases. "Sushi for the senior, raw fish and veg cleverly disguised by sticky rice." She handed him the cardboard wrapped package and a pair of chopsticks. "I know you can handle these because I've seen you eat noodles with them and you're a master."

"You bet," he replied as he took everything from her.

"And chicken Caesar for me, plus cutlery. Oh, and...." She put down her package and took two plastic glasses out of the back, handed one to Finn, and then unearthed a full bottle of white wine. "Not exactly prime vintage, but it's just for lunch and to loosen you up a bit, so…."

She didn't finish, but Finn all of a sudden realized why she'd been so eager to go along with his idea of having wine with lunch.

"I've been sworn to secrecy by the Crown," Finn rebutted, not without a little cheek. "Like you have your doctor-patient confidentiality, right? Does anything I tell you need to be repeated to Carlton?"

"Not a word. I made that very clear to him this morning. He gets my assessment of your capacity to come back to work. That's all."

Finn took the bottle from her and looked at it. Not his usual fare, but then what he usually drank came with a cork, not a screw top. He poured them a glass each anyway before tackling his sushi.

"So what happened, Finn? In court yesterday."

Finn sighed, taking his time to chew the sushi roll in his mouth, but nerves made him taste little of the delicate flavors. "We had the jury on our side. We'd shown them the monster behind the calm, collected man in the dock. We'd even been allowed to explain to them he'd done this sort of thing before, but the defense had made it very clear that he'd served his time for his crime, and since he'd been a free man for more than three years, they'd also tried to explain he'd been rehabilitated. We knew we needed to let the jury hear the horror story the victim's mother had told us to nail the verdict, and then it would be cut-and-dried. Only once she was in the witness box, she looked scared and intimidated. I knew I had to tread carefully, but she changed her story. All of a sudden our child molester was a model stepdad, who was discreet around her son and who had never been alone with him or who had never laid a finger on her, although two separate A&E reports show she was beaten, most likely by him. No matter how hard I prodded her, she wouldn't say a bad word about him. I admit I badgered her a bit. I think he somehow got to her, and because of the abuse she was scared enough of him to change her story. I thought if I made her scared of me and of how I'd react to her changing her story, I could intimidate her enough to tell the truth."

Ayse nodded. "I've seen you do this before in court and it's very effective, but you're always in control, Finn. What is it about this case that's so special?"

Finn took a sip from his wine to stall for time. "He was going to get away with molesting an innocent ten-year-old boy, Ayse."

"Oh, come on, you've lost cases before. Remember that case where the bigoted DI discredited Tommy Drummond on the stand for no other reason than that he caught him snogging his boyfriend outside a bar in Soho. Off duty. That was another rape case you didn't win, and you didn't take a swing at the other gay DS who claimed the DI was the most tolerant boss he'd ever worked for."

"That was different." Finn started gathering the empty wrappers from the food they'd eaten, just to ignore the incessant stare Ayse was giving him.

"You're not a bigot like that DI, Finn. In fact you love working with Tommy on a case. I swear your eyes light up when he walks into the room."

"That's not true! Tommy's a really good detective. His cases are always well documented, and he works hard at finding all the evidence we need. I even see Stevie act surprised by what Tommy comes up with sometimes, and she's got more experience than all of us put together. Give Tommy a few years and he'll make DI, I'm sure."

"Finn, are you gay?"

Finn looked at her briefly and saw what must be her most compassionate and accepting expression before he looked away. "No," he said dismissively, hoping he sounded convincing enough. "I don't see the relevance of this, of my sexual...."

"Orientation," Ayse offered, finishing the sentence for him.

"Yes, I don't see what my sexual... orientation has to do with my capability of doing my job."

"You're right," Ayse admitted. "If you were gay, you'd still be the best Senior Prosecutor at the CPS. And personally it's none of my business, but for my assessment I want to form an image of you that is as complete as possible. Even if you'd answered 'yes,' it would never end up in my report, but it would give me an indication of how open or closed off you are and of how much you trust me."

She waited for a few moments, but however awkward the silence, Finn didn't know how to fill it.

"I want to know what makes you tick, Finn, but we don't need to cover all the ground today. We'll get back to it at a later session."

"I said 'no,' so I didn't exactly omit answering your question."

She smiled. "I knew you shrewd lawyer types would be able to wiggle yourself out of it. But will your answer stand up in court?"

Finn didn't answer her. He felt relieved when she got up from the bench.

"Can we make another appointment for tomorrow? Say at four?"

"It's not like I have anyplace else to go."

"Right," she replied. "Don't you have any hobbies, Finn?"

"Don't have the time for hobbies usually."

"Married to the job, eh?"

"Pretty much."

"Makes for a jealous wife, the job," she said, leaving Finn behind to stew over that.

Chapter Three

FINN

AGAIN FINN barely slept that night. He kept having nightmares and then waking up sweat soaked, not remembering what had upset him enough to rouse him from his sleep. Hoping the talk with Ayse later would get him an okay from her so he could return to work, Finn spent the day the way he usually spent his Sunday mornings: cleaning his flat and doing his laundry. Although he'd grown up in a house with servants, he preferred not to have strangers around to do chores he could easily do himself. His flat was spacious but easily maintained since he was barely there for more than sleep. Ironing his shirts was something he'd learned to do at university, and he'd found it an excellent way to give himself time to think. He'd come up with many a solution to a case while making sure his professional attire was immaculate.

At precisely four in the afternoon, Finn secured his bike to the rail outside of Ayse's practice and rang the doorbell.

His conversation with Ayse started pretty much where they'd ended the day before, with the exception of his sexual orientation. Ayse didn't touch the subject and instead focused on the cases that had led to Finn's meltdown.

"It's like every case that crosses my desk these days is either domestic violence, rape, or child molestation. I find myself actually looking forward to a straight-up robbery-homicide or a negligent manslaughter case. Something straightforward."

"You'd be bored to death after a day, Finn. You usually give those cases to Armen, right?"

"I wouldn't now. It's been one after the other, and the victims are treated more cruelly and the aggressors are more shrewd and screwed up than before, it seems. And you know what else I'd like? Someone in that dock showing remorse. Before this last case, we convicted a man of raping half a dozen women, and even after the jury found him guilty, all he showed was pride. His only sorrow was that he wasn't allowed to continue."

"You were a defense lawyer before you joined the CPS, right?"

Finn nodded. "The CPS prefers their prosecutors to have defense experience because it helps us better understand all the tactics defense uses."

"Makes sense. Couldn't have been easy for you."

"It was valuable experience." Finn didn't know where her line of questioning was going, but it was safe ground, so he indulged her.

"You have such a passion for defending the victims, I have a hard time seeing you defend a criminal."

"Not all suspects are guilty." Finn was starting to see what Ayse was aiming for now. He wouldn't be much of a prosecutor if he didn't catch on sooner rather than later. She was trying to find ways of explaining his behavior to Carlton, and his need to give the victims a voice would certainly score him some points. Then again, Carlton and he went further back than he and Ayse did, and he was sure Carlton knew exactly why he'd made Finn his Senior Prosecutor and by doing so had passed up more than one prosecutor who had seniority over Finn.

"How did you do defending the real criminals, then?"

Finn smiled. "I was very good at predicting who would be convicted and who would get off." He still felt rather smug about that. "It was always a combination of who was the prosecutor, who was the judge, and whether or not I felt they'd actually done the crime. The office I worked at started betting on my predictions."

"I don't believe you actually answered my question, Finn."

"I got the cases I was sure would be a walk in the park—"

"The innocent suspects," Ayse interrupted.

"And the cases I was sure no lawyer, however shrewd, could ever win."

"The ones caught red-handed?"

"And the ones everyone, including the judge and most of the jury, would be prejudiced against. I was a junior, fresh out of Oxford, so I got mostly the ones who couldn't afford representation: the homeless people, the hopeless petty criminals, you know."

"The underdogs."

"Newly out of university, we were rarely made the lead in a case unless it wasn't expected to bring in any money. Then, if you lost the case, it was no great shame, but if you won, the firm would be complimented on their excellent judgment in picking new barristers."

"Did you ever make a name for yourself at that time?"

"If you're asking whether I ever won any of the unwinnable cases, then no, but I did like trying. Especially with the homeless people. I wanted to give them the best possible defense."

When Finn looked at Ayse, she was smiling at him in what Finn could only interpret as her proud-mother look. Was she actually proud of him? "What?" he asked her innocently.

"Do you have any idea how you come across at the office?"

Finn was taken aback by the question. He'd never wondered what his colleagues thought of him. "I hope they feel I'm a consummate professional."

"What else?"

"I don't know."

"If all you wanted to be was a consummate professional, do you think your meltdown damaged that?"

"Yes," Finn answered quietly. "Probably."

"Do you think they know about your altruism?"

"You can't stay a prosecutor without at least a little of that."

Ayse didn't react, so he felt he needed to elaborate.

"It's not like I couldn't make more money being a defense lawyer. Especially with my experience in the CPS, any firm would be happy to snap me up. Or I could start my own firm. Would be a gold mine."

"But you don't need the money." It wasn't a question.

"I bought my flat with the inheritance from my parents, and there's still a substantial sum left in the bank."

"Not to mention you don't take up your vacation days, so you can't spend it on that."

"Guilty as charged."

"Carlton's suggestion was I tell you to take an airplane to some Caribbean island and take up some of those vacation days."

Finn grunted but didn't answer.

"I told him he could suggest that to you himself."

"He knows I won't do it. What am I to do on a fucking Caribbean island?"

Ayse giggled. "Carlton used almost exactly those words."

"But more colorful?"

"No, less, actually. I don't think he feels you're capable of using curse words."

"Oh, dear."

"Prim and proper is what he thinks you are."

"Maybe he's right," Finn said, thinking about Carlton not using his usually rather peppered language when he mimicked him.

"In any case, I suggested to Carlton he lets you come back to the office to work on your cases."

"Seriously?"

"I told him it is your safe haven. But he's not going to let you go to court."

"What? How can I work on my cases and not see them all the way to court?"

"Armen. You're to coach him. For the time being."

"He's not ready."

"Come now, Finn. You've let him ask questions during some of your cases. He's good. Not as good as you, but all he lacks is experience."

"But he's not ready to be lead in these cases!"

"That's where you come in. You help him with strategy, walk him through his line of questioning."

"You sound like you've never stepped foot in a courtroom. I don't rehearse these questions. Most of them are born from a witness's demeanor or his other answers. You need to think on your feet in court."

"Calm down, Finn. You're not helping your case. It's this or full-on suspension. At least this way you can still feel useful and stay on top of your cases."

"I don't suppose I can sit second chair?"

"No. No court appearance whatsoever. For the time being."

"Until when?"

"Until you can convince Carlton that there will not be a repeat of two days ago."

"I can say now it won't happen again."

"I can't take this to Carlton, Finn. The conditions are you keep seeing me on a regular basis, meaning as often as I deem necessary, and if you do that, you can come and work on your cases at the office. If Carlton and I feel you can handle it, you will also get new cases."

"So I'm at your mercy?"

"Pretty much," Ayse said with some glee. "Do you trust me, Finn?"

"Yes."

"Then it shouldn't be the torture you make it out to be."

THE NEXT morning Finn walked into his office before eight. Despite the fact it was Saturday, he was let in, since the doorman was used to seeing him come into work on which was, strictly speaking, a day off. It also meant Ayse had talked to Carlton, and Carlton had extended his permission. Finn hadn't slept any better than previous nights, but his anxiety had been replaced by excitement. He'd never realized how much he loved his work, and although he wouldn't get to do his favorite part, he'd still get to do everything else. He was still allowed to figure out the truth.

It was quiet in the office on a Saturday morning, and Finn found the case files of the current cases on Armen's desk, with the more "delicate elements" in the locked cabinet in his office. They weren't as meticulously organized as they would be if he'd placed them there himself, but he knew everything would be there. Armen was messy but brilliant nevertheless. Finn knew his system but was glad he spent his Saturday mornings with his wife and two young children and left him to work in peace.

"MORNIN'."

Finn looked up from his desk and the file he was reading. "Tommy."

"Thought I'd find you here. The boss said you'd be in this mornin'. That's your boss, not mine."

Finn smiled at Tommy and then remembered what Ayse had told him, that his eyes lit up every time Tommy walked into the room. He'd never thought about it, basically because he never allowed himself to think about Tommy that way.

Finn had never felt any attraction to women. He liked working with them, but that's about where it ended. He didn't have any friends outside of work, and even the ones he considered friends in the workplace barely extended beyond a companionable lunch and a propensity to organize impromptu meetings to discuss the different angles of a case. What he did with them wasn't what other people would call socializing, and Finn knew that. He'd always told himself he didn't need it and that he preferred his own company over needing to accommodate for another person. If that made him selfish, then so be it.

His attraction to men was of a different caliber, though. He knew it was there and blissfully chose to ignore it. Over the years he'd worked with quite a few men who'd drawn his attention. Many of them were policemen, and all of them were young, smart, and ambitious. Finn had never acted on those feelings, and he seriously doubted any of them had ever known. Why would they? Finn was always extra careful not to treat them differently or let his eyes wander.

Now he wondered if he wasn't more obvious than he'd always thought. Ayse hadn't mentioned any other men besides Tommy. Was Tommy special? Tommy was rattling on about what had happened in the last three days, and Finn realized he wasn't paying attention. Instead he was looking at Tommy's bright blue eyes, always sparkling with mischief, and today was no different. He was enthusiastically reciting how they'd conducted a search of a skip and found credit card receipts putting their suspect at a hotel room he'd claimed never to have visited. Finn hoped he'd find Tommy and Stevie's notes in the files he had yet to read, because Tommy's animated voice and the dimples in his cheeks were preventing Finn from registering the details he usually relied on so heavily in court. Not that he was going to be allowed to present this evidence himself, but he might have to coach Armen through it.

Finn blinked a few times to kick his brain into gear. This wouldn't do. How could one question from Ayse topple his world so much? He'd answered the gay question to the best of his ability, and that's how he was going to defend himself if Ayse called him on it, but now it seemed the evidence had presented itself rather differently. The general definition of a gay man was a man attracted to men rather than women, and Finn had to admit to himself he did fall into that category. It didn't matter that he'd never acted on those feelings and never would. If Ayse ever brought the subject up again, he was going to have to level with her. He'd find a way to talk himself out of the questions that would inevitably follow, but he wouldn't lie to her.

"You're not even listenin' to me, are ya?" Tommy asked in his rather strong South London accent. There was no malice in his voice. In fact Finn thought he looked rather amused. "Maybe it wasn't such a good idea to come back to work today. Should've taken the weekend off, I reckon."

"No, I reckon it was a very good idea," Finn answered, using similar words to the ones Tommy had used but not even attempting to mimic his juicy accent. He didn't want to mock Tommy, and how could an Eton boy like him ever wrap his tongue around those sounds anyway? He knew he was out of his depth when it came to sounding like a man of the street. Whenever Tommy and Stevie got into a word match—which they often did, even in the office of their esteemed Senior Prosecutor—Finn would sometimes lose track because they seemed to speak something quite far removed from the Queen's English. He loved the sound of it and could listen to them for hours.

Tommy was gesturing something along the lines of "What's up?" signaling to Finn he'd spaced out again.

"It's quiet on Saturdays, and I reckoned I'd need to catch up on my reading," he said, finishing his earlier train of thought.

"Did it do any good?"

"I was coming along fine until you showed up."

"You should've said somethin'. I would have left you alone, but I reckoned since you usually ask us to come here to tell you in our own words, you'd want to find out what you missed."

Finn smiled at Tommy. "And you were right. I'm just a little distracted, and I'm sorry. Why don't I make it up to you? Fancy going down the pub for lunch?" Finn heard himself say the words as if it wasn't his mouth uttering them. He was surprised by his own gall. Maybe Tommy was right, and it was too early for him to return to work.

Tommy was stunned into silence. One corner of his mouth curled up, and he looked Finn up and down as if he was only now seeing him for the first time. "Why, guv'. Are you paying?"

Finn couldn't back down now. "Sure." He was too unsure about his proposition to be confident, though. "Unless you have other plans?"

For a moment Finn thought Tommy was going to treat it as a joke and back out, but he didn't. "No, no other plans."

Finn saw another side of Tommy, though. He didn't seem to be his confident self and talked a lot less than he usually did as Finn got up from behind his desk to put his coat on. Even their short walk around the corner was spent in silence, and Finn couldn't help wondering what Tommy was thinking. He wasn't about to attempt to find out, though. Since he had no intention of doing anything with his attraction, he didn't want to lead Tommy on. He simply wanted to buy him lunch to thank him for his consideration, coming by the office on his day off to update him on their progress.

Once there Tommy loosened up a bit after the cook brought around their orders of fish and chips. He sprinkled plenty of salt and vinegar on both and proceeded to eat, barely waiting to swallow before speaking. "You know we were worried about you, right?"

"There was no need, but thank you," Finn replied politely.

"We were worried they were going to sack you," Tommy continued, stuffing his mouth with the white fish. "Office wouldn't be the same without you." He continued talking with his mouth full, but Finn forgave him.

"Thanks, Tommy, but Chief Carlton is on my side. He had no choice but to suspend me, and I need to get some help." He hesitated for a moment and then decided not to tell Tommy about his visits to Ayse. "I'll be back in court after sufficient time has passed. In the meantime Armen is taking my cases. He'll present the evidence you collected."

"That's all fine and good, but he's not you, Finn."

Finn startled at hearing Tommy call him by his first name. Inside the office of the prosecutors, they went with the public school etiquette of calling people by their last names, but Tommy always seemed to find ways to circumnavigate the name issue. Until now. Then Finn realized Tommy had called him by his first name in the cloaking room after the incident as well.

"It's got nothin' to do with him being so young and all, and he's a good prosecutor. He's been learning from the best long enough to have picked up some of your tricks, I reckon, but people expect to see you. We expect to see you too."

Tommy was looking at his chips instead of his table companion, but Finn could have sworn he was blushing. Could it be that Tommy fancied him? Surely this couldn't be the case.

"I'll be glad to be reinstated as well, Tommy."

They finished their pints and said their good-byes, each wishing the other a good weekend before walking out of the pub together. They'd barely set foot on the pavement when they literally bumped into Ayse.

"Why, Tommy, Finn, both of you hanging around the corner of the office on your day off? You boys need to get a life." She looked from Finn to Tommy before settling her eyes on Finn again. Finn could practically read her mind, but she wasn't going to say anything right there on the street. To his surprise, Tommy was staring at the pavement as if he'd been caught doing something he shouldn't have. Finn wished he could ask Tommy why he avoided Ayse's gaze and why he was so nervous he was balancing from his toes to his heels and back again, but he couldn't. He knew what Ayse's favorite topic was going to be on Monday, though.

TOMMY

IT WAS strange walking into that pretty Turkish psychiatrist who often gave expert witness testimony in Finn's cases. She'd given him a strange look as if she knew why he was there but didn't know why he was with Finn. Maybe she was jealous? Maybe she meant more to Finn than they could be open about since they worked together? Besides seeing the appeal of her mocha skin against Finn's milky complexion, Tommy couldn't imagine Finn with a woman. Oh yes, he was smitten by the man for sure. He also saw the truth in what she'd said. He had to get a life. Most likely without his favorite prosecutor in it.

Chapter Four

FINN

NOW FINN was working again, his sessions with Ayse were moved to early evening, but Finn found himself looking for excuses to work late. The problem was, especially now he didn't have arguments to prepare for, he had little to do after Armen left to tuck his kids into bed, so he was going to have to face the firing squad.

"You're late, Mister Senior Prosecutor," Ayse said by way of greeting as she let him into her flat. "And don't give me the excuse of needing to catch up at work. You can do that on the days you don't have an appointment to see me."

Finn could tell she was trying hard to be the strict schoolteacher, but it wasn't in her nature.

"I'd think you had lots to tell me!" It was, however, in her nature to enjoy watching him squirm.

"Oh, I don't know," Finn replied, trying to play dumb as he followed her to the lounge.

"Cup of tea?"

"Sure." Anything to postpone the inevitable.

Finn heard her rattling kitchen cabinets as she made him tea.

"You and Tommy seemed to be progressing quickly," she shouted from the other room.

Finn was glad the distance between the two rooms allowed him to compose himself. His mind wasn't coming up with any witty answers, though. "I bought him lunch for coming in on his day off to brief me on what I'd missed. Was the least I could do."

"So it wasn't a date, then?"

Ayse's voice was a lot closer all of a sudden. In fact she was standing in front of him, offering him tea in a delicate Royal Doulton cup.

"No, Ayse, of course it wasn't a date."

"I know you told me you weren't gay."

"About that…." He waited until she was seated opposite him. "I wasn't entirely truthful, but I didn't lie."

"Which is it?"

Finn shrugged.

She gave him her most compassionate stare. "It's like me telling you I'm a little bit pregnant. There's no such thing. Either I am or I am not. Either you told me the truth or you didn't."

"You're pregnant?"

"Don't change the subject!"

"You're the one who brought it up!" It answered his internal question about why she hadn't drunk the wine they'd shared on their first session in the courtyard, though.

"Fine, yes, I'm pregnant. Now can we get on with it? We're not here to talk about me. You were saying something about telling me the truth?"

Finn tried to remember whether he'd ever heard her talk about her and Charlie trying for children, but he knew that was beside the point. "I told you a version of the truth."

Ayse raised both her eyebrows.

"I've never been attracted to women, but I do occasionally fancy a man. I've never acted on it, though, and I'm not about to start now."

"Never? Not even with a woman?"

Finn shook his head. "I never saw the point."

"You really are married to your work, aren't you?"

"'Fraid so."

"Never?" Ayse repeated. "Not even…."

"Not even a snog, Ayse." He sort of felt sorry for her, since she clearly couldn't fathom something that was completely normal for him. "I've never performed any intimate acts on or with another person, male or female."

"You make it sound so clinical, Finn! I'm talking about making love, sharing yourself with another person. It's a basic human need to be touched, Finn. How do you…."

"Handle it? I don't. Don't need to. I'm used to it. I can't imagine myself doing those things you mentioned."

She got up from her chair and crouched down in front of him. He automatically tensed up as she reached out and touched his hand. When he didn't flinch back too much, she enveloped his hands with hers, even though his were much bigger.

"I understand the fear of intimacy, Finn, but every living thing needs to be touched. Even delicate flowers bloom better when they're handled."

"I'm not a delicate flower," he said with a chuckle. At least his sense of humor was returning.

"I know you're not. Even before all this, I thought you were one of the strongest people I knew, and I see no need to adjust that idea."

Finn nodded, looking at their entwined hands.

"There is such a thing as asexuality. It's recognized as a sexual orientation, just like gay or straight. As strange as it sounds to us sexual beings, there are people who have absolutely no desire to be intimate with another person. They don't experience lust or lustful feelings. It doesn't mean they don't have the need for physical contact. Have you ever tried massage?"

Finn rolled his eyes at the speed with which she was expressing her thoughts. "No, Ayse. I haven't." He was surprised at how dismissive he sounded.

"Anyway, there's something to think about before our meeting on Thursday. I do want to talk some more about this fear of intimacy then, Finn."

Finn took a deep breath and released it with a sigh.

"I never said this was going to be a walk in the park."

"No, you didn't."

"We'll get there eventually."

Ayse changed the subject to less delicate topics, but Finn still wasn't looking forward to Thursday.

THAT NIGHT he dreamed of Tommy. He'd sort of expected a dream the night after their lunch, but instead it happened after he'd told Ayse about it, and it was far more intimate than he'd expected as well. He'd never seen Tommy without his clothes on. Tommy always wore trousers and shirts that pretty much covered his body. In Finn's dream Tommy had a tattoo on his shoulder that curved around it and brought out what Finn imagined was a nice set of muscles. He kissed it, and Tommy had leaned into the touch, enticing Finn to wrap his arms around Tommy's narrow waist and washboard stomach until he could pull the DS against him and rub his groin against Tommy's arse.

At that moment Finn had woken up, his stomach sticky from his release. Although this was a rare occurrence—and the first time in his life he actually remembered the cause of it—he didn't do what he always did and rush into a shower. Instead he curled himself up and closed his eyes, trying to recapture the feeling of holding Tommy close. It was gone, though. He could no longer feel the other man's skin or smell his manly scent so close. And he had to acknowledge what his dream had made abundantly clear to him, that he was definitely attracted to the man and that he wasn't asexual. His dream had been decidedly lustful. He wanted Tommy for more than entertaining conversation.

After a while of not being able to sleep, Finn got up from his bed and walked to the bathroom, where he washed the remnants of his dream off his stomach and changed his PJ bottoms. Sleep evaded him, though, and he was cycling to work by seven in the morning.

HE'D JUST caught up reviewing Armen's case files when he got a call from Stevie, asking whether it was okay for them to come by the office to review a new case and discuss the subject who was detained because of it. At first Finn was excited about the visit, but then he realized he'd have to face Tommy, and he wasn't sure he was ready for that. Before he could get too nervous, the two sergeants breezed into his office. Armen was in court, so Finn couldn't let him handle it. Besides, his curiosity won over his anxiety as Stevie took the lead in telling him what had happened the day before.

"We picked up a suspect this morning from that battery case in St. James's Park last week. He hasn't confessed yet, but we think—" And with this she looked at Tommy. "—we have enough evidence for you to charge him with GBH."

"So give me the details," Finn asked as he sat down on his desk, facing the two police officers.

Tommy proceeded to show him pictures of a man's bruised knuckles, his headshot, and CCTV pictures of him walking into the park and then running out again several minutes later, looking around as if to see whether anyone spotted him.

"It's all pretty circumstantial. Defense will argue he was in the right place at the wrong time and will most likely come up with a reason why his knuckles are bruised, even when the suspect is keeping mum now. We need more."

"The lab is examining the DNA evidence from underneath the victim's fingernails and trying to match it with the suspect's," Tommy added. "Our suspect has scratch marks consistent with defensive wounds."

Finn looked at Tommy, and all he saw was the image from his dream, of Tommy without his shirt on. He shook his head to dispel the image. Right then, it was easier to fix his attention on Stevie, who was a tall, middle-aged woman who'd never progressed further than DS because she didn't always play by the rules and refused to conform to what most superintendents considered to be a female cop. In fact she acted like most of her male counterparts, and this confused the hell out of most of her superiors. Finn suspected that was why she got along so well with Tommy.

"So we'll need to let him go, then, until the lab comes through?" Stevie asked with her usual no-nonsense, slightly arrogant expression.

"Does he have representation yet?" Finn asked.

"He does," Stevie replied.

"In that case you don't have a lot of choice. His solicitor will demand he be released. We might as well keep him on our side until we actually have reason to remand his client," Finn stated.

"Sure enough, guv'."

Both DSs walked out of his office, but when Finn looked up from his papers, Tommy was standing in front of his desk.

"Did you forget to tell me anything?"

"I, eh, wanted to ask you if you were coming to the pub later."

Finn shrugged.

"Armen just called Stevie to tell her he won his first solo case and invited us to McConnell's since we did most of the investigation work. I thought you'd want to celebrate with us... him."

Finn caught Tommy's slip of the tongue but decided to let it slide. "I should be there for him, being his mentor and all."

"Yes," Tommy replied. "You should."

He had that twinkle in his eye that Finn always thought was mischief, and Finn knew he was a goner. He even let it slide that Armen had called Stevie and not him to announce his first big victory.

TOMMY

MCCONNELL'S WAS crowded, even for a Friday night. He could barely hear himself think, let alone carry on a conversation. This was a copper's pub, not a lawyer's bar, which meant asking for a half pint was frowned upon and they didn't make fancy drinks. It was lager, bitter, stout, or Scotch. For anything else they'd direct you across the street to the Half Circle, where you could not only get cocktails but halfway decent food as well. Here just about all you could get to combat hunger pains was a packet of crisps.

Armen was the center of attention and was clearly enjoying every minute of it. It was his party, after all. Stevie was telling tall tales in the corner for the three people close enough to hear her. Tommy was sitting on a bench behind one of the tables with a half-full pint of lager in front of him when Finn walked in. He gestured at him and scooted a little closer to the other occupant of the bench, a woman he didn't know, to make room for him. Finn seemed to be grateful at finding a familiar face without attracting too much attention. He'd barely sat down before a pint was thrust in front of him. Armen winked at him and then carried on the rowdy conversation he was having with three or four of Tommy's work colleagues.

Finn smiled and then shook his head at Tommy. He said something to Tommy he didn't quite catch, so Tommy gestured that he hadn't understood.

"I'm seeing a different side of Armen," Finn repeated, shouting this time.

"He's on cloud nine!" Tommy agreed.

"I remember my first big win too."

Tommy drank some more from his pint and remained next to Finn, not knowing what to say. He could feel the warmth of Finn's leg against his and was tempted to put his hand on Finn's knee but didn't think it would be welcome. After all, he still didn't know whether Finn swung his way. He reckoned the ball was in Finn's court, since Finn knew Tommy was gay. It didn't make the proximity any easier, though.

Finn was barely drinking his beer, and the noise was getting to Tommy. "Want to get out of here?" He had to repeat it to Finn, but after that, Finn nodded. He finished his pint at record-breaking speed and followed Tommy outside.

"Phew," Finn said as they made it to the small awning where some of the smokers had gathered. "The fresh air feels good."

"Bit nippy," Tommy replied, watching their breath come out all foggy.

Finn chuckled. "I shouldn't have drunk that beer so fast." To prove his point he swayed a bit, and Tommy grabbed him.

"Well, you're a cheap date," Tommy quipped.

Finn giggled, and Tommy thought it was the funniest sound coming from the prosecutor. It also made him look adorable.

"Think you can walk a bit?"

"Sure," Finn said.

They started walking toward the river where it was quieter and passed a few couples making out against the buildings on the darker side of the street. Tommy saw Finn looking at them with melancholy in his eyes, and he decided to take a flying leap.

"Ah, young love. So naïve."

Finn looked at him sideways. "I seem to have missed out on that."

"All work and no play makes even Finn a dull boy."

"I suppose."

Tommy looked at his walking partner, but Finn was staring at the pavement in front of his feet as they slowly walked on. "So is there anyone in your life?"

Finn didn't seem unsettled by the intrusive question. "No. Ayse thinks I'm married to my work."

"Are you?"

"Well, I'm not married to anyone else."

"Would you want to be?" Tommy realized what little alcohol he had in his system made him brave. The darkness of the streets also helped in that respect.

"Not married, no, and if you'd asked me this last week, I would have said I was fine on my own, but with everything that happened in the meantime…."

"I'm a good listener," Tommy blurted out. They'd reached the underpass and walked toward the banister where they could look across the Thames.

Finn stopped there. "I've had too much time to think, Tommy."

"And that's a bad thing?"

"It is when you're not used to it. I... I've been talking to someone. Carlton made me after what happened. It's brought some things to the surface I've been trying to keep buried."

"You have skeletons in your closet?" Tommy tried.

"Wouldn't go that far." Finn chuckled. "It made me realize I come home to an empty flat every evening and my most prolific hobby is taking work home."

"That *is* sad," Tommy agreed. *And lonely* he wanted to add.

"So do you have a boyfriend?"

Tommy smiled at the forward question. "No. Never really had anyone serious. If you don't count my teenage drama."

"Drama?"

"Well, technically I wasn't a teenager anymore when she was born, but I have a twelve-year-old daughter."

Finn looked at Tommy as if he'd just said something totally unbelievable. And maybe he had. "I didn't know that."

"Kasey lives with her mum and stepdad. She shows up at my flat when she's had a row with her mother and then stays over. I give her mum a call to say not to worry, and I make sure she makes it to school the next day. That's about it. It happens maybe four or five times a year."

"Does she know you're...?"

"Gay?" Tommy chuckled. "She thinks it's *kewl*," Tommy exaggerated. "She's a good kid. Her mum is trying hard not to be a gran at thirty-two, but yeah."

Tommy could swear Finn had moved closer. The night air was chilly, but the heat radiating off Finn was positively tropical. His arm was brushing against his, and Tommy had to restrain himself from taking Finn's hand.

"I never thanked you for making sure my little courtroom drama didn't get too out of hand. Don't think I could have lived down being escorted out by the ushers," Finn said in a soft voice.

"Instead you were taken away by ambulance men. Don't know which is worse," Tommy answered, trying to sound casual. When it didn't lift Finn's spirits, he looked at him. "I wish I could have done more."

Finn shrugged. "I lost it in there. You came to my rescue, took me into the robing room and helped me calm down."

"So that was the robing room? One of those lockers is yours?"

Finn nodded and looked at Tommy as he turned away from the river and leaned his backside against the banister.

Finn seemed to move closer, and Tommy couldn't resist doing the same. His heart rate sped up as Finn let go of the banister to turn toward him just a little, and Tommy nodded, hoping that showed both that he was open to the overture and that he understood what Finn was trying to do.

The brush of Finn's lips against his was fleeting and way too soft to call it a kiss.

"I'm sorry."

"Why?" Tommy asked.

"I didn't mean to…."

"Kiss me?"

Finn sighed, eyes directed up.

"You have no idea how many times I've wanted you to do that. I didn't want to presume you were into me at all, so I never made that move. I reckoned you knew where I stood."

Finn bit his lips. "It's not because you're gay that you're into me either, Tommy."

"I know." Tommy looked at Finn, who was still avoiding eye contact. "So will you kiss me properly, then?"

Finn was breathing more heavily than normal, and Tommy detected some stress. "What's wrong?"

"I've… I don't… I've never done this before."

"Kiss a man?"

Finn nodded briskly.

It explained a lot, Tommy found. "A kiss is a kiss." He shrugged. "Unless it really means something. But it's just like kissing a woman, only if you do a lot of it, you get whisker burn."

Finn smiled, and Tommy felt his heart take flight.

"I need for us to take it slow."

"I can do slow," Tommy replied.

Finn leaned against him again and put another chaste kiss on Tommy's lips. This time he lingered longer, and Tommy wanted to grab and devour him but decided that would go against what Finn wanted tonight. He'd have to make do with the feeling of Finn's soft lips against his and his masculine, faintly cologned scent under his nose. The pressure of Finn's chest against his was an added bonus. And then Finn pulled away.

"See, that wasn't so hard, now was it?"

Finn shook his head, his smile still present. "I like you a lot, Tommy Drummond."

Tommy swallowed. So his crush wasn't as unrequited as he thought, after all.

Chapter Five

FINN

HE WALKED back to the CPS offices with a spring in his step. He hadn't felt much like partying but wanted Armen to feel like he supported him for the full 100 percent, so he'd gone to the pub.

Riding his bicycle back home, he tried to replay in his head what happened after seeing Tommy. Had he really kissed him? Ayse would be proud, only he wasn't going to tell her. This was between him and Tommy, nobody else. For one, if Carlton found out, he'd prevent Tommy from investigating Finn's cases so there would be no conflict of interest. He couldn't have that. Tommy was the best investigator he knew, and Finn had asked him to join the Central Criminal Court Trials Unit on more than one occasion.

That night his dream of Tommy was back, and this time it didn't surprise him. He now knew what it was like to kiss him and had felt Tommy's chest through their layers of clothing. If anything, he had a better image to dream about. He didn't wake up with a start, but with an intense feeling of longing to know what it would really feel like to have Tommy that close for more than a quick snog. It had been obvious from the night before that Tommy was open to them trying to go further, and at the same time, some of Finn's anxiety was subdued by Tommy's patience and restraint at pushing Finn's boundaries.

As Finn lay awake, the doubts crept in. How long would he be able to try Tommy's patience? Would Tommy understand there was a reason he'd kept himself from human contact, physical human contact, for all of his adult life? Would he ever be able to truly tell Tommy about it?

As he got out of bed, he resolved to play it by ear. Maybe it wouldn't be necessary to explain everything to Tommy. He had a hard enough time explaining it to himself.

AROUND LUNCHTIME Finn couldn't stay cooped up in his office for one minute longer. Carlton had gone to lunch, and Armen was in court. He'd been poring over case files all morning, and Carlton kept telling him to savor this, now he actually had the time to go through everything with a fine-toothed comb, but Finn's enjoyment of work came when he argued his case in court, not when he was preparing for it by reading the endless volumes of material the Met had prepared together with his coworkers at the CPS.

He was putting his coat on when a curt knock followed by the opening of his door made his heart skip a beat. Tommy was paying him a visit.

"What brings you here?"

"Guess I caught you just in time. Won't keep you long."

Finn smiled and started taking his coat off again. "No problem. I was just going out for some fresh air."

"In that case, can I interest you in a little field research?"

"Stevie not with you?" Finn asked instead of answering Tommy's question.

"I just left her where I'd like to take you. She's got the car, so we'll need to take the Tube."

"We could take a cab?" Finn suggested.

"Naah, wouldn't want to put it on the CPS's tab. I… eh. I'm not here entirely for work business only."

Finn smiled, feeling his face heat up. Sometimes he cursed his fair complexion. "Were you planning on making a pit stop on your way to this field research area?"

This time it was Tommy's turn to blush. He also chuckled and looked away, his hands resting on his hips, which spread his jacket and gave Finn a view of his flat stomach and well-filled groin area.

"Stevie will wonder where I am. So no, but let's say *your* presence isn't *strictly* necessary. I just assumed you weren't as busy as you usually were, so when I suggested to Stevie you might like to see this crime scene firsthand she agreed."

Finn peeled his eyes away from Tommy's enticing body when he heard that Stevie was in on it.

"Well, I did want to see *you*. Preferably alone." This time Tommy was looking straight at him, and all hints of shyness were gone. He clearly wanted there to be no misunderstanding.

"Would you close the door behind you, then?"

Tommy nodded, Finn's favorite mischievous Tommy expression on his face, as he shut the door, first with his hand, then by leaning against it. Tommy's hands remained on his hips, and Finn walked toward him, not exactly brimming with confidence. Tommy's face remained a picture of "come hither," though. It gave Finn the confidence to close the space between them and line up his body with Tommy's. He was an inch or two taller than Tommy, but Tommy was broader, more muscled. Still they seemed to fit together well.

Tommy moved his hands to Finn's hips and drew him closer until Finn too was leaning against the door. Finn didn't know what to do other than kiss Tommy. He hated feeling this out of his depth, but at the same time it was exhilarating. Tommy wanted him. Tommy had taken the Underground to come see him with some feeble excuse, and now they were making out in his office. If anyone caught them there....

Tommy's hands moved to cup Finn's face, and Finn finally found his anchor by resting his hands where Tommy's had been just moments earlier. Tommy's tongue gently coaxed Finn's lips apart, and Finn let it happen. He could taste Tommy now, and it made his heart race. How could a simple kiss be this enticing, erotic, mind-blowing?

And then Finn realized Tommy had him firmly in his grip and he had no way out. He put his hands on the door and pushed himself away. Tommy looked a little perplexed, and Finn could only turn away and walk to his window. The calming view of the river and the other side of the embankment settled his breathing.

"I'm sorry. You asked for patience, and I didn't give it to you," Tommy said behind him.

Finn sighed but didn't turn around. "I wanted it too, Tommy."

Finn tried not to freeze when he felt Tommy's hand on the small of his back. Instead he savored the warmth it emanated. Ayse was right yet again. He craved to be touched, not just by anyone but by someone he trusted, and for some reason he trusted Tommy, although he had no rational explanation for it. He didn't look over his shoulder as a second hand joined the first, and then the warmth spread to Finn's shoulder as Tommy rested his chin on it.

"You have some view from here."

"You've been to my office before," Finn said, trying to feel soothed by the touch rather than unnerved.

"Yes," Tommy replied. Finn thought he could hear him smile. "But I've never looked out the window. I'm always looking at you."

A tickle near his ear and a slow intake of breath near it told Finn Tommy was inhaling his smell. He remembered the first time he'd smelled Tommy and understood the attraction, so he let his head fall back a little and leaned into the touch. He turned his head sideways and caught some of Tommy's distinct scent too. It turned him on, and he was glad he wasn't pressed against Tommy anymore.

Then Tommy pulled away from him. The gesture wasn't abrupt, more a little reluctant as if Tommy didn't really want to let go just yet. It helped Finn pull himself together, though. Tommy was at the door before Finn dared to turn around.

"So shall we go to the crime scene, then? Forensics have gone over it already. All the pictures and most of the evidence has been taken. Stevie's wrapping up our paperwork."

Finn nodded. "Yes, let's go see this firsthand."

TOMMY

THE UNDERGROUND was crowded because of the lunch hour. Not that there were any really quiet moments during business hours, but as they walked into the station, he could tell the trains were going to be packed. They managed to slip into one just as the doors closed, and they were pressed together, trying to keep their balance as the trains hustled over the bumpy track.

The way they were standing, Tommy could smell Finn, and it instantly made him hard, just like it had at Finn's office, only this time they were facing each other, and it was only going to be a matter of time before Finn caught on. Restraining himself wasn't easy at the best of times and had only got worse after that first kiss at the embankment of the Thames. From that moment on he knew his feelings were returned, but he'd also been told in no uncertain terms to be patient. Being Finn's first man held a certain attraction, and he looked forward to aiding in Finn's education, but right then, those feelings were most unwelcome.

A sudden jolt as the carriage took a sharp turn at breakneck speed made all the occupants grab for the nearest safety rail, and it pushed Finn even tighter against Tommy. The look on Finn's face was a mixture of surprise and wonder. His mouth was slightly open, and his eyes were wide. Tommy smiled and theatrically rolled his eyes at Finn, which made Finn smile even broader.

"I'm sorry," he mouthed at Finn.

Finn shrugged.

"But can you blame me?" he said equally silently.

Instead of answering, Finn bit his lip.

And then Tommy felt a hand over his distended crotch. Automatically he looked down, but both Finn's jacket and his were obscuring his view. As the hand slowly kneaded him, he looked around to see if anyone was spotting their interaction, but everyone was minding their own business. Did the hand belong to the shy and sexually insecure man he thought Finn was? In any case he was doing a good job bringing him off.

Tommy leaned forward so he was closer to Finn's ear. Whispering was no use, so he spoke in his normal voice, hoping nobody was close enough to hear. "If you don't stop, I'm going to pop like a champagne cork."

The hand didn't stop, and as Tommy moved back to look at Finn, he could see Finn wasn't about to stop at all.

"Do you want me to?" Finn asked.

Before Tommy could answer, the train slowed and stopped at the station. They had to move to let people off, and Tommy felt the warmth of Finn's hand disappear. When the doors closed and they started moving again, Finn was too far away from him. Tommy tried not to look at him and instead pictured the horrific crime scene he'd left earlier in an attempt to let his arousal abate. He only hoped he didn't have a big wet stain at the front of his trousers.

FINN

"SO BRING me up to speed?" Finn said to Stevie as he walked into the posh duplex in Belgravia. He tried to focus on Tommy's partner instead of Tommy because he felt a little guilty about what he'd just done to him on the train. It wasn't like him to be that forward, but the crowd in the train had provided more privacy than they'd had at his office, and he'd felt the sudden urge to do something about the hardness pressed against his thigh when Tommy had been pushed against him. Seeing Tommy's eyes glaze over had given him a sense of control, and he both wished he'd never done it and that he'd finished Tommy off.

"No forced entry, so the perp knew our victims, or at least gained entrance into the apartment legally," Stevie said as she handed Finn a white jumpsuit to put on.

"Victims? Plural?"

"One man, one woman. The ME thinks both victims were sexually assaulted around the time of death. There is DNA all over the place, and she's interested to see how many donors she can identify. Our hope is three or four."

"So one or two assailants?"

"Both vics were tied up, so technically one rather strong and forceful perp could have done it. Especially if he carried a weapon."

"Any evidence suggesting what he carried?" Finn asked as he felt himself slip into his professional mode. He could do this.

"Nothing to conclude gun or knife. Neither victim shows clear knife or gunshot wounds."

"How long have they been dead?"

"ME estimates death occurred in the early hours of the morning. The doorman called it in at two this afternoon when he was supposed to bring the car around for them to leave and they didn't respond."

With all three of them dressed in the regulation protective clothing, they started walking around the clearly affluent flat. There were signs of a struggle, with a knocked-over lamp and a broken vase in one corner of the sitting room, but it all seemed minor for what Stevie had described to him. One of the forensics team was investigating a bloody fingerprint on a doorframe, but that was about all the evidence Finn could see.

"This way, guv'," Stevie suggested. They followed her into one of the bedrooms, where a much larger bloodbath was evident, even though the bodies of the victims had already been removed. Finn treaded carefully, since he was unaccustomed to being invited to a crime scene this close to the time of the events. Usually, if a visit was in order for Finn, he'd make it after all the evidence was turned over to the CPS, and this could be weeks rather than days after the crime.

Finn tried to suppress a shiver.

"The pictures forensics take don't do this justice," Tommy said quietly.

"I can almost feel the hatred," Finn replied. He took a deep breath to compose himself. "So what is the theory? I could be wrong, but this doesn't look like a robbery."

"Sex games gone bad, maybe?" Stevie said as if she'd just asked them what they wanted on their sandwiches for lunch. "There's ropes and belts for tying up—"

"Hang on," Finn interrupted. "I thought you said no knife wounds? The amount of blood I see here suggests these people were gutted."

"ME isn't sure what they used. A knife is a possibility, but the wounds were deep, with little superficial damage. She thought it could have been done by a screwdriver or an ice pick. They're going to have to rinse the bodies off to find out, apparently."

Finn swallowed to keep the bile from rising. He'd stick to crime scene photos from now on.

Tommy clearly wasn't afflicted by the same involuntary response. He was scanning the room.

Finn decided keeping his focus on Tommy was a much better choice, after all.

"See anything interestin', guv'?"

Finn startled at Stevie grinning at him. "I don't usually get to see the fresh crime scenes," Finn replied quickly, trying to hide the fact he'd been caught eyeing Tommy. "He seems to feel right at home here." He gestured his head at Tommy, who was crouching near an odd-shaped bloodstain.

"Yeah, he does. Born to it," Stevie replied with an all too knowing smirk across her face.

"So you're thinking these two people invited a third or maybe fourth person into their bedroom, and it got so out of hand that this person or persons ended up gutting their hosts?"

"It's one explanation," Stevie said calmly.

"And the other?"

"The perp might not have been invited. When I leaned on the doorman, he reported a missing spare key. Apparently it'd been gone for a few weeks and he was waiting for a replacement."

"Is the doorman a suspect?"

"Everyone's a suspect, guv'. You know that," Stevie replied with a sparse smile. "But if you ask my opinion, then it's unlikely. My guess is on the sex games angle." She dangled a clean pair of leather cuffs from her latexed hand.

Finn nodded. He did value Stevie's opinion. Stevie had the best gut instinct Finn had ever encountered. Finn started walking around the apartment again, deliberately watching his step and without touching anything. Tommy wasn't as careful, simply because he was obviously a lot more used to doing this than Finn was. Finn admired Tommy's single-mindedness and realized instantly they shared the same level of concentration.

Only now that concentration was out the window. Finn's mind kept wandering to what happened on the Tube over here, and how bold he'd been to touch Tommy so intimately. At the time it seemed like something Tommy was open to, and Finn had acted on an almost incontrollable urge. This was what scared him. He didn't know how to act around Tommy. He had no clue how to take it from where they were—which was hardly more than a little kissing and some holding—to something approaching a physical relationship. Technically, he knew Tommy would want sex at some point. Purely mechanically, he knew how that would work, but he had no idea how to convey his intentions to Tommy and had even less of a clue what Tommy's were.

So what possessed him to grope Tommy like that? In public, no less. It was so far out of character he didn't even recognize himself in those actions. It wasn't like him to force himself onto anyone like that, robbing from them any choice in the matter. It went against everything he believed in, yet it didn't take a stellar memory to recall that they'd been his actions.

"Tommy, can we talk when you're done?"

"Yes, of course," Tommy replied, turning to Finn with a faint smile on his face. "I'll square it with Stevie, but I think we've seen all we need to see."

Finn watched him walk over to his partner and nod to her as they conversed. Finn didn't try very hard to understand them. He could tell from their expressions they were talking about work.

"All done," Tommy announced as he approached Finn again. "Want to grab some nosh?"

Finn looked around to see whether anyone was in earshot. The forensics team were packing up, and Stevie was at the other side of the room. "I want to apologize for the Underground... thing." *Very eloquent, Mister Prosecutor.*

"You mean the... eh...?" Tommy looked around as well, probably for the same reason Finn had. "Your... very, eh, warm... hand?"

Finn released a nervous chuckle. "I don't usually do those sorts of things."

"I didn't think you did."

"Please don't take this the wrong way. I...." *Don't know how to behave around you?* No, that wouldn't do. "Can we start at the beginning again?"

Tommy leaned a little closer, watching that Stevie stayed far enough away from them. "The kissing was a good start. I liked that. But maybe we can try some of that groping in a more private place?"

Finn feared he was turning crimson. "I promise I won't do that again."

Tommy smiled and looked at him sideways. "Please don't promise that."

A little taken aback, Finn stared at him.

Tommy put his hand, out of view from everyone still around, on Finn's stomach and leaned close enough to whisper in his ear. "Somewhere more private, I hope to repeat the experience. Your hand felt nice."

Finn tried to keep himself together. Tommy's hand felt nice too. He could feel its heat through his fine white shirt and already dreaded the moment Tommy would take it away. Anyone seeing them standing like they were would notice the intimacy, though. When a door slammed shut in the next room, Tommy took a step back, and their connection was broken.

Almost as an afterthought, he turned back toward Finn. "Cooking for two is more fun than just for me. Did you have plans for tonight?"

Finn automatically shook his head. He kept himself busy at work these days, but there wasn't enough reading for him to need to take it home with him like he used to do all the time when he still spent half his days in court. The thought of a free evening at his flat was less appealing than what Tommy was offering. Yet joining Tommy at his created another difficulty. They were steering toward more intimacy, and that scared Finn.

Chapter Six

TOMMY

FINN WAS leaning against the counter, trying to look relaxed. "Seriously. I could burn water given half a chance."

Tommy raised his eyebrows. "So what do you eat in the evening?"

Finn shrugged, taking a sip from his red wine. "Anything I can pick up between Southwark Bridge and Kensington? I don't actually eat at home a lot. I often work late."

"But a man's got to eat." He let his gaze wander over Finn's lean frame, which this one time wasn't covered by flowing court robes or his ever present half-length coat and scarf. Finn was wearing a clearly expensive white shirt that fit him perfectly and was tucked into black dress trousers that were in turn held up by a thin black leather belt. The way his arms were crossed, with one hand elegantly holding the wineglass, left little to Tommy's imagination. He couldn't help mentally undressing the man standing in his kitchen.

"Oh, I eat. When I don't forget."

Tommy tossed the searing pan he'd just added the vegetables to before pouring in the oyster sauce. It had a lot of garlic in it, which was not something he'd put in his mouth before a date, but he reckoned they were both going to eat it, so it didn't really matter. The dish didn't take a lot of time to heat up, so he picked a spoon out of the drawer and scooped some up before walking over to Finn.

"Here, taste this." Holding his hand under Finn's chin, he offered the spoon for Finn to lick.

Clearly hot, Finn was struggling not to burn his mouth. He waved his hand before his opened mouth before tasting it. "This is excellent. You can't get anything this good at a takeaway."

Tommy smiled, flattered. "Oh, come on. You sound like you need to get on my good side." He turned to his pan, stirred the contents once more to make sure all the rice noodles were thoroughly covered with oyster sauce, and then proceeded to divide the stir-fry between two bowls. Finn opened the drawer Tommy had taken the spoon out of. "There are chopsticks in the drawer next to it," Tommy said, taking both bowls into the sitting room where the dinner table was. He put them on the place mats that were always there to cover up the rather stained wooden surface, and by the time he'd unearthed some matching napkins, Finn was in the room with him with two sets of chopsticks.

"Cloth napkins," Finn remarked with a smirk. "Fancy for an impromptu supper."

Tommy didn't reply. What could he say? That in his mother's house they didn't even have napkins, let alone cloth ones matching his place mats, and used to wipe their mouths with their sleeves? He pointed at the chair usually reserved for visitors and sat down on the one closest to the kitchen. He watched with fascination as Finn closed his eyes and breathed in.

"This smells utterly delicious."

"Dig in," Tommy suggested, as he picked up his chopsticks. Tommy had shared food with Finn on other occasions, usually at the CPS offices shortly before an important case was to go to trial. More often than not Armen and Stevie were present, and supper consisted of the local Chinese takeaway, and they ate out of the plastic boxes the food came in. He'd admired Finn's dexterity with chopsticks even then, especially because Finn never seemed to enjoy his food for more than mere sustenance. He was always tossing ideas back and forth and still working while he ate. Not tonight. Tommy watched Finn slip little morsels of food into his mouth and taste them as if he wanted to capture every single identifiable flavor. He was so entranced he almost forgot to eat himself. At the same time he felt flattered. It didn't feel like Finn was trying to get on his good side. Finn was simply indulging himself in the food Tommy had cooked for him in the ten short minutes he'd spent behind his stove. The only sounds that came from Finn were a series of barely audible, clearly appreciative murmurs.

As Tommy took another bite, he felt his cock stir, thinking of what Finn would be like if he was really allowing himself to be spoiled. He entertained the thought of Finn naked on his bed putting other things in his mouth besides food and moaning appreciatively then as well.

"I couldn't eat another bite, sadly," Finn said, pushing his empty bowl a little farther up the table. "We have a kitchen at the CPS offices.

Next time you're coming by to work on a case, I won't be asking you to pop around to the takeaway but will demand you make this for us."

Tommy smiled, knowing flattery when he heard it. "Next time all of you can come around here to work and I'll feed you." He got up from the table and took the bowls into the kitchen.

"That's an option too." Finn followed close by.

Tommy simply put the bowls in the kitchen sink, along with the chopsticks and the wok.

"You wash, I dry?" Finn suggested.

"I can do it later."

"Won't take long."

Finn grabbed the kitchen towel from the peg and held it up, so Tommy opened the tap and waited for the water to become hot. It felt oddly domestic, even more so than when he was cooking for Finn. As he washed the bowls, rinsed them under the running tap, and then handed them to Finn, he knew their touches weren't accidental. The apprehension about what was going to happen after they were done was growing, and he felt more and more aroused as the seconds ticked away. Fortunately he'd changed the sheets on his bed that morning.

After reaching up to put the bowls away, he came face-to-face with Finn and was pulled into a tight hug. It felt good to be held, and Tommy enjoyed Finn's commanding strength. When Finn let up a bit, Tommy could look him in the eye, and he did marginally the same as their first time at the underpass: he nodded at Finn to give him permission to kiss him. Their kiss was a little like the first time as well. It started hesitant and chaste, only this time it became a lot more heated a lot faster, and Tommy found himself pulling Finn even closer, knowing full well Finn would be able to feel his arousal. And just like earlier that day at Finn's office, that's what seemed to make Finn pull away.

"Not slow enough?" Tommy asked, immediately wanting to take his words back when he read in Finn's face that the answer was yes.

"I better go."

"Finn! Please don't... go." He knew he sounded lame. And needy. But he really didn't want Finn to leave yet. "It's early yet, and we can just talk, in there, on the sofa."

Finn seemed to think about it. "Thank you for dinner. It's been ages since I've had a home-cooked meal. It was a treat."

Tommy knew he was being let down. He also knew he had no right to beg Finn to stay. "I didn't weird you out with the crime scene, I hope?"

Finn chuckled. "No. However grueling, I think it would help me prosecute the case. If it was given to me, of course. As things stand, if my office gets it, Carlton will probably assign Armen."

"Then he'll need your coaching, because I think this will be a bit above his level of experience."

"I'll need to do a lot more song and dance for Carlton to let me anywhere near a judge or a witness again."

"So tell that cute psychiatrist what she needs to hear."

Finn smiled as he moved to the hallway to grab his coat. "If only I knew what she needed. She's on my side, but she doesn't think I'm ready yet either."

"Does it count that I think you're ready?"

Finn put on his coat and wrapped his scarf around his neck. "You're biased."

Tommy was left standing in his hallway after Finn closed the front door behind him.

THE NEXT morning when Tommy arrived at the station, Stevie called him to ask him to cover for her. She'd been summoned to her son's school and would be in later, so Tommy decided to tackle the paperwork for the Belgravia murders. A call to the medical examiner's office revealed that the murder weapon was confirmed to be an ice pick. Finding this a curious choice of weapon, Tommy charged up his computer and opened HOLMES in the hope of finding murder cases with similarities. Contrary to most searches through the Metropolitan Police database, this one gave him swift results. Seven cases popped up. There were three old cases from the nineties, all robberies where the assailant used an ice pick. A man had been apprehended for those, but he'd died of an overdose before he'd been put in front of a judge. The other four were unsolved. All of them had occurred in the last two years, and they showed a growing level of violence.

Tommy took notes. The earliest one had been an attack on a young woman. She'd been raped at knifepoint. Or more exactly, at ice-pick point. And she'd survived. He took down her details and decided to pay her a visit once Stevie got back.

The second victim had been flagged, a male police constable on traffic duty, a mere two months out of training. Raped, then murdered with a single stab to the chest. Tommy frowned. Assailants who raped indiscriminate of gender were rare. Unless it was their way of asserting dominance. Rape was often about power, but most rapists stuck to one gender. If this crime was committed by the same perp as the others, it was a first for Tommy.

The third victim was a homeless man, found by tourists in a back street in the theater district. He'd also been raped, then murdered. Multiple stab wounds this time. Definitely less controlled than the PC.

When Tommy opened the pictures from the fourth case, he knew this was the same perp as the Belgravia murders. A law student had been murdered in his student flat. There were no signs of a struggle in the rest of the small apartment, but the bedroom was a bloodbath. The young man had been raped and then gutted after being tied to the bed with leather cuffs.

"That looks familiar."

Tommy jumped and only then realized it was Stevie creeping up on him.

"It's not from Belgravia."

"I gathered that."

"It's from an open case from about four months ago. A student."

Stevie looked over his shoulder and commandeered Tommy's mouse before flicking through the photos. "Wouldn't surprise me if that was done by the same perp as our case."

"I agree."

"Miss Fielding, how nice of you to join us today."

They both looked up into the stern face of their DI.

"I think we have a serial killer on our hands, sir," Tommy said quickly before the DSI could go on about Stevie being late. "I found several recent cases with a similar MO in HOLMES but with escalating violence." He got up and grabbed his jacket from the back of his seat. "We're on our way to the CPS to report it."

"No," the DSI replied curtly. "Bring me your findings, and we'll take it through the proper channels." He didn't wait for an answer.

Stevie looked at Tommy with large eyes. "I thought he'd be happy with a break in the case?"

"He doesn't want us to take it to Finn. Proper channels? That means he wants to take credit for it."

"Technically, he should," Stevie said, still looking in the direction of where their DSI had walked away.

"But he usually wants to know what we'll charge the perp with before we go see him. Which means conferring with a prosecutor first."

Stevie threw Tommy an amused look. "You just want to go see Finn DeHavilland."

Chapter Seven

FINN

"SIT DOWN, DeHavilland," Bill Carlton demanded in his usual won't-take-no-for-an-answer manner that made him the formidable force he was in the CPS. "How are your talks with Dr. Kartal going?"

"Well enough, I suppose." Finn was on guard. He hadn't been given a reason why Carlton had asked to speak with him, simply that it had to be his first stop as he arrived at the office. He'd been uncharacteristically late after another sleepless night and more regrets than he could deal with, which he was now, reasonably successfully, trying not to think about anymore.

"Dr. Kartal was instrumental in allowing you back to resume at least part of your responsibilities here, so she speaks quite highly of you. I suspect she has a soft spot for you, which is why I didn't follow all of her advice."

"Which advice was that?"

"I can't tell you the details—"

"Don't dangle a carrot," Finn interrupted, thankful that his years at the CPS, mostly under the wing of Carlton, had given him leave to speak frankly to the man—who was his superior, after all.

"She wanted you to resume work as soon as possible because she feared you'd lose the rudder if you didn't. Something about you living for your work and not having any hobbies. You should come golfing with me at the weekend, Finn."

"I think I'll pass, but thank you for the kind offer." He picked an imaginary piece of fluff from his wool trousers.

Carlton raised an eyebrow at him, clearly not buying Finn's rehearsed and overly polite answer. "Very well. Dr. Kartal seems to believe you can handle as big a case load as always, but I wasn't ready to let you loose on the unsuspecting public just yet, which is why I kept you out of court."

"You do know I have seven pending cases I would never have given to Armen to handle? He's not ready for the big ones yet."

"He won his first big case alone. He seems more ready than you assume." Carlton stared at Finn with icy cold determination. "But since you won't be spending any time in court, you're free to pursue a long-term case."

"Long-term case?"

"And a very delicate one as well. I'm relying on total confidentiality. Not a word to anyone about this, not even Armen."

"I'll need more information than that, Carlton."

"I thought you'd be jumping at the offer of a thorough investigation like this." Carlton turned around and took his bottle of Scotch out of his cabinet, along with two glasses.

"Not for me, thanks. Isn't it a bit early for that?"

Carlton cocked his head.

"You know you can't butter me up with liquor, Bill." Finn didn't often use his boss's first name, but he found that occasionally it brought the message home.

"Very well." Carlton put the bottle and glasses away again and sat down opposite Finn. "I think you're the perfect candidate for this job, and since you have spare time I don't think you can afford to relinquish your duty on this one. Nor would you want to once I tell you what this is about."

TOMMY

"THE BOSS said we should look at it as a promotion," Stevie said, sitting outside the office of the man who was to become their new DSI.

"Then why does it feel like we've been put on the back burner?"

Stevie shrugged. "Let's just hear him out."

"I just think it's strange that we're being reassigned right after we catch a break in a big case. No explanation given."

Stevie looked more at ease than Tommy felt. "It wasn't like we found the perp. We just tied some more cases to him." She sighed. "At least we know this one. Stanton isn't a bad bloke. The boss must have had his reasons for picking us out of the litter, and I bet it's for something good."

Tommy wasn't so sure, but he had the sudden craving to call Finn and ask him for advice. Only he couldn't, now could he? He had the man's mobile number all right, but that didn't mean he could call on a whim.

"Gentlemen." A booming voice in the corridor called Tommy back to attention. "Please come into my office."

Tommy eyed their new super. Gray suit with expensive-looking black shoes underneath. When he turned around he was sporting a black turtleneck sweater under fair skin and hair, alert dark eyes, and a cleanly shaven face. He was still all business, just like he'd been a year ago when they worked together briefly.

"Sit." He pointed at the two chairs in front of his desk. "Tea?"

"Yeah, sure. All the trimmin's for me," Stevie replied with a smile. Tommy simply nodded.

Stanton poured three mugs from a side cabinet inside his office and handed them one each, unceremoniously putting down the milk and sugar on his desk for them to help themselves. Then he sat down behind his desk.

"Let me get right to the point. I'm heading a special task force and commissioned two sergeants with ample experience to work on my team. This will mean you will be temporarily assigned to the Central Criminal Court Trials Unit. You will be given time to do the tasks necessary but will need to spend some time on your other cases as well, so as not to arouse too much suspicion. You will work closely with the CPS on this to make sure all interrogations and subsequent arrests are completely without scrutiny."

Tommy felt his eyes on him specifically.

"According to your file this shouldn't be a problem."

Tommy didn't know how to reply. There were two of them. Why was the super scrutinizing him? Clearly he couldn't know about just how close he was getting to one certain member of the Crown Prosecution Service.

"Of course, guv'," Stevie replied in her usual jovial manner. "We've moonlighted for them before. And in Serious Crimes we always liaise with the CPS. Only way to make sure we don't get branded in court afterwards. But then you know that."

"So what is this all about?" Tommy asked, much more restrained than Stevie had been.

The superintendent waited to proceed, looking from Tommy to Stevie and back at Tommy. "We have reason to believe a senior investigator at the Yard has fabricated evidence in more than a dozen cases, sometimes leading to convictions based on false evidence. We need you to reexamine some of these cases for two reasons. First we want to indict the investigator and anyone else who helped him falsify the evidence, and secondly your investigations might be used to reopen certain cases, if necessary." He waited to let it all sink in. "So you see how your working together with the CPS will be crucial to this. As will your confidentiality. The senior investigator is still at work right now. He's a DI and outranks both of you. He's also not aware he's being investigated, so direct contact will be out of the question."

"Isn't this supposed to be a job for the DPS? Doesn't the Yard have its own oversight committee?" Stevie asked, her face suddenly solemn.

"There has been an investigation by the Directorate of Professional Standards, but it revealed very little. The prosecutor therefore thinks someone at the DPS is in on the fraud."

"So this is just one prosecutor thinking he's been wronged?" Now it was Tommy's turn to ask for some answers. He was already dreading not being able to tell Finn about this.

"There is enough evidence presented to warrant further investigation. And yes, this comes from one prosecutor, but he built a strong case. It's up to us to make it stick. Are you two up for it?"

Tommy looked at Stevie, who was already grinning like the cat that got the cream. He knew Stevie loved a good, juicy case like this, and so did he, but it was going to put a lot of stress on them, with keeping everything very hush-hush. Stevie nodded at him, asking for permission to take on the case. Tommy smiled briefly.

"We'll do it," Stevie said with a grin. "Hope this also means a pay rise. Three children don't pay for themselves."

DSI Mark Stanton got up from behind his desk with a big smile. "Let's go liaise with your prosecutor, then. He has everything you'll need to get started."

Tommy had a brisk thirty-minute walk along the Strand to think about how his day had turned out. It was one to remember, any way you wanted to look at it. DSI Stanton didn't slow down for one minute, though. Tommy had a pretty good physique and could have easily run the distance, but he was surprised how well Stanton managed to keep up. He and Stevie walked quite a bit every day, but usually at a more leisurely pace. From the Strand they had to walk across the bridge to

Southwark. Tommy wasn't surprised to be led down the familiar corridors of the CPS building.

They could have gone into any of the many prosecutors' offices but were directed to one Tommy had never been to, Chief Crown Prosecutor William Carlton's.

"Good to see you, Mark. And you brought your team?"

"Stephanie Fielding and Thomas Drummond, both sergeants in good standing and apparently quite renowned for their discretion," Stanton replied by way of introduction.

Tommy saw Stevie cringe at hearing her Christian name.

Carlton stepped aside, and Tommy's gaze fell on Finn. For a moment they exchanged nods of recognition.

"And you know Finn DeHavilland, of course."

"'Course we do," Stevie replied, always the first to answer.

Bill Carlton nodded at their visitors. "Then let's not waste anyone's precious time. Finn, like we agreed. Can you do the briefing?"

Carlton sat down on the edge of his desk, and Finn walked around it, closer to where Tommy and Stevie were sitting. He put his hand on an enormous stack of folders with papers piling out of them from three sides.

"We have reason to believe a senior Scotland Yard investigator is fabricating evidence and passing it to the CPS as legally obtained. Some of this evidence has been used in court and has resulted in convictions. Some of it has been dismissed in court, and some has resulted in us deciding not to pursue a suspect because it exonerates him or her." He looked at Carlton for a moment, then continued. "All these investigations will have to be redone, but with the utmost discretion until we can have enough solid evidence to convict the investigator. Chief Prosecutor Carlton and I have decided to focus on a few cases that seem cut-and-dried to make the indictment stick, but we need to gather as much information as possible, because when this gets blown open, most of the trials involved will have to be redone as well, and previously dismissed cases will actually need to go to trial. This has the potential to cause a large dent in the CPS's finances, but this should be secondary to getting a fraudulent cop off the street."

Tommy loved seeing the fire return to Finn. He'd missed that these past weeks after the court meltdown, but now it seemed Finn had found his second wind. "And we do your legwork? Talk to victims, suspects? As if it was an open case?" Tommy asked.

"Exactly," Finn answered. "Only you have to be both discreet and casual about it. Neither the victim nor the suspect can know the cases have been reopened, because technically, they haven't."

"So we're moonlightin'?" Stevie asked.

"Kind of, yes."

"We'll need copies of the cases," Stevie stated.

"Because of the discretion needed for these cases, you will work out of Finn's office for the time being," Carlton said. "We can't risk letting case files of closed cases hang around a police station."

Tommy wanted to protest that they handled case files every day, but he decided against opening his mouth since he reckoned Finn would have talked it through with his boss before they were informed. He saw the benefit of working out of Finn's office, with the possible exception that there would be other people around and that the more time he spent with Finn, the harder it would be to hide that they knew each other a little too well to be just work colleagues. On the other hand, if the night before was anything to go by, their "relationship" had hit a major snag and working with Finn at all was going to be awkward, so he almost didn't dare look at him.

"I suppose since we're used to coming around here to ask the prosecutors for advice, it won't arouse suspicion if we spent a lot of time here," Tommy said.

"So when do we start?" Stevie asked, chipper as ever.

"We're still working out which cases take priority. I suggest you return here tomorrow morning and I'll give you your first assignments."

"Works for me." Stevie got up from her seat.

"And in case you're wondering what my place in all this is?" Mark Stanton asked. "I'll be clearing the time you need with my colleagues and keeping up appearances toward the brass. To them it will look like I am supervising you, but in truth you'll report only to Mr. DeHavilland. I'll only come into play when people start breathing down your necks. I'll also be able to indicate when you're coming too close to the truth, because high up, alarm bells will start going off, and they might make life hard for you."

"Good to know," Tommy said, nodding at Stanton.

They all shook hands and walked out of the ostentatious office. Tommy noticed Finn following them into the corridor, but he didn't want to look at him. He didn't know if DSI Stanton had any idea how well he knew Finn, and Tommy wasn't about to put himself into a situation he had to talk himself out of. "I'll be right back," he told Stevie before turning the corner to the loos.

Tommy had barely finished peeing when Finn entered. He stood next to him as he unzipped.

"Didn't mean to spring this on you without warning, but I've never seen the Met work this quickly. I reported the anomalies to Carlton months ago, keeping him up to date on all the strange happenings I'd discovered, but he didn't do anything with them. Then this morning he assigned me to the case, asking me which police detectives I trusted to work with."

"And you gave them my name," Tommy continued flatly.

"You and Stevie are rock solid. You're thorough and discreet. You were the first team that came to mind."

"I suppose I should be flattered that you're this good at keeping your personal life separated from your work," Tommy said, zipping up and turning away from him to wash his hands.

Finn followed him to the washbasin. "I'm sorry if this is awkward for you, Tommy, but because of the nature of this case and the fact it will need to stay between us and no one else, the only one I could think of working this closely with was you. And Stevie of course."

Tommy heard the jump in Finn's voice as he tried to keep to the facts but failed. It also cracked his armor. "I don't hold anything against you, Finn. I'm not entirely sure what exactly happened, but... we can work together. I don't doubt that."

Finn nodded, and Tommy wished he knew a way to make Finn turn back into the confident man he'd been just minutes earlier in his boss's office. He put his hand over Finn's. "We'll talk later, right?"

Finn nodded. "I'll call you."

Outside in the corridor, Stevie was waiting for him. She was leaning on one of the filing cabinets and flirting with a pretty redheaded secretary. Although she had an ex-husband for every one of her children, Stevie's flirting wasn't totally out of context for Tommy.

When Tommy approached she nodded her good-byes to her conversation partner. "Ready to go?"

Tommy nodded. As they walked outside, he knew he had to confide in Stevie before they ended up working so closely with Finn Stevie would be able to draw her own conclusions.

"Stevie," Tommy said as he held her back before walking toward Southwark Bridge. "I need to tell you something."

She stopped and raised an eyebrow at him.

"Finn DeHavilland and I—"

"Have been making googly eyes at each other ever since your misconduct trial. I know. Have you slept with him yet?"

Tommy was stunned into silence by her question.

"I'm nobody to judge, Tom. My oldest son's father is the DPS officer who investigated the first shooting I was involved in. We met on the job, and he was married at the time. I was still a uniform then. He got me in the family way, divorced his wife, and married me just before I popped. We were separated by the time I returned to work. I know how it goes when you work closely with a good-looking man. Sparks fly. Just never imagined DeHavilland was your type."

Tommy chuckled. "I haven't slept with him."

"So he's playing hard to get? He won't resist you long if we're working out of his office. We'll just have to agree to a sign if you want me out of your space."

"We'll figure something out when it's necessary. You know him, Stevie. He's all work and no play in his office. Nothing's likely to happen when we're working."

Stevie checked him up and down and sported a look Tommy interpreted as almost maternal.

"If there's anything I can do…?"

"I'll let you know."

FINN

HE LIKED working late. He'd missed that in the weeks since his meltdown. Now with the six assigned cases to plow through, he had an excuse to stay behind after everyone had gone home. The sheer volume of some of the case files he'd need to lug home made it that he often preferred to stay until ten or eleven in his office and then go home to sleep. He'd overcome his apprehension about cycling home in the dark a long time ago.

The other upside was that the office was quiet. No distractions. When he grew tired, he would get up and gaze over the slow-flowing Thames and feel calm descend upon him.

He was just poring over a case they'd decided two years earlier not to prosecute when his phone rang. His personal mobile.

Tommy.

Why would he call at this hour? Right. He'd said he'd call and time had slipped away from him.

"Tommy?"

The noise on the other side of the phone connection made it hard to hear the voice.

"I'm watching my building go up in flames, Finn."

"What?" Finn said, fearing that what he heard was that Tommy had narrowly escaped being fried alive.

"My flat. Everything in it. And everyone else's too. Eleven people homeless, including me. It's massive, Finn. I'll be lucky if I can find my front door, let alone anything else. Firemen think it's going to collapse."

Finn was already standing, grabbing his coat. "Are you hurt?"

"No, it was already blazing when I arrived. I was at my mum's when one of the neighbors called me."

"Stay there. I'm picking you up."

Finn ran out the door, then retraced his steps to lock his office. Too many documents in the files open on his desk were considered confidential and delicate.

Once outside he contemplated taking his bike home before grabbing a cab but then reckoned he could always take the Underground to work in the morning. A black cab with its roof light on turning into the street sealed his fate. He'd go see to Tommy and then figure out what to do with his bike.

Chapter Eight

FINN

AT THIS late hour, it didn't take the cabbie long to drive to Tommy's address.

"Bloody hell, guv'. What's this, then?"

"Fire," Finn replied superfluously as he paid the fare. "I'm picking up a friend who was evacuated."

"I'm off duty," the cabbie replied. "Mind if I come see? I'll drive you both back."

Finn nodded before walking in the direction of the blaze.

There were fire trucks and ambulances standing nearby. Some were treating occupants with minor injuries. There was one man wearing an oxygen mask and lying on a stretcher inside an ambulance, but he had a decent gut, so Finn knew it wasn't Tommy. Still, he was relieved to see Tommy standing at a safe distance, watching the fire blaze on.

As he walked closer, Tommy noticed him and looked his way. His eyes were watery, and he sniveled, his hands tucked into his jacket. All Finn wanted to do was grab him and pull him close, but he didn't know how welcome that gesture would be, so he didn't.

"You okay?"

Tommy nodded. "It's all gone, though. I tried to go inside to rescue Mrs. Severn's dog, but the fire was too intense. That was before it was this bad. I can only hope the mutt got out somehow."

Finn nodded compassionately, trying to be inconspicuous as he looked Tommy over for fire damage and didn't find any. Tommy turned toward him. All Finn could do was wrap his arms around Tommy and rub his back. It felt so good it was criminal. Even after Tommy looked up at the blaze again, he didn't pull away, and Finn kept holding him close. Nobody paid them any attention. Finn didn't scold Tommy for running into the blaze and potentially risking his life for a dog that wasn't even his own and was just glad he'd come out of it without any damage.

In the distance Finn could see the cabbie watching the firemen work. "When you're ready to go, we have transportation. The guy who brought me here is watching from there." He pointed at the cabbie.

"He's probably an arsonist," Tommy commented with a chuckle.

"Who knows?"

Tommy looked at the building one more time. Finn agreed with Tommy it was going to be totally uninhabitable once the fire had been put out.

"Do you have anyplace else to stay?"

Tommy shrugged. "Mum's place is tiny. I don't want to put her out. I could sleep on Stevie's sofa. Wouldn't be the first time."

"Come home with me," Finn suggested without hesitation. "Have you eaten?"

Tommy nodded. "Shepherd's pie at Mum's."

"That's better than what I had."

Tommy threw him a questioning look.

"Leftover pasta salad from lunch."

Tommy smiled. "I should cook you a decent meal."

"Maybe you should," Finn agreed. "Some other day."

It was only as they started walking toward their driver that Tommy left Finn's arms, and for the first time that evening, Finn felt the cold of the autumn night air.

TOMMY

ON THE way home, Tommy was totally depleted. In the back of the cab, he sagged down to the seat, and as soon as he sensed Finn's warmth next to him, it was drawing him in like a magnet. He wanted to feel the soothing arms around him again and leaned against Finn's shoulder. Finn put his arm around Tommy, seemingly without thinking.

"I probably smell of the fire."

"Always had a thing for barbecues," Finn quipped.

He kissed Tommy's hair, and Tommy felt safe, even though he could see the cabbie eyeing them in his rearview mirror.

"So, anything irreplaceable?" Finn asked after a long silence.

"I'm homeless, Finn," Tommy said, sounding more harsh than he intended.

"I know," Finn whispered, rubbing Tommy's hair as he would to soothe a young child. "You're not out on the street," Finn eventually said as if he'd needed to think about it first. "I have a spare room. You can use that until you're back on your feet."

"The fire chief said he'd call me if the building was safe to go into, maybe tomorrow or the day after, and I could see what could be rescued. I'm not expecting to find anything."

"Clothes can be replaced. Furniture too. Even a TV or DVDs can be found everywhere."

Tommy just nodded, relaxing more and more into Finn's embrace. There was something incredibly comforting in just being held. Tommy wanted more, but he knew he'd have to forgo the mindless comforts of sex. He'd spent enough time with Finn to know a kiss was obtainable, but anything more seemed insurmountable, yet he found himself truly enjoying the total absence of performance anxiety. Finn didn't expect anything more from him than a little tenderness and some company. If someone had told him even six weeks ago that he was going to develop feelings for a man he'd never even seen naked, he'd have laughed out loud. Now he knew it wasn't just possible, it was really happening.

"I don't want to outstay my welcome," Tommy said. "Throw me out before I start taking up too much space in your bachelor life, okay?"

Finn nodded against Tommy's hair, and he didn't even need to look up to see that Finn was a little intimidated by the prospect of inviting Tommy to stay the night with him. By the time the cab stopped in front of Finn's Kensington flat, Finn was so tightly wired Tommy thought he could play him like a violin.

FINN

"WELCOME TO my humble abode."

Tommy nodded, looking calm despite the traumatic evening. "If this is humble, you must be related to Her Majesty."

"Well, I do work for the Crown," Finn answered with a chuckle. He saw Tommy look around. Was he nervous?

As he let Tommy walk into the hallway first, Finn couldn't imagine that Tommy's stomach clenched as much as his or that his muscles twitched so badly he couldn't stop flexing them. This was worse than the first time he'd stood up in court. Worse even than his first high profile case where he knew that, right after the jury's verdict, he was going to need to address a whole fleet of reporters.

"This way," Finn said as he led the way farther into his house. As he reached up to hang up his coat, his hand trembled. He felt Tommy close behind him.

"Don't be nervous," Tommy whispered in his ear.

His left hand was on Finn's shoulder, and Finn felt a hand brush over his ribs under his upheld arm. Was Tommy going to hug him? The seemingly casual touch made his stomach clench even more. The connection disappeared as quickly as it came, and Finn smiled as he saw why he'd jumped. Tommy was handing him his coat to hang up, while remaining behind Finn. Finn shook the fright out of him. "Let me hang that up for you." He took the coat, but as he reached up again, Tommy wrapped his arm around Finn's waist, and all Finn could do was hold on to his coatrack. His whole body was tense with need, but at the same time he was afraid, afraid of what might happen between them, afraid of what wouldn't happen between them, and afraid of disappointing Tommy, who had experience Finn sorely lacked.

"Relax," Tommy said, placing a soft kiss on the side of Finn's neck. "You know I won't do anything you don't want to do."

"That's what I'm afraid of," Finn said, his voice croaking.

"You're never afraid," Tommy said as if it was a fact of life.

"I'm not a bad actor in front of a judge or a jury," Finn replied, his voice not as steady as he would have liked, "but there I know what I'm up against." He was incredibly grateful that Tommy's hands weren't moving so he could keep a semblance of control over his own body. "Here I'm not exactly on familiar grounds." *Understatement of the century*. The warmth from Tommy's hands was seeping through the fabric of Finn's starched shirt, and it felt so good he could hardly think straight.

"I know," Tommy said.

They had, after all, talked about this without going into much detail. Finn hoped that Tommy simply thought he had no experience with men. That he had no experience with women either hadn't come up in conversation.

"Can I take a shower?" Tommy asked as he finally let go of Finn. "I must smell of soot."

"I'll pop your clothes in the washer," Finn suggested.

"Through there?" Tommy asked as he pointed in the direction of one of the closed doors that were visible in the small hallway.

"This way, actually." Finn led the way to his bathroom, which was large enough to accommodate both a shower and a bath. Although nobody but Finn ever came there, he was now glad for his slightly OCD manner of keeping it pristine at all times.

Tommy whistled. "If this is anything to go by, I'd like to see the rest of the flat too."

"You will," Finn replied proudly. "I'll give you the grand tour after you've freshened up. Towels are in there, and I'll get you a robe to put on. Be right back."

Finn went out into the hallway and pulled a neatly wrapped package out of the linen closet. He knew exactly what was in it—the burgundy bathrobe his mother had bought him the last Christmas they'd celebrated together. He hadn't bothered taking the plastic wrapper off it because he had a perfectly fine bathrobe in use already.

He knocked on the bathroom door.

"Come in."

Finn opened the door and couldn't not stare. Tommy was standing in the middle of the room in just his tight white-and-blue striped briefs, his clothes in a pile at his feet. He wasn't at all self-conscious about his near nakedness as he bent down to pick them up, and Finn felt like his feet were nailed to his hardwood floors.

Tommy exchanged the pile of clothes for the robe. "Fluffy," he remarked. "You shouldn't have taken out a new one. I'm just a guy from a council flat. You shouldn't spoil me or you'll never be rid of me."

Finn wanted to say he absolutely wanted a chance to spoil Tommy, but the words got stuck in his throat. So much for being known for his eloquence. Where was that particular skill when he needed it?

Tommy put on the robe and then turned away from Finn to step out of his underwear. Part of Finn was sad for having been denied the visual, but another part was grateful. It was going to be hard enough to sleep thinking that the object of his desires was just a thin wall away from him, or knowing he'd been naked in his bathroom.

"I'll go wash these," Finn said by way of good-bye after letting Tommy add the underpants to the pile. He left the bathroom and entered the smaller room next to it where his washer and dryer were located. He heard the shower being turned on and realized he'd been holding his breath. As he added soap and fabric softener, he did the same breathing exercise he always performed in the robing room at the Old Bailey before he had to go into court to present closing arguments, only he missed part of the ritual of putting on his collar and wig. Still, it had the effect of calming some of his nerves.

With Tommy's clothes in the washer, Finn went into his kitchen to make them a cup of tea. It was the least he could do to help Tommy get over the ordeal of the last few hours. While the kettle was on, he went into his bedroom to look for pajamas for Tommy to sleep in. Given his mother's propensity for giving him useful gifts—and her lack of imagination—he had several of those in the unused stages as well. He'd just put them in the guest room together with the sheets he needed to make up the guest bed when his kettle announced that the water was boiling. Just moments later the water in the bathroom was turned off, and just as Finn poured the hot water into his teapot, Tommy walked into the kitchen.

"I followed where the sounds were coming from."

Finn looked at Tommy and tried hard not to remember that he was naked underneath the robe. "Tea will take another few minutes," he said, turning away from Tommy to get the milk and sugar. "I don't have biscuits to go with this, I'm afraid."

Tommy smiled and shrugged.

"We can go into the sitting room if you like."

Tommy gestured for Finn to lead the way, and Finn took the tea and cups out in a tray, deftly opening the door between the kitchen and the sitting room with his shoulder.

The sitting room was sparsely furnished, with a large leather settee in one corner and a rarely used flat-screen TV against the far wall. Finn instantly realized they were both going to have to sit on the same couch, and the nerves he'd so successfully tamed earlier were back in full force. They sat down, and as Finn started pouring the tea, he felt Tommy's hand on his knee. From the corner of his eye, he saw the robe slide off Tommy's knee, and he was pleasantly surprised by the hairy leg that popped into view. He'd seen most of Tommy's physique earlier in the bathroom, of course, but he'd felt too self-conscious to stare, and now he wished he'd feasted his eyes a little more. Then again, his perfectly cut dress pants were feeling uncharacteristically tight around his groin, and he was grateful to be sitting down and leaning forward so he could hide what Tommy's proximity was doing to him. Having a clearer picture of a naked Tommy would only fuel his imagination more, and this was not something he needed.

Tommy took a careful sip from his tea and groaned. "You have no idea how good this tastes."

Finn held out his cup. "Yes, I do."

Suddenly Tommy came close enough to enter Finn's personal space. "There's one thing that would feel even better."

Finn knew what Tommy meant, but he feigned innocence. "And what would that be?"

Tommy put his hand, warm from holding his tea mug, against Finn's jaw and pulled him closer so he could kiss him. They'd done this before, but this was the first time he'd done it to Tommy as he was one fluffy burgundy robe away from being stark naked. That thought made him hesitant, to put it mildly. At first Finn didn't kiss him back, but despite all of his fears and apprehensions, this felt so right he couldn't remain passive. He managed to put away his hot mug by touch only and was happy it didn't crash to the floor, before realizing he didn't know what to do with his hand. Tommy took care of that for him by grabbing it and placing it over his knee. Finn was distracted by the feeling of another man's hairy skin under his fingers, but that thought was taken away when Tommy moved his hand higher up Finn's thigh. The realization that Tommy was going to encounter evidence of his arousal was enough for Finn to pull away. Instantly he understood what this looked like, but he needed to create some distance between them, so he went as far as getting up from the couch.

"I'm sorry. I didn't mean to reject you so blatantly, but...."

"I was moving too fast. I'm the one who should be apologizing." Tommy also stood up, but he didn't move closer. "It's been an emotional night."

Finn was grateful that the robe falling into place obscured more of Tommy's enticing body, but he couldn't stop his eyes from wandering.

"I know the first time with a man isn't easy," Tommy said, taking a step closer. "I've been there. I had girlfriends in school, like I said I even got one pregnant, and all the while, I knew what I really wanted was a man, but I didn't dare date one."

He took another step in Finn's direction, and Finn could smell Tommy's damp hair and the shower gel he'd used. This time Finn didn't even flinch, and Tommy took the last step to close the gap between them.

"If I'm just your experiment, please tell me. I don't mind."

Tommy's mouth was close to Finn's ear, and Finn could feel the fine stubble on Tommy's skin.

"I won't stop you, but I won't invest myself either. We can just fuck and have it over with, and that's fine with me too. I just want to know where we stand."

Finn's head was full of all sorts of conflicting feelings. What Tommy was offering him was a chance to do this on his own terms, but Finn didn't want a one-night stand. If he'd wanted just sex he could have done that ages ago, and with men he wouldn't need to work with on a daily basis. There was something about Tommy that told him he could trust him, though, trust him with taking care of him, trust him to understand this wasn't going to be easy. But how could he explain to Tommy that he'd been quite content with his celibate life up to now? How could he explain it to Tommy without revealing the reason?

"I don't want just a one-night stand, Tommy. That's why we were moving too fast." Okay, a little white lie never hurt anyone, especially not because it was a lie of omission, and even juries could be persuaded to forgive those. He put his hand on the back of Tommy's neck and slowly brought their lips together. This time Tommy wasn't rushing him, mimicking whatever Finn did without taking initiative. It made Finn grow bolder, deepening the kiss and eventually adding a hand to the small of Tommy's back.

Tommy moved into the touch, lining up his body with Finn's. He wasn't exactly passive, but Finn got the feeling he could control what happened between them, although at the same time he was wildly out of his depth. Years of denying any sort of romantic feelings meant he hadn't a clue how these sort of interactions occurred. Although Tommy's hard body was distracting him, his mind took the easy way out and fled to safer ground.

In court, Finn had easily forgone questioning a woman when the witness had to recall how her relationship with the man in the dock had progressed from a chance meeting to a full-blown sexual relationship.

Finn had casually let Armen take over, knowing he had no idea how to ask the witness the right questions. Armen had gladly stepped in, leaving Finn with the feeling he'd killed two birds with one stone. He could remain the tough-as-nails prosecutor, leaving the "softer" questions to his younger counterpart, and he could save face.

"Everything all right?"

Tommy's voice brought Finn back to the here and now. He was still standing in front of his unlit fireplace, his arms around Tommy in the same way Tommy was holding him, but they were no longer kissing. Finn's head was resting on Tommy's shoulder, and he was inhaling Tommy's freshly washed scent.

"I'm sorry."

"No need," Tommy replied gamely. He raised his hand to cup Finn's jaw and look him in the eye. "You stopped moving for the longest time. I thought you'd fallen asleep or something."

Finn smiled. He didn't know what to do, so he opted for what was becoming safe behavior, and he quickly kissed Tommy. "Let's have our tea before it gets cold."

Tommy made sure his robe covered up anything untoward when he sat down, and again Finn felt grateful for small favors. They picked up their mugs and drank from the rapidly cooling tea.

"Top up?" Finn asked, reaching for the teapot.

"Yeah," Tommy answered, holding out his mug. He waited until Finn finished pouring and then sat back, one arm over the backrest of the couch they were sharing. "So if you don't want a one-night stand, then what did you have in mind?"

Finn swallowed as if his mouth had just been stuffed full of cotton wool. He'd always known Tommy was direct, but it still took him aback. He had no idea how to answer that, so he didn't. Instead he stared into his tea. Even when Tommy scooted closer, he didn't look up.

"You're safe. I'm not going to jump you," Tommy said to soothe him. "I'm just not very good at guessing. I like to know, you know?"

"I'm… I'm too distracted by you," Finn said, barely understanding himself what he meant by that.

Tommy got up and held out his hand as if to tell Finn to stay where he was. He disappeared into the corridor and returned about a minute later wearing the pajamas Finn had put out for him, with the robe securely tied over them. The only things not covered were his hands, feet, and face. The fluffy robe, thanks to the way Tommy had tied it, covered even his neck.

"Less distraction, right?"

Finn chuckled, feeling some of the tension in his body drain away.

"I just need to know one thing."

Finn nodded.

"You are actually interested in taking this further, right? You just need me to be really patient?"

Despite his fair complexion, Finn didn't blush easily, he really didn't, but Tommy's understanding, his acceptance, were a bit too much. He so wanted to reward him, only he was too scared.

"Not infinitely," he eventually answered. "I'll understand completely if my need for taking it slow exceeds your patience."

Tommy leaned back against the backrest of the couch. "You'd be surprised how patient I can be."

"I thought it was all about getting off, when men come together?"

Tommy smiled softly, and Finn suddenly realized how tired he looked. "I did that. I know a few clubs not too far from work where you can go for just that. Walk in and pick up a guy to have sex with."

Finn tried not to look shocked. He was a man of the world. He knew men did this. It was the principal reason why he had resigned himself to staying celibate. The last thing he wanted was something meaningless. Which was why he never pictured Tommy as one of the men who would go for that sort of thing.

Tommy sighed, bringing Finn back with the game. "It grows old very quickly."

"One-night stands?"

Tommy nodded. "Yeah."

Finn still didn't know how to react. How out of his depth could he be? This was turning into one confusing evening. On the one hand, he had the object of his affections right there in his house. He'd imagined this, had worked out scenarios in his head about what he'd do if Tommy was in his flat, and now that he was there, he realized his fear was even more crippling than he'd imagined.

When he looked over at Tommy, he saw he'd fallen asleep. His head resting against the backrest, Tommy looked totally relaxed. The dimples in his cheeks were gone, and his usually fairly thin lips looked curvier and somehow plumper. He also looked... harmless. It wasn't that he didn't trust Tommy when he said he'd never do anything Finn didn't want to do, but Finn couldn't simply shake the flight reactions he'd developed since he was a young child. They appeared whenever Tommy did even the slightest thing more than kiss him, no matter how much he actually wanted Tommy there.

Sitting here on the couch with him asleep finally gave Finn the chance to indulge in a little unashamed staring. Despite the fluffy robe and slightly too long pajamas, Finn could imagine Tommy's flat stomach, nicely developed arms, chest, and strong thighs. He had nice feet too, with neatly trimmed toenails and clearly visible tendons. He was tempted to touch what little bare skin he could see but instantly felt bad about wanting to take advantage of Tommy when he was at his most vulnerable. So he just sat there, looking and trying not to feel bad about enjoying the sight before him.

Then Tommy stirred. "Mmmh, sorry about that." He wiped his hand over his face and then scratched his hair, making it stand to all sides. "I make a lousy houseguest, falling asleep on you in the middle of a conversation."

"After the day you've had, you're entitled to it. But maybe I should put you to bed."

Tommy's mischievous smile appeared, and Finn realized what he'd just suggested. Before he could react to it, Tommy said, "I'd like that" in a voice Finn could swear was dripping with sex.

"I still have to make the spare bed," Finn said to escape Tommy's look. He got up and walked to the guest room, but he found Tommy following him. Once inside he picked up the bed linen, but Tommy pulled it out of his hands.

"You don't need to."

"I can't let you sleep in here without sheets."

Tommy cocked his head as if to ask Finn whether he was thick. When Finn didn't react, he smiled. "I could just sleep in your bed."

"I'm not...."

"You're not used to sharing. Yes, I know." Tommy sighed, sounding resigned. "I won't push you. I'll sleep in here tonight." He threw the sheets on the bed and started unfolding them so they could make the bed.

Finn knew he wouldn't sleep a wink if he'd taken Tommy up on his offer to sleep in his bed. "If you need anything, don't hesitate to knock on my door. I'm a light sleeper. Or just help yourself." *To me*, Finn added only in his head. He'd never dare to actually say it.

"I will," Tommy replied with a faint smile. "Good night."

"Good night."

Alone in his room, Finn sat on the side of his bed. Tommy had practically offered himself on a silver plate. He'd even said all the right things, how he was sick of one-night stands and was ready for something more permanent and how he was going to be patient and understanding. It was no use wanting more. He knew he couldn't do anything anyway.

OF COURSE he dreamed of Tommy again. Their kisses had become more intense, and Finn's chance to feast his eyes and feel some of Tommy's body underneath him had fueled more vivid images. It was only in his dream that he realized the image of Tommy had changed. Gone was the tattoo wrapping around Tommy's shoulder. Tommy had no tattoo. At least not there.

This time when he woke, he hadn't come yet, so he was lying awake on his back, staring up at the ceiling, wondering if he should finish himself off. He so rarely masturbated, and the reason for that was that what little release it gave him was always replaced by disgust. It was bigger than himself. And the last thing he wanted was to feel the bile rise when the image of a near-naked Tommy was still fresh in his mind. He didn't want to associate Tommy with the memories that made him who he was in the privacy of his own little cocoon. No, Tommy had to remain pure in his mind, so he waited for his arousal to abate. It did, eventually, but sleep evaded him. He continued staring up at the ceiling, listening to his quiet flat, when the smallest of sounds invaded the silence. For a moment he thought it was his upstairs neighbor who had brought home a date, but then he realized the sounds came from inside his own flat. Slow, even, rhythmical sounds, coming from the guest room.

Chapter Nine

TOMMY

HE'D WOKEN to images of his flat burning and the neighbor's dog fried. Not a total nightmare but close enough to make him lie awake now. Despite the disturbing memories, he also woke to a morning erection. And it wasn't even light yet. He experimentally ran his hand over it and rubbed it a little. It felt good. Maybe if he wanked he could sleep some more. Reaching to the side of the bed he grabbed some paper tissues from the nightstand so he wouldn't soil his borrowed pajamas and pulled the bottoms down. Finn had really thought of everything.

Finn.

The kissing was nice. They were progressing. But despite all his talk of being sick of casual encounters, it was getting hard not pushing Finn to a bed and simply ravishing him. Only in his dreams. He was pretty sure Finn would never forgive him if he did that. So this was all he had for now, wanking to the memories of that thin, sinewy body lying half on top of him, of those kisses, sometimes hesitant, sometimes more daring. And then there was the memory of that hand on him in the full commuter train. A hand that knew what it was doing. So uncharacteristically Finn's hand. That was the memory that made him stiff as a board. Tommy tried to keep his movements slow and as quiet as possible, because this house was the quietest flat he'd ever been to. He could only hope Finn was asleep in the next room, because even the rustle of the sheets sounded like it could wake the dead. He pushed the sheet away and looked down at his erection standing up proudly. He cupped his balls and then pushed down underneath them. As he moved his foreskin with his left hand, he circled his hole with his right. He started wondering whether his prosecutor was a top or a bottom. Whether he'd want to fuck him or whether he'd ask Tommy to fuck him. Either way suited him. He didn't bottom often, but for Finn he would. As long as he spoke to him in that low, slightly raspy voice of his. He could hear it now. "You're so tight. So hot."

Tommy gasped as he shot his release into his hand and then realized that if Finn was awake, he would have heard him. Well, it was too late now. Feeling limp limbed, he took the tissue and wiped his hands, then bundled it up and put it on the nightstand. He'd have to find a way to dispose of it in the morning, but right then he simply wanted to enjoy the warm, fuzzy feeling of having had a mind-blowing orgasm courtesy of a Crown Prosecutor. Well, sort of.

FINN

PANTING WASN'T easy when you were biting your lips, but Finn had to.

It's all good. This is a good feeling, Finn. Just let it wash over you. Tommy did what every healthy young man does all the time, even though you so rarely indulge in it. But how could you resist now?

He lay there listening to calm return to his house. No more rhythmical movements. No more muffled whimpers and soft moans. He imagined Tommy lying in the guest bed in his full glory, naked, still half aroused, maybe even with the glistening trail of his release still evident on his stomach. Part of him wished he'd been the cause of that release. Part of him hoped he'd be able to be just that one day.

The feeling of nausea that usually accompanied his rare ventures into self-satisfaction didn't come, though. It somewhat surprised him. Instead he simply felt empty and needy. Damn Ayse for planting the seed in him that he needed human touch. Now he couldn't go back again. He got out of bed and walked to the corridor. He startled as he saw Tommy do exactly the same.

"You're awake."

"I could say the same about you," Tommy replied. He leaned a little closer. "Did I wake you up?"

"Oh, no," Finn answered, feigning innocence. "I'm an insomniac."

"I usually sleep like a baby. Guess the fire is still bothering me."

Tommy was close enough so Finn could smell the sex on him. It was arousing to say the least. Almost unconsciously he bridged some of the remaining distance and found himself being kissed in the dark corridor.

"Come back to my room," Finn whispered against Tommy's mouth.

"I doubt you'll get a lot of sleep if I do," Tommy said, not moving away from Finn.

"We'll need to sleep, but maybe we can sleep together."

Tommy nodded and kissed him again.

TOMMY

HE COULDN'T believe his luck. Finn wanted to sleep with him. Of course he remembered Finn's plea to take it slow, so he knew the chance of this being any more than a lot of kissing and a few stolen gropes would be slim at best, but he knew he could take whatever Finn was willing to give him.

Finn took his hand and led him to his room. The only light there was the streetlight that shone through the curtains from outside, and once Finn let go of him, Tommy waited patiently to be invited further. The invitation came in the form of Finn crawling under the covers and opening them for Tommy to slip inside. Even in the dim light of the room, Tommy could see Finn's apprehension, so Tommy stayed on his side of the bed until Finn moved a little closer.

"I've been told it's not healthy to deny myself someone else's touch."

Tommy chuckled nervously. He really didn't want to cross any of Finn's boundaries, but if holding him was all he would get to do, he could live with that. For now. "Come here," he said with a croak in his voice. Finn scooted even closer as Tommy put his arms around him and simply held him. It lasted for several minutes until Finn looked at him and kissed him.

"She's right. It does feel good."

FINN

SLOWLY IT started dawning on him that music was playing. Softly, very much in the background, as if it didn't want to intrude. He felt something stir beside him. Not some*thing*, some*one*. And he felt safe. Warm. Didn't want to open his eyes or move in case that someone would disappear as if he'd been a dream. When his mind started to whir into action, he realized music playing in his bedroom was unfamiliar because he never slept until his alarm went off.

"You Are So Beautiful." Joe Cocker. How appropriate.

Finn didn't need to open his eyes to know who was beside him in bed. It made him tense up just a little, but only for a moment. Tommy was making weak protest noises next to him, and he could smell him. Damn. All man, slightly musky, just a hint of sweat. Tommy, who had eagerly taken up Finn's invitation to sleep beside him, who had kissed him tenderly, then more passionately, but who had pushed his boundaries only as far as Finn had let him. Tommy, who was beautiful indeed. Unruly, often curly brown hair that he clearly straightened occasionally. Bright blue eyes. Dimples in his cheeks when he smiled, and he smiled a lot. Tommy, who looked absolutely content just to sleep with him, close, limbs entwined. It was intimate but not too much. How did he know how far Finn was able to go? They'd slept in pajamas—soft cotton trousers and matching shirts—more clothes than he'd seen Tommy in that evening when he was about to step into the shower.

Finn smiled as he realized Tommy was sleeping in borrowed apparel. Finn's apparel. Striped. A gift from Mother. Not exactly Finn's taste, but the moment Tommy had emerged from the guest room wearing it, he knew he liked it on him.

Tommy's hand was reaching for him, and Finn rolled closer. Tommy pulled him the last of the way in.

"Sleep well?" Tommy groaned.

"Don't remember the last time I needed an alarm to wake up, so yes, I suppose I slept well."

"Me too."

Only now did Finn dare to open his eyes. So it wasn't a dream. Tommy was really there. His hair was mussed up even more than usual. He had a crease on the side of his forehead, probably from the bed linen. Finn could spend all morning looking at that man.

Tommy opened his eyes briefly, only to close them again as he moaned appreciatively and pressed his lips against Finn's in a messy kiss. Finn grabbed the back of Tommy's head and kissed him back, which made Tommy moan even more. Finn could feel Tommy's tight, muscled body press against his, and he became aware of a few other things as well. Tommy was grinding his groin against his, and it was arousing as hell. As he stopped kissing and Tommy's lips rubbed against his cheek, then his eyebrow, Finn realized Tommy was aroused too as he felt hardness pushing against his stomach. He swallowed, as he had to keep telling himself this was Tommy and Tommy didn't mean any harm. Tommy was just doing what men did, rutting against him until he'd spend his passion.

Suddenly all Finn could think about was running away, but with Tommy draped on top of him, he found he couldn't. Instead, he froze up.

It took Tommy just a few moments to catch on.

Tommy was panting, his eyes closed, his expression pained, and then all of a sudden he stopped grinding. Tommy opened his eyes and looked at Finn. He opened his mouth and then closed it again.

"Christ, Finn, I'm sorry." Tommy rolled off him, settling on his side facing Finn.

"Don't be," Finn replied automatically. He couldn't keep looking into Tommy's gorgeous blue eyes, which were sad and full of regret and maybe a little pity too. Finn couldn't get over the fact he hadn't been able to control his adverse response. This was Tommy, his Tommy, and the one man he knew would never hurt him.

"Finn," Tommy breathed more than said. He wiped a strand of hair away from Finn's forehead with such tenderness Finn felt his eyes flood with tears. The touch had been so light, so fleeting that Finn wondered if he'd imagined it. He turned away and sat on the side of the bed with his back to Tommy so he wouldn't see him cry. Was he ever going to be able to do this with someone? If he couldn't even relax around Tommy, how could he ever hope for any intimacy?

"I'll get up, give you some space," Tommy said.

Finn wanted to beg him not to. He wanted to reach back and grab Tommy and pull him down to the bed again, kiss him as if his life depended on it and continue where they'd left off, but he was still frozen, impotent, scared. Despite the fright, Finn was still hard, his erect cock pushing against the soft cotton of his pajama bottoms, asking to be freed from its confines. But all he could do was let his arms drop between his legs in an attempt to hide from the feelings of shame that always rose up whenever he saw himself through someone else's eyes, a middle-aged man who couldn't get close to a lover without seizing up. So he let Tommy leave and listened to him putter around the unfamiliar place trying to get ready for work.

Finn got his clothes together and tried not to bump into Tommy until he was washed and dressed. The awkward confrontation came just ten minutes or so after the debacle that was an attempt at morning sex.

"My clothes feel nice. They smell good too," Tommy said when Finn walked into the kitchen. "Thanks for washing them."

"I should have ironed your shirt."

Tommy shrugged. "I never iron my shirts. I just hang them from a hanger in my bathroom."

"Still," Finn replied, unable to finish his sentence.

"I'll... I'll look for another place to stay for tonight. I could probably crash on Stevie's couch. God knows I have in the past. If she doesn't have company, she doesn't mind."

"Tommy." Finn took a step closer. "I meant what I'd said. You can stay here. It'll probably take a while before they let you into your flat again."

"If ever."

"If ever," Finn repeated. "Until you can find a new place, the guest room is yours."

Tommy looked up at Finn, not even trying to avoid his gaze. "Thanks. Especially...." He faintly pointed in the direction of the bedroom.

"You did nothing wrong," Finn said honestly. "You pushed, and I...." *I crumbled*, Finn wanted to say, but he hated stating the obvious. "I wanted it too. I just never thought... I hoped it would be enough to stave off the demons, but...." Finn looked up at the ceiling, silently cursing his inability to finish a single sentence. "I left you hanging."

To Finn's surprise, Tommy smiled. "In that respect one-night stands are better. I usually get off." He shrugged and took a step into Finn's personal space. "But I generally don't sleep like a baby with my hookups, and you have no idea what a good night's sleep is worth to me."

Tommy's voice sounded seductive and low and went right to Finn's groin. When he looked sideways, Tommy planted a sweet kiss on his cheek and then walked away. "Sorry, I can't stay. You might be allowed to be late for work, but I'm on the clock. Even the new super won't like it when I slack."

TOMMY

HE'D KEPT his cool as long as he was in Finn's house. On the Tube, waiting for the train, he kicked himself for losing it. How could he have betrayed Finn's trust so much? How could he have done this to that man? He'd quite possibly lost any credit he'd had. Would Finn ever trust him again?

Finn hadn't really told him about his demons before, but Tommy had spent enough hours talking to the man to know they were there. At first Tommy had thought they had to do with Finn venturing on a first indulgence for a taste in men, but then Tommy had stumbled on something much deeper. He'd encountered a deep-rooted fear of intimacy in Finn that had only surfaced when he'd made a move on him. That was the first time he'd been rejected.

None had hurt so much as this morning, though. And it had nothing to do with waking up piss proud and feeling it was a good idea to work it out on the man sleeping next to him, and everything to do with knowing Finn would probably freak but figuring, in the early light of day, it wouldn't get that far.

So he was relegated to the guest room again after being so good the night before that Finn had invited him into his bedroom. Practically. As Tommy recalled, he'd still had to nudge him ever so carefully. But Finn had taken the bait, and Tommy'd been good and had stopped the seduction after the kissing, despite a tent that could house an army regiment in his pajamas. The talking and cuddling had its own merits, though. Finn had finally relaxed, his face less tense, his limbs a little more slack, and his cute smile had pierced through his armor. They'd kissed some more, and Finn had tentatively started a discovery of Tommy's shoulder and arm. Tommy had no idea why Finn had lingered there for so long, but he'd let him, caressing him and basically making him feel very self-conscious. Tommy had wanted to indulge him, though, the scrutiny curiously tickling his ego. They hadn't gotten any further before they'd both fallen asleep, pretty much in each other's arms. And then Tommy had blown every inch of progress they'd made.

The busy Tube train took his mind off what he'd left behind, which was, technically, a good thing, but it also reminded him that he had a lot to do today. Not only did he need to check out his burned-down flat, but he also had to go out and buy himself some new clothes. It wouldn't do to have Finn wash the same threads every night. That's when he remembered the underwear he was wearing was Finn's. Stevie would never let him live it down, but then Stevie would never know, would she?

"So where did you sleep last night?" Stevie asked as she stuck his head inside their office. "Boss told me your place burned down."

"Morning to you too, Stevie."

"My couch is yours. You know that, right?"

Tommy smiled at his partner. "I got a better offer."

"I admit I don't offer all the trimmin's, but then you wouldn't want me to either, right? But if it's a place to rest you seek, you know where I live."

Tommy smiled at Stevie's unassuming way of showing her support. He'd always known he could count on her, but it was still nice to be told.

"I stayed at Finn's," Tommy divulged quietly.

"Finn as in DeHavilland? Our CP? It's about time."

"He's neither yours nor mine, Stevie." Tommy sighed.

"I bet you're sorrier than me about that fact," Stevie replied without batting an eyelash. "Guess I was right he wasn't the sort to put out quickly, then," Stevie mumbled.

"What?"

Stevie raised her head. "Well, you confessed you and him were an item, but now it seems that was premature. Somewhat. Is he really playing that hard to get? Seems like something an Eton boy would do to a simple copper from a council flat."

"Stevie," Tommy cautioned. He wasn't about to tell her about his sex life. Or lack thereof. Especially not in light of what had happened that morning. "Listen. I... called him. He once told me if I ever needed anything... and you had company, right?"

"Nobody important enough to leave you standing in the cold, sonny boy. Three divorces have made my priorities crystal clear to me."

Tommy nodded his understanding. "So weren't we supposed to go to the CPS offices to check out our new case files?"

"Nope. Stanton said someone from his office called it off."

Tommy couldn't help feeling rejected a second time. "So we're back on the Belgravia murder case?"

"It's only one day. Finn's secretary said he needed more time to prepare, so we're supposed to go tomorrow."

"But what's keeping us from working the Belgravia case, then? There was one survivor among the ice-pick murders. The first girl. I want to go see her."

"Can't. We're off the case. It's gone back to Serious Sexual Offences, who were assigned in the first place."

Tommy sighed. "That's bloody unfair!" he muttered.

Their backup orders were to act as if nothing particular was going on, so they did some follow-up visits around town, and Tommy managed to buy himself some dress trousers and a smart jacket at a charity shop and a few shirts that were on sale at Debenhams. He'd grabbed a packet of white-with-purple-stripes boxer briefs on his way to the cash register.

"You're going to look way too smart for us coppers, sonny," Stevie said while she was waiting in line with Tommy. "Or are you dressing up for our CP?"

Tommy rolled his eyes at Stevie, but at the same time he wondered just how transparent he was. Although he'd always admired Finn's dress sense, he knew not to try to emulate it. He simply wouldn't get away with it, and on top of that he didn't have the salary to compete anyway. Not that a CP was that well paid. Finn came from money, and Tommy was sure he had quite a nest egg tucked away somewhere. He just had to look at the apartment he'd slept in the night before. Even the kitchen chairs were antiques.

When he looked at Stevie, he realized she was giving him her most teasing look.

"He's not going to see what I dress up in, so it doesn't matter. Unless you know something I don't know. Do we need to go see him?"

"No." Stevie shook her head. "We're summoned to see the boss."

"What did you do now, Stevie?" Tommy teased.

Stevie smirked. "Maybe it's something you did for a change."

The visit to DSI Mark Stanton's office didn't last long. They were told the official reason why they were taken off the case they were investigating was to free up time for the work they'd be doing alongside Finn. If anyone asked, they were to refer to the fact that they only got the case in the interim until Serious Sexual Offences had been able to free up a team of their own.

Tommy almost felt sorry for himself. It had all the makings of a nice, juicy case, and now they were relegated to going through old papers again.

Chapter Ten

FINN

HE'D HAD an extra day to go over the six cases and prepare for the arrival of Tommy and Stevie, but he was a perfectionist, and he was nowhere near ready. When he saw them make their way between the desks to the back where the offices of the senior staff were located, he put on his game face and decided he wasn't going to show his insecurities to them.

As usual, Stevie walked first. She had a big stride for a woman, but then she had longer legs than most women too, and she wasn't the type to hide away her unusually large stature. Tommy followed behind her. Despite being almost a head shorter, he had no problem keeping up with her.

Finn noticed Tommy looked good, and he was wearing clothes he hadn't seen before.

"Stevie, Tommy," Finn greeted them.

"Ready for duty, guv'," Stevie said.

"That's good to hear," Finn said, peeling his gaze away from Tommy. He gestured at the long table he'd asked be put into his spacious office. "I've laid out the six cases we'll be starting with. I suggest you acquaint yourself with them before we decide on a course of action."

Stevie cocked her head. "This asks for plenty of coffee. Shall I bring some for everyone?"

The men nodded. As soon as she was out of earshot, Finn cautiously approached Tommy. "I expected you last night."

Tommy didn't look at him directly. "No, you didn't. You needed space, and so I took Stevie up on her offer and slept on her sofa."

"You can't keep doing that, Tommy. It's okay for one night, but not until you find a new flat. And you know how hard it is to find something affordable on short notice in the city."

Tommy nodded in agreement.

"My offer still stands. My guest room is yours for as long as you need it." He walked away to grab a file off one of the stacks but changed his mind and turned back to face Tommy, who was pretending to read as well. "You were right about the space I needed, but that doesn't mean I don't want to help you have a roof over your head. I don't do much more at home than sleep, so you won't be in my way."

"I won't be home early either. Since we'll be working together."

Finn couldn't help but smile at Tommy, and Tommy mimicked his expression.

"Come home with me tonight."

"Okay," Tommy agreed.

Finn didn't get the chance to react, because Stevie walked into the office carrying three mugs of coffee. Finn rushed to hold the door open for her and took one of the mugs.

"So are you going to tell us who the corrupt copper is?" Stevie asked when she handed Finn his mug.

Finn cocked his head. "I can't."

"How are we supposed to investigate if we don't know who we're investigating?"

"That's why we're going over the case files first," Finn said. "I want to know whether I'm seeing coincidences that aren't there. I need fresh eyes to go over them with me, and if you two see what I see, then I know they aren't coincidences."

"If you say so, guv'."

"Well, Stevie, it's impossible to unknow something. Once I tell you, you will be biased. And call me Finn when we're in here, okay? Tommy does."

"Yeah, but Tommy knows you intimately," Stevie quipped while she looked at Tommy.

Finn's heart skipped a beat. What had Tommy told his partner?

Stevie turned to look at Finn. "I can't imagine he calls you Mr. DeHavilland if you're sharing a… flat."

Finn smiled at Stevie, both because of her teasing and because he was relieved she took it well, whatever Tommy had divulged to her.

"So we read these six case files and tell you what jumps out at us?" Tommy asked.

"Exactly."

Stevie and Tommy started at opposite ends of the table. As he watched them meticulously go over the papers and notes contained in the files, Finn realized postponing today had been a waste of time. The preparation he'd done yesterday had had only one purpose, and that was to prepare himself for working with Tommy again, but Tommy's easy forgiveness for their debacle had made that futile. If only he'd known that before.

Finn took out his old notebooks and looked through the parts he'd marked the day before. Those were the parts pertaining to the six cases now under review. He tried to concentrate but soon found himself distracted by Tommy's dedicated note taking. He knew Tommy was left-handed, but seeing him contort his hand to jot down notes in his book seemed infinitely more fascinating than his own scribbles. Luckily, neither Stevie nor Tommy noticed his daydreaming.

At precisely twelve, Stevie closed her file. "I have a lunch date. I will be back in exactly half an hour. Just giving you boys fair warning."

"Well, that explains why she was all dressed up this morning," Tommy said as soon as she'd closed the door behind her.

"Who is she seeing?"

"Your ginger secretary."

"Natalie?"

Tommy nodded in agreement.

"I thought Stevie…. Hasn't she been married… like, a few times?"

"Mmh," Tommy acknowledged. "Don't think she'll be doing that again."

"Because she's into women now?"

"Because third time lucky didn't work for her."

"Oh." Finn didn't want to come across as totally thick, but he wasn't sure if Stevie was now a lesbian or bisexual, or…. Did it matter? It wasn't like he had any intention of seducing her.

"Want to go out for lunch?" Tommy asked.

"We could order in a sandwich," Finn suggested.

"Doesn't Natalie usually get you those?"

"She does. Okay, let's go get some ourselves."

TOMMY

HE WAS happy they were back on speaking terms, but Finn still seemed a little awkward.

Fifteen minutes after leaving the office they were sitting in a secluded courtyard behind the CPS offices on a worn bench in the sunshine, eating sandwiches from Pret a Manger.

"I had the feeling Stevie confused the hell out of you today."

Finn shrugged and swallowed his bite before speaking. "She just seems so... I don't know... easygoing?"

"About pursuing Natalie?"

"Don't get me wrong. I like Stevie. She's great. But she has three kids from three marriages and now she's into women all of a sudden?"

Tommy just had to laugh. "Stevie falls in love easily. Period. Doesn't matter if it's men or women. Sadly for her when the first flutters of love are over, she just as easily moves on. Like three husbands realized a little too well."

"Are you like that?"

"Are you asking me whether I move on to the next conquest easily?"

"Well, no, but that's a question I'd like to know the answer to as well."

"I don't. I've only been in love once, I think."

"You think?"

Tommy wondered if he should be totally honest with Finn or lie by omission. He wasn't sure Finn was ready for the whole truth and nothing but the truth. "I've had crushes, like anyone else, I presume, but they don't happen that often to me." Before he dug himself any deeper, he knew he had to change the subject somewhat. "So what was the question you were really asking?"

"Whether you were like Stevie and it didn't matter what sex your partner was."

Okay, this was safer ground. "Technically, it doesn't matter all that much, but I do seem to end up falling for men more than women."

Finn's smile indicated this was what he wanted to hear.

"But I'd think twice before I married anyone," Tommy added with a wink.

"Until you found Mr. Right?"

"Whoever Mr. Right is, yeah."

Finn looked at his watch. "We should be getting back."

"We can always talk more tonight."

"Exactly."

Crisis averted. Tommy was relieved they'd talked privately before he had to go back to Finn's flat again.

Chapter Eleven

FINN

HE ACTUALLY came home earlier than he'd told Tommy. He'd brought some work with him, not the corrupt copper case but some reading he had to do for Armen, and contemplated getting some Thai food on the way. Only, he had no idea when Tommy was going to arrive, so he reckoned he might as well wait and call out for it later.

At exactly seven his doorbell rang. When he opened it, Tommy was there carrying two bags full of groceries.

"Since I'm not paying rent, I thought I'd keep you fed," Tommy simply stated. He seemed in good spirits, at least much better than that morning. "You haven't eaten yet, I hope?"

"No, was just about to call for takeaway."

"Mate, how you stay so trim on bad food, I don't know. Don't you ever cook?"

Finn shrugged. "Don't see the point if it's just for me."

"Well, there's two of us now, so if you don't mind me making a mess of your kitchen, I'm cooking us supper."

"Be my guest," Finn replied, holding out his hand in the general direction of his kitchen.

"So what else do you make besides a stir-fry?" he asked as he helped Tommy unpack enough food to feed an army for the rest of the week. His fridge had never been this stocked before.

"I can make lots of stuff. Mum taught me. She worked nights, and we didn't have the money to get takeaway, so as soon as I was old enough to not set the kitchen on fire, she showed me how to make basic stuff. I found I actually like cooking. Even if it's just for myself."

Finn felt a little guilty about taking the easy way out. "I grew up with servants and no access to an actual kitchen unless I was home alone and the kitchen maid was left to look after me."

"How sad," Tommy replied with a smile.

"Are you mocking me?" Finn asked half seriously.

Tommy moved to stand next to him at the counter, bumped him with his hip, and then placed a quick, innocent kiss on Finn's lips. "Yes." A broad smile splayed over his face as he took out the onions and ground beef. "Can I trust you to peel an onion?"

"I can try," Finn replied, trying to keep up the banter, but the kiss, however chaste, had changed the air in the room and made it heavy once more. Maybe it was just Finn projecting his feelings on Tommy, but he knew when Tommy turned around to get some of the vegetables that the time for banter was over. He showed Tommy where to find a skillet and a cooking pot and let Tommy work on his side of the kitchen. The silence was hard to stomach, though. Finn knew he had to address the elephant in the room.

"Do you know that yesterday morning was the first time I ever woke up with someone?"

"First time as in…?"

"First time ever. I own a double bed, but I'm the only one who's ever slept in it. Until yesterday." Finn looked at the onion he was peeling and felt his eyes shoot full of tears. He could blame the onion, of course. Who didn't cry peeling onions, for heaven's sake? He sniffed and continued chopping. "And you know what? I liked it. I never thought I would, but I liked it. It wasn't half as awkward as I thought it would be."

"If only I'd kept my hands to myself, hey?"

"No, Tommy." Finn put his knife down and leaned on the counter, his gaze trailing to a spot near wall. "That one's on me. You did nothing wrong."

"So you keep telling me."

"Because it's the truth."

"Evidence never lies, My Lord," Tommy said, mimicking how Finn spoke to the judges in court.

Finn turned toward Tommy, needing all his courage to look him in the eye. It was almost a relief that Tommy was still looking the other way. "In this case the evidence is open to interpretation. Unless you can read minds, and the last time I looked that was a very rare condition."

"So how should I interpret it, then?"

"I'm the one who couldn't handle it, Tommy. I'm the only one at fault here."

"So you've decided you're not into men, after all?"

Finn shook his head, a slight smile on his face. "I like men. There, I said it. Another first. I've never liked women. At least not in my bed. I love working with them, but I'm not attracted to them in that way."

"And I was the first man you slept with?"

Finn nodded.

"I don't get it."

"One and one is still two, Tommy."

"You mean you've never...." Tommy dropped his knife and turned to face Finn. "Is that why it's so hard for you to...?"

Finn had never seen Tommy at a loss like that. He wanted to comfort him but had no idea how to do that. All he had was his experience with distressed witnesses, and with them it helped to stay calm and collected and true to himself. And act kind. This was what he did with Tommy.

"No, that isn't why it's so hard. I suppose it isn't easy to embark on a personal life for the first time at my age, but then again, I thought you would guide me through it. I trusted you to. And you tried. I have to give you that. There were other things making that impossible for me yesterday morning. Maybe one day I'll be able to explain them to you."

"Tell me what to do, then."

"You're doing it. You're here."

"That's easy when I have no place else to go."

Finn chuckled. "There is always Stevie's couch."

Tommy let his gaze trail down. He also spoke uncharacteristically quietly. "Your bed was a lot nicer than Stevie's couch."

"Was there ever any doubt?" Finn hoped Tommy would smile back at him, but he didn't. His face softened a bit, but that was all Finn had to go by. "You can sleep in there again." Now it was his turn to feel his voice crack. "I enjoyed what we did right up to me freezing up on you."

"Are you sure?"

For the first time in what felt like ages, Tommy looked up at Finn, and Finn saw the insecurity in the otherwise positive sergeant.

"No, but if I don't try... it's like getting back on the horse, right? Only you don't hurt the horse's feelings by falling off. I'm afraid I hurt yours by my reaction."

"I just didn't know what it meant. I thought it was the end of the experiment. I thought you'd tried it with a bloke who's got experience and it didn't feel right and you didn't know how to tell me. Even our kiss just here confirmed that."

"That wasn't a kiss," Finn said, trying to sound more confident than he felt. "This is how I wanted you to kiss me." Finn took Tommy's head between his hands, consciously forgetting that his hands must smell of onion, and pulled him closer so their mouths could touch. He didn't hold back, kissing Tommy with all the fervor he could muster. He could feel how he pushed Tommy against the counter with his hips and, as Tommy returned the kiss, how he became pliable under his hands. When they broke apart, they were panting.

Tommy was the first one to speak. "I thought I'd ruined everything."

"If anything was ruined it was all on me, Tommy." It felt good to hold him like this. It brought back memories of sharing the bed with him and sleeping in his arms, and Finn hoped they could do it again. Preferably tonight.

"If I don't get back to dinner, I'll ruin that, and there's no way you can take credit for that disaster."

"Fair enough," Finn said, letting him go, albeit reluctantly.

They worked almost silently, the only conversation being Tommy's instructions for what Finn could do to help him. Finn spent most of his time in the kitchen cleaning up after Tommy, but he didn't mind. It made him feel useful and oddly domestic as well.

Tommy made them spaghetti, but like nothing Finn had ever tasted. It was a weird recipe with lots of hot spices and canned pineapple, but it tasted so delicious he ate way too much. Again. Only this time there was plenty left over as well.

"That'll taste good cold too," Tommy persuaded him.

Finn raised an eyebrow.

"It will. And maybe one day I'll get my measurements right and actually cook for two."

"I think you got your measurements just right," Finn replied, rubbing his distended stomach. "Want to watch a movie as we digest this?"

"Sounds like a plan."

Finn owned a flat-screen TV mostly for the purpose of watching the news. He rarely, if ever, watched films or series, but Tommy deftly flipped through the channels and found some action movie with Nicholas Cage.

"This good for you?"

Finn nodded as he watched Tommy settle on the couch. He wasn't all that interested in the movie but found himself enthralled by the man sitting next to him. He picked up a file he needed to read but was unable to concentrate as Tommy's body occasionally came into contact with his, and he felt a strange calm settle over him. He could get used to this, this quiet sharing of living space, this total lack of need to talk. He'd always imagined that sharing his flat or even his life with someone would be stressful and leave him craving his solitude, but being with Tommy, especially when Tommy's attention wasn't focused on him, was effortless.

Finn returned his attention to his case file, concentration coming a little easier to him now, until he felt Tommy's hand in his. He looked up into Tommy's blue eyes and actually felt butterflies in his stomach.

"I'm sorry, but I need to go to bed if I'm supposed to be a functional human being in the morning. You see, I'm summoned to the office of this really demanding prosecutor for a hush-hush case, and I need to be at my best."

Finn's hands ached to touch the dimples in Tommy's cheeks, but instead he just smiled at him. "He's not so tough when you get to know him."

Tommy leaned over him and placed a rather chaste kiss on his mouth. "Night." He got up and walked toward the hallway.

"Tommy," Finn called out to make him stop. "Will you sleep in my bed again? Please?"

Tommy, who had never stopped smiling, simply nodded before walking off.

TOMMY

HE PICKED up the bags he'd left in the hallway earlier and took them to the guest room. Yes, Finn had asked him to sleep in his room again, and he would, but treating Finn's bedroom as his own was an entirely different game. So he appropriated a half-empty wardrobe in the guest room as his own and hung up the trousers and jacket he'd bought together with his new shirts before venturing into the bathroom for a quick wash.

Standing in front of the insanely large bathroom mirror, he checked himself out as he took his clothes off. He wasn't bad looking, he supposed. He ran when he found the time, went to the gym occasionally, and was blessed with a naturally muscled physique. If he could change anything, he'd want to be a little taller, but all in all, he was fairly happy with the way he looked. He ran his hand through his hair and across his scruff. Should he shave? He hadn't shaved since the fire, simply because he didn't have anything to shave with. He'd only bought new razors and shaving cream this evening, but he was dead tired. The stubble had already grown softer, and it wasn't like he was going to get laid. After yesterday's debacle, he could scratch that off his list. But Finn had asked him to sleep with him, and if the night before was any indication, they wouldn't be sleeping on their own side of the bed.

As Tommy remembered what had happened, he found himself growing aroused. Finn wasn't nearly as muscled as he was. He was more the lean, sinewy type, which just happened to be what Tommy usually went for in a man. For a moment he wondered how flexible Finn's body was and then shook his head to dispel those thoughts. He knew he couldn't go there, but the damage was done. He stuck his hand inside his briefs and squeezed his erection. If he didn't do something to satisfy the craving, he was going to find his control slipping again, just like yesterday morning. So he pulled down his briefs until he was standing naked in the bathroom. Closing his eyes he imagined Finn's mouth on him, kissing and licking his way down to his erection. In his dreams Finn was aroused too, aroused enough to banish his demons and actually have sex with him.

Tommy opened his eyes with a start. The image of Finn on his knees, sucking him off, was all wrong. Yes, it aroused him, but it didn't fit. Not that he didn't want it, but he just couldn't imagine the tall, single-minded prosecutor doing it. The memory of them making out was better, as long as he stayed away from the moment Finn froze up. Until then, it had been pretty magical.

Tommy kept touching himself, imagining that it was Finn's hand, not his own. It was surprisingly easy to remember what Finn's hands felt like (soft, yet strong), how he touched him (a little hesitantly at times), and how it conflicted with his kiss (openmouthed and eager). He wanted it to happen again. Soon. Tommy banished any thoughts about why their attempt was cut short and instead played out another scenario. This time they were both naked, lying on Finn's bed. Finn was in control, sporting a confidence Tommy had only ever seen after a court victory. His hands were confident too, exploring Tommy's body like Tommy was exploring Finn's. Touchy, grabby, intimate hands, soon joined by lips and tongues. Tommy could so imagine the movements Finn's lean but strong body made as it attempted to get closer to its mate's. In his dreams it was Finn's hand on him, bringing him to full erection, while Tommy was allowed to do the same to Finn. "Let me fuck you," Tommy heard his imaginary Finn say. "Hard and fast so you can still feel me in the morning."

Tommy thrust hard into his own hand, imagining Finn doing exactly what he'd said he'd do. That first thrust had been voluntary, but the three following were purely reactionary to the amazing feeling shooting through his groin. He came hard, leaving him panting as he watched his release drip down the pristine, whitewashed furniture of Finn's bathroom. He took his time catching his breath as he cleaned it up and then started wondering how his imagination made him so eager to bottom for Finn when this wasn't something he normally did. Was it just that he liked the confident Finn better than the quiet, brooding one, or did it simply tell him this was the Finn he wanted to see?

Deciding this wasn't a question he was easily going to find an answer for, Tommy pulled on his sleep attire and looked in the mirror one more time. The scruff would have to do for now. At least he wasn't terribly scratchy.

Chapter Twelve

TOMMY

COMPARED TO the day before, Stevie, always confident and self-assured, looked to have taken it up a notch. Not that she was wearing a skirt—the only time Tommy had ever seen her wear one was when he'd gone to church for the confirmation service for Stevie's oldest daughter—but she did look more elegant, and she was definitely wearing makeup. Tommy was convinced Stevie did it for Natalie, Finn's secretary. Maybe they'd moved past the flirting stage, maybe not. He wasn't going to ask her. Stevie was the one who could extract information from a stone. No way was he going to get personal information from her unless she volunteered it. Which didn't mean Tommy hadn't noticed. The other reason not to ask her was that she would probably rebut with asking him about Finn, and he certainly wasn't going to give her that info.

Not when he'd only crawled out of the Crown Prosecutor's arms a mere two hours earlier. The feelings he had for Finn continued to surprise him. There had been no naked skin and only casual kisses, and nothing blatantly sexual about their interactions, but he felt more like they were moving toward a relationship than he'd ever felt with anyone else. Then again, the men he'd shared his bed with had never been more than an easy lay. Finn definitely wasn't that.

"Good morning," Finn greeted them, opening his door while they were still walking toward it. He stepped aside to let them into an office that was organized differently from yesterday. Instead of one long table, it contained six smaller ones, one for every case file. No wonder he'd left that early this morning.

"Tommy, walk on so I can close the door, please? What goes on in here isn't for the eyes and ears of the rest of the office."

Tommy nodded and walked inside, surveying the huge whiteboard occupying most of one wall. He hadn't seen it before and wondered when Finn had had the time to have it installed. The six stacks of files had been tidied again as if they hadn't rummaged through them the day before. This time there were boxes underneath each table of the kind they used to bring files to the Central Archive. Some of them were overflowing even underneath the table.

"You see we have our work cut out for us," Finn continued. "Now we've read through the files it's time to find similarities between these cases. Any cross reference we can find might be important. We can place them on the board there." He pointed to the six case numbers on the whiteboard. Finn lowered the blinds on the windows facing the rest of the office. "I've also made our security more stringent. This office is to remain locked at all times. I will personally open and close it, and if I leave, you two will need to vacate it as well. I am the only one who can give anyone other than us three access to this room."

"Chief's orders?" Stevie asked.

"My orders. Even Carlton will need my permission. I've discussed this with him already, so you know he knows the rules. Don't let him tell you otherwise. I want us to be able to work unhindered and without mincing words."

"Does this mean you trust us more than you do your own boss?" Tommy asked.

Finn stared at him intensely. "Maybe."

He didn't break eye contact until it made Tommy uncomfortable, which was a feat, because this was Tommy's strong point when he was interrogating witnesses. This glimpse into Finn's determination reminded Tommy of the daring encounter on the Tube. Just like then, Finn surprised him, and Tommy simply relented.

"I already explained how important discretion is in this case. The detective we're trying to nail got away with things because he had help. Possibly from high up. It is entirely plausible that some of these cases had implications beyond what we find in these pages. I seriously doubt all we need to know is in these files, but these are the files Carlton allowed me to look into. This is where the two of you come in. You'll need to be my eyes and ears as well as my legs out there."

"Not to mention we still need to cover cases outside of what we do here so nobody becomes suspicious," Stevie reminded Finn.

"Of course." Finn cocked his head. "Let's get started so you can go see your DSI this afternoon to ask what else you need to do so as not to blow your cover."

FINN

FINN WAS going to have to learn to keep a level head around Tommy. He was starting to realize that working together was not going to be very efficient if he didn't. If preventing himself from staring at the handsome man was hard before, now that he'd felt him under his hands, stroked his flat stomach and straight back, albeit through a thin layer of cotton, he found his eyes perpetually glued to Tommy. On top of that Stevie was giving him curious looks. What was she up to?

They were both hard workers, and keywords as well as links between the cases had appeared on the whiteboard opposite the long table. Questions were flying back and forth about arresting officers and supervisors and judges. No question about prosecutors. All cases were Finn's, either as primary prosecutor or as supervisor.

Around one o'clock, Stevie folded her case file. "I don't know about you, but I'm hungry. Anything I can bring you boys?"

Finn looked up. "BLT?"

"Sounds good to me," Tommy chimed in.

"Be back in a sec."

Finn waited until she was gone. "Is she usually this courteous?"

"I think you bring out the best in her."

Finn wasn't sure that was true, but he didn't mind being alone with Tommy. "She probably has a date with Natalie."

They exchanged knowing looks.

"So have you heard from your insurance about your flat?"

"Have you ever known insurance case officers to work that quickly?"

Finn chuckled. "Not really."

"So what do you want for supper tonight?"

"I'll probably still be here when it's time for supper." Finn sighed, wishing he could just go home in time and walk into a house that smelled of cooking, but he'd already been truant yesterday. He couldn't make a habit out of it. Not even for Tommy. Besides, this case was too important to give up to whimsy.

"No idea when we'll be back. Depends on what the DCI has in store for us."

Finn wanted to take a chance. What could go wrong? The blinds were drawn, everyone had received the message they were to stay out of his office, and Stevie was on a food run. He grabbed a startled Tommy by the back of his neck and kissed him.

"Well, Mister Crown Prosecutor," Tommy said with a chuckle as Finn broke the kiss. "Is this how you ensure cooperation from all the policemen you work with?"

Finn felt himself flush, but he was in charge here. Certainly he could come up with a witty comeback? "Oh, policewomen too."

Tommy pushed him against a filing cabinet and kissed him back. "So this is the reason for all that security. So you'd have a place to snog me."

"Guilty as charged," Finn replied without creating distance between them.

"If I didn't know any better, I'd think you'd instructed Natalie to come on to Stevie so we'd get time for this."

"My powers only extend to certain people, Tom." Although Finn's instinct in intimate situations was always to let Tommy lead, Tommy seemed to like it when he took charge. He just wished he felt confident enough to do it more. "Besides, I'd think Armen was more her type. Dark and mysterious?"

A curt knock on the door made them scatter. Finn looked to see if Tommy was presentable before barking, "Enter!" Then he remembered he should have actually gone to the door.

"I brought you lunch, sir," Natalie said through the closed door.

Finn walked over to open it and accept what she handed him. "I thought you'd be out with Stevie."

"Oh, no, sir. I can't possibly spend every lunch with Sergeant Fielding."

"Please note that if you so wish you may spend your lunchtime with Sergeant Fielding when we break during the day."

Like a true redhead, she flushed all the way down to her ample cleavage.

"Noted, sir."

Finn turned around holding the sandwiches while Natalie closed the door behind her. "So tell me what you found before you and Stevie need to leave to tend to your other duties."

Tommy went over to the board and drew a box in the middle. He traced solid lines from five of the cases and a dotted line from the sixth to the center box. Then he wrote "Frank Farraday" in the middle box.

Finn used his napkin to wipe out the name.

"Wrong?"

"No, Tommy, you've just confirmed that my suspicions are correct."

TOMMY

WHEN HE came home—how quickly had Finn's flat become home to him?—it was already dark outside, but the lights inside the flat were lit. Finn had actually beat him to the punch.

"You look haggard," Finn said without as much as a hello. "Everything okay?"

Tommy let himself drop into the sofa like a dead weight without taking into consideration it wasn't his sofa, strictly speaking. "We had to pick up a district nurse today. I feel like I should take a shower to get his scent off me. It's a case that would have ended up on your desk."

Finn threw him a questioning look as he sat down at the other end of the couch.

"Thirty-year-old man who couldn't keep his grubby hands to himself. I can only hope his victims won't remember what's been done to them."

"Little ones?"

Tommy could hear the apprehension in Finn's voice.

"The oldest was five."

"Oh God."

"I know."

They sat together in silence for long moments. Then Tommy felt he had to break it. "These men with positions of power over young children. It's nauseating." He looked over at Finn, who seemed calm but absent. "Social workers, nurses, community care assistants." He kept looking at Finn, hoping he'd react, but he didn't. He felt he needed to say something, though. "I understood your helplessness when you had your meltdown, Finn."

Finn looked up with a start. "You did?"

He nodded. "I told you I was raised by a single mum in a council flat, right?"

Finn nodded.

"She had to work three part-time jobs to keep us fed and dressed. She never complained, always kept her head up. By the time I was eight I was fixing breakfast for me and my sisters and heating up whatever Mum had left for us in the fridge when we got home. There were days when she'd be out of the house by seven and wouldn't be back until eight or nine in the evening. To this day it's a freaking miracle we turned out okay."

"You're a smart cookie."

Tommy raised his eyebrow at Finn and chuckled at the expression. "Most men I grew up with ended in jail or worse. Most of the girls my age in our tenement are practically grannies by now." He shrugged. "Anyway, we had a community center. It was a place to hang out and get out of the cold more than anything. They didn't have the funds to actually do things with us, but it was run by a pretty charismatic guy who managed to get us a Ping-Pong table and an old beat-up snooker table and who would have tea for us if we wanted. It was reasonably warm and dry, but above all it was a safe place.

"And then one day he called me into his office and wanted me to sit next to him. He put his hand on my knee and kept moving it up my thigh. I was uncomfortable but didn't know how to react. After that I looked for excuses not to be alone with him. I thought I was the only one until one of my friends jumped in front of a train."

To Tommy's surprise, Finn veered up. "I'll make us a cup of tea. Did you eat yet?"

Tommy let him go. He wondered why it was such a touchy subject and then concluded that it was probably still as upsetting for Finn to hear these stories as it was to hear his witness cover up for them in the witness box. He followed Finn to the kitchen.

"I'll fix us an omelet or something," Tommy said to Finn's back. "I think we still have eggs."

Finn didn't react.

"I didn't mean to upset you, Finn."

"You didn't," Finn answered immediately. Then, after a pregnant pause, "Did he do more to you than just touch your thigh?"

Tommy stood next to him, not looking at Finn. "Not really. He just seemed to look at me in a funny way. As if he wanted to ask me something but didn't know how. It wasn't until I started going out to gay bars that I recognized that look."

"Good."

"I stopped going to the center after my friend killed himself."

Finn continued making the tea.

"So shall I make us that omelet now?"

Finn nodded.

The food was almost done when Finn spoke again. "I'm sorry you had to go through that. Don't take this the wrong way, but I'm glad it was your friend and not you who got... hurt."

Tommy smiled at Finn. "Me too." He started cleaning up the cooking area while Finn set the table.

"Do you know that district nurse had a record? No arrest was made, but he was detained for questioning less than a year ago. The record was sketchy at best. According to the file, the interrogation was taped, but the tape was missing from the records. I need to go to the Central Archive to ask what might have happened to it."

"Who were the officers in charge of the interrogation?"

"You're going to like this. Frank Farraday and a constable who is now on traffic duty."

"You'll probably find out the constable is the one who made the tape disappear and Farraday didn't even get a reprimand."

"Sounds like you know this guy well?"

Finn turned to face Tommy, his lips two thin lines. "Be careful, Tommy."

"I'm always careful. How dangerous is this dirty copper?"

Finn cocked his head.

"Does his influence really stretch that far?"

Finn inhaled deeply. "I think so."

Chapter Thirteen

FINN

HE WAS getting used to walking into his apartment to find every light on and clanging coming from the kitchen. Usually it smelled pretty nice too. The aroma drifting into the hallway gave Finn ideas of Thai food. Was there no end to Tommy's culinary prowess? He couldn't wait to sneak up on him (not possible, but Tommy didn't mind pretending) and give him a good snuggle (from behind, while Tommy was stirring the pots, or in this case probably the wok), followed by a kiss that would invariably curl his toes (just short enough not to burn anything). Finn enjoyed eating together as well, amazed at how he still found things to talk about even now his life consisted mainly of chewing through endless boxes of case files and writing case summaries. Tommy was just that easy to be with.

As Finn crossed the sitting room on his way to the kitchen, he noticed a girl in a school uniform sitting on the sofa. The wavy brown hair looked familiar. Was this Kasey?

"Hi," he tried.

She looked up from the pop star magazine she was leafing through.

"Who are you?" she asked suspiciously.

"I'm Finn." He didn't bother supplying a last name.

"Oh."

Oh? "And you are Kasey?"

"How did you know my name?"

"Tommy's told me about you."

"Oh."

Teenage vocab clearly wasn't improving. "So you've come to visit your dad?"

"Mum's being a pain. He probably told you about her too, right?"

"Yes, he did."

"So he's living here now?"

"You know his flat burned down?"

"The whole building. It's gutted!" she said with obvious schadenfreude. "It looks like it was bombed or something."

"So, yes."

"You shagging him?"

Finn was a little taken aback by her question, but years of keeping a straight face in court clearly helped now as well. "I don't think that's any of your business, young lady."

"He's my dad. I'm entitled to know."

Finn gave her a mock stern look, one he'd used quite often and very effectively in court. "Even dads are allowed to keep some secrets from their daughters."

"I know he's gay. He told me, and Mum explained that he's only sleepin' with blokes now," she stated with teenage arrogance.

Finn didn't detect any hurtfulness, though.

"And I've seen him with boyfriends before. He would sometimes have them over when I arrived at his old flat, and then he'd send them away. Suppose he can't now since this is your place."

"We'll both stay here tonight. And you're welcome as well. Did you call your mum to tell her where you were?"

"Dad will. He always does, even if I don't want him to."

"Your mum is responsible for you, so she's entitled to know that you are safe for the night."

She shrugged, clearly not caring either way.

"So what's he making us for dinner?"

Kasey looked up from the magazine she was still leafing through. "Some stir-fry."

"Smells delicious."

"I suppose," she said. "It's better than anything Mum can come up with, anyway."

Now there was a seal of approval. "I'll go say hi to him, okay?"

"Give him a good snog from me, then," she said with obvious glee, and Finn recognized not only Tommy's sense of humor but the same dimples in her cheeks as well.

Finn chuckled as he walked to the kitchen.

Tommy was standing behind the cooker, adding vegetables to the stir-fry and making the wok hiss. Finn put his hand between Tommy's shoulder blades.

"Hi."

As soon as Tommy acknowledged his presence, Finn wrapped his arms around him and gave him a full-body hug from behind, making all of the day's troubles evaporate.

"Have you met our guest?"

Finn nodded, his chin on Tommy's shoulder.

"I should have called, but she showed up at the station just before I left."

"It's okay. She can stay in the guest room. Did you call her mum yet?"

"I should probably sleep on the couch."

"Why?" Finn asked lightheartedly. "She thinks we're shagging anyway, and it's not like she'll walk in on us doing anything." He wasn't proud of the slow progress they were making in the physical department, but it was easier to joke than it was to feel down about it.

"I never let anyone stay over while she was at my place."

"Yes, she told me."

Tommy shook his head. "My daughter, the keeper of secrets."

Finn chuckled and hugged Tommy tighter. "She's fine with you being gay, Tommy."

"I know."

Finn was a little surprised with how not fine Tommy was with his daughter knowing it, though. Or was he just uncomfortable with her being witness to it? "She's old enough to ask very personal questions of someone she's just met, so I think she's also old enough to understand her dad is allowed to share a bedroom with… someone."

Tommy didn't answer, and that somehow worried Finn. It was a reassurance that Tommy's reluctance to sleep with him was clearly a pattern between father and daughter, but Finn sensed there was more to this than Tommy was letting on.

"Would you share my bed if I'd been a woman?"

Tommy took the wok off the fire and put it down with a clang. He then pushed Finn away from him and turned around. "I'm not ashamed of you, Finn, but like you said, she asks very private questions, and I don't want to lie to her."

"I know! So tell her it's none of her business."

"She's my daughter."

Finn could see the despair in Tommy's face.

"I want to tell her that it's love. Whether it's between a man and a woman or between two men, it's the same thing. I want her to grow up less of a bigot than her mother is. Well, I blame her stepfather, actually. He's the one who gives her a hard time every time she runs off to stay with her 'faggot father.'"

"I never call you that."

Both men turned to the kitchen door and saw Kasey standing there.

"I know you don't, K."

"He just doesn't like me running away. He doesn't get that it's chaos at our house and at yours it's always quieter. Even here it's calm. Nobody yells. At least they didn't until you two started fighting over me."

"We weren't…," they both started.

"Fighting," Tommy finished.

"So can I stay?"

"'Course you can," Tommy replied, looking for confirmation from Finn.

Finn looked at Tommy. "Why don't you go make up the guest bed, and I'll set the table so we can have dinner?"

When they returned, Finn had dinner on the table and Kasey seemed more relaxed. With both men in the same room, she seemed less inclined to ask personal questions and resorted to one-word answers whenever Finn or Tommy tried to engage her. They ended up casually talking about how their day went and more or less ignored her, which she didn't seem to mind.

Finn retreated to his home office while Tommy and Kasey did the dishes, and he lost track of time until Tommy invited him to come to sleep.

"I like her," Finn said as they were stripping down to their underwear in the bedroom. "Not to mention, I can see the resemblance."

"Kasey?"

Finn nodded. "She's got your hair, your dimples, and your eyes."

"My dimples?" Tommy asked.

Finn had never seen him so self-conscious. He moved closer and ran his finger over Tommy's cheek where Tommy's fingers had just left. Tommy smiled, and there they were. Finn poked the one underneath his finger. Tommy reciprocated by grabbing him around the waist, lifting him, and dropping him on the bed.

"Never took you for a caveman," Finn said, temporarily out of breath because of the sudden assault.

Tommy looked Finn in the eyes. "That wasn't caveman. I don't think you're ready for my caveman."

Finn chuckled, but he stopped when Tommy rested his head on his chest. With most of Tommy's weight on him, it felt incredibly intimate, much more than the lying close they'd been doing every night since Tommy had moved in. Finn combed his fingers through Tommy's hair and left his hand there, after which Tommy inserted his hand underneath the cotton T-shirt Finn was wearing. For a moment Finn felt his muscles tense up, but then he made a conscious effort to relax. He trusted Tommy to sleep next to him. Why wouldn't he trust him to touch his bare skin?

Finn kissed Tommy's forehead, and Tommy closed his eyes. It was chilly in the bedroom, and the overhead light was still on, but Finn didn't want to move to remedy any of that. Tommy clearly wanted this, and Finn knew exactly what that need felt like. He remembered Ayse's words about every human being needing physical contact, and he tried to remember what it was like when he wasn't getting any of it. He found he couldn't but knew without reservation he never wanted to experience that time again. He gently caressed Tommy's face, making him open his eyes.

"Come here."

Tommy stretched out so he could kiss Finn. Finn almost immediately upped the ante and kissed him back with as much fervor as he could manage until Tommy pulled away.

"You're making me all hot and bothered," Tommy said with a sigh.

"I thought that was the idea."

Tommy looked regretful, and Finn knew he was going to be turned down. It was strange that it was now Tommy's turn and not the other way around.

"Not with Kasey here."

Finn nodded but felt a little disappointed anyway. They got off the bed, turned down the bedding, and extinguished the light before crawling under the covers. It was awkward between them all of a sudden, and they lay side by side for long, silent minutes.

"What's wrong, Tommy?"

"Nothing."

Finn turned on his side so he was facing Tommy. "Can't we even sleep in each other's arms now she's here?" As soon as the words left his mouth he realized how jealous and spiteful they sounded. "I didn't mean to say that. What I meant is, I just want to hold you. I want to sleep with you like we've been sleeping all this time. I like holding you, and I like being held."

Tommy looked at Finn with sad eyes before burrowing into his arms. "I wish she was a cuddler, Finn."

"Kasey?"

"Yes. Last time I held her she was six or seven. Now she jumps even when I accidentally touch her."

"She's a teenager. Didn't you go all awkward when you were her age?"

"I suppose. Did you?"

"Why do you think I have such problems with intimacy? I grew up with nannies and servants. And a mother who didn't have the first clue what to do with a child and who would fire every nanny who developed a relationship with me. Add to that a father who felt his son had to be strong and stoic above all—"

"Well, he did a good job for you. You needed his training for the courtroom."

"Except when the dam breaks and the flood is catastrophic. In retrospect I'm surprised it took this long."

Tommy snuggled closer, positioning himself like before, half on top of Finn. "But you like holding me."

Finn kissed Tommy's forehead and tried to prevent the tears welling up in his eyes from dripping onto Tommy.

Chapter Fourteen

TOMMY

AFTER YET another day only half spent at Finn's office, with the other half running around for other cases, it was raining cats and dogs by the time Tommy reached Finn's apartment, and he was soaked to the bone. He took off his coat in the hall and shook the rain out of his hair before running into the guestroom for a dry sweater. Seeing Finn's tan coat and black cap on the hook near the door, he shook his head. He couldn't believe Finn was out running in this weather. He checked his watch and saw it was close to seven. Finn would be home soon, he was sure, so he could start dinner. He brought the soaked-through paper grocery bags into the kitchen and started taking out all the vegetables needed for the soup he was going to make. Luckily the shop girl at the bakery had had the foresight to wrap the focaccia bread in plastic. Otherwise that would be ruined for sure.

With the vegetables chopped and the pot about to start bubbling on the stove, Tommy picked up all the discarded vegetable cuts and went to put them in the bin when he saw it was overflowing. He grunted but knew it would make sense to take it out to the collection bin outside, only he didn't want to put on his soaking wet coat again. Then he remembered Finn's coat and cap. The coat would be on the small side, but he was sure it fit well enough for a quick run outside.

After donning the borrowed attire, he took the waste outside and was pleasantly surprised to find the rain had stopped.

FINN

IT HAD started raining shortly after he'd started on his run, but he'd persevered. Between Tommy living in his apartment and regular counseling sessions with Ayse, he'd found plenty of excuses not to go running, but since he'd come home early and Tommy wasn't there yet, he'd braved the inclement weather. Now it was dark and dry again as he rounded the corner to his flat. He smiled and stopped in view of his building to catch his breath and see the telltale signs of occupation. Just about every light in his apartment was on, which meant Tommy was home, and that invariably made him smile.

"Tommy?" Finn called out as he opened the front door. There was no reply, but Finn followed his nose to the kitchen where a pot was steaming away on the stove. When he lifted the lid, everything was boiling madly, so he lowered the heat a bit until it was just simmering. He'd learned enough to know he could do this without ruining Tommy's food. "Tommy?" he shouted again. Still no reply as he walked toward the bathroom, hoping to find his boyfriend in the shower. Since the bathroom was empty he decided he might as well get clean before dinner was ready. When he reemerged and Tommy was still nowhere to be found, he started to become worried. He put on clean, and more importantly dry, clothes and took out his mobile to call Tommy.

"This is Tommy Drummond, leave a message."

Voice mail. Dammit.

"Hi, love, it's me," Finn spoke. "Where are you?" He disconnected the call almost immediately and redialed, this time to reach Stevie.

After only two rings, she picked up. "He's not here, swee'heart."

Finn chuckled. "How did you know I called for Tommy?"

"Why else would you call me? We were done about half six. I'm sure he left just the same as me."

"Thanks, Stevie. Give my love to the kids."

Finn sighed as the call ended, and then he sat deflated on the dining room chair. Where could Tommy be? He called Tommy's mobile again with the same result and then called Ayse.

The call was picked up after several rings, but quite a racket assaulted him.

"Be quiet for a moment! I'm answering a call!" The noise damped somewhat, and Finn heard a door close. "I'm sorry about that. Finn?"

"Yes, it's me. Did I call at a bad time?"

"No, just a house full of family. My sister and her mongrels. What's wrong?"

Finn smiled. "Why would anything be wrong?"

"Because when I'm at home you either call me to reschedule our appointment or when something happened with Tommy."

"Nothing happened with Tommy, at least I don't think so. I came home to a house with all the lights on but no Tommy. The soup he made is on the stove, so I'm sure he just ran out for something he forgot to bring from the shops, but I've been home for half an hour now and he still isn't back."

"Well, taste the soup, and if the veggies are done, turn off the heat. Otherwise you'll end up with mush."

Finn walked to the kitchen and did just that. "You're a godsend."

"Did you call his mobile?"

"Twice. Voice mail every time."

"That is strange. Maybe he's on the Tube and doesn't have service? Did you walk around the flat while calling? When Charlie's home I can never reach him on his phone because he always forgets to take the bloody thing with him. He's not used to carrying it when he's on a mission, so he always forgets about it when he's home."

Finn knew Ayse was only trying to soothe him, but it was working. "I'll give it a try. Now go see that your sister's children don't break down your flat. I'll talk to you tomorrow."

Although Finn knew Tommy was pretty attached to his mobile and never went anywhere without it, he tried to do what Ayse had suggested and dialed repeatedly while walking around the flat to listen for Tommy's *Avengers* ringtone. He didn't hear it anywhere, so he decided to walk out onto the terrace to see if he could spot him coming down the road. There wasn't a soul around, so he dialed again, and then he heard it. It was a faint sound, and it stopped when voice mail picked up, so he dialed again. The sound hadn't become clearer, which meant the mobile hadn't moved. Finn ran to the front door and grabbed for his coat, only to realize it was missing, and so was his cap. He didn't go in search of it, thinking he probably wouldn't need to go far. As soon as he stepped down onto the pavement he dialed again and followed the sound to the back alley.

There, under the glaring streetlight, Finn saw a slumped-down body wearing his coat.

"Tommy!"

He crouched down on the street next to him, feeling the rainwater soak into his trousers, but he ignored it. Tommy was hurt. That was plain as day, even under the cold light. There were already bruises around his eyes, his lip was split, and his eyes were closed.

"Tommy, wake up." Finn put his hand on Tommy's stomach, shook him, and then felt the wetness under his hand. When he withdrew it, it was dark. "Bloody hell, Tom. What did they do to you?" He pulled the coat apart and then the shirt underneath and saw the pool of blood just underneath Tommy's ribs. He pushed his hand on top of it to stop the flow and cursed as he scrambled around for his mobile and couldn't find it. His eye fell on a gleaming piece of metal and realized he must have dropped his phone as he sank down to the ground to tend to Tommy. It was too far to reach, but he knew Tommy's only chance was to dial 999, so he let go of Tommy's wound just long enough to reach for it.

"Emergency. Which service do you require?"

"My friend was beaten up."

"I'll put you through to the ambulance service, sir."

It didn't take long to get connected. "Ambulance service. How may I help you?"

"My friend was beaten up," Finn repeated, trying to stay as calm as possible.

"Is he hurt badly, sir?" a calm, friendly voice on the other side of the line asked.

Finn tried to remember everything that was important about calling 999, and although he'd interrogated enough witnesses on the stand who'd done it all wrong, he now drew a blank himself. "Yes, he is. I'm in Kensington." He gave his address. "He's unconscious and bleeding from his stomach. Please get here quickly. I can't get up to lead them to the scene because I can't take my hand off the wound. I'm underneath a streetlamp in the back alley."

He barely heard the rest of the conversation and hoped the dispatcher hadn't given him any instructions, because he knew he would have missed them. He threw down the phone and tried to remember what else he needed to do. Check for a pulse. Yes, he remembered how to do that. He just didn't know how to interpret it. He could feel a heartbeat, so that calmed him down some, but the shirt Tommy was wearing was soaked in his blood, and Finn had no idea how much longer the emergency services would be. As he waited and continued talking to Tommy, he inwardly kicked himself for not going out in search of him earlier and maybe preventing the attack or getting help to him sooner. He hoped Tommy would make it and his regret wouldn't turn to anguish.

Although Finn was happy to see the flashing blue lights of the ambulance arrive in the alley, it didn't diminish his worry. He knew Tommy wasn't out of the woods yet, and he tried to give the ambulance men as much information as he could before they whisked him away. As he walked back to his flat, all he wanted to do was call Ayse to talk to her, but he knew she had her hands full with her family, so he called Stevie.

"I'll drive you to 'ospital," Stevie answered as soon as Finn explained to her what happened. "And I'll ask the unis to come to the scene. Maybe they can find out what happened."

For some reason Stevie's no-nonsense reasoning calmed Finn down more than anything.

SEVERAL HOURS, many cups of tea, and a few calls from Stevie later, updating him on the investigation, Finn was still sitting in the A&E waiting room in his clothes soaked in Tommy's blood. He was wiping his hands over his face and scratching his hair to stay awake when Ayse walked in.

"Finn! Why didn't you call me?"

"You had family over, and I know how important—"

"Bollocks," she cursed. "If I'd known it was this bad, I would have come right away!"

She punched Finn's arm, and the fact it hurt made Finn smile.

"Who called you?"

"Stevie did. She told me where you were and how tired you sounded and that I was the only person she could think of besides Tommy who could make you feel better."

He got up from his seat and then realized what he looked like. Ayse pulled him into her arms anyway.

"Your clothes," Finn protested. He had to admit it felt good, though.

"Oh, Finn," she soothed. "Who cares about that?" She squeezed him again before letting him go. "Can I get you anything? Coffee? Tea?"

"I've had some tea, thanks."

"How's Tommy?" Her forehead was creased, and she clearly braced herself for impact.

"Still alive, last I heard. He's in theater."

She sat down next to him.

"They beat and stabbed him. I never saw so much blood. Well, actually, I did. At a crime scene Tommy took me to, but both victims were dead."

Ayse rubbed his back, and he couldn't find words to tell her how good that felt. "He'd gone out to the back to put the trash in the bin and...." He didn't know what else happened. "Stevie doesn't think it's a robbery because they didn't take his wallet or his mobile."

"Stevie got the Met involved. That's good, right?"

Finn nodded. "At least that part's covered. She's not hopeful they'll ever find who did it, though. There's supposed to be CCTV footage, but it was dark out. The chance they'll actually be able to recognize a face is practically nonexistent."

"Why don't I take you home for a shower and a change of clothes and then I'll bring you back here to see Tommy?"

"I can't leave."

Ayse held out her hand. "Then give me your key and I'll go find you a change of clothes. I promise I won't snoop around in your sex toys drawer."

Finn looked at her as if to ask whether what he heard was actually what she'd said, but her smug face said it all. Even in these dire circumstances he had to admit it was funny, so he smiled.

"I don't think there's anything about me in my house that will surprise you anymore, Dr. Kartal." He handed her the keys.

"I'll be back in a little while. Will you be okay?"

Finn nodded and watched her leave.

IT WAS almost morning when the surgeon finally brought them some good news. Finn had washed in the toilet washbasin and changed into the clothes Ayse had brought him before he'd dozed off, sitting in a chair and leaning against the wall with Ayse in his arms. They were still smiling about hearing that Tommy was going to be all right when Stevie walked in with a woman Finn didn't know in tow.

"Any news yet, mate?" Stevie asked.

Finn nodded, looking at the strange woman before turning back to Stevie. "They just told us he's out of surgery and doing well. He's in Intensive Care so we can't see him until this afternoon, but they found where he was bleeding from and managed to stop it. He'll need some blood and time to heal, but they were pretty positive."

He looked at Ayse for confirmation, and she nodded.

"That's good news, innit?" Stevie said with a smile.

"Are you going to introduce us, Stevie?" Finn asked a little hesitantly.

"Of course. Finn, this is Maggie Drummond, Tommy's mum. Maggie, this is Tommy's... Finn DeHavilland."

Maggie extended her hand and vigorously shook Finn's. "Tommy's told me so much about you."

From the corner of his eye Finn saw Stevie gesture at Ayse, and after Ayse patted him on the shoulder, she left with Stevie.

"Why don't we sit here," Finn suggested.

"You found Tommy?" Maggie asked.

"He, ehm.... Tommy is living with me, after the fire." *Right, very eloquent, Mister Prosecutor.* Then again, Stevie didn't know how to introduce him to Tommy's mother, and Finn knew exactly how that felt. He had no idea how much she knew about Tommy's private life. She looked exactly how Finn had imagined her from Tommy's stories, though. He could see the resemblance, although it was nowhere near as close as the way Kasey resembled her father. Mrs. Drummond was short and compact, with perfectly coiffed hair he was sure had been tinted to take care of gray hairs. She looked worried and very much in control of her emotions at the same time.

"Are you his boyfriend?"

Finn saw no malice in her. She just wanted to know. Although their relationship wasn't exactly set in stone yet, Finn had a feeling about what she wanted to hear. "We're trying to make a go of it, yes."

She smiled. "He told me about having a crush on you. He started telling me about this Crown Prosecutor, and I kept thinking you were a bit too posh for my Tommy, but then you let him move in with you after the fire, and I thought you couldn't be half bad if that's what you did for him."

"He's a great… friend."

"Only a friend?"

Finn chuckled at seeing her disappointment. "We're working on it. Together."

She grabbed his hand and smiled. "Aaaw, it's so nice these days to see young people working at a relationship. Too many times you see them throwing it away, and I keep telling my youngest nobody's perfect. She could take a page out of my Tommy's book, she could."

Finn smiled. "She probably could."

She perked up some more. "So are they not lettin' you see him because you're not, what do they say? His domestic partner?"

"Yes," Finn replied.

"But I'm his mum. Would it help if I told them who I was and asked to see him? I bet they'd let his mother in, right? And then I can take you along."

Finn felt good about this. "You know, they probably would."

She got up and gave a determined nod. Finn could so see where Tommy got his fire.

"Come along, then. I'm not giving them time to say no."

Finn wasn't really surprised when the nursing staff went out of their way to let her see her son. What surprised him more was that she wouldn't take no for an answer when they told her she couldn't bring Finn. It was crystal clear to him how she'd managed to bring up her children alone.

"They're as good as married, these two. He's a Crown Prosecutor, and he's my son's partner. He's been out there all night waiting to see him. How can you not find it in your heart to let him see his boyfriend?"

Finn almost wanted the ground to open up and swallow him. This sort of attention was exactly what he didn't want. But then the diligent nurse manning the door wavered.

"Very well, but only for a few minutes. He's asleep, but even so he needs his rest."

When they entered the room Tommy was in, Maggie gasped. "Oh God, is that really my Tommy?"

Finn swallowed hard. Tommy's face was swollen and bruised. One side of his face looked like raw meat, black and blue, his eye swollen shut. The other side had a large bruise over his jaw and a split lip, which was stitched up. Finn didn't recognize the face either, but he did recognize the hand that wasn't in a cast. Tommy's knuckles were scraped, but the hand was definitely Tommy's. Finn caressed it gently as they stood and looked at him, listening to the soft beeps all around his bed.

Chapter Fifteen

FINN

THE FOLLOWING day Finn returned during visiting hours and sat by the bed. He was surprised Tommy was still asleep.

"We've been doing tests to see why he isn't waking up, but so far everything is negative," the nurse reassured him. "Maybe he's got the sort of body that just hibernates as long as it isn't up to par."

"Is that common?" Finn asked worriedly.

"I've seen it before," she assured him.

Finn had a hard time leaving, but he arranged his work so he could spend every time he was allowed with Tommy.

On the third day after the attack, Finn was starting to give up hope. Tommy hadn't shown any sign of waking up yet. He reacted to pain, which was encouraging according to the nursing staff, but other than that, he remained totally impassive. Right from the first day, Finn would talk to him all the time they were alone. He'd tell him about his day and the cases he was working on and could actually speak about, and he'd repeat as often as he could that he needed Tommy to come back to work with him. He soon ran out of things to say, though. It didn't help that he wanted to shake Tommy to wake him up but didn't dare. Instead Finn poured his heart out to Tommy.

"Remember when you told me about that caseworker in the community center who'd felt you up?" Finn paused to give Tommy the chance to answer, even though he knew he wouldn't. "I so wanted to tell you I knew what that was like. Only it didn't happen like with you. It didn't stop after one time. I didn't protest. I wasn't as strong as you, and I never said I didn't want it." Finn tried to swallow away the tears that trickled down his throat. He had to pause to collect himself before continuing.

"It went on for years, Tommy. He was a friend of my mother's. I had to call him uncle, although he was neither a brother of my mother's or my father's. Uncle Malcolm. He seduced me. Gave me the candy my mother wouldn't give me and the attention I so wanted from my parents but never got. Then after some time he warned me never to tell anyone what happened in the boathouse. I avoided it after that, but he found me everywhere, and over the course of his many visits I ran out of places to hide. The older I got the more daring he became and the more...." Finn couldn't even say it.

"Tommy, he's the reason I sometimes can't bear to be touched. It's because of him that I've never been able to let anyone close. No matter how hard I try, when I see you look at me in a certain way, all I can see is how he used to look at me, with his hungry smirk and his lustful eyes. Every time you put your hand on me, touch me, however tender and caring, I can only feel Malcolm's grabby hands. It's bigger than me, Tommy, and I don't know how I'll ever get over that feeling. I so want to. I so want to be able to be the man you deserve."

Finn startled when he heard someone clear her throat behind him. He looked up, momentarily unashamed about the tears streaming down his face, only to see Ayse standing near the entrance of the room.

"I couldn't help overhearing you, Finn."

"Fuck." Finn wiped his face. "I suppose it's for the best. I could never tell you if I knew you were listening."

"Like you're telling Tommy because you know he can't hear you?"

Finn nodded.

"It's good to tell someone, even if the only one listening is you." She moved a chair next to Finn, sat down, and took his hand without looking at him. "I've suspected for a long time you were an abuse survivor, Finn. And you are that. You're a survivor. You've studied hard, you are very successful at what you do, and at least in your professional life you don't shy away from the cases that could possibly bring back bad memories."

"What gave me away?" Finn asked with a croak in his voice.

"Your overdeveloped sense of righteousness. Your tireless effort to bring the bad people of this world to justice. Some people call that naiveté or idealism, but I've always suspected it went a lot deeper with you. He never got his day in court, did he?"

Finn shook his head in question, his forehead furrowed, feigning ignorance.

"Your abuser. The man who did this to you."

Finn bit his upper lip. "He ran away to the Philippines. He never stopped abusing young men, boys, I'm sure. It's just easier there."

Ayse was frowning too, now. "Did you ever tell anyone before you told Tommy?"

Finn snorted. "I told my mother. She said I was lying. That I was a horrible child for having such cruel fantasies. Fantasies!"

"How old were you then?"

"Fourteen."

"Is that when he stopped doing this to you?"

"She bought him a ticket to go and leave the country."

"So she got him away from you. Isn't that what a mother is supposed to do?"

What? Finn couldn't believe what Ayse was saying. "She should have gone to the police. She should have reported it to the authorities so he could be put on trial." Finn was getting riled up by the fact Ayse stayed so incredibly calm. How could she? This man had ruined his life!

"Finn, this was what? Almost thirty years ago, right? Nowadays we have policemen trained to deal with child abuse. We have magistrates who know how to get people like this convicted, but back then? In the circles you grew up in? It was covered up. It was deemed too much of a scandal to do anything else. I'm not trying to side with her, but she did what she was raised to do. Besides, she probably wanted to spare you. Back then people thought that if you didn't speak about it, it would go away."

Finn shook his head. What Ayse told him had calmed him because deep down he knew she was right. It didn't mean he had to like it or even agree with it, but what was the use of being angry at his mother? She was dead and couldn't defend herself or her actions anymore.

"Because of what that man did to me for eight years, Ayse. Eight years! I was six when this started! Because of what he did I can't even let Tommy come near me. He loves me. It's the only explanation for why he sticks around even though I freeze up every time he tries to push me to do more than kiss. But I'm broken. Beyond repair. When I realized I liked men, not women, I felt disgusted with myself. I was afraid I was going to be like him. A pervert who abused little children to get off. So I shut that part of me away. I stopped wanting."

"I think you're safe to let yourself want, Finn."

"I can't. You know the statistics as well as I do. Almost all the child abusers we put away were abused themselves!"

"Yes, but what you're conveniently forgetting is that only a small percentage of victims become aggressors themselves." This time she looked him in the eye. "That's why I said you were a survivor. Correct me if I'm wrong, but I seriously doubt you've ever had lustful feelings for a child, right?"

Finn shook his head.

"Instead you fell in love with what the more open-minded people at his station consider the epitome of manhood. Tommy's a grown man. He's almost thirty years old. He's a father. He's strong and in control. He's done exactly what you did and made something of himself. He's a detective sergeant and on his way to an inspector's exam. He dug himself out of that council flat and into a real, responsible job, and he's got the same sense of righteousness you have. He doesn't do this for the fame or the money. He does this to put the bad people behind bars. That's why you're attracted to him. That's why you couldn't resist falling in love with him. You share a sense of values and beliefs. You share a passion. My theory is that you fell in love with him the moment he first walked through your door. Only you didn't know it until he'd been so cruelly outed by his boss, and then you knew you could help him and felt compelled to do so by a force stronger than yourself. That's love, Finn. You're just lucky that he feels the same way about you."

Somehow what Ayse was saying made perfect sense. He squeezed her hand and nodded, since that was about all he was capable of.

Then he heard a groan come from the bed, and he turned to look at Tommy. The eye that wasn't swollen shut was open but looked unfocused. He was mumbling something Finn couldn't make out.

"You're in hospital, Tommy. You were beaten and stabbed."

Tommy tried to sit up but fell back to the bed with a pained expression on his face.

"Don't move too much or you might pop your stitches."

"Who?"

"We don't know yet," Finn replied, surprised by his own calmness. "But we're trying to find out. Stevie's on the case." This seemed to calm Tommy down as well. "You're going to be fine. You look and probably feel like you were flattened by a cement truck, but it's nothing that won't heal. Whatever they stabbed you with nicked an artery, so I almost lost you, but the doctors got here in time."

Tommy's open eye focused on Finn, and Finn smiled. "I met your mum. You're right. She's quite a lady."

A hint of a smile broke on Tommy's face as he closed his eye. "Sleep. I'll be here when you wake up."

Finn sat next to Tommy's bed, holding his hand and listening to the soft beep of the little clamp that was over his finger and that registered his heartbeat and breathing. They'd explained that as long as it stayed above 95 percent, he was fine. Finn stopped looking at the display and just listened for the changing pitch of the beeps.

"I think he's asleep, Finn. Let me take you for a breath of fresh air, just for ten minutes or so."

Finn didn't reply immediately. He looked at Tommy and saw he seemed much more relaxed than before. He knew what Tommy looked like when he was simply sleeping, and this was a lot closer to that than what he'd looked like before, so he got up. "Okay, just for a few minutes. Let me tell the nurse where I am."

Finn walked to the duty nurse. "He was awake for a few moments. Opened his eyes. Spoke a few words. He's asleep again."

She smiled at him. "That's good news. We knew it would only be a matter of time. I'll go and check on him in a minute."

Finn pointed outside. "I'm just going out for some fresh air. I'll be right back."

She nodded and then went back to her paperwork.

Ayse was already holding the door to the corridor open. "Do you want some coffee?"

"No, I'm going right back in. This hospital coffee is no good anyway. And their tea is even worse, if you can believe it."

Ayse hooked her arm underneath Finn's and strolled along with him. "You've made some sort of breakthrough tonight, Finn. It won't be smooth sailing from here on in, in fact you might feel it makes everything harder for a short while, but I want you to continue to come see me. I'm not a relationship counselor, but I still want to be your listening ear. And I'll start you off with some advice. Tell Tommy again, this time when he's awake and giving you his full attention."

Finn shook his head. He couldn't tell Tommy.

"Finn, don't dismiss it. It won't be easy telling him, but Tommy's not an insensitive person. If you tell him, even if it's just the highlighted version, he'll understand why you blow hot and cold around him, why you jerk away from his touch, and why you can't take this further right now. It will buy you time with him."

"Or he'll just see me for what I am. Damaged goods."

"You're not beyond repair, Finn." Ayse stopped in the middle of the deserted corridor and forced him to face her by grabbing his shoulders. "But you can't do this alone. Tommy will help you heal, and I'll be on hand to talk to."

"I don't know where to start."

"Ask him to teach you."

"Teach me?"

"He knows you're inexperienced. I know very few men who can resist offering slow and thorough instruction."

Finn smiled. "You're a pervert, Dr. Kartal."

She shook her head, smiling even more widely than Finn. "No, I'm not. I'm simply telling you to take advantage of the situation. Isn't that what you are renowned for?"

"That's in court."

"And this is real life. I know. But what have you got to lose?"

They said their good-byes, and walking back to Tommy's room, Finn contemplated Ayse's words. It wasn't going to be easy, but maybe she was right. He'd have to find the right moment to tell Tommy, though, and he knew he'd be hard pressed to find the nerve.

Chapter Sixteen

TOMMY

THE FIRST few days in hospital Tommy's head felt like it was stuffed with cotton wool instead of brain matter. No matter how hard he tried, he couldn't recall how he'd managed to land himself in hospital in the first place. He vaguely remembered Finn telling him he'd been mugged in the alley behind Finn's flat. The nurse explained he had a severe concussion, a broken left arm, cracked ribs, a hairline fracture in his jaw and one around his eye socket, and a four-inch scar on his right side from the repair job the doctors had had to do because of the stab wound he'd received. One of his other vague memories was of Finn telling him they'd only just made it to hospital in time to save him. He could only imagine how much of Finn's legendary control was left intact after that ordeal.

Tommy also dreamed a lot, and sometimes it was hard to distinguish his dreams from reality. One of those dreams was of a doctor calling his time of death like you saw in the movies and then of Finn crashing to the ground crying. Finn needed him and Finn loved him; there was no doubt about that. After all, Finn slept on that damned uncomfortable-looking chair next to his bed every night and then went to work the next morning, only to come back in the afternoon with a trolley full of case files to review while he was keeping him company.

When one of the doctors checking his wound decided Tommy was fit enough to go home, he called Finn, and Finn was there within the hour. He still hoped he wouldn't outstay his welcome at Finn's flat, but on the other hand, there was no place he'd rather be.

FINN

HE WAS infinitely grateful he could bring Tommy home and didn't have to leave him to his own devices in a place where there was nobody to take care of him. Yes, he had to work during the day, but at least he could help Tommy up in the morning and make sure he had a decent meal and some company in the evening. The rest would sort itself out. If necessary he could bring work home. Especially in the first few days.

"Finn, please," Tommy pleaded as he watched Finn nervously dart between the cab and his front door while Tommy stood to the side, trying to keep his precarious balance against the corner of the steps leading to the front door. Before Tommy tried to walk up, Finn was there.

"Careful now. Watch your step."

"Stop right there, mister," Tommy said with an even, soft voice but with clear frustration leaking from it. "You're making me dizzy. Calm down. I'm not an invalid."

Tommy's movements were measured, careful, and very slow.

Finn wanted to help, but he didn't know how. He wanted to tell Tommy that yes, right now he was an invalid, but it wasn't anything that couldn't heal, so he didn't say anything. He knew he was fussing and fidgeting, which was, he had to admit, a little out of character, but he couldn't help himself. He'd almost lost the man who meant the world to him, and seeing him suffer made him squirm. He did, however, make a conscious effort to act calmer.

They somehow made it into the flat with a bag of groceries, Tommy's bag of mostly nightclothes, and an exhausted Tommy, all in one go.

"Sit or lie down, whichever feels most comfortable. I'll make us something to eat."

"Is that safe? I barely survived the mugging, and now you're going to poison me with your cooking? You should order something they can bring to the house," Tommy suggested, his voice flat and so devoid of the humor the words suggested that Finn walked back into the sitting room to see how serious Tommy was. "I'm kidding," Tommy added for good measure, his facial expression hard to read because of the state of his injuries.

"I'm making spaghetti."

"Oh, that's safe, then." Tommy sat down ever so slowly, and Finn resisted helping him with all his might.

"It's something I can heat up. I can work a microwave, you know."

"I know."

Finn brought in the food on a tray table he'd had stashed away from when his mother was sick. He reckoned it would make eating easier for Tommy, since his preferred left arm was in a cast and he'd need to eat with his right.

"Do you need me to cut it up for you, or will you manage?"

"I'll manage," Tommy said as he looked at the store-bought spaghetti.

"They told me you couldn't chew much with your broken jaw, but on second thought, lasagna would have been easier to work."

Tommy smiled somewhat. "There are more days to come."

They ate in silence, Finn trying hard to kill any urge to help Tommy out. It worried him that Tommy ate only a few bites before putting his fork down and sighing.

"Tired?"

Tommy nodded. "It's crazy how everything costs so much more energy."

"Your bed is made," Finn said.

"It better be, since I'm sleeping in yours."

"Wouldn't you be more comfortable sleeping alone? You know I'm not a placid sleeper. I'll wake you every time I move."

Tommy looked at him with his good eye. The one that had been swollen shut for the longest time was now open as well but very bloodshot, and it looked strange, so Finn focused on the light blue one.

"You don't want me there?"

"I want you to be comfortable."

"And I want a warm body next to me, someone who can help me up if I need to pee. I'm being entirely selfish."

Finn put the unfinished plates away, together with the tray table, and moved closer to Tommy. Ever so carefully, he put his arm around Tommy's shoulders and then saw him wince.

"Don't you dare pull away from me. My whole body hurts, but I'll gladly suffer it if it means you'll hold me."

It took some maneuvering, but eventually they settled with Tommy lying back to chest with Finn, with Finn's arm draped over him so he could put his hand on Tommy's chest. Tommy's left arm was hung over the backrest of the sofa so it remained elevated, and his feet were up.

Finn flicked on the TV so they could watch the news, and he slowly felt Tommy relax until he knew he was asleep. Nothing on TV interested him, but he needed to practice what he was going to tell Tommy, and it felt easier to do this with the TV voices in the background.

"I'm sorry I always pull away from you, Tommy. It has nothing to do with you, but more with what a man named Malcolm did to me when I was a child. Every time we start something there's a voice inside me telling me what we're doing is wrong. I know it isn't real, but he made it wrong for me."

"You told me before," Tommy murmured.

Finn's heart stopped. He tried not to gasp. Tommy was still relaxed, lying against him.

"He didn't love you, Finn. I do."

Finn wiped the tears away from his face, at the same time trying not to move so he'd wake Tommy further. "I didn't know you were awake."

Tommy sat up slowly, wincing with most of the moves he made before turning his entire body in Finn's direction. He looked sad, but then his expressions were still hard to read. "I didn't know whether it was something I'd dreamed or whether it was real until you told me now." He put his good hand on Finn's leg. "In any case, I'm glad you told me, because I was beating myself up over what I was doing wrong every time you jerked away from me."

"You did everything right, Tommy," Finn said with a raspy voice. "It's me. I want you so much it hurts, and then you indulge me, and all I can think of is that he used to do that to me too, and it makes it all sordid. Even fantasizing feels wrong because I want you to do to me what he did to me then, and I hated what he did, so how could I want that?"

Tommy's lips tensed, and the dimples appeared in his cheeks, although he wasn't smiling. "You're going to have to separate the two, Finn." He paused as if he was thinking. "It may be the same movements, but my intentions are totally opposite of his. Besides, you never consented to him, and I would never do anything to you that you didn't consent to. You're going to have to trust yourself to say stop when it's something you don't want. And I promise I will listen to you."

Finn softly placed his lips against Tommy's, careful not to hurt his already bruised mouth. "I think I should put you to bed. You were already sleeping."

"Only if you join me."

Finn chuckled out of unease. "You drive a mean bargain."

"I promise I'll let you leave if we keep each other awake," Tommy said softly. "But as you just saw here, you relax me enough to allow me to rest."

Finn conceded, nodding at Tommy as he held out his hand to help Tommy up.

TOMMY

WALKING WAS hard. So was breathing. He was grateful both his legs were in decent condition, because between his ribs, arm, and jaw he was utterly miserable. And as much as he liked Finn being close by, he hated being so dependent on him. During his last day in hospital, he'd simply decided to turn that dependency into something positive. He was going to use it to get closer to Finn.

Now that Finn had told him about the abuse, Tommy understood where that idea had come from. It had been niggling in the back of his head for days that he had to find a way to become totally innocuous to Finn, and now he knew why. Tommy had investigated enough child abuse cases to know that Finn's abuser, a friend of the family, had used the power he had over Finn to do unspeakable things to him and had then preyed on his shame and fear of his parents to make sure little Finn never spoke of it to anyone.

Tommy was looking at Finn as Finn was helping him undress. Tommy liked Finn's hands. They were soft yet strong, with neat, well maintained fingernails that didn't look quite so perfect they seemed manicured. Finn seemed less nervous than he usually was when they were in such close proximity, but his mouth was tense with concentration, and his gaze was firmly planted on the buttons of Tommy's jeans as he was undoing them, careful not to brush over any intimate parts.

Tommy couldn't help but smile. He let Finn work without trying to help him, simply because he wanted to keep feeling Finn's hands on him. He had to will himself not to get aroused too much, though. The last thing Finn needed now was a man who sprung wood at the slightest occasion. The pain and discomfort helped. And sadly, so did Finn's abuse confession. At the same time it calmed him to know why Finn was the man he was. And that he'd been doing the right thing all along.

"Are you ready to lie down?"

Tommy nodded. "I'll need my meds. Sorry, I think they're still in my bag."

Finn gently kissed his forehead. "Will you be okay on your own for a moment?"

"There's nothing wrong with my legs."

Finn looked down. "You're right. Be right back."

Tommy slowly turned around and pulled the duvet off the bed so he could sit down. As soon as he did, his ribs protested, and when he tried to support them with his left hand, the annoying cast hit just the right spot. Or the wrong one in Tommy's case, because tears shot into his eyes.

"Fuck!" Tommy tried not to shout too loudly.

"Here, this will help." Finn handed him his pills and then a glass of water.

Tommy swallowed them dry and then drank from the glass.

Finn took the glass back before crouching in front of him. "How long until the pain pills kick in?"

"'Bout half an hour?" Tommy's eyes wandered to Finn's hands, which were caressing his naked knees. "Too long in any case."

"When did you last take them?"

"This morning."

Finn shook his head, and Tommy saw the worry.

"I didn't want to be out of it too much tonight."

"Let's get you comfortable."

Finn was surprisingly good at helping him find a comfortable position, but he needed to be prompted again to join Tommy in bed. Tommy wanted him there, though. After days in a hospital bed, he needed the comfort of Finn's warm body next to him. It was the only thing that made him feel alive.

Chapter Seventeen

TOMMY

THEY WERE lying side by side, Tommy's injured left arm elevated by a pillow, his right arm supporting Finn as he occasionally leaned over Tommy to kiss him. Finn's right hand was resting on the bare skin of Tommy's stomach, as his T-shirt was pulled up to about his nipples.

"Just do it, Finn. Slide your hand down. You want to, right?"

"It's all wrong. You're injured. You can barely move."

"There's nothing wrong with it. The pain is going away. I can move better now." They both looked at Finn's hand. "Just do it. I promise I'll tell you to stop if it feels wrong."

Finn nodded, but at the same time he looked terrified. "You know I've never...."

"Just stop when I tell you to stop," Tommy interrupted. "And if I don't, that means you're doing it right."

Tommy tried hard not to tense up too much under Finn's hand, but the anticipation was killing him. Maybe it was the drugs that made him horny. Maybe it was the fact that he knew wanking with his right hand was no good. "Right there. A little lower. I won't break, Finn."

Finn giggled almost silently, kissing Tommy again as he let his hand slip under the elastic of Tommy's briefs. "Oh God," Finn sighed against Tommy's mouth at about the same time Tommy gasped at feeling Finn's hand on his semierect cock.

"Move," Tommy moaned.

"Can I just enjoy the feeling for a moment?"

Tommy sighed, part exasperation, part frustration. "You have one too!"

Finn giggled again, and Tommy fervently hoped they could keep this investigation bit slow and relaxed. He wanted to savor it for as long as he could, hoping only his impatience would curtail it.

"I very rarely—" *Kiss*. "—touch it in any—" *Kiss*. "—sort of—" *Kiss*. "—pleasurable way."

"So you're saying," Tommy murmured against Finn's temple, "that you need a manual?"

Finn chuckled, and his whole body participated. He pulled up his shoulders, threw his head back momentarily, and squeezed his hand just a little. It was enough for Tommy's cock to fill a little more.

"Just move your hand. Slowly. Up and down. A little more pressure. Yeah. Oh, that's good." Tommy let himself slowly drift away on a cloud of bliss, and they exchanged sloppy kisses while he tried to enjoy what little skin-to-skin contact they had, since Finn was still wearing a T-shirt and briefs. For some reason Finn's hesitant actions and inexperienced moves made Tommy even more eager. All he had to do was keep his hands to himself and let Finn get on with his exploring. The latter was easy; the former wasn't. He was a very tactile lover, and sex wasn't sex if he didn't get his hands on some naked skin. As it was, he tried to enjoy the hand job, which was more eagerness than skill, and tried to think of the higher purpose. At least it helped his stamina.

"You feel good," Finn whispered.

"Isn't that supposed to be my line?" Tommy joked.

"It feels good? What I'm doing?"

"Frickin' stellar." All aches and pains forgotten, he kissed Finn hard just to prove his point and pulled Finn's body closer to his. He hoped it wasn't just his imagination when he felt Finn rubbing his groin against his hip. "Will you let me do this to you?"

Finn kissed him back with abandon, but when he stopped, he rubbed his nose over Tommy's, and Tommy took that as a no.

His hands were itching to touch Finn's bare skin, but he knew what they were doing now was already so far out of Finn's comfort zone it could be classified as a miracle, so Tommy didn't push.

"Go on. Don't stop, then," he urged him on since Finn's movements had stilled. "That part of me isn't hurting as much as the rest."

Finn smiled against Tommy's mouth and squeezed his hand at the same time.

Subtle it was not, but the sensuality of the encounter and the fact that he'd pined for Finn for so long, aggravated by the kissing-and-nothing-more, made Tommy hornier than he normally would be. Of course, the self-imposed abstinence helped too, since he hadn't felt anything other than his own hand in months now. Tommy tried to focus on feeling Finn's sinewy body close to him and not on the pain Finn's rubbing up against him caused. He knew the wonderful feeling in his groin could drown out some of the aches of his injuries. "A little faster," he groaned, and Finn complied. Tommy knew he wouldn't last long, knew it by how his body was involuntarily pushing into Finn's hand and how he was desperately trying to get closer to him, yet when his groin exploded, midkiss and eyes closed, it still took him by surprise.

Finn moving away from him right after wasn't exactly expected either.

"Don't go," Tommy called after him, his body still twitching and his chest heaving, making his ribs ache. He only just managed to grasp at Finn's T-shirt. "Don't run. Stay here and hold me a little while longer." Looking at Finn's confusion made Tommy realize he sounded just like his ex-girlfriend after he'd made his quick getaway years ago. "Didn't mean to sound so desperate," he was quick to add.

"I just wanted to get you cleaned up. And me," Finn said, holding out his hand.

Tommy raised his arm over his eyes and nodded. He guessed a little TLC after the act wasn't on the books yet.

When Finn returned, it was with a warm washcloth, and his actions felt soothing and kind. Only Tommy didn't want kindness.

Finn hesitated after he was done and then unceremoniously tucked him back into his briefs.

"Come here." Tommy gestured.

"What do we do now?" Finn asked softly.

"We lie close together and try to sleep," Tommy answered. "Unless you let me take care of you the way you took care of me?"

Finn shook his head.

"Then crawl under the covers with me so we can get warm."

"Your ribs okay?"

Tommy looked down at his black-and-blue torso and nodded. "Blowing your wad is a great pain reliever." He didn't think Finn was going to take him up on the offer of sleeping together, so he was a little surprised when Finn got up to turn off the light in the bathroom and then slipped into bed next to him, pulling the covers up over both of them. Tommy could tell Finn was unsure how to cuddle without hurting him, but he gave him the space to figure it out. They eventually found a position that suited both of them, with Finn lying on his side close to Tommy. Tommy turned his head a little toward Finn so he could inhale his scent and found himself slowly drifting off.

A little while later, the room still dark, Tommy woke to Finn breathing heavily into his ear. The breathing was restrained, as were the sounds Finn was trying to prevent himself from uttering. It took Tommy a minute to erase the medicated clouds from his head so he could understand what Finn was doing. The small, frantic movements against his thigh didn't need a lot imagination on Tommy's part to become a turn-on again. He knew if he said anything or let on that he was awake Finn would stop, and he felt guilty enough for being the only one to reach his climax earlier to stay utterly silent. It wasn't easy since his cock was filling up at the thought of Finn masturbating against him, and he desperately wanted to kiss him, but he also didn't want to take away the pleasure Finn would feel at coming to completion.

Finn whimpered and shook before he stilled, only to start shivering again.

Tommy moved for the first time since he'd awoken and used his good arm, still tucked around Finn's shoulder, to pull Finn closer and kiss his hair. "It's okay. You needed that."

Finn gasped and tried to pull away, but Tommy held him close. "You did absolutely nothing wrong, Finn."

When Tommy kissed Finn's face he could taste tears. "There's nothing wrong with needing this, love."

"Then why do I feel dirty?"

"Turn on the light and we'll talk."

"No lights," Finn said curtly. "I need to clean us up."

"It's okay, Finn," Tommy repeated. "It's just a little sticky, but there's nothing dirty about it. It'll wash off in the morning. Just enjoy this."

Finn was wound tight as a spring, so Tommy kept rubbing his shoulder until Finn finally relaxed.

THE NEXT morning, Tommy woke up alone. He was sore and had a hard time getting up, but he desperately had to pee, so he had no choice. By the time he emerged from the toilet he was able to walk without stumbling again. He encountered Finn walking toward the bedroom with a tray.

"Morning."

Finn smiled at him. "Hope you like porridge. That's about all I can make for breakfast."

"Sounds lovely. Comfort food, right?"

"And I added some of those blueberries you like so much."

"Yummy," Tommy replied. "I'd probably be more comfortable in the kitchen than sitting on the bed on account of the ribs."

"Oh yes, of course." Finn turned around and backtracked to the kitchen, where Tommy tried to lower himself to the wooden kitchen chair without groaning too much. To Tommy's surprise, the porridge looked nice and creamy, and the blueberries were just the right ripeness. Almost by command, his stomach growled.

"Guess that was a sign of approval."

Finn smiled nervously. "Maybe you should taste it first."

Tommy had to use his right hand to scoop up some of the porridge with his spoon, and Finn's expectant look didn't help him to do that in any sort of elegant way. "Can't wait until I can use my left hand again," Tommy said by way of apology. To his surprise, the porridge was just the right consistency and sweetness. "This is excellent, Finn."

"He says without hiding his surprise," Finn quipped.

Tommy laughed, more at seeing Finn take it with a sense of humor than anything else. He had to cut it short because of the stabbing pain in his chest, though. He noticed the pain pills Finn had prepared for him and took them, hoping he'd feel better soon. "It really is good. I love porridge, but I rarely make it myself."

"It's about all I'll make for myself."

Tommy smiled at Finn as he scooped up a spoonful of the breakfast pudding laden with blueberries. "We'll have to remedy that."

"Are you going to teach me to cook?"

For a few moments Tommy simply looked at Finn and saw the confident, fun, and at times slightly cocky man he'd had a crush on for the last year. There was little evidence of the damaged and insecure man he'd found hidden under the veneer and had gotten to know better in the past weeks, and he wondered how to reclaim some more of the former. He knew he'd have to stop staring at Finn for starters. "At least I should teach you the basics. How *not* to burn water would be a start. The added perk being that maybe I can come home to a home-cooked dinner for once in my life."

"Sounds like a plan," Finn said.

Suddenly Finn got a predatory look in his eyes, and Tommy tensed up at seeing him approach. With an elegant flick of his finger, Finn brushed over Tommy's chin, and he licked at his finger before leaning forward and kissing Tommy.

"You had something on your chin," Finn explained.

"Wouldn't want to waste any of the good stuff."

Finn's kiss was confident and dominant, and besides Finn's delicious taste, all Tommy could think about was that Finn must feel good about the leap they'd taken during the night. Despite his aching body, Tommy was eager to repeat last night's interaction, but he needed a soft place, not a hard chair to support him.

"Can we maybe move this to somewhere more comfortable?" Tommy suggested as soon as Finn gave him a moment to catch his breath.

"We just got out of bed," Finn said.

Tommy saw him blushing, and he put down his spoon to pull Finn closer. "It's Sunday. We don't have to live by the clock."

FINN

IT WAS as if a bigger force was guiding him. And it made the guilt flare up even more than before. Tommy's body was covered in bruises; his lip was split and his jaw hurting. Finn could see that every time he had to open his mouth to ladle a spoon of porridge in. The porridge had been a hit, and Finn was secretly proud of himself, but it didn't take away the fact that all he could think of was repeating what they'd done in bed during the night. He wanted nothing more than to relive the feeling of power he'd experienced when he made Tommy moan and plead for more and the ecstasy he'd felt as he rubbed himself against Tommy's relaxed body while inhaling the heady mix of sweat and musk emanating from Tommy's skin. Even after he'd spent his lust, after Tommy had awoken and without even a hint of recrimination had accepted what Finn had done to him, after Tommy had taken him in his arms and kissed him, the craving had still been there. Even hours later, in the light of day, Finn was still half-hard. Seeing Tommy stumble into the kitchen, underwear a bit crumpled and hair sticking out all over the place, had made the lust flare up again. He wanted to ravage Tommy.

He wanted to touch him and taste him and make him produce the same delicious sounds again, yet there was something warring inside him.

He didn't want to be the man who snuck around. He didn't want to be the man who had to wait until Tommy had fallen asleep to be able to do something about his raging hard-on. He wanted to share that experience with Tommy, but he didn't know how, and now Tommy was offering it to him. Would he be able to do it now?

Finn watched as Tommy got up from his chair with some difficulty, walked in the direction of the corridor, and turned around. "So are you coming?"

Finn didn't hesitate. He wanted this. He *needed* this. Ignoring the warning bells, ignoring the tension in his body and the flight reaction in his mind, he followed Tommy into the bedroom.

The bed was still a mess of crumpled sheets, and Tommy didn't bother straightening any of them before climbing in. Finn joined him, lying next to him before kissing him, because this was the only thing he could do without mixed feelings. This time there were no instructions from Tommy on what to do, and Finn felt at a loss. Tommy was rubbing up against him, and it definitely felt good, but despite his earlier experience, which was pretty positive overall, Finn still hesitated before touching Tommy without Tommy's permission. He could feel Tommy's arousal, his hard, swollen cock, against his stomach and didn't need to reassure himself he was equally aroused, but somehow he couldn't bring himself to push his hand between their bodies.

Tommy had no such apprehensions.

Finn gasped as he felt Tommy's calloused hand grasp him, and then he lost it. He pushed inside the fist and came without warning, his body shaking against Tommy's. When he opened his eyes, he saw Tommy's surprised expression, and all he could do to hold himself together was to run. He had to be alone, seek cover in the bathroom and close the door. Away from Tommy. Away from his shame.

Chapter Eighteen

TOMMY

"YOU OKAY?"

Tommy stood in front of the closed bathroom door, his arousal and the cut-short encounter in the bedroom feeling like a bad dream. Well, it wasn't too bad, just a little confusing.

Tommy knocked on the door again.

"Just cleaning up a bit," Finn said. His voice sounded casual, but Tommy feared it was the practiced kind of casual. There was nothing he could do now, so he went into the guest room, where he knew there was a small washbasin where he could clean up a bit as well.

Tommy returned to Finn's bedroom and sat on the side of the bed, waiting. He heard some rumbling coming from the bathroom, figuring it was Finn taking things out of the medicine cabinet or something like that.

And then fear gripped him.

Finn had intimacy issues. Finn was an abuse survivor, and Tommy had taken him way out of his comfort zone. But they'd done this before. They'd sort of made love in the middle of the night and then again just now. What had been different? Tommy went over the events of the night before and then over what had just happened, and it hit him. Last night Finn hadn't wanted Tommy to reciprocate the hand job. This morning Tommy had taken matters into his own hand. Literally.

Damn.

Tommy got up, realizing it had been a while since he'd heard any sounds coming from the bathroom.

"Finn?"

No answer.

"Finn, please talk to me."

"Just give me a minute."

Finn's voice sounded shaky, yet Tommy sighed in relief and returned to the bedroom. He was making a mountain out of a molehill. Finn was a grown man, a grown man who functioned fine in society. Obviously a little setback in his private life wouldn't make him suicidal all of a sudden. Tommy kicked himself for being a drama queen.

He looked at the bedside clock: 10:48. He'd give him five minutes. Okay, maybe ten.

After three minutes he walked out of the bedroom, the waiting driving him crazy. He was going into the kitchen to make himself a cup of tea.

With two cups in his right hand, he walked back into the bedroom to check the clock—10:57, so he'd given Finn ample time.

"Finn, I made tea!"

No answer.

He put down the mugs, walked over to the bathroom door, and knocked.

"Finn?"

Again, no answer. He tried the door handle, but the door was locked.

"Finn, talk to me or I'm breaking down the door." He shook himself at his desperate words, but he knew that Finn only had to give a sign of life and he'd cease his actions.

But there was only silence.

Tommy braced himself to throw his left shoulder against the door, like he normally would, but then realized this was his most bruised side, including three broken ribs, so he threw his right shoulder against the door instead. Pain wracked his body, but the door didn't budge.

"Finn, for heaven's sake, bloody answer me!"

Tommy knew something was wrong. Finn had hurt himself, taken tablets, slashed his wrists. He had to know, and dialing 999 wasn't going to bring anyone here on time. He'd have to do it himself.

He took a step away from the door, and with a swift kick of his foot he knocked the door open.

Finn was sitting behind the shower stall against the crowfoot bath, knees pulled up and arms wrapped around his head.

"Finn, it's me. Tommy."

Tommy couldn't see any blood. Finn was dripping wet, probably from the shower, but he was still wearing his briefs and undershirt as if he'd forgotten to undress. When Tommy tried to touch Finn, he scrambled away as if he wanted to crawl inside the wall behind him.

It dawned on Tommy that he was the last person Finn wanted to interact with, because he'd done this to him.

He, DS Tommy Drummond, had turned Finn DeHavilland, commanding Crown Prosecutor, into a trembling puddle of misery.

Tommy took a towel out of the cupboard and put it at Finn's feet. "Try to get warm and dry, Finn. I'll find someone to help you."

Tommy knew he had only one course of action open to him. He had to call Ayse.

AYSE ARRIVED fifteen minutes later, her hair looking like she'd tied it together in a hurry but otherwise as impeccably dressed as if she had a court appointment. Tommy opened the door in his fluffy burgundy bath robe. Underneath he'd managed to half dress himself, but it had taken more effort than he'd imagined.

Ayse threw him a concerned look. "You look at least half as much of a mess as you described Finn being in."

Tommy nodded.

"Where is he?"

Tommy showed her the bathroom but didn't go inside. From the door he could see Finn hadn't moved. He knew any intervention from his side would be counterproductive, so he went back into the sitting room, since this was as far from Finn's bedroom and the bathroom as he could go without leaving the flat.

He could hear the murmur of Ayse's soothing voice even there but couldn't hear what she was saying. When he finally heard Finn's low voice answer, he released a sigh and felt some of the tension drain from him.

Tommy was sitting with his hand over his face, trying to pull himself together, when Ayse entered the sitting room. "Does he have a robe or something I can throw over him to make him feel a little warmer?"

Tommy nodded. "It's on a peg on the inside of the bedroom door."

He heard some movement in the rest of the flat and some more subdued talking but nothing he could place. The minutes on the sitting room clock were ticking by so slowly Tommy felt like he was in a time warp. Then the sounds stopped altogether, which made him even more apprehensive. He knew he had to trust Ayse, though. He eventually walked from the sitting room to the kitchen and took his cup of now cold tea to empty it in the sink.

"Is that tea?" he heard behind him, startling him to the point he almost dropped his mug.

He turned around to see Ayse standing in the doorway.

"Sorry I snuck up on you like that."

Tommy shook his head to tell her it was all right. "I'll make you some fresh. This is stone cold."

Ayse stood next to him. "Could you tell me what happened?"

"I don't know," Tommy answered evasively. In truth he wasn't sure.

"I'm not asking you what you did to him, if anything. I'm just asking for your side of the story. Finn is a little confused."

"I… we…." Tommy sighed in frustration. Was she seriously asking him for intimate details?

"Listen," she started. "Let's forget for a moment that you're a copper, Finn's a prosecutor, and I'm probably Finn's only real friend, not counting you."

"I don't know if I'm his friend anymore."

Ayse nodded and bit her lip. "Then let's agree that there is doctor-patient confidentiality between you and me as well as Finn and me. Meaning I won't tell him about what we talked about any more than I'll tell you about what Finn told me. Unless you give me express permission."

Tommy knew Finn trusted Ayse implicitly. He also knew from what little Finn had told him that Ayse had been made privy to a lot more intimate details than he'd ever told anyone. Maybe she could tell him what he'd done wrong. He just didn't know where to start. The kettle whistled, so Tommy occupied himself making tea.

"Think Finn might want one?" Tommy asked.

"Probably, but leave him be for a little while. We can make more later."

They took their mugs into the sitting room.

"So can you tell me what happened between the two of you? Maybe start last night?"

"He brought me home from the hospital. I was in pain, drugged up to my eyeballs with painkillers, so I was a little cranky and a lot more brave than I would usually be. He made me dinner, and I fell asleep on the couch, so he wanted to put me to bed, but I didn't want to sleep alone. Flat on my back on a bed, I can hardly move, so I wanted someone close to help me if I needed it. I swear, anything more intimate was out of the question as far as I was concerned." That part was easy, but Tommy wasn't sure how he was going to explain the rest. "Somehow we started kissing, which isn't that unusual. I knew Finn could handle the kissing, because that's all we've been doing so far."

Ayse nodded, her face unreadable.

"It became more intimate. Seems I wasn't the only brave one last night. It was mostly Finn. I just lay there, wanting to do more but afraid that if I made a move Finn would stop. It was entirely selfish on my part."

Tommy hesitated, unsure whether she needed to know more, but she only nodded for him to continue.

"He, ehm, finished me off." He couldn't even look at her while he said it, only braved a quick glance in her direction. She didn't respond to what he said at all, so Tommy deduced he had to tell her more. "He wouldn't let me do anything to him, wouldn't let me… reciprocate."

"Go on."

"I don't know what else…."

"He woke you up in the middle of the night?"

Damn, she was good. She was comparing their stories. Finn's account against his. So this was how a suspect felt. "He told you."

"He did, but I'd like to hear your side of it."

"I don't know…." Tommy shook his head. How could he tell her about something that intimate?

"He was masturbating while you were asleep, and it woke you up," she said matter-of-factly.

Tommy nodded, still unable to look her in the eye.

"Finn wanted you to know he felt very accepted by what you did then."

"He does? I mean, he did?"

Ayse smiled. "Yes. He was afraid you would turn away from him, and instead you took him in your arms and made him feel safe. Do you have any idea how important that safety is to Finn?"

Tommy didn't really understand what she meant, so he shrugged.

"For years as he was growing up, he didn't have a safe place in the house. And he had no one to turn to. He tried to tell his mother what Malcolm was doing to him, and she brushed him away. He was basically told his bad feelings about the whole thing were inconsequential. These were his formative years, where a sense of self was established and where he should have figured out his sexuality. For him, both were confusing and dangerous. Most people who lived through what he went through drop out of school and are unable to keep a job or any sort of relationship with another human being going. It's a miracle he functions at all in society, but he's managed because he's found an occupation where he doesn't need to be himself. He's a tool of the law, a tool of the Crown. That's all he lives for. He doesn't have a personal life because he can't face having one. He doesn't know how. You changed all that."

"You mean I ruined it all for him."

"No, Tommy. For the first time ever, he wants to live for more than his job."

"But why…?" Tommy pointed in the general direction of the bedroom. "Why is he so miserable, then? He couldn't even look at me or talk to me. What did I do wrong?" He felt tears sting in the back of his throat, thinking about how Finn had fled from him and had ended up curled into a ball on his bathroom floor as if Tommy had raped him all over again.

"You opened a Pandora's box," Ayse said calmly and without even a hint of recrimination in her voice. "He wants nothing more than to enjoy being with you, but every time he opens a little window into his soul, all the evil he's kept at bay since he was six years old floods out."

Tommy tried to imagine what it must be like for Finn but came up empty. And then he realized what he'd done that morning. In itself it wasn't wrong, but given what little he knew about Finn's abuser, it made sense that Finn's confusion triggered something to connect the wrong dots.

"I touched him this morning."

Ayse leaned forward. "And he reacted strangely to that?"

"Not really," Tommy replied, his mind whirring. "He, ehm, responded a bit too quickly. That's all." *God, why couldn't he just say Finn had come?*

Ayse smiled knowingly, and Tommy felt relieved. Maybe he didn't have to spell it out for her after all.

"This is discovery time for him, Tommy. We did this when we were teenagers. He never got the chance, so he's doing it now. With a vengeance." She got up from her seat. "I'm going to go talk to him again. One possible solution would be that you move out of here and find your own place again, returning the safety of his flat to him. That way he's always got his safe haven to return to."

"I'll go looking as soon as I'm on my feet again," Tommy said, feeling sad but understanding what Ayse was saying. He doubted his relationship with Finn, if you could call it that, would survive, but he wanted Finn to be happy again.

"No need, really," she said as if all the puzzle pieces were falling into place. "With the baby on the way, I'm moving to a bigger house that's been in Charlie's family for a while. You can sublet my flat for the time being. Who knows? You might not need it for long."

FINN

AYSE HAD put him in the guest room, but he'd moved back to his bedroom and got under the covers of his bed to warm up again. Tommy's scent still clung to the sheets, and somehow, after his talk with Ayse, feeling Tommy near felt okay again as long as he wasn't physically there. After he'd stopped shivering, he'd even become bored enough to pick up a file he was supposed to have been reviewing. In truth, he was worried about what Ayse and Tommy were talking about, and to keep his mind off it, he'd picked up his staple distraction, work.

"After everything you've been through today, you're reading work stuff? More abuse cases? Finn, you're incorrigible."

Finn smiled at seeing Ayse at the entrance of his room. She gestured at him, asking silently if it was okay that she enter, and he nodded. She walked inside, closed the door, and sat next to him on the bed.

"How's Tommy?" Finn asked.

"You've been through hell today, and you ask me how *he*'s been?"

Finn nodded.

"Insanely worried about what he did to you."

Finn sucked in his lips. "You did tell him he did nothing wrong, right?"

"I think you should tell him that."

"How?"

"Just explain it to him. I tried to tell him about losing your footing because you have no safety net, no coping skills for what is happening between the two of you right now. I've asked him to give you space to explore, be the teenager you never had the chance to be, but I think it would be easier for him to understand this coming from you. Oh, and I suggested he sublet my flat so you two could have your own space again."

"Ayse," Finn lamented. "I want to be with him. Our relationship was not going anywhere until he moved in here."

Ayse took his hand. "Trust me on this, Finn. He loves you every bit as much as you love him. It will be for the better."

"Since I'm so ignorant where relationships are concerned, maybe you should explain that one to me as well."

She smiled. "Go on a date. Take him to see one of those art house films you always tell me you want to see but never get around to. Have a picnic in the park. Drive down to Brighton and spend a weekend together in some dilapidated hotel on the seashore."

"You caught us after our first date."

She snorted. "Fish and chips at the pub? Finn, he may be a guy from a council flat, but even he is higher maintenance than that."

"And it's bloody November. I'm not taking him to the park so we can freeze our bollocks off."

"Finn, language!" she quipped.

They both laughed.

"Don't know if we're ready for a weekend away yet," Finn said contemplatively. "But I don't think I can live without him either." He sighed, exasperated. "What happened is my fault, Ayse. He's an obsession. I can't keep my hands off him. Even now when he's hurt and tired, all I want to do is be with him and touch him, and at the same time I know it'll end badly."

"All the more reason why you need to learn distance. You need to get a grip on the fact that he'll still be there even if you're not together. Besides, a relationship is more than sex." She took Finn's hand. "You have a lot of catching up to do, but you don't need to do it all right now. Take your time."

"And what if his patience runs out?"

"I'm pretty sure it will be beneficial for him as well to take it a bit slower. I think he's already proven he can wait. Just keep the channels of communication open. Shouldn't be hard since you're both working on the same case, right?"

Finn nodded. "I can't throw him out, though."

"You won't have to."

Finn looked up at Ayse. "You did it for me?"

"He's a smart guy. I explained to him you needed your space, and he immediately said he'd go looking for another place to live."

"But I don't want him to leave," Finn said, practically whining.

Ayse squeezed his hand. "I know, darling."

Chapter Nineteen

TOMMY

IT DIDN'T take Tommy long to pack his things. After all, he only had one bag of clothes and some toiletries to take with him.

To his surprise, as he was about to leave, Finn handed him another bag. When Tommy opened it he saw it contained sheets for a large bed, some very fluffy towels, and the robe he'd been wearing at the flat.

"I can't take these, Finn."

"Yes, you can," Finn replied, sounding resolute. "A man only needs so many towels, and you've seen my airing cupboard. It's positively bursting with stuff I've never used."

"Bought for you by your mother."

"She was the practical sort. And not very imaginative in the gift department."

Tommy could tell Finn was keeping a brave face. For a moment he thought he was just projecting his feelings, but then he saw Finn's eyes go all glassy.

"I like to think you're comfortable."

Tommy took a step in Finn's direction and saw him struggle, his lips pursed and jaw tense. Tears threatened to run down his cheeks. Tommy wanted to hold Finn one last time, but he feared it would do more harm than good, so he simply took the bag of towels from Finn and gave him a quick peck on the cheek. "I'm not giving up on you, Finn. We're only giving each other a little space."

Finn nodded and swallowed hard as they separated. Tommy took the trolley he'd borrowed from Finn together with the bag and pulled it along with his right hand as he allowed Finn to open the front door.

"I'll see you next week."

Tommy nodded without looking at Finn and made his way to Ayse's waiting car.

FINN

FINN COULDN'T even look at Ayse as Tommy got into her car. He closed the door and sank down against it even before the car drove off.

The reasoning behind Tommy leaving was sound. They needed space to discover each other, and living together at this precarious point of their relationship wasn't good, especially not for him. But Finn physically hurt. Tommy was barely gone, and he already missed him. Sitting on the cold tile floor in his hallway, legs pulled up, head in hands, and elbows resting on his knees, Finn allowed the tears to flow. It eased some of the pressure inside his chest, but at the same time he felt utterly lost. How had the last few weeks changed his whole outlook on life? Before that he'd never seen himself as someone who could share his living space with another human being, yet Tommy added so much to it, he never felt like he was getting in the way.

As his tears started drying up, Finn listened to the sounds of his flat, or more precisely to the silence. For the first time ever he dreaded the thought that this was all there was. This was not what he wanted. He craved a partner, someone to share things with. These past weeks he'd gone out of his way to be home in time simply to spend the evening with Tommy. Sometimes all they did was eat together and watch a movie, but it always felt nice to have someone else there. But it needed to be Tommy. Nobody else would do.

Finn got up from the cold tiles and walked to the kitchen. He had to find a way to deserve Tommy. He was going to have to work on banishing his demons, because Tommy needed a man who could love him back for the full 100 percent.

TOMMY

ON MONDAY Tommy couldn't wait any longer. He hadn't seen Finn since Thursday, and although he had no real reason to go to the CPS offices, he knew he had to see him, even if it was just for one minute. Although he was technically on sick leave, the uniformed policeman at the door let him sign in without question, which Tommy was grateful for. He didn't want to make up a reason just for the sake of it.

As he walked between the desks of the administrative staff, he saw Finn in the conference room, which had large windows separating them from the other staff rooms. He slowed his step to look at the man he was in love with and the reason he'd fallen so hard for him. The Finn he was looking at was in control and relaxed and so far removed from the other side he'd seen in the past weeks, it made his stomach flutter again. At the same time Tommy realized that living alone did seem to suit Finn better than living with him.

Finn was sitting on one of the desks, papers in hand. His facial expression was animated as he spoke to the people facing him, and he appeared quite relaxed, although the discussion seemed serious. The blinds in part of the conference room were drawn, so Tommy moved to the side to see that Finn was speaking to Armen, Carlton, and Ayse. Armen was gathering his papers while Carlton and Finn were conversing when Finn looked to the side and caught Tommy's eye. He stopped midsentence, smiled at him, and gestured him to come inside.

Tommy opened the door and caught Ayse's smile before turning to Finn. "I didn't mean to disturb you."

"You weren't," Finn said with an unreadable expression. He turned to Carlton. "Was there anything else you wanted to discuss?"

"No, no, I think we were done," Carlton replied. Tommy felt the tension in the room but had no idea what it was about. Ayse and Finn were exchanging looks behind Armen's back.

"Armen, if you need help on the Armitage case, let me know?"

"I think I have everything," he said as he eyed Tommy suspiciously and left the room.

Tommy gestured at the door. "If I came at a bad time, I can come back later or tomorrow."

"No," Finn said. "Close the door and sit down." Again he looked at Ayse, and it made Tommy uncomfortable. When Finn looked through the window to the rest of the office before sitting across from Tommy and Ayse, Tommy felt something prickle at the back of his neck.

"We need to keep what is said here under wraps," Finn said, his voice soft as if they could be overheard. He turned to Tommy. "I have reason to believe the corrupt cop case we were assigned to is larger than we thought."

"Should we be discussing this, then?" Tommy asked. "I'm not part of the legal team. I'm just the cop doing the investigating, and not much of that right now either. And if I need to be here, we should call Stevie as well."

"Let's go for a walk," Finn suggested. He went to his office to get his coat and handed Ayse hers. He didn't speak until they were outside on the street. "Stevie will talk to you about this, but there are trails leading from your attacker to my office."

"Meaning?"

Finn directed them into an alley that led to a small, secluded garden. "I have reason to believe you were attacked to discredit you and possibly me, depending on how much they know about us."

Tommy looked at Ayse, who was gazing around to see whether anyone was within earshot, and then back at Finn. "They know who attacked me?"

"No, but there is CCTV footage of your attack. And there is footage of a man wearing pretty much the same attire as your attacker walking into the Old Bailey and speaking to Armen, just hours before you were attacked."

Tommy tried to stay in control of his emotions. "Clothes don't prove anything, Finn. You know that." His ribs were still taped and his arm was in a cast, but the pain was becoming more manageable. Although his memories of that night were still sketchy, the attack was far from forgotten. "And what does what happened to me have to do with our case?"

Finn looked at Ayse. "Ayse and I have been talking about more than my rehabilitation during our therapy sessions. I needed someone not involved to bounce ideas off. You can consider her part of the inner circle now." He took a deep breath before continuing. "We were given just six cases to review, right?"

Tommy nodded.

"Luckily, I'm an obsessive note taker, and I've isolated at least another thirty to forty more we need to take a look at. They have certain things in common, but one thing that's for sure is that there is no way one man could do all the covering up. We're certain he must have had people on the inside doing that for him, both in the CPS and in the Met. So there are very few people we can trust."

"So Armen is out? Stevie and I are in?"

Finn nodded.

"And Ayse is in."

"She's profiling the suspect for me. And helping me figure out what we can expect him to do next."

Tommy felt a pang of jealousy seeing how Finn was looking at Ayse. If he didn't know any better he'd call it love. "How about Carlton?" Tommy asked, trying to stay focused on the case and not the way Ayse was throwing admiring glances at his lover.

"That's where I need to tread carefully. Almost on a daily basis, he's in my office asking about my progress. I realize once the cat is out of the bag it will be a high profile case—"

"Not to mention, he's concerned about the mental health of the prosecutor who's running it," Ayse interrupted.

Finn rolled his eyes and smiled at her, adding to the bad feelings stirring in Tommy's gut.

"You can't say I'm not following his orders to see my psychiatrist."

Tommy looked away from the two of them. Given what he knew about Finn, it was silly to believe there was anything more going on between them than a growing trust, but despite knowing it was for Finn's good, moving out of Finn's house had ripped his heart out. And like a silly kid, he wanted Finn to look at him that way too.

"In any case," Finn continued, "I need to keep him up to date on our progress, but I'm reluctant to tell him everything."

Tommy threw him a surprised look. He knew how high Finn's praise of Carlton ran, and he'd never heard any criticism about Carlton from Finn before.

"He's in a position to steer how our department works. He's instrumental in dropping charges or deciding not to prosecute certain cases. Technically, as senior prosecutor, I call the shots on the cases assigned to me, but these last eighteen months or so, I've been overruled more than once. Those are the cases I want to go over again first. He could be a willing or an unwilling participant. I'm not accusing him of any wrongdoing because I don't have a single shred of evidence, but we need to keep the inner circle as small as possible. I'll decide what information to feed him, how, and when."

Tommy could see how that made sense. "And how do we know *you're* in the clear, Mister DeHavilland?" Tommy said to lighten the mood, if not everyone's then at least his own. "Carlton put you on the case. If he's got something to hide, maybe he put his best asset forward?"

Finn chuckled. "That's why I like you, as coppers go. You have an open mind."

He leaned closer to Tommy to the point Tommy thought he was going to get kissed right there in the secret garden.

"But I'll keep you around because you're on desk duty, right?"

Tommy nodded. "I can't do much." He held up his left arm. "I can barely write. I doubt if anyone can read my signature on the sign-in sheet at the front desk."

"All I need is a second pair of eyes to help me go through boxes and boxes of files over at the archive. I'll do the heavy lifting and the note taking. And in the meantime, I'll get to ogle you."

Tommy felt a flush creep up his neck and watched Ayse giggle. She got up before he could say anything as a rebuttal.

"I'm going home," she said, still smiling. "I have boxes to unpack. Tommy, I have enough work at the house tonight, so I won't be coming to the flat. Just to say you have all the privacy in the world."

She said it with her hand on Finn's shoulder, and Finn smiled up at her as if he didn't know it was directed at the two of them.

They watched her walk out, and then Finn turned to Tommy.

"So you need help with *your* boxes?"

"You know as well as I do that unpacking *all* my things took exactly fifteen minutes." Tommy hated how bitter he sounded.

"Then let me take you out to dinner."

"Are you sure?"

Finn took Tommy's unbandaged hand and simply held it. "I miss you."

Tommy leaned a little closer, inviting Finn to kiss him. To his surprise, he did, albeit rather chastely.

"Okay," Tommy said as they broke apart. "But we're going Dutch."

Finn smiled.

FINN

IT WAS strange how picking Tommy up from Ayse's flat, which was temporarily Tommy's, of course, felt like a date. They'd both gone home to change, and now Finn was ringing Tommy's doorbell while a London cabbie waited patiently near the curb.

When Tommy appeared, he was still struggling to get his left arm, cast and all, through the arm of his jacket. "I will be happy to see the last of this," he told Finn on the way down to the pavement. Then he stopped. "You look good, Mister Prosecutor."

"Stop calling me that," Finn said, smiling at the compliment nevertheless.

"I've always had a soft spot for the cap." Tommy reached up to stroke the velvet cap Finn was wearing.

In the cab over to the restaurant where Finn had reserved a table, he couldn't stop looking at Tommy. The swelling in his face was almost completely gone, and all he could still see was the red line above his lip and two yellowish patches, one around his left eye, the other along his jawline. He was sitting to his left, so he couldn't take Tommy's hand. Instead he resolved to let the back of his hand brush over Tommy's thigh. Finn ached to touch Tommy, even here in the near public of the London cab, but he didn't dare. He was going to have to find a way to get used to more than kissing before trying that again.

The restaurant was small and packed with mostly theater crowd. It was decorated with silk drapings in bright colors, which were toned down by the subdued lighting from the copper chandeliers. Ayse had suggested she book the table, so Finn wasn't surprised when they were taken to a table a little in the back and away from most of the noise.

"Ayse told me this was the place where her husband always took her when they were dating."

"Man's got taste," Tommy replied.

The waiter arrived with menus, but he didn't hand them over. "Doctor Kartal suggested you take the chef's menu. Would this be to your liking?"

Finn looked at Tommy.

Tommy's eyes lit up. "Want to live dangerously?"

"Isn't that what we've been doing?"

Tommy smiled, and Finn turned to the waiter.

"Sounds like a good idea."

"With the appropriate wines?"

"I can't have more than one glass," Tommy answered, lifting his injured arm. "Too many meds."

"Just one glass each, then," Finn told the waiter. "Red?" he asked Tommy.

"Definitely."

After the waiter left, Tommy turned to Finn. "I thought you'd booked the table."

"Ayse did. What can I say? She's not just counseling me for work."

Tommy took Finn's hand. "That's good to hear."

"You don't mind?"

"She knows everything anyway. And she told me there's doctor-patient confidentiality both ways." He looked straight at Finn. "If her support is what you need, I'm all for it."

"She's my rock, but she's not here tonight. Tonight it's just you and me."

"That's good to hear too."

The food the waiter brought was delicious. There wasn't one main course, but lots of little plates with tastes of what Finn deduced was most of the menu. He suspected Ayse called that particular restaurant because she knew they'd have to share everything on the plates and would have lots to discuss about the different, exotic tastes of the Middle Eastern cuisine. Although neither had been great travelers, Tommy because of budget restraints and Finn because he'd only ever lived for his job, Finn was surprised how much Tommy knew about the herbs the chef had used.

By the time they were both stuffed to the gills, Finn realized they hadn't talked about the case at all, which was a good thing. He was pleased to find out they never seemed to run out of things to say to each other.

"Ready to go?" Finn didn't wait for an answer but gestured at the waiter to bring the check. When he brought it, Tommy snatched it. "Oh no!"

"I thought we were going Dutch?"

Finn shook his head. "I'm paying for this one. Next date is on you."

"I can't afford anything this fancy."

Finn looked at Tommy. "You can cook for me as soon as that arm works again."

"That's not the same," Tommy replied, still holding on to the bill.

"No, it isn't. It's much better than anything we can get at a restaurant."

Tommy grew quiet. "Seriously?"

Finn nodded, slipping his credit card next to the bill still in Tommy's hand.

"I think I like being a kept man," Tommy admitted. "To some extent."

The outside air was crisp, and they could see their breath. "My house isn't that far from here. We could walk if you're not too tired," Finn suggested.

"I'm fine. As long as I don't need to run, I'm good. The ribs still ache when I need to do more than just breathe."

Finn snaked his arm underneath Tommy's and gave him a quick peck on the cheek. "We'll just pretend to be old-age pensioners then and stroll home."

"Well, you're wearing the right cap for it," Tommy teased.

Finn nudged him with his elbow.

"Ow, watch the ribs."

"I'm sorry," Finn said, not letting go of Tommy.

"The broken ribs are on the other side."

"Tease."

They continued strolling leisurely when suddenly they were accosted from behind.

"Oi." A big man ran around them and stopped them in their tracks. "You two poofs?"

Finn didn't respond, hoping he'd go away.

The bully poked Tommy. "I asked you a question."

"So you're rude and then expect us to answer you?" Tommy said. "Think again."

Finn's cap was knocked off his head, and he swiftly turned to see his assailant. All he could make out was that it was a kid on a bike. When he scanned the street, his cap was nowhere to be found.

"You think you're strong, hey?" the big lug of a man still standing in front of them said. "Think again. We didn't beat you up because we chose not to. There." He started walking backward. "Next time you feel the need to cuddle ya boyfriend, we won't be so forgivin'."

A car stopped next to them, and the lug got in the backseat. With his raised middle finger through the open window, the car sped off.

Finn ran his hand over his short hair. "Stupid bugger."

"They took your cap."

Finn pinched his lips. "It's just a cap. Don't worry. I thought we were going to get bashed."

"I suppose that's a new one for you."

Finn looked at Tommy. "This happened to you before?"

"Once or twice. You always get heckled at some point, but the later it gets and the more alcohol plays a part, the more chance of violence. This doesn't feel like an ordinary incident, though."

"Oh?"

Tommy sighed. "Most guys who do this are working class, poor blokes. They don't get picked up by BMWs, even in this area of town."

"You're right. I was still too startled by that punk stealing my cap, but I did think the car was unusual."

"You have some way of keeping notes? I remember a partial license plate."

Finn fished his notebook out of his jacket pocket.

"LH 11 K. Something or other. Don't remember the last two letters."

"Car registered in the Wimbledon area between March and August 2011," Finn murmured. "I wonder how many dark BMWs are among the plates where the random letters start with a K?"

"You know your vehicle registration plates, Mister Crown Prosecutor."

"We can check it out later. Now let's go home."

Despite the attack they continued to walk arm in arm until they reached Finn's house. "Come inside for a nightcap?"

"I want to catch the Tube. I better leave."

Finn nodded, pretending to understand. He was just turning around to unlock his door when Tommy stopped him. Tommy looked at him for many long moments and then lunged forward to kiss him. Finn raised his hands to cup Tommy's head so he could kiss him back. Stuck between his front door and Tommy, Finn was getting so turned on the world around him could explode and he wouldn't notice.

All too soon Tommy pulled back and licked his lips. "I have to go. Otherwise I'm going to take you up on your offer."

"Would that be so bad?"

Tommy shrugged. "It would defeat the purpose for me living in Ayse's apartment. We need to figure this out without sharing a living space, remember?"

Finn nodded, reluctantly allowing Tommy to leave. He watched him walk away, down the street toward the Tube station. "I'll pick you up tomorrow. You are coming with me to the archive, right?"

Tommy turned around and raised his thumb.

Finn didn't walk inside before Tommy rounded the corner.

Chapter Twenty

TOMMY

THE METROPOLITAN Police Archive was guarded as if it were the Tower of London and the contents were the crown jewels.

"I've only ever been here to check evidence in," Tommy admitted as they walked up to the entrance. "You don't get past that little room there." He pointed through the glass door to his right of the sign-in desk.

"I've actually checked things out, but we can only do that for open cases. And we can't reopen any of these without charges, so for now we'll need to request and sign for everything we look at, and they won't let us look at more than one case at a time."

"How are we supposed to compare things, then?" Tommy asked, squinting at the bright winter sun shining over the awning on the building.

Finn knocked on the side of his briefcase. "Aren't you happy I'm a very astute note taker?"

"Ecstatic," Tommy replied without enthusiasm as he waited for Finn to push open the entrance door and hold it so they could walk through.

"Finn DeHavilland, Senior Crown Prosecutor," Finn announced to the uniformed policeman sitting at the reception desk. "This is Detective Sergeant Thomas Drummond of the Serious Crimes Command. We have an appointment to review evidence on a number of cases."

"Yes, sir," the man replied after checking their credentials. He picked up his phone and dialed a number. He spoke briefly and then put the phone down before getting up. "Please put your items on the table."

Finn handed his briefcase over and took off his coat, then gestured at Tommy to take his off while the guard searched through Finn's things. He even took a momentary interest in Tommy's cast. "You are expected in room 24C two floors down," the man said after he was done and had handed everything back they were allowed to take inside. He buzzed them in, and Finn opened the door to the corridor. They walked silently to the lifts and waited for them to reach the underground floor.

Tommy could tell Finn was an old hand at this. He also enjoyed seeing the confident and determined Finn who felt right at home and could talk anyone under the table without batting an eyelash. He'd seen too little of this side of him in the last weeks and silently hoped Carlton would let Finn back in court soon so he'd get to see more of it.

For now they'd have to weed through endless dead cases, looking for the needle in the haystack that could get their suspect indicted. The problem was they didn't know what they were looking for.

THE ROOM they were shown into looked like an interrogation room, with a large table in the middle and chairs on either side. There was also a smaller table to the side. Finn requested his first case from the uniformed man who'd shown them in, and Tommy was taken aback that they were locked inside the room when he left to retrieve it.

"There's also no cell phone reception here," Finn said as if he was reading Tommy's mind. "They take security very seriously."

"Obviously."

"They inventoried everything we brought in. I can bring my notes, but you noticed they kept our mobile phones and anything large enough to conceal bits of evidence."

"Well, mobiles are practically portable scanners these days."

They stopped talking when they heard the lock turn, and the same man who'd shown them in walked inside with a trolley containing two evidence boxes like the ones Tommy had seen underneath the table at Finn's office. It took the policeman and Finn several minutes to go over the manifesto to make sure both were on the same page as to what Finn was supposed to return to him later.

The broken arm was frustrating Tommy to no end. He hated having to rely on Finn for everything from hauling the boxes onto the table to unpacking the evidence to taking notes on what they'd found. And in tune with Finn's thoroughness, they were taking a lot of notes, because it took quite a few cases before they started seeing similarities.

"Here's his name again," Finn said. "Frank Farraday."

"What did he do for this case?"

"He interrogated the suspect's partner." Finn rummaged through the box. "No tape of the interrogation. According to the transcript the interrogation took place at her home."

"That's unusual," Tommy said. "If you interrogate someone that close to the suspect, you take them into the station to get accurate records."

"According to this, she couldn't leave because she had nobody to look after the children," Finn said, reading from the transcript.

"So you call for a WPC—oops, can't call them that anymore—you call for a police constable, of any sex, to babysit for an hour while you do the interrogation. Under the best possible circumstances. Or you take the kids with you and leave them with a junior constable." Tommy got up to look at the transcript with Finn. "Who was his second?"

Finn looked it up and jotted it down. "Timothy MacAuley. PC."

"A junior? The name doesn't sound familiar."

Finn put the file back and took out others. "This one has a tape. Audio only. The suspect himself." He put the tape in the playback unit and switched it on. They listened for about three minutes.

"Sounds pretty standard," Tommy remarked.

"This guy wasn't very talkative in court either, if I recall."

"Did you win the case?"

Finn shook his head. "A vital part of evidence was disallowed and one of the witnesses was discredited. The jury acquitted him."

"Did he do it?"

Finn shrugged. "Can't be sure."

"Gut instinct?"

"Stalking and intimidation are always hard to prove. He was a very manipulative yet intriguing man. Nicely groomed, seductive too. I got the sense he could have had our discredited witness eating out of his hand if he'd been patient and said the right words, but he got off on scaring her. It was subtle."

"Could have gone either way, then?"

Finn pursed his lips. "If it hadn't been our witness's second attempt at getting a man indicted for something like that, I think I could have got to him."

Tommy laughed. "Glad your professional pride wasn't hurt too much."

Finn shrugged. "I think we have everything we need for this case. Let's call up for another."

They repacked the box, and the officer who'd brought them this case exchanged it for the next set of evidence boxes, after which they both signed for access. Tommy had more than once thought that if he would contest his signature in court, he could probably get away with it, because he couldn't write legibly right-handed if he had a gun to his head.

They worked about the same with all the cases, unpacking them, going over the content, and checking for familiar names and strange occurrences.

"Frank Farraday again," Tommy said with a smirk. His face turned sour. "Looks like he followed the book this time. We have taped evidence." They listened to a muddled conversation with a woman who had a distinct accent and a rather nasal-sounding voice.

"Looks like his skills at setting up a recorder aren't very good," Finn remarked. "Too bad we can't charge him with that."

Tommy looked at Finn's concentrated gaze. He was listening a lot more carefully to this recording than he had with the other testimonies. Tommy tried to figure out why that was, since the conversation itself seemed mundane, common, a simple confirmation of what clearly had been said before, off the record.

He waited for the tape to finish. "What was different about this tape?"

"Different?" Finn parroted as if he'd been dragged away from his thoughts. "The voice sounds familiar, but I can't place it." He wrote something down in his notebook.

"Linda Smith," Tommy read from the file.

"That's a big giveaway," Finn said with a smile. He took note of it anyway. "Second?"

"DI Marchand." Tommy's voice slowed as he read it.

"Isn't that your…."

"My very own little arsehole of a bigoted Napoleonic ex-boss, yes."

Finn sniggered. "How colorful."

Tommy glared at Finn but couldn't hold it for very long. "I know. Things changed for the better after that. Not in the least the attention I got from you."

Finn put his arm around Tommy's shoulders and rested his head against his temple for just a moment, then went back to his case files. It felt like a show of support, though, and that was all he needed.

FINN

THE FLEETING touch was all he could manage. He wanted more, of course, but they were working, and ravaging Tommy in a locked room in the basement of Central Archive was a bit much, he thought. Besides, he'd promised Ayse to learn to spend time with Tommy without constantly craving physical closeness. It wasn't working yet, though.

"So, this case with the district nurse that Farraday was involved with?"

Tommy looked up. "The file is still at the station. Stevie could look it up for us."

"There was a missing interrogation tape there as well?"

Tommy confirmed with a nod. "Think it would pull more weight if you asked what happened to it? Stevie said she wasn't getting anywhere."

"We'll go outside for lunch and call her for the case number so we can request it," Finn suggested. "Maybe if I pretend I don't know this is part of one of your running investigations, I'll get somewhere."

GOING THROUGH the files was tedious work but not without results. They didn't find anything to put Farraday away for life, but cumulatively there was plenty to get him suspended or even sacked from his job.

"So do we have enough to make a case?" Tommy asked as he helped put another file back in its box.

"I find it hard to believe this is all there is. He's done this for years and got away with making evidence disappear. I'm sure if we talk to some of these former suspects, we'll find he probably fabricated some of this evidence as well. On this massive scale, he needs to have help from above, hence the reason for all the secrecy, only why would someone cover up for him if he was just a bad cop? There has to be more."

Tommy nodded. "Maybe we're looking in the wrong place?"

"It has to be in these files. What are we not seeing?"

"Maybe Stevie and me should go talk to some of these people and try to form a picture of who this Farraday is. Maybe we can talk to some of the constables who worked with him as well?"

"I don't want you in harm's way, Tom."

Tommy sighed, and his silence told Finn he was going overboard.

"I just don't want you to get hurt any more than you already are."

"That's very sweet of you, but this is exactly why they don't allow couples to partner up."

Finn cocked his head, knowing full well Tommy was right.

"I'm a cop, Finn. Sometimes we end up in dangerous situations. Do you think I like being on sick leave and letting Stevie go it alone? And it's not like either of us have been hurt that many times. Maybe a scrape or a bruise left or right, that's all."

"Let's go outside for lunch so we can call Stevie."

AS SOON as they'd received the case number from Stevie, Finn had gone back to the front desk, asking for the evidence to be delivered to their room. Then he went back outside to sit in the lukewarm sun with Tommy, who'd bought them salads for lunch.

"One option would be to get Farraday suspended on the evidence 'problem,' and this would buy us time to dig deeper," Tommy suggested, using his right hand to make an air quote.

"Mmmh, the Capone prosecution. It's a tough call. On the one hand it would prevent him from doing more damage, but on the other hand it would make it much harder to catch him in the act, and everything we've found is circumstantial in the sense that he's always got a partner in crime who can be blamed for it."

"But the one thing every case has in common is Farraday."

"The defense would only have to find one case where evidence was fabricated or lost where Farraday was nowhere on the books and my case would be blown out of the water. I can't take that risk."

"Would it help if we got people to testify to the fraud?"

"Possibly. But if he's as manipulative as they say he is, it's going to be hard to find those witnesses."

"Between Stevie and me, I think we can persuade a few people."

"You need to be allowed to go back to work first to be able to do that, Tommy."

"Let's go dig through some more files, then!"

TOMMY

AS THEY entered the evidence room, the uniformed policeman who'd brought them all their other boxes entered with just one plastic bag. "This is all we could find for the case you requested, sir. The rest of it has been on loan to the Westminster office of the Serious Crimes Command. Signing officer is DSI Mark Stanton."

"And why was this tape not kept with the evidence box?"

Tommy was amused by Finn's commanding tone. For that reason alone he'd prayed the constable would mess something up.

"Find out the reason this was not included in the box. ASAP."

Finn didn't shout, but Tommy knew if he'd been on the receiving end of that command he'd run as quickly as he could. Okay, and he might be a little turned on as well.

"I can't believe this," Finn murmured, more to himself than to Tommy as soon as the policeman left. "If this is the way they deal with evidence, I'm taking on the entire Central Archive."

"Let's listen to the tape to hear if there's anything useful on there, okay?" Tommy said, hoping to soothe Finn.

Finn inserted the tape into the listening device. His eyes lit up as soon as the voices became clear. "This is the same woman's voice we heard earlier. Northern accent, possibly Scottish."

"The one you thought you recognized?"

Finn nodded. "I still can't place her, but I'm sure I've heard her before. I mean before the first tape."

"Let's listen to what she has to say."

"He was ever so kind. Helped me out with the kids and ev'rything."

"Did you ever encounter anything that made you suspicious of him?"

"Oh no, why would I? He took care of the littl'uns when I was flat on me back. They loved him to bits."

"Did you ever see suspicious bruises on the children's arms or legs or buttocks?"

"Kids get into all sorts of scrapes, sir. No harm there. Nothing he did to them, in any case. Told ya, they loved him. Always happy when he came by the 'ouse."

"End of interrogation. Detective Inspector Frank Farraday present for the entirety of the custodial interrogation of Miss Elisa McCann. Tuesday, April 2, 2013."

A buzzer at the door announced their policeman was back.

"Mr. DeHavilland. As you requested I found the reason why this tape wasn't included in the evidence box signed out by the Westminster SCC. It was brought to the Central Archive after the rest of the evidence was signed out, sir."

Finn nodded. "Thank you, Constable."

"Will that be all, sir?"

"Yes. You can take the tape back. Can this be reunited with the rest of the evidence?"

"It's not customary, sir."

"Obviously not, but I'd like it nevertheless," Finn continued in his commanding manner.

The constable took the tape, resealed it in the evidence bag, and took it with him.

"This sounds suspiciously like evidence tampering," Tommy said.

"Only we can't prove it." Finn sighed. "If I suggest this to a judge, the defense will say the tape had been mislaid and had only recently been found. Farraday or his supervisor will get a slap on the wrist, and that will be the end of it."

"We should go over to the station and talk to Stevie. She has the rest of the evidence and can tell us whether the tape is documented or not."

"I'm taking you home, Tommy. You aren't supposed to be working, and you look exhausted."

Tommy had to admit Finn was right. He was ready for a nap, not for more work.

Chapter Twenty-One

TOMMY

"Finn?"

"Ehm?"

"Come inside with me?" Tommy felt like a teenager asking his boyfriend to come up to his room to make out. When Finn didn't immediately react, his insecurity went up a notch again. Then he remembered Ayse's words that Finn needed time to do what they'd done as teenagers because he'd never had that time to take it slow and explore. It dawned on Tommy that he hadn't had that time either. His exploration with girls had been because it was expected of him. He'd never minded the sex, but it had always been a rush to get it over with and an even bigger rush to get out of whatever place she was in, because afterward he never knew what to say or do. When he'd finally grown the courage to try men, that too had been fast-paced and only aimed at sexual satisfaction. Everything he'd shared with Finn so far had been all about the slow exploration Ayse had hinted that Finn needed. And clearly he needed that too.

"I think it's too soon, Tommy."

"Okay," Tommy replied with a nod, trying not to look too disappointed. He'd hoped that knowing *why* Finn needed the slow pace would change things for the better, but it clearly hadn't, and Tommy started thinking again that they'd never make it.

"You look like I just took your favorite toy away."

Tommy met Finn's eyes and saw him smiling. His thin lips barely masked his nervousness, but he seemed much more self-assured than he usually was when they were alone together.

"I miss you, Finn."

Finn's smile disappeared, and his eyes became moist. He was clearly searching for the right thing to say, but no words came out, at least not at first. "What will happen when I come up with you?"

"We talk. Spend time together. And then whatever you like."

"And what about what *you* like?"

Tommy looked at the cabbie who'd driven them from the Central Archive to his sublet and was clearly wanting to leave. "Let's pay the fare and talk about this in more intimate circumstances, okay?"

He kicked himself for his choice of words, but Finn didn't appear to have a problem with them as he got out of the cab and took his wallet out to pay.

Tommy in turn didn't wait for Finn and unlocked his front door. To his surprise, Finn was close behind him. As he let Finn inside his flat he looked nervous, but no more than Tommy felt.

"It still looks like Ayse's place."

Tommy chuckled. "It still is. It will take some time before I can buy furniture of my own, so I'm really grateful that she's subletting it fully furnished." He walked on to the kitchen. "Should I make us some tea?" He didn't wait for Finn's answer. He needed to make a cup of tea to have something to do.

"You might not need to buy any furniture, Tommy."

Finn joined him in the kitchen, standing very much like they stood that very first time at the underpass next to the Thames after Armen's party. Just like then they were facing in opposite directions as Finn was leaning against the counter.

"I think I know a way we can make it work between us."

Finn's voice was soft, soothing, and surprisingly in control, Tommy thought. "I've spent a lot of time talking to Ayse about this to figure out what parts of what we do set me in full flight mode."

Tommy must have looked in a total panic, because Finn put his hand on Tommy's cast-covered arm.

"Don't worry. I didn't go into details with her. I don't think she'd want me to either."

"I'm sure she hears all sorts of things from her clients."

Finn chuckled. "We're friends, Tommy. It's hard enough for me to go to her for Carlton to allow me to work again. She knows about the… abuse, but I don't tell her what we do or don't do in bed."

Tommy couldn't resist letting out a breath.

"My talks with her have allowed me to learn a lot about myself, though, and although I'm not all that big on soul-searching, I have been thinking a lot about how we can get past our impasse."

Tommy was almost afraid to hope.

"That is if you still want to give it a go with me."

"More than anything," Tommy replied, trying very hard not to simply wrap his arms around Finn and kiss him silly. Instead he poured the near-boiling water into his teapot and looked at his kitchen counter instead of Finn.

"Good."

"So what did you come up with?"

"Could we agree on no sex? At all."

Tommy bit the inside of his lip around the still healing scar, welcoming the pain, which was nothing compared to what Finn had just told him. "Sure," he replied. "But I thought we were already doing that?" He knew he sounded cold and distant, but it was better than sounding bitter. Tommy took his teapot into the sitting room.

"I'm glad we could agree on that," Finn said, following him with the two mugs, milk, and sugar Tommy had taken out of the cupboard but couldn't carry.

For the first time inside the flat, Tommy turned toward Finn. "Just call it a friendship, then, not a relationship. So it's a good thing, after all, we're not living together anymore. At least that's past us."

"No! Tommy, you misunderstood me."

"I understood perfectly that sex is not for you. Fine. But I can't live without at least a glimmer of hope, Finn. I love you, and that makes me almost infinitely patient, but I need to know that somewhere in the future, even if that means a year from now, you won't run away from me and turn into a puddle of misery because I touched you. I hate to be this shallow, but I need the physical side of a relationship too. I need the sex just as much as I need the cuddling and the holding and the kissing." By now he was almost standing on the other side of the sitting room and no longer facing Finn.

"Will you let me answer that?"

Tommy sighed. He knew he'd been rambling, but he was also glad it was off his chest. Finn's calm reply soothed him too. "Yes. I'm sorry. I won't interrupt again."

"I need the holding and the cuddling and the kissing too, Tommy."

Tommy wanted to interject "But not the sex" and then remembered his promise.

"In fact, that's the bit that was working for me. It was staring me right in the face all the time and I didn't see it. He never just kissed me or held me for the sake of tenderness, Tom. It was all a means to an end. Something to blackmail me with. He groped me and made me do things to him, but the closest thing to hugging was when he forced me to sit in his lap."

Tommy cringed at hearing Finn talk about his abuser, but he tried not to show it.

"If you're willing to help...."

Finn didn't finish his sentence, so Tommy thought he was waiting for confirmation from him. He nodded.

"I need you to teach me how to enjoy that touch, Tommy."

"And how do you want me to do that?"

Finn chuckled nervously. "I wracked my brain trying to find ways to get skin-to-skin contact without it turning sexual, and all I could come up with was massage. According to Ayse it's a known remedy for people with intimacy issues to get used to being touched without the fear of it becoming too intimate."

Tommy held up his dominant arm. "I see a practical impediment."

Finn nodded. "Yes, I know. I thought of that too, and then I pictured *I* could start massaging *you*, and then I realized that would be difficult too because of—"

"My ribs." Tommy nodded.

Finn cocked his head. "I guess this will try both our patience."

Tommy slowly walked closer to Finn. "Stay anyway."

"I should go back to work. And we have work in the morning as well."

"We're going to be spending time at the archive again, right?"

Finn nodded, and Tommy took another step closer.

"So stay, and it'll spare you the effort of picking me up in the morning." He stepped into Finn's personal space and could tell Finn was hesitating. "The bed in the guest room is made up."

"But I don't want to sleep in the guest room."

Before Tommy could invite him to his own bedroom, Finn kissed him with so much fervor he forgot his painful lip and felt the passion trickle down all the way to his toes.

FINN

IT FELT so damn good to kiss Tommy he didn't know how he'd survived the past week without seeing him and then all day at the archive in his presence barely even touching him. It gave him hope, but he knew he'd been this comfortable before and even then hadn't been able to pull off advancing their relationship.

It was almost a blessing when Tommy pushed him away. "You're breaking your own rules, mate."

"Yes, I am. You're right."

He tried to take a step back, but Tommy didn't let him. For a moment his flight reaction kicked in, and then he felt himself relax again. Tommy looked at ease as well, and Finn knew that if he really put some effort into it, Tommy would relinquish his hold. He didn't struggle.

"If you're sleeping in my bed tonight, I'll take you up on your offer." Tommy let go of him and moved away.

Finn wasn't sure which offer Tommy meant.

"The massage. I'll rub your shoulders as best I can with my right hand, and you can rub mine. I have only one problem."

"Which is?" Finn asked hesitantly.

"I won't be able to hide my arousal. I agreed to this not turning sexual, so I won't do anything with it, but it will be there." He looked away from Finn momentarily to pick up his cup of tea and take a drink from it. "Christ, I sprang a stiffie just kissing you. I'm pretty sure having your hands on me will only make it worse. So you're going to have to trust me that I won't do anything with it."

Finn nodded, remembering what he did to bring Tommy off the night before his second meltdown. It made him aroused too, despite what happened afterward. "I trust you."

"So bring your cup and follow me."

To his surprise, Finn felt fairly calm following Tommy to his bedroom. He *did* trust Tommy; he just didn't trust himself. The bed was made up with familiar-looking sheets, although he'd never seen them out of their wrapper before. Other than that the room was sparsely furnished. Tommy pulled the straight-back chair from under the vanity and turned it around before straddling it. He took his sweater and T-shirt off in one go, helping it past his cast, and then bent down to open a drawer and pull out a small bottle.

"Lube?" Finn asked, not without humor.

"Lotion," Tommy answered with a mock-annoyed smile.

Finn took the bottle from Tommy, squirted some of it on his hands, and warmed it before reaching for Tommy's shoulders. He hesitated to put his hands on Tommy's bare skin.

This was silly.

He'd touched Tommy before. More intimately than this even. He'd had his hand on Tommy's cock and had felt him come. What was more intimate than that? Granted, with other parts of his body there had almost always been at least one thin layer of cotton separating his skin and Tommy's.

He rubbed his hands together again, adding some more lotion from the bottle and warming it again. He closed his eyes and put his hands on Tommy's shoulders. The skin there was soft, enticing, cooler than he'd imagined. His hands took over, like muscle memory, and he gently kneaded the taut muscles running from Tommy's spinal cord to his shoulder joint, taking extra care near the protruding bones in the middle.

Tommy softly moaning brought Finn back to the present.

"You're good at this."

"One of my nannies had a whiplash injury. She was always in pain in the evening, and she taught me how to do it."

Tommy moved his head around to flex his neck. "Never realized how tense I was until now. If you ever see her again, tell her that her instruction was excellent."

"I'll tell her I have a lover who appreciates it," Finn said with a smile on his face.

Tommy looked up at him through the mirror with such a blissful look that Finn's arousal, which had started with the kissing and had only got worse from the touching, didn't abate one bit. He mentally suppressed it, though. They'd agreed it wouldn't turn sexual, no matter what, so instead of kissing him on the mouth like he wanted to, he kissed Tommy on the forehead and was rewarded with another soft moan.

"This feels so great you could put me right to sleep."

Finn continued to knead along Tommy's spine as Tommy let his head drop forward.

"We should probably switch before you turn me completely to putty."

Reluctantly, Finn pulled his hands away and stepped back so Tommy could get up. When Tommy looked him in the eye, his face was so sultry it shot right to Finn's groin. Finn was glad he could sit down facing away from Tommy before he had to take his shirt off.

"Can you…?" Tommy asked, handing the flask to Finn. Finn squirted some lotion into Tommy's right hand and then put it on the vanity. "It's going to be cold for a moment. I can't warm it like you did."

"It's fine," Finn replied, placing his arms on the back of the chair and trying to relax. The lotion was cold indeed, but it didn't last long. There was little finesse to Tommy's movements, but Finn found himself not minding. The idea of Tommy's hand on his skin, the care with which Tommy tried to rub him with his nondominant hand made him lean into the touch, craving more. He tried not to think of Tommy behind him, his chest and arms bare, and closed his eyes so he could just enjoy the sensation. He soon found himself enjoying the contact a little too much and had to direct his mind to his court cases for fear that he would turn around and pull Tommy into his arms, which would violate their agreement.

"You're cute when you're purring," Tommy whispered in his ear.

Finn chuckled. "Even with one hand you're pretty good at this."

Tommy moved away from him. "Wait until you let me show you just how good." He didn't linger and instead started gathering the clothes he'd discarded and putting them on the other chair in the room.

Finn did the same with his and found himself looking for an opening. He didn't want to take anything for granted. "Is your invitation still open?"

Tommy stopped what he was doing, a soft smile on his face. "For you to stay here?"

Finn nodded.

"Of course. You can sleep in the guest room."

Finn tried not to look disappointed as he finished gathering his clothes.

"Or you can stay here with me."

Finn couldn't help perking up, and judging from Tommy's chuckle, he wasn't hiding it very well.

"Our agreement stays in place, right?"

Finn nodded. His heart said he wanted to chuck the agreement, but his mind called him on it. He knew the chance of yet another disaster was still there, and he didn't want to try Tommy's patience too much.

"Let's eat first. I have soup left from yesterday, and the bread you bought before we drove home would go well with that."

Finn agreed, feeling relieved that eating would release some of the tension he was feeling. As always the dinner was delicious, and Finn knew he could get used to simple, nourishing dinners like Tommy cooked them. But first he was going to have to deserve them.

They'd barely finished the dishes when Tommy yawned.

"Let's put you to bed, because I don't want you to keel over and hurt yourself more."

Tommy mumbled something Finn didn't understand, but he got the general idea that Tommy agreed with him.

In the bedroom Tommy threw him a pair of gray flannel boxer briefs and a T-shirt of the same color. "They might be a tad big for you, but they're clean."

"Thanks. I'll put them on later when I come to bed."

Tommy turned around and started changing into nightwear. He wasn't hiding, but he was discreet nevertheless. Finn got a quick glance at Tommy's naked arse from behind and had to look away. If there was ever any doubt....

"I'm going to work in the sitting room. I'll try not to wake you when I come in here."

"It's just reading, right?"

Finn nodded. "And some note-taking, of course."

"Do it in here."

"I don't want to keep you awake."

"Nothing could keep me awake tonight, Finn. Not even the man I love sitting in bed next to me reading papers."

"All right, if you're sure."

He ran into the sitting room to retrieve his briefcase and quickly returned to change, while Tommy watched him from the bed. He joined Tommy a little hesitantly. He didn't know why he had such apprehensions now. They'd slept together for weeks before they'd had sex, and he should be less—not more—afraid now they'd agreed nothing was going to happen.

As soon as Finn was in the bed beside him, Tommy sought to find a comfortable position and closed his eyes. Finn smiled at his own silly feelings and took his papers in hand. It was almost three hours later when he finally turned off the light.

"Come here," Tommy whispered.

"Didn't meant to wake you," Finn replied, equally as soft.

He moved closer so Tommy could kiss him. It was a chaste kiss, without teeth or tongue, but it brought Finn easily into Tommy's arms, where he eventually settled with his head on Tommy's shoulder.

Chapter Twenty-Two

FINN

"NIGHTMARE?" TOMMY asked, sleepily turning toward Finn.

"No," Finn replied as he continued to stare at the ceiling.

"So you're just an—" *Yawn.* "—insomniac."

"I can't stop thinking about that woman's voice. I know I've heard it before."

"Well, when you become chief, you can ask your secretary to put your notes in a computer, and then you can run a search." Tommy didn't even open his eyes and yawned again. "Until then you'll need to go through all of your notebooks, and since they're in your office and not in my flat, there's nothing you can do short of getting up and pedaling to your office. So sleep."

He pulled Finn closer, and Finn turned on his side so Tommy could spoon him. It was so comfortable it was as if they'd been doing this for years. The warmth against his back and the slow, rhythmical breathing behind him made him eventually doze off.

THE NEXT morning he was at the office a little later than usual and found a note on his desk to see Carlton as soon as he got in. He hadn't been inside for two days, so it wasn't a big surprise that Carlton wanted an update.

He hurried over, but as he walked up to the door he saw Carlton had company. Through the large windows of the office, blinds half closed showed there was a woman inside Finn didn't know. He was about to turn away when the conversation she and Carlton were having turned loud. She was clearly upset about something, and Carlton was trying to stay calm while appeasing her. It wasn't working, and the more upset she became, the more flushed Carlton got.

Feeling self-conscious about what he'd just seen, Finn walked the few paces to the coffee stand to pour himself a cup of tea. That way he couldn't see directly inside, but he still had a view of the door so he could see when his boss was free. Just moments after he'd taken a first sip of his tea, the woman walked outside with a determined step, and Carlton gestured at Finn to come inside.

"Finn, sit. Drink?"

"No, thank you," Finn replied, holding up his cup.

"What did you find at the archive?" Carlton asked as if it was just a normal morning and he hadn't just had a fight with someone in his office. Then again, it was none of Finn's business.

"Nothing concrete," Finn answered evasively. He wanted to know what Carlton was fishing for before he gave him anything.

Carlton poured himself a tiny Scotch.

At nine in the morning.

"I thought you'd have exhausted your leads on the cases I gave you, since you requested other ones to review."

Finn knew Carlton had his spies everywhere, and the archive was an obvious place, but he was surprised Carlton was letting him see his hand this early in the game. "You know how it goes, Bill. You see something in one case and remember something like that happened in another case you handled, so you want to look that one over as well, just to be sure."

Carlton nodded, emptying his glass. "Your notes didn't cover what you needed to know?"

"I found the connection in my notes," Finn replied staying purposely vague. "But the details aren't in there because I'm looking at the case in conjunction with others, not as a stand-alone case I need to prosecute."

"I see."

Finn saw it too. This wasn't just friendly interest. He knew this was becoming a high profile case. Getting a Scotland Yard detective prosecuted for fraud had the potential to blemish the entire Metropolitan Police. It had to be handled with kid gloves. Any wrongdoings during the proceedings would reflect badly on Bill Carlton in the first place and only on Finn in the second. It was understandable that he'd want to keep a close eye on the goings-on. Finn had a niggling doubt about Carlton, though. Just like he had the feeling he was being spoon-fed little bits of information, only enough to keep him going but maybe not quite enough for him to crack the case.

"Bill, will you let me be lead on this if it goes to court?"

Carlton's eyes narrowed. "That depends. On whether you can be trusted in open court."

"I've been following your instruction and have been seeing Dr. Kartal on a regular basis. This case against Frank Farraday is delicate and will be tried in open court, although his defense will try to ask for closed proceedings. You can't let Armen handle this. He knows nothing about the case and isn't experienced enough for it."

"Of course not. But there are other more experienced prosecutors."

"They don't know the case."

"So what will you have him indicted with?"

"A growing number of charges of misconduct in public office by willfully engaging in conduct amounting to an abuse of public trust. We're still digging through cases to figure out how many cases I can charge him with."

"This is not your usual fare, Finn."

"You allowed me to get started on this case. You knew full well it was an unusual investigation for both me and the sergeants I was assigned, but we're doing our jobs."

Finn didn't think he was imagining Carlton growing a bit paler, but he continued nevertheless. "I'll draw up the necessary papers for the DPS to dismiss him from duty, and then the criminal investigation can go to court. But I think we should take our time with this one. This isn't about one corrupt cop. He must have help higher up. Otherwise he couldn't get away with it."

"The longer we wait, the more he can do wrong, Finn. When will you be ready to charge him?" Carlton asked.

"I suspect we'll have enough to get him dismissed from the force in about two weeks, but—"

"Prepare your case, and then I'll decide who takes lead on this one."

"No," Finn said resolutely. "If you won't let me take lead, the next two weeks the lead prosecutor will need to be by my side. This isn't some GBH we're prosecuting. A single mistake can topple the whole investigation."

Carlton smiled, but it didn't reach his eyes. "In that case I better give it to you so you're not responsible for anyone else getting egg on their face."

Finn was fuming but only on the inside. His instincts, that Carlton was not on his side, were right. However, he got what he wanted. At least partially. "I won't let the Crown down," Finn said by way of acknowledgement. He nodded at Carlton before leaving his office and walked back to his own.

On the way out Armen crossed his path.

"Armen, do you have a minute?"

"Certainly."

They continued to Finn's office. "Do you remember the day DS Tommy Drummond was assaulted outside my flat?"

"Vaguely."

"Do you remember a stranger coming up to you in the Old Bailey and handing you an envelope?"

"How did you know?"

Finn gestured him inside, opened his laptop, and clicked on the link to the CCTV footage he'd saved there.

Armen nodded. "Yes, of course. There was nothing of consequence inside. I thought it was strange, but it felt like some sort of prank."

"What did you do with the envelope or its contents?"

"I threw them away."

"What was inside?"

"A handwritten note asking me to take a picture inside the courthouse with my mobile phone. Of course I didn't."

"Did you recognize the man?"

"I barely saw him. Is he a suspect?"

"The man who stabbed DS Drummond that evening was wearing the same clothes. We— I was hoping it was someone you knew, so we'd have a lead on the stabbing."

"Sorry, sir, I honestly thought it was a prank."

"Very well. That's all." Finn rummaged through the papers on his desk to hide his disappointment. Armen took the hint and left.

TOMMY

IT FELT strange to sit in front of his new DSI's office without Stevie. When they were told that Mark Stanton was going to be their new boss, neither he nor Stevie minded the switch. Stanton had been the interim DSI when their bigoted boss had been suspended for trying to get Tommy kicked off the Met, and their cooperation had been a good one.

One phone call had changed Tommy's idea of him, though, and nothing was ever going to be the same.

"Come in, DS Drummond. Sit. Cup o' tea?"

Tommy hated these little get-togethers, even more so because Stanton always seemed so kind. Being summoned to come alone and find an excuse to leave Stevie to her own devices was easier now he was on sick leave than it was before the assault, but that didn't make these conversations any easier.

"No, thanks."

"Well, we won't be long. I know you're busy. How's the arm? And are your ribs healing nicely?"

"They're fine. Still a little sore in the morning but otherwise good enough to work."

"That's good news. I have to say you did a nice job remaining my eyes and ears where our prosecutor is concerned while you were away from work. Did the doc clear you?"

Tommy swallowed away the bile. "Yes, he did. Light duty only for now."

"I'm sure you can find something light to do. DeHavilland still taking you to the Central Archive?"

Tommy nodded.

"You do realize this is for everyone's protection, not least of all Finn DeHavilland's, right?"

Tommy nodded again, not believing a word of what he was saying.

"So where is the case going? What have the three of you unearthed?"

"We're still digging through old case files, trying to find connections."

"And?"

"Finn…. Our prosecutor… has phenomenal memory. The cases and details he remembers—"

"Cut to the chase, Tommy. I know he's good. He's a friggin' senior Crown Prosecutor. You don't become one because you're a pretty face. Tell me what you've found. Remember I have my connections at the Central Archive."

What could he tell him that was innocuous? The license plate? No, that was too much detail. He had to give him something, though.

"We're making a list of all the police officers who signed the interrogation statements of different cases."

"And are there any similarities between all these cases? Tommy, I picked you because you are a great sergeant. So why do I need to ask you the questions I ask a first-week constable? Do I need to explain what kind of report I ask of you?'

"No, you don't, sir."

Stanton sighed deeply, and Tommy knew he was going to have to give him something substantial soon.

"Very well," Stanton sighed again. "Next time I want a full report on your progress. Or would you prefer to give it to me in writing?"

"No," Tommy replied resolutely. The last thing he wanted was a paper trail of what was going on here. "I'll get you something when I have something to report. Right now we're still in the dark."

"Of course," he replied in such a manner that Tommy knew he didn't believe him.

Stanton dismissed him with a wave of his hand, and he couldn't get out of there fast enough. Outside Stanton's office he picked up a cup of water to wash away the taste of bile in his mouth but found he couldn't. He needed to trust Stanton, but that trust crumbled after every one of these "meetings." He was between a rock and a hard place and had nowhere to turn.

Chapter Twenty-Three

TOMMY

WITH TOMMY officially back at work, Stevie suggested they spend their first day at Finn's office bringing everyone up to speed.

"Can I start?" Stevie asked even before they'd set themselves down at the central table. "The investigation into Tommy's stabbing?"

"By all means," Finn replied.

"We had CCTV footage from the back alley but no discernable faces. Assailant was alone, presumable a male in his thirties, possibly early forties. He wore a hoodie and jeans with some sort of combat boots. He accosted Tommy from the back, stabbing him right-handedly with a long, narrow, pointed object, like an ice pick."

"Not a knife?"

"The surgeon said definitely not a knife because it only cut a long, narrow tunnel and didn't inflict any damage to the side. The intent was to go deep and inflict damage there. According to his report it was something most closely resembling an ice pick, which is an unusual object, since few people stab large blocks of ice these days, but the surgeon is no medical examiner, so I talked to our ME, and she agrees it's most likely an ice pick. Which led me to Portobello Road and the people selling nicknacks on the street. They're not large sellers, ice picks, these days, which is no surprise. One bloke said he sold a Victorian one for fifty quid a few weeks ago but couldn't give me a description of the buyer. Of course, there's also no receipt. So that was a dead end."

Tommy subconsciously put his hand over the healing wound on his right side, right under the ribs.

"Good news is our Tommy put up a fight. As clearly visible in the CCTV, he turned to face his assailant and punched him in the stomach. The guy reciprocated and gave him a right uppercut, which accounts for the broken jaw and the split lip on the left side of his face. When Tommy went down, no doubt because of the blood loss, his assailant continued to kick him until he stopped moving. I reckon Tommy's lucky to be alive, and part of that, in me 'umble opinion, is the fact he got away from the ice pick."

"Why do you say that?" Finn asked.

"The couple in Belgravia wasn't so lucky."

Both Finn and Tommy nodded.

"According to the ME, the weapon there was an ice pick as well."

"But we were taken off the case," Tommy added.

Stevie smiled. "Yes, we were. But when the name Frank Farraday fell, I did some digging anyway. We were assigned that case in the first place because Frank Farraday had called in sick that morning. They were short-staffed at the posh stations, so they asked us, Serious Crimes, to cover for Sex Offences, since they reckoned we'd know how to behave and it was a homicide anyway." She waggled her eyebrows theatrically. "In any case, ME says it was a crime of passion. Both victims were stabbed over fifty times. He didn't want to call it rape, because of the fact they'd been found tied up with the kind of leather used in sex games, but both the male and female had been roughly anally penetrated."

Tommy watched both Finn and Stevie pull a face as if they could feel it.

"So sex games gone awry is still an option?" Finn asked.

"Something went friggin' wrong all right," Stevie agreed.

"What if the ice pick makes us assume both the murders and Tommy's assault were perpetrated by the same man? What does this tell us?" Finn asked.

"Either the perp saw us do the investigating and feels Tommy found something incriminating, or it was a coincidence."

Finn shook his head. "I don't believe in coincidences."

Tommy raised his hand. "Let's not forget the possibility that Finn was the intended victim of my mugging. I was wearing his coat and cap. And Finn was at the crime scene as well."

Finn and Stevie looked at Tommy. Tommy's mind was going full blast, and he knew he was going to ramble incoherently, but these two were the only people who could help him make sense of the jumbled ideas in his mind.

"The perp saw Finn enter the crime scene. It's incredibly unusual for someone from the Crown Prosecution Service to visit a fresh crime scene unless evidence is found that cannot be captured in a picture or an evidence bag and that could lead to a swift arrest of a suspect. So what if our perp thought he'd been found out because Finn was there?"

"He couldn't exactly walk into the crime scene, which was crawling with police officers and Forensic Services," Stevie added.

"But he could have been outside, watching the proceedings."

Stevie snorted. "He did a bloody good job staying so calm after such a passionate murder."

"You see it in serial killers all the time," Finn supplied. "They come off their killing high and are very much in control. Maybe he enjoyed the attention the crime was getting, seeing all these people work the scene? There's a reason you coppers scan onlookers at a cordoned-off crime scene. But with Tommy's stabbing he *was* very much in control," Finn added, almost as an afterthought.

"Not if you saw the footage. It starts off in control, but when Tommy goes down, he starts kicking him, and that is pure frustration."

Tommy could see Finn thinking, as if he was going through the motions of reconstructing the scene. "Tommy's face was visible thanks to the streetlamp. Maybe our perp realized it wasn't me and the kicking is him taking his frustration out on Tommy?"

"That could fit," Tommy replied. "But the only thing relating the two crimes is our conjecture."

"And the ice pick," Stevie interrupted. "And let's not forget the man very much looking like Tommy's assailant walking up to Armen Nagocyan in the Old Bailey that afternoon."

Finn nodded. "I asked Armen about it, and he said the man gave him an envelope with a note in it, but it didn't make sense, so he discarded it."

"This note?" Stevie asked as she slapped a piece of paper wrapped in a clear evidence envelope on the table between them.

Finn looked at it. "Possibly. The words on it are what Armen told me it said. Where did you get it?"

"Lucky for us they don't empty the bins every day. From the footage inside the corridor it was clear what bin Armen dropped the envelope in, so that narrowed it down. Had to sift through a lot of waste. You can't imagine what sort of stuff gets discarded inside the Old Bailey. Not sure what good it will do us, but it was such a strange occurrence I reckoned it might not be a dud in the long run."

"Has this been processed, Stevie? Ink? Fingerprints? Paper?"

Stevie shook her head. "Chain of custody was broken."

Finn sighed. "I agree. Even if I make Armen testify he received this note, defense will argue there is no way to be sure that this is the exact note because Armen dropped it in the bin."

Stevie looked apologetic, although there was nothing she could change about it.

"So tell me about our corrupt copper case?" she asked.

"Tommy and I have weeded through many an evidence box at the Central Archive. If you start putting them all together, it's easy to see the mistakes, if you can call them that. Either this guy is terribly lax all around, or these 'mistakes' are intentional."

"Since he's a Rape and Serious Sexual Offences officer, all the cases are rape, domestic abuse, and sometimes child abuse," Tommy continued. "Some of the evidence speaks of a taped confession, and then there is none. Sometimes there is a written record of equipment malfunction. If we had that much malfunctioning we wouldn't be able to do our job. He consistently finds ways around doing his sworn duty. The written accounts are full of excuses. Testimony couldn't be taped because the victim refused. Or the victim couldn't come to the station for one reason or another. What surprises me is that his DSI signed off on these cases. Half of them have leads that were never followed up on. I'm only a sergeant, but I wouldn't dare go to any supervisor with this."

Stevie nodded.

"We're still looking into our suspicion that he fabricated some of his taped confessions. But our biggest problem is time," Finn said. "Carlton wants me to hand this over to DPS within the next fortnight."

"Fuck, Finn." Tommy gawked. "We've barely scratched the surface!"

Finn briefly put his hand on Tommy's knee and squeezed it. "I know. Carlton wants this man off the force with as little fuss as possible, but I know that if we dig deeper, we can drag down half his department. And maybe beyond that."

"I suppose we can still do this after DPS starts his proceedings," Tommy said without much conviction.

"They'll have time to cover their tracks." Finn sighed. "My hands are tied."

"Will they let you at least go to court?"

Finn nodded. "Carlton promised me it would be my case."

Tommy smiled and was grateful for small mercies.

"At least one corrupt copper will be off the streets," Stevie added. "Even if his supervisors go scot-free."

"So is this the end of our cooperation?" Tommy asked with some trepidation.

"I'll write my report for the DPS at night. During the day we keep digging at the Central Archive. Tommy, you and Stevie need to talk to some of the interrogated suspects and witnesses. See if any of those are willing to take the stand, but remember we need to keep quiet who will be testifying for us. I wouldn't trust anyone in Farraday's entourage not to try to squeeze the witnesses."

"We'll reconvene here every morning to plan our work?" Tommy asked.

Finn nodded. "This will remain our headquarters. So far I have no evidence that someone is leaking what's been said here, so I think it's a safe place."

So far. Tommy dismissed the thought that if it ever surfaced that some things were leaked, he'd be the source. This was another instance he was tempted to disclose his weekly meetings with Stanton, but he knew Finn wouldn't take it well. Finn trusted him and it wouldn't just ruin their working relationship, but their private one as well. He'd simply have to be careful what he fed Stanton. And hope that their DSI really had Finn's safety in mind and not his downfall.

"Do you need me at the archive?" Tommy asked, pulling himself together again. "I have a list of people we can go talk to to check how much of what Farraday wrote in the files is true."

"I can go it alone for today. We'll check in again tomorrow."

Tommy nodded and got up from the table. "I want to take a look at the other ice pick assaults and murders too."

"Do it discreetly, Tom. If this is all the same man, I don't want it to reach his ears."

FINN

TOMMY'S IDEA that his own mugging somehow tied Frank Faraday to the ice pick murders wouldn't leave Finn alone. He could think of only one person who could help him in that respect. Ayse.

"Did we have an appointment?" Ayse asked as she opened the door to her office for Finn.

"No. I was wondering if you had ten minutes for me?"

"Sure," she replied with a wide smile. "Fifteen or twenty even if you want. How's Tommy doing?"

"Back at work, so okay, I suppose."

"How's the dating going?" She led him inside and sat down on the sofa. Finn joined her.

"We almost got mugged after our dinner."

"Ouch!"

"No harm done. They tried to scare us, nothing more."

"Good."

"It got me thinking, though," Finn admitted.

"What about?"

Finn inhaled to focus his attention. "You know who we're investigating, right?"

She nodded.

"What sort of man is he? What can I expect when I face him in court?"

"If you feel he's deliberately making mistakes, it depends. Either he's just a bad cop who wants to pretend to be more important or—"

"His files are not perfect enough for that," Finn interrupted her.

"In that case, do you think he's sabotaging the investigation out of laziness or because he's hiding something?"

"I suspect he's fabricating evidence, so that doesn't exactly constitute laziness. It's much easier to ask a person questions and record them than it is to make things up."

"But if you make them up, you are in charge of how the investigation goes. So you're looking at a manipulative man who wants full control over every situation. He'd rather hide evidence than hope for a good outcome of a trial, unless it's a cut-and-dried case."

"Or he's involved," Finn suggested.

"What haven't you told me?"

"Can we go outside for a walk?" He nodded at the window to the street.

Ayse narrowed her eyes and then grabbed her coat. "Let's go."

They walked briskly for a few minutes until they arrived in quieter streets. Ayse slowed to a stroll. "So you're being paranoid, which makes me think you found something very important."

Finn took her arm as he continued walking at a leisurely pace. "Stevie found out that Tommy was assaulted with an ice pick, not a knife. And another case with an ice pick surfaced. A case Tommy invited me to the crime scene for."

"How exciting. To be allowed to visit a crime scene."

Finn gave her a death stare, and her smile dimmed.

"It was a blood bath. A man and a women brutally raped and murdered."

"With an ice pick," Ayse provided.

"If I didn't know any better I'd think you were jealous of what I saw. I tell you, don't be."

She squeezed her mouth shut, but Finn could tell she tried not to smile.

"Our subject's name came up. It was supposed to be his case, but he'd called in sick. It made me wonder if the reason he'd manipulated all that evidence was that he was somehow involved in those cases and worried he might be incriminated."

"Does anything in his file indicate he has a fetish for ice picks?"

"Oh no." Finn shook his hands at her. "I don't mean he's involved with Tommy's assault or the Belgravia double murder. I was wondering if he could be involved in the rape cases he botched."

"It's a possibility. It isn't unheard of for police officers to end up doing crimes themselves. After all, they're inherently fascinated by it and know what to do without getting caught."

"So how do I lure him out?"

"You can try to appeal to his pride, tell him you admire his ingenuity. But I think you have a better shot at looking for patterns. If he's really a serial rapist or even a peeping tom, then his crimes will gradually become worse. It may start with accosting a victim and holding her down, then the next victim may be tied up while he masturbates on her, gradually progressing to forceful penetration. Most serial rapists become more and more violent, though. Sometimes something goes wrong when they restrain their victims and they kill by accident, finding the rush even bigger than when they simply rape her. Others go consciously in search of that bigger rush, but a man who continues to rape victims eventually will kill."

"So you're saying I should look at connections between the Belgravia homicides and our man?"

Ayse raised her eyebrows at Finn. "At least to see if you can figure out how he could have botched the investigation the way he did all the others. I'm not saying he's a killer or even a rapist, but it could be an interesting exercise."

"The problem is I don't have the time for interesting exercises. Carlton has given me exactly a fortnight to close the investigation and hand it over to DPS."

"Well, you better get cracking, then."

"Tommy found other unsolved crimes perpetrated with an ice pick. If you put them on a timeline, it does suggest escalating violence. To save time I'll keep the cases separate. Once Farraday is off the force we'll have time to dig into the murders."

"Well, you can always call me for input. I'll bill it to Carlton and tell him I'm still seeing you as a patient."

Finn smiled. "You don't do that anyway?"

"Let's make it legitimate, then. Are you ready to go back to court?"

"I can't wait, frankly."

"Good. Now walk me back to my office and you can go on your way to wherever you were going."

"Central Archive."

Ayse yawned theatrically.

"I know. It was more fun when I could do it together with Tommy."

"But Tommy is out talking to people for you. You'll see him tonight, right?"

"Maybe."

"Call him. Ask him to dinner. I can recommend another place for you if you like."

Finn smiled and deposited Ayse back at her office. "I think I can find a nice restaurant for us."

She stood on her toes and kissed him on the cheek. "He's worth it, Finn."

"I know."

Chapter Twenty-Four

FINN

EVEN AFTER Finn had submitted his papers to the Directorate of Professional Standards, he knew something was missing. He'd spent the last two weeks at his office, only going home to sleep and only seeing Tommy in an official capacity. He'd noticed Tommy's cast being taken off and his usual swagger reappearing in his step as his body healed and the aches left him. At the same time they'd barely exchanged a stolen kiss, and Finn couldn't wait for another date with him to reaffirm they were actually still together.

Although he was happy the investigation had been his sole focus for the last fortnight, he was also itching to get back into court. Carlton had reluctantly confirmed that prosecuting Frank Farraday was going to be his case, and he hoped the DPS would swiftly fire Farraday so the criminal case could rush out of the starting blocks.

He couldn't stop thinking if they'd had more time they could have built a better case, but consoled himself that once the papers were submitted he'd be able to find the time to continue the investigation into who had done all the covering up.

With the evidence they had, Farraday's DSI was the only man they could include in the charges, and only for negligence, not for the charges Farraday would be indicted for. It would depend on the DPS whether or not he'd be sacked for that or only reprimanded. Finn was pretty sure all he could hope for in the case of the DSI was a demotion, but Farraday's job as a detective had to end up on the chopping block.

As he waited for the DPS to announce their decision, it soon became apparent that free time was nonexistent. Carlton unexpectedly lifted his ban on Finn's court appearances, but Finn was given the types of cases that would normally go to a junior. Knowing he needed to win Carlton's trust, he went through the motions, appearing in court for the "for mention" cases, where no defendants or witnesses were present but timelines were set for evidence to be presented, or where the prosecution was called on by defense to perform certain actions. Finn could do those court appearances in his sleep, but the preparations for them made sure he was working long hours most days of the week.

Occasionally a slow day would pop up, and every time that happened, Finn craved to pick up his phone and call Tommy, but he knew from Natalie that Tommy and Stevie were also kept more than busy by their DSI. Afraid he'd be turned down because Tommy was too busy, he never got around to calling Tommy.

And then the news came.

Farraday was sacked from the Met and his DSI was demoted, just like they'd expected. Finn had been given the all clear for criminal prosecution, and his appearance in magistrate's court was scheduled. He needed to celebrate this first step with Tommy.

His mobile in hand, he lost the nerve to call first and decided to proceed immediately to Ayse's former flat, still the place where Tommy was living. He raced up the steps and had barely rung the doorbell when Tommy appeared.

"I just heard. They believed your arguments."

Finn nodded as Tommy grabbed his scarf and pulled him into the corridor. Finn didn't even have time to close the front door because he was enveloped by Tommy's arms and held tight. He hugged Tommy back until a middle-aged lady appeared in the staircase next to them.

"Evenin', Mrs. Setters," Tommy said as he let go of Finn but took his hand and dragged him inside his flat.

"She's okay. Don't think she was quite prepared for what she saw, but she won't give me grief about it."

"That's good to hear," Finn replied, a little perplexed. "Wouldn't want you to get into trouble with the neighbors."

"It's so good to see you."

Tommy kissed Finn with such abandon, Finn was afraid he was going to lose his footing.

"Natalie's been keeping us up to date with what Carlton is making you do and how busy you are."

"She told me Stanton's doing the same with you two."

"You can't imagine the cold cases we've been digging through. And none of them anywhere near the Farraday case. Stevie's earlier adoration for Stanton is hitting an all-time low, I tell you."

"And you?"

Tommy seemed to hesitate. "He's all right… I suppose, but that doesn't matter now. Let's stop talking about work. I finally have you here again!" Tommy pushed Finn to the couch, and in no time he was all over him, straddling Finn while they were kissing. It was as if the weeks of being apart had never happened.

Finn had no idea of the passage of time but didn't really care. Tommy was in his arms, and he was in his safe place, on the couch, with both of them fully dressed and Tommy not making any effort to change that. They only stopped long enough for Tommy to rid Finn of his new cap, scarf, and winter coat. Even when Tommy moved away, he didn't mind.

Finn looked at Tommy's thoroughly kissed lips and sighed.

"What?"

"Nothing," Finn replied, smiling. *How lucky can one man get?* His body was humming, and he could still feel Tommy's groping hands on him, although they were now sitting next to each other on the sofa.

"Not nothing," Tommy said smugly. "You're all flushed, Mister Prosecutor."

Finn turned toward Tommy again and rubbed his thumb over Tommy's swollen lips. "You look like you had a fling with a Hoover."

Tommy giggled silently. "And guess who the Hoover is?"

At that moment, Finn's mobile sprung to life. He reluctantly pulled away from Tommy and got up to answer it.

"Finn DeHavilland," he said curtly.

"Finn, it's me."

"Ayse? Are you okay? You sound…."

"I'm sorry to call you at this hour, but I'm in A&E at Westminster. Charlie's not here and I didn't know who else to call and…."

"I'll be right there." He grabbed his coat from the other sofa and put it on. When he turned around, Tommy was standing next to him, and it dawned on him he hadn't said anything to him. "Put your coat on. Ayse's in A&E, and she's all alone." Finn exhaled. "If you want to. You don't need to come, but she needs me."

"I'll drive," Tommy said as he grabbed his coat.

At Westminster A&E Finn asked to see Ayse.

"And your name?" the duty nurse asked sternly.

"Finn DeHavilland."

"And who's he?"

"Tommy Drummond," Tommy volunteered.

Finn smiled at Tommy's expression. He clearly didn't like to be spoken about as if he wasn't there, and Finn couldn't blame him.

The nurse studied her clipboard. "You're both on the list. Follow me."

"Both of us?" Tommy whispered at Finn behind the nurse's back.

Finn shrugged but couldn't prevent a smile.

They were shown into a room where Ayse was lying on the bed with her eyes closed and a drip in her arm. As Finn approached, she looked at him. When she saw Tommy, she smiled broadly.

"I'm sorry I disturbed your night."

Finn shook his head. "What happened?"

"I was driving home, and I got rear-ended. The other car was driving so fast he knocked my car into the wall."

"Oh God. The baby?"

"My airbag blew up so I thought I was safe, but I got stomach cramps, and when I told the ambulance crew I was pregnant, they said their policy was to get pregnant women checked out anyway."

"Good," Finn said, feeling just a little bit of the tension drain out of him. "Is he okay?" Finn pointed at her belly.

"*She*'s okay for now. They gave me some medication to relax, and I'm not allowed to get out of bed for a few days. Which is why I called you." She hesitated. "Charlie's on the other side of the world, my family isn't much help, as you know, and I really want to go home, but they'll only let me if there is someone in the house to take care of me. I'm only allowed to get up to go to the toilet, so I need a minion to fetch me things and feed me, that sort of thing."

"I'll call Carlton and tell him I'm working from home for a few days. He won't like it, but any junior can cover my court appearances. This takes precedence."

"Tommy can stay as well," Ayse said with a twinkle in her eye. "My house is huge. There's plenty of room."

"Ayse," Finn warned her, his teeth clenched.

Tommy put his hand on Finn's shoulder. "Why don't I sort things out with the warden—" He gestured outside. "—and you two can make plans for the rest of the week." He didn't wait for an answer and walked out.

"So how are you and Tommy doing?"

Finn shook his head and widened his eyes. "You call me here, telling me you had an accident that could have killed you *and* your baby, and then you ask me about my love life?"

Ayse giggled. "Come on, Finn. Even you know you two are meant for each other. You know you can live together. To be honest, that's something neither you nor I expected."

"I know."

"So do it."

Finn gave her a mock mean stare. "You're the one who said it would be a good thing to live apart for a while and actually go out on dates."

"And is it working?"

"Kind of."

"Only kind of?"

"Ayse!"

"I know. Stop meddling." She smiled smugly. "It's working, though."

He growled at her, which made her laugh. "We've barely seen each other these past weeks. Work is keeping both of us way too busy."

"All the more reason to ask him to move in with you again. If you don't I'll tell him I have to let go of the apartment, and then he'll have no choice."

He could see her holding her bulging stomach as she laughed, and he added his hand on top of hers. It made her stop and look at him.

"You need to take care of this little one. That's your only priority. Let me deal with Tommy."

"Gladly," she said with a wink. "I only have one guest room since the other one is converted to a nursery. I'm sure you can share, right?"

Finn smiled. Maybe it was a good thing. He hoped.

Chapter Twenty-Five

TOMMY

HE STARED at the screen. This was too much of a coincidence. He had to tell Finn about it but didn't want to do it over his mobile phone. The tabloid phone-tapping scandal had shown them it was possible, and they had started exchanging ideas about the case in only a few well-thought-out places.

Tommy jotted down the details of what was on the screen, then turned off the computer, got up, and grabbed his coat.

"Where are you goin'?" Stevie asked.

"Home. I'm taking some overtime." He hated lying to Stevie, but Stanton's office was right next to theirs, and he couldn't talk about it here at the station.

"Good on ya. See you tomorrow."

All the way home on the Tube, Tommy tried to think of what Finn was going to say when he told him about what was on the piece of paper in his inside pocket. He knew Finn's prosecutor side would crop up, going through all the reasons why this piece of evidence wouldn't stand up in court. He just hoped Finn would hear him out.

The last 500 yards between the Tube station and Ayse's house, Tommy called Finn's mobile. "Can I talk to you in the garden?" It was becoming code for "I have evidence that could mean something."

When he walked through the garden gate, Finn was there, tiptoeing in his half-length brown coat and thick scarf. "We have to find a warmer place to do this in."

Tommy didn't reply. Instead he held up a note for Finn to read.

"Fifty-nine Danville Terrace," Finn read aloud. "Why is that familiar?"

Tommy cocked his head, waiting for Finn to catch up.

"It's Frank Farraday's address, isn't it?"

Tommy nodded.

"So why is that important?"

"The woman who ran into Ayse's car?"

"Don't tell me she lives at…."

Tommy nodded again.

"You're kidding."

This time Tommy shook his head. "What coincidence is it that makes Farraday's girlfriend crash into a car of someone we know?"

When Finn didn't immediately answer, Tommy raised his eyes to the ceiling. "Come on, Finn, think like a prosecutor. You don't believe in coincidence, remember?"

Tommy could see the wheels turning in Finn's head.

"He sent his girlfriend out to crash her car into Ayse's?"

"That's my take on it."

"Or she was frustrated by him being sacked because of the evidence we gathered?" Finn suggested.

"But why take on Ayse, then?"

"Because he knows she's working on the case with us?"

Tommy scoffed. "We're back to him being behind this."

"Ayse's not an investigator or a prosecutor."

"No, but she's on the CPS payroll. Maybe he thinks if something happened to her it would destabilize you?" Tommy pursed his lips.

Deep lines formed over Finn's brow. "Someone outside the CPS offices knows Ayse's my counselor, and they think I divulged certain matters regarding the case to her?"

"They don't need to know she's your counselor. It's easy enough to know she's your friend. You've been seen with her all over London. Someone who doesn't know her very well might even think she's your girlfriend and you're the father of her baby. Even if they think she's just your friend, she is on the CPS payroll, so you might be a little freer with her about the facts of this case."

Finn sighed. "This is leading us nowhere. They are targeting people in my vicinity. That's clear now."

"There's another thing. Remember the license plate on that BMW that picked up our harasser?"

"Vaguely," Finn admitted.

"The car that crashed into Ayse's Mini Cooper is an old model Vauxhall Vectra, but the plate contains the letters and numbers of the one we saw. Vehicle registration for that plate isn't a Vauxhall, though."

"Or a BMW, I presume?"

"Nope."

"We need to dig deeper, but I can't introduce this into the case against Farraday."

"Why not?"

"The prosecution's stance has been turned over to the defense. All we can prosecute him for is misconduct in public office."

"Will he get prison time for that?"

"Most likely. This is a high profile crime."

"Then we have time to build another case against him? We can start looking into the girlfriend?"

Finn grabbed Tommy's arm. "Be careful, Tommy. He knows we're onto him. He's like a caged animal right now, and he's free to roam the streets with no job to go to. Be on the lookout for him."

"Stevie and I will start in the morning. Right now I'm taking advantage of the fact the two of us will be sharing living space."

FINN

HE COULDN'T stop staring at Tommy, sleeping next to him.

They'd spent the evening in front of the TV, keeping Ayse company, but Ayse had gone to bed after 9:00 p.m., and they'd settled into their guest room as well.

Now Tommy was sound asleep, and Flynn was lying awake worrying. Part of him wanted to protect Tommy, but he knew that would only drive Tommy away. Part and parcel of being in love with a police detective was the fact he couldn't wrap him in cotton wool. Like Tommy had made it clear to him before, they got into dire situations sometimes, and they were well equipped to deal with most of them. Only what if sleeping with him made Tommy a target for someone out to hurt a Crown Prosecutor?

Finn turned away from Tommy and tried to find a comfortable enough position to fall asleep.

"Ayse's fine. Go to sleep, Finn," Tommy murmured.

Finn smiled, and Tommy draped an arm over Finn's chest. Finn raised his arm to accommodate him, and Tommy snuggled even closer.

"You're going to have to get some sleep, love," Tommy mumbled, this time close to Finn's ear.

"I know. But you know me. Insomniac first class."

Tommy kissed him on the neck. "Although I could do with some uninterrupted sleep, I'm glad we're sleeping together again."

"So am I."

They changed position again, and this time the warmth of Tommy's chest against his back lulled Finn to sleep. He could so get used to this.

TOMMY

ALMOST WITHOUT talking about it, Tommy and Stevie had agreed to continue investigating Frank Farraday and the reason he was falsifying records and creating evidence at every possible free moment they had in between assignments from DSI Stanton. Keeping it a secret from Stanton wasn't easy, though.

One of the suspects on Tommy's to-do list was a young woman who had reported her sister being raped but who had withdrawn her testimony. The sister had been a reluctant witness and had never wanted to give any details about the alleged rape to the Met, but she had told her sister about it, and the sister had gone to the police.

"Miss Shaw," Tommy started as soon as she opened the door. "We're DS Fielding and DS Drummond of the Metropolitan Police. We're doing follow-up on some cases and would like to talk to you about the investigation into your sister's rape."

"I 'ave nothing further to say about that," she replied in a nasal voice with a distinct Northern accent. Tommy immediately recognized the voice from the tapes they'd listened to at the Central Archive. A voice Finn had recognized but had been unable to place. Tommy knew he had to earn her trust so she would come to the station with them and have her voice recorded along with her identification, like standard procedure required.

"The detective who did the investigation is under review, ma'am," Tommy continued, keeping his voice soft and low. "We've been asked to talk to some of his earlier contacts to ask them how he went about his business."

"You mean Frank Farraday?" she asked, changing her demeanor from reserved to defiant.

"Yes, we do," Stevie replied. "If you remember him that well, his investigation wasn't as cursory as his records portray. Would you talk to us about him?"

She looked at Tommy, then back at Stevie. "I'll talk to you," she told Stevie. She let them into the house, directing Tommy to the sitting room and Stevie into the kitchen. They spoke in murmurs, so Tommy couldn't hear what was being said. It wasn't that he didn't trust Stevie. They simply hadn't talked about a course of action, and Stevie didn't know how important this witness was because she hadn't heard the two counterfeit tapes.

Tommy sat down on the sofa and texted Stevie in the hope she'd look at her phone when it beeped. When he still hadn't heard anything back fifteen minutes later, he contemplated barging in on the two women. He had paced a groove into the lime green carpet by the time Stevie entered the sitting room.

"I convinced her to come to the station with us for a statement. Call Finn. I think we hit the mother lode."

FINN ARRIVED just as Stevie was preparing everything in the interrogation room and trying to make Ronnie Shaw feel relaxed enough to talk. Tommy could listen to their casual conversation through the speaker as he kept himself behind the one-way glass.

"So who is this?" Finn asked.

"Veronica Shaw, aka Ronnie Shaw. About a year ago she reported a rape to the police. Farraday was put on the case, but it never went anywhere because Ronnie claimed her sister was the victim, but the sister refused to cooperate. Ronnie was interrogated, or so it says in the file, but equipment failure was stated as the reason why there was no recording. We rang her doorbell, and as soon as she replied to one of our questions I recognized her voice. I think she's the nasal-sounding Northern girl on two of the counterfeit tapes."

"So why aren't you in there with them?"

Tommy cocked his head. "She only wanted to talk to Stevie. It's her prerogative."

"But according to your partner our Ronnie has quite a story to tell?"

"Apparently. I was left in the dark, hence the reason I'm here behind the glass. I want her to repeat what she told Stevie, but somehow she doesn't trust me enough to do it with me in the room."

"She's clearly a poor judge of character," Finn said with a smile. He put his hand on the small of Tommy's back, and Tommy pushed against it just a little. Finn pulled away when the door behind them opened.

"Who did you bring in?" Stanton asked.

Given he'd kept this from his DSI, Tommy thought it was best to stay as close to the truth as he could. "Ms. Shaw was a witness to a rape."

"And why isn't Sex Crimes taking this?"

Tommy knew he had to go for broke. "They did. Frank Farraday did."

"I should have known it would be something like that. Mr. DeHavilland, don't keep my detectives from their work too long. Drummond, I want to listen to that interrogation tape when you're done." He grabbed the door handle and then walked back to Tommy. "Why aren't you in there with them?"

"The witness expressed a desire to speak to DS Fielding only, sir."

Stanton sighed. "Very well." He walked out and let the door close by itself. Tommy was glad for silencer hinges, but he coughed away his relief at Stanton's fast exit anyway. Luckily Finn didn't catch the unease of their interaction. He didn't trust Stanton and Finn in a room together. "So is Ayse all right at home?" Tommy asked as soon as he had his heart rate under control again.

"Her doctor gave her the all clear this morning and she went straight back to work," Finn replied. "It was a good thing I had to leave as well. I could call a cab and get both of us to the office, or she would have walked."

"She's worse than you are."

"I recall you being just as eager after your mugging, Tommy."

"Let's, ehm, listen to what she has to say," Tommy suggested to change the subject back to the two women behind the glass. "Stevie was serious when she told me this was important."

"Could you tell me about the first time you met Frank Farraday?"

"It was after I filed the report about me sister's rape."

"He came to talk to you at your home?"

"Yes."

"Did he bring you to the police station?"

Ronnie nodded.

"Did he record your conversation?"

"Yes."

"Was there anything unusual about the taping?"

"He stopped and started a few times. And he asked strange questions."

"Strange how?"

"He asked random questions. Things that were beside the point. When I asked him why he was asking those questions, he stopped the tape."

"You're right. It's her. The woman in the tapes," Finn confirmed.

"What was his off the record reply?"

"That they were control questions, like with a lie detector test."

"Is that the term he used? Lie detector test?"

"Good question," Tommy told Finn. "Farraday would call it a polygraph, unless he was trying to appease the witness. The term lie detector test is used in American crime series, though."

"The BBC uses it too," Finn added. "But those tests don't hold up in criminal court. Farraday should know that."

Tommy looked at Finn. "I don't think that's the point, Finn. I think he was trying to get certain answers from her so he could edit her replies and make it look like someone else's tape."

"I think this warrants an investigation by forensics."

"In that case I hope your court appearance isn't any time soon, because they take their time."

Finn bit his lip. "Her testimony would probably be enough."

"Is that the last time you saw him, Ronnie?"

"No. Two days later he was back at my house. Told me he had a few things to go over with me. So I invited him in."

"Did he tape your conversation?"

"Oh, no. He...."

"Just tell me again what you told me in your kitchen."

Ronnie shook her head.

"Interrogation of Veronica Shaw halted 4:32 p.m. DS Fielding present."

Stevie stopped the tape. *"Farraday no longer works for the Met. Which means he no longer has access to any of this information."*

"He said he had important people in his pocket. People high up."

"Did he tell you who?"

"No."

"Finn DeHavilland, are you there?"

Finn pushed the button on the intercom. "Yes, I am."

"I'd like to use a different tape for the rest of the interrogation. Can you use the first tape for the running investigation?"

"Yes."

"And you'll need the second tape for the second court case."

"We can just not use the last part until we need it, Stevie," Finn said.

Tommy pressed the intercom nob as soon as Finn let go of it. *"We'll need to hand this tape over to Stanton. If we use a different tape, we can keep that one between us."*

Tommy looked at Finn, and Finn nodded. "Agreed."

"Who else is listening to this?" Ronnie asked.

"Senior Crown Prosecutor Finn DeHavilland. He's the first voice you heard. He's also the man prosecuting DI Farraday. And DS Drummond, who was with me at your house."

"Nobody else?"

"Is there anyone else in there with you two?"

"No," Finn replied.

"Can I trust them?"

"Yes, you can."

"I'll repeat what I told you at the house, but not on tape."

Stevie looked in the direction of the mirror.

"Do it," Finn answered.

"Okay, tell me again."

Ronnie looked at the mirror and then back at Stevie. *"He tried to seduce me. I told him I wasn't interested. He told me that if I wanted to help my sister I had to do what he asked."*

"What did he ask of you, Ronnie?"

"He told me not to move and not to speak. I couldn't make a sound. And then he raped me."

"Did he tie you up or threaten you?"

"He held something sharp against my neck. After he was gone I thought it could have been a pen or something, but at the time I was convinced it was a knife. He kept it there until he was done. And then

he told me that I was better than my sister. He said she couldn't do what he asked and he almost had to kill her. He also said that if I ever told anyone, he'd dispose of my sister. I believed him."

"Oh, fuck," Finn said. "She needs to commit this to tape."

"I think we'll need to prove to her that we can get him behind bars first."

Chapter Twenty-Six

FINN

DESPITE HAVING an admission from a woman that Farraday had raped her and her sister, Finn had to prosecute the case he'd set in motion months earlier. He was fairly certain he could get Farraday put in prison for at least a year, and that would give them the time to flesh out the rape charges, but it meant he had to focus on this case and this case alone.

As he donned his robes and collar and put on his wig, he held on to the fact he was allowed to go back to court and actually do more than administration. Nevertheless it was going to be a slow, tedious few days of asking witness after witness the same questions.

Finn straightened his back, lifted his chin, and stretched his jaw. He was going to do what he did best and do it with the utmost restraint and dignity. As far as he was concerned the meltdown was never going to happen again, not even if a witness changed their testimony while facing Frank Farraday.

BY THE second afternoon of the trial, Finn was having to redress his focus with every different witness, because they all started melting into each other.

Finn turned toward the dock where Frank was sitting. "Did you ever speak to this man?"

"First time I saw him was sitting there," the witness replied.

"Who took your statement on the matter?"

"Nobody. A copper called and said he'd come 'round, but he never did."

Finn lifted a folder for the court to see. "Let the record show in exhibit fifty-nine two there is a statement in the records attributed to this witness." He gave the opened folder to the usher and waited for him to give it to the witness. He then addressed the woman on the stand. "Can you testify that this is not your statement?"

She briefly looked at the papers. "I told you, I didn't give a statement."

"Please turn to the last page," he instructed. "And this is not your signature?"

"It's my name but not my handwriting."

"Thank you." Finn turned to the judge. "I have no further questions for this witness."

Finn sat down. As the witness left the stand and another witness was called, he took the next folder from his papers and reacquainted himself with yet another person coming in to augment the case and show the jury the extent of the defendant's disdain for the public he was supposed to protect. When he was sure he knew what questions to ask, he looked behind him at the public gallery in the hope of seeing a familiar face. It was a little early for Tommy to show up, but he could hope.

Then his breath caught in his throat. It couldn't be.

His mind was saying the elderly man sitting hunched over must have died of old age by now, somewhere in his tropical paradise filled with enticing young boys, but his heart knew it was him all right. "Uncle" Malcolm. Finn looked away and closed his eyes. With some difficulty he banned the nightmarish thoughts and tried to recall Tommy's voice telling him he couldn't hurt him anymore. His mind knew, of course. He was an adult now. Taller and stronger than the frail man sitting on the bench.

Finn veered up. "My Lord, before the next witness arrives, could I request you to suspend work for today?"

The judge looked at his watch and most likely saw what Finn knew, that they had thirty minutes at most left of the court day. "Your reason for this, Mr. DeHavilland?"

Finn wanted to run home and talk to Tommy for some courage, but then a thought niggled at the back of his mind. "On second thought, let's finish the two witnesses that were called."

"Very well."

The two witnesses spoke very much of the same. One had talked to the defendant but not about the case her statement was attributed to, and the other had never met the defendant. The questioning was over with ten minutes to spare, and the judge called it a day.

Finn texted Tommy from the robing room. "Are you home yet?"

"On my way. You done?"

"Yes. Just getting ready to leave the Old Bailey."

"Okay, bring your robe home."

Finn smiled at Tommy's naughty-sounding message, but he couldn't indulge in it. He called him instead. "I have something serious to talk to you about. Your place or mine?"

"Come on over."

"Don't start dinner yet."

"Okay," Tommy replied calmly. "See you in about half an hour, then?"

"Yes, that'll be about right."

FINN BURST into the flat and walked resolutely to the kitchen, where he thought he'd find Tommy. He wasn't there. He returned to the hallway to see Tommy come out of the bathroom, where he grabbed him and held him tight. Tommy didn't resist and even hugged him back after the first surprise.

"Lovely to see you too." Tommy smiled when Finn stopped squeezing the air out of his lungs. Finn's face must have shown his agony, because Tommy's voice changed to concerned. "What happened?"

Finn shook his head and grabbed Tommy's hand to drag him into the sitting room, where he gestured him to sit. Finn remained standing.

"Could this all be a setup, Tom?"

"As in conspiracy? Tell me what happened."

Finn paced. "I was doing fairly routine questioning of witnesses to show the jury the extent of the fraud. I could see them sitting there, some looking bored, some looking angry. I knew they were on the Crown's side. I was contemplating not even calling our star witness."

"Ronnie Shaw."

"Yes." Finn took a deep breath. "And then I looked at the public gallery, and there he was."

Tommy raised his eyebrows.

"Uncle Malcolm."

"Oh God." Tommy veered up from his seat.

"There is only one reason that man could have been brought there."

Tommy nodded.

"Someone thought bringing him in would make me lose it. The judge would have to declare a mistrial."

"Only if you lost it again. Tell me you didn't?" Tommy stood up.

Finn inhaled deeply. "I didn't. I asked the judge to halt proceedings for the day, but then the wickedness behind it all revealed itself to me, and I realized that I had to keep going as if I'd never seen him."

Tommy smiled. "I'm proud of you."

Finn grabbed him into a hug again. "I kept thinking of you telling me he couldn't hurt me anymore. The fact is he still could."

Tommy pulled out of the embrace and held Finn at arm's distance. "No, he can't. You're older and stronger, and you know who you are now. And you have me." That last sentence was spoken so soft, Finn almost didn't hear it.

"I know."

"So what's all this about a setup?"

"The only reason Malcolm would have been there is to make me lose it. And all the pieces of the puzzle fell into place. All through this investigation, we've been boycotted. They knew that if this went to trial, the evidence would be overwhelming. So they tried very hard to make sure it wouldn't get that far. A high profile case would go to the Senior Prosecutor. Me. So they set me up to show I was unstable, then let me get on with my work so I'd be declared fit to take the case if it ever went to court."

"So if they couldn't stop it going before a judge, they had ammunition to declare a mistrial, but only if the senior was a lunatic," Tommy added.

"Thank you," Finn said, not without amusement.

"I didn't say you were. A lunatic." Tommy smiled. "But that's going a bit far, isn't it?" He sat back down, and Finn joined him.

"The attack on you."

"Yes," Tommy said hesitantly.

"It was dark. You were wearing my coat."

"And your cap, 'cause it was raining."

"I'm sure it was me they thought they were attacking."

"I suppose it's possible," Tommy reluctantly agreed. "But what could have been the purpose? I've had some time to think about this. I'm sure that if you were incapacitated, they would have found someone else to take the Crown's position. Carlton could have taken your place!"

"It would have bought them time. Maybe that's all they needed."
Finn bothered his upper lip with his finger. "The arson attack."

"My flat."

"Yes. What if that was the deterrent for you? What if they wanted
you to stop investigating?"

Tommy frowned. "If they were watching the flat they would have
seen me go in but not leave, because I left by the back door. It's a
shortcut to where I'd parked my car. The mugging." Tommy shook his
head at Finn.

"Mugging?"

"Stevie and Natalie. She took her to a fancy restaurant, and they
were mugged. She filed a report, but nobody ever found anything. They
were threatened by a guy with a knife. Stevie gave him her purse, and
he took out her wallet and saw the pictures of her kids. He then went on
to tell her he knew where to find her children and would do something
to them if she reported this. After he ran away, she followed and found
her purse, with all her money and her cards still inside, at the end of the
road. Right there on the pavement."

"Why didn't she tell me?"

Tommy shrugged. "It was just something that happened. At the
time we didn't think it was relevant. Stevie felt it was just a random
mugging, and she was joking about how stupid the guy was for
dropping the purse."

"Now it seems all he intended to do was intimidate Stevie."

"And he wasn't very good at that either. We get this occasionally.
You go to a suspect's house. He feels trapped and threatens to come
find you when he gets out. I guess you could say we're used to it."

Finn put his hand on Tommy's knee. "I'm usually not the favorite
person of the thugs we convict either."

"You think our near gay-bashing was a part of this too?"

"Almost had to be. It sounds almost as silly as Stevie's mugging.
But that's how we found the car. And the stolen license plate."

"Leaves you wondering why they stole your cap. I liked that cap,"
Tommy mused.

"It was a kid. Maybe he needed to prove himself by bringing
some evidence?"

"If Farraday is behind all this he's either not the sharpest tool in
the box or he has stupid accomplices. The mugging and the near

bashing were just… idiotic. Who would think those would stop us from prosecuting?"

"I'm still glad to have a copper in the house." Finn leaned against Tommy, and Tommy put his arm around Finn's shoulders.

"Technically I'm not in your house."

Finn turned around and gave Tommy a peck on the lips. "You're right. So maybe you should move in with me again."

"Are you ready for me?"

Finn smiled and returned to leaning against Tommy. "I don't know, but it seems silly to keep paying for two houses when we only just occupy one at a time anyway."

"So tell me about seeing Malcolm."

"Can we just have dinner? And better conversation? Something not work related?"

Tommy kissed Finn's hair. "Sure. It's just omelet tonight. We have yesterday's leftover veg, and it's a quick dinner."

"Sounds perfect."

TOMMY

HE REGISTERED Finn moving in the bed next to him but didn't open his eyes. Finn was a restless sleeper at best, but seeing Malcolm again had made him toss and turn to the point where Tommy wondered if he'd get any sleep if he didn't move to the spare room. Early during the night he'd decided that giving up one night's rest was a small sacrifice for showing Finn that he wasn't the sort to give up. He was going to stand by Finn no matter what happened.

Finn grunted and sat up. Tommy didn't need to open his eyes to know that. Finn's nightmares were increasing in frequency, but by now Tommy could handle them in his sleep.

"Breathe, Finn," he murmured, reaching out to touch the no doubt soaked back of Finn's pajama top. To his surprise, he encountered naked skin, so he opened his eyes. "You okay?"

Almost immediately he got an armful of Finn, and he pulled him closer. "Sssh, it's okay. I'm here."

"I know," Finn said in his low, slightly raspy voice. "Can I turn on the light?"

Tommy nodded, although what he really wanted to ask was for Finn to go back to sleep. When Finn flicked on the bedside lamp, Tommy had to fight the bright light.

"What's wrong?" As he adjusted to the light, the blurry pictures in front of his eyes became more clear, and he saw Finn was stark naked.

"Nothing's wrong."

As Finn sat up, Tommy couldn't help but feast his eyes. Although they'd been living together off and on for months, Finn was fiercely protective of his privacy, and Tommy had only seen Finn fully naked a few times when he'd caught him stepping in or out of the shower. He'd never been allowed to actually drink in the sight of the sinewy frame and the dusting of very fine hair all over Finn's pale, smooth skin.

"Well, you truly are a natural blond, aren't you?" Tommy joked.

Finn looked embarrassed. "Don't laugh."

"I'd never laugh at you." He put his hand on Finn's thigh. "Come here if you don't want me to drool all over you."

Finn lay down, snuggling into Tommy's arms as he often did at night.

"Why did you want the lights on if you didn't want me to look at you?"

Finn didn't answer. Instead he kissed Tommy, and Tommy simply enjoyed feeling Finn's naked skin against his chest.

"I want to see you," Finn said as he slowly moved down Tommy's body.

Tommy had a pretty good idea what Finn was aiming for as Finn pulled down the elastic of his boxer briefs. "Are you sure?"

Finn nodded. "Unless you don't want me to?"

Tommy smiled, a little befuddled about Finn's sudden action to up the ante. "Of course I want you to, but…." *My question is, are you ready for this?* He didn't voice his concerns, because he didn't get the time. Finn was kissing his stomach, right down to where his treasure trail fanned out into his pubic hair, and his cock was growing heavier by the second. He resolved to just let Finn have his way with him, not interrupting him or urging him on, but he couldn't stifle a moan when Finn enveloped his cock with his mouth. After so many months of doing little more than fumbling around and then wanking in the shower afterward, Tommy had to raise his arm over his eyes to steal himself away from the visual. The sensation and knowledge of what Finn was doing to him and knowing what a leap this was for Finn made it all the more powerful. Tommy knew that if he just let go, it would all be over in ten seconds flat. It didn't matter that Finn's inexperience showed. It mattered even less that Finn was trying too hard. The one idea still present in Tommy's mind was that he wanted it to last. Who knew when Finn would be up for this again?

"Finn, stop for a moment."

He didn't.

"Finn, please stop!"

Finn looked up at him. At the corner of his mouth was a glistening drop of saliva that he wiped away, seemingly unconsciously, with his thumb.

What made Tommy pull him closer was the look in his eyes, though. "I'm not angry with you. We were rushing it. I want us to take our time."

This seemed to settle Finn, and his confidence returned. "I wanted to do this for you."

"I don't want you to do anything just for me, Finn."

"I liked it too." Finn looked almost guilty, but his self-assuredness didn't vanish.

"Will you let me do it to you as well this time?"

"What do you mean, this time? I've never done this. To anyone."

"I know, but I remember how you wouldn't let me do anything to you."

"I'll let you now."

Tommy didn't want to question Finn's resolve. He felt a little apprehensive, though. After the last debacle where he'd had to call Ayse to let her verify Finn was okay, they'd done little more than kiss and cuddle. This seemed to be Finn's comfort zone. Now Finn was taking a giant leap outside of that. "Just take it slow. Take your time."

Finn nodded as he pulled Tommy's boxer briefs down again. His confidence wasn't quite as strong as before Tommy had interrupted him, but he went straight for his prize anyway. Tommy, not used to being quite this passive, had to remind himself of the need to remain as innocuous as possible to Finn, which meant he couldn't lead him and couldn't really touch him unless he asked. Fortunately, the heat had died down some, and keeping an eye on Finn to look for signs that he was uncomfortable prevented him from coming as soon as he felt Finn's mouth on him. It did mean this time he couldn't look away from what Finn was doing, and soon enough Finn's ministrations—and the visual stimulation—had Tommy teetering on the edge.

"Close, Finn. You're making me...."

It took just one unashamed look from Finn to send him crashing over the precipice. Finn seemed fascinated by what he'd caused, and just as Tommy was scraping his mind together again enough to ask Finn whether he wanted him to do the same to him, Finn raised himself above him and came with his cock in his own hand, and almost no sound, adding to the milky white droplets already fanned out over Tommy's stomach.

Tommy looked up at him, silently praying that all would be well and Finn wouldn't be overcome by disgust or regret, but he seemed calm and surprisingly in control as he moved to get out of bed.

"Stay, Finn." Tommy grabbed Finn's arm and almost immediately let him go when he saw Finn looking at it.

"You're all sticky. We can't sleep like that."

"Then let me."

Finn didn't move away from the bed as Tommy got up. Seeing Finn so relaxed brought on the urge to kiss him. When Tommy moved closer and Finn didn't back away, he softly placed his lips on Finn's. Tommy couldn't find the right words to express how he felt and hoped his kiss said enough.

When he walked to the bathroom, Finn followed, and they cleaned up without saying a word.

Tommy wasn't surprised that Finn put on his pajamas again before crawling back into bed. "You were right," Finn said as he snuggled closer to Tommy.

"Right about what?"

"That I am safe now. That he couldn't hurt me anymore."

"Oh, yes. Well, you *are* safe." *Baby steps*, Tommy reminded himself since the lovemaking had still been pretty one-sided, but at least he didn't have to run to the bathroom to finish himself off this time. And Finn seemed happy, which in turn made Tommy happy.

"Seeing him again made me remember your words, and then on my way home I thought I had to test it. At first I wanted to do what I'd done before, touch you while you were asleep, but then I thought I'd still be sneaking around. I wanted it to be out in the open."

"You didn't seem scared this time."

"Like you said, he couldn't hurt me anymore. What we do *is* different."

Tommy felt himself desperately wanting to sleep. "I know you probably want to talk about this, but we both have work in the morning." He looked at the alarm clock. "And the morning is about two hours away."

"We should try to sleep."

"Think you can?"

"Yes. I think I can now."

Finn was asleep before Tommy was, which was also a first. Tommy simply relaxed against Finn's warm skin, knowing everything would be okay.

Chapter Twenty-Seven

FINN

AFTER A long and tedious week—the only bright point being the text message announcing that Ayse had given birth to a perfect baby girl—sentencing was a godsend. As was expected by the overwhelming evidence, Frank Farraday was told he'd spend the next twenty-six months in HMP Wandsworth. What started out as a Friday without surprises didn't end that way, though.

After Farraday was led away, it was still early enough in the day for Finn to return to his office. He was in the middle of packing away his evidence with the help of Natalie when a shrill woman's voice could be clearly heard through the office.

"Well, I'm glad it's the middle of the day and most people are out of the office for Friday lunch," Natalie said with an uncomfortable smile.

"You said he wouldn't need to do time! You promised."

"Is that coming from Carlton's office?" Finn asked, trying not to look too amused. The blinds on his own office had been opened again, so he didn't need to stick his head out of it to look into Carlton's. The woman doing the shouting was the same woman he'd seen in Carlton's office earlier. Because Carlton's office door was closed Finn couldn't hear what Carlton was saying, but he instantly knew this was a delicate situation.

"Nat, can you go around the office to make sure there's nobody within earshot, please? If anyone is still here, make up some excuse. It's Friday. The sun is shining. Everyone needs some fresh air. You'll think of something."

"Yes, sir."

Natalie walked outside, and Finn moved a little closer to Carlton's office in the hope he could catch Carlton's eye to warn him he could be heard. Bill Carlton was solely focused on the woman, though. She looked to be about Carlton's age, with neatly coiffed hair and a floral dress underneath a tan mac.

"He doesn't belong in prison, Bill. You said so yourself!"

She was still shouting and obviously well acquainted with him, since they were on a first-name basis.

"Ella, calm down. The whole office can hear us."

"I don't care!"

"Well, I do," Carlton replied in his usual calm manner.

Finn could see from his flushed complexion he was fighting to keep his composure.

"It is nobody's business but our own. Let's get out of here and to a more private location."

He tried to grab her arm, but she resisted. "Frank is your son! You promised you'd look out for him!"

Finn's mind was whirring. Bill didn't have a son. He had three daughters, all grown up, one of them a defense barrister with her eye on a position at the CPS. *Oh my!* Frank as in Farraday? Was Bill Frank's father?

"I tried, Ella, but Frank became too careless. There was nothing I could do. The evidence was simply too overwhelming."

"You never cared for him. Or me for that matter."

"I cared for him enough to break the law for him. I cared enough to almost sacrifice the best Crown Prosecutor the CPS has. This could not just cause me to lose my job, but I might well end up in prison, right alongside him."

Finn had heard enough. He took a step back into his office and partially closed one of the blinds so Carlton wouldn't immediately notice his presence. He heard a door open and saw "Ella" leave, pacing to the exit with a determined step. Carlton remained inside, pouring himself a substantial scotch.

Finn grabbed his mobile phone and called Tommy.

"Drummond."

"There's been a development. See me in the secret garden?"

"I'm about ten minutes away."

Finn snuck out of the office without Carlton noticing.

"YOU SOUNDED worried," Tommy said as he walked toward the bench Finn was standing next to. He silently held out a wrapped sandwich.

Finn swatted it away. "You could say that."

"Congrats on the verdict, by the way. You did your homework, and it paid off. So where's the fire?"

Finn looked around to see if anyone was within earshot. Despite the radiant weather, the secluded garden was deserted. "Carlton is part of the conspiracy." He gave Tommy a quick rundown of the conversation he'd overheard.

Tommy took a huge bite out of his club sandwich. "Not surprising." He chewed and swallowed.

Finn raised his eyebrows.

"Well, to think up this whole scheme to discredit you, someone on the inside must have been in on it. You sure you don't want any of this?"

"I can't eat right now," Finn replied. "But I never expected Carlton. He's my boss. I've looked up to him for… decades. He got me interested in working for the CPS. He was my mentor, my prime example."

Tommy cocked his head. "He's a highly functioning alcoholic who hasn't taken on a case in years. On the other hand, he's been giving you child abuse cases for a long time. Doesn't he understand how these affect you?"

Finn shook his head. "I never told him about Malcolm. There was never any need."

"Well, if you ask me, he knew somehow."

"Maybe I was just good at my job, Tommy." Finn closed his eyes right after he spoke Tommy's name, because he knew how bitter he'd sounded.

Tommy grabbed his hand. "Of course you're good at your job. But these cases gnaw at you after a while. I worked child abuse before serious crimes, remember. I couldn't hack it. Not all day every day. We still get enough of those cases as it is. And every time I'm grateful it's not Kasey."

"Maybe Carlton reckoned since I didn't have a family, it would be easier for me."

"It would only be easier for you if you didn't have a heart, Finn. Stop making excuses for him. At the very least he knew what was going on and didn't do anything about it. I think you should confront him and get a full confession out of him."

Tommy pulled Finn down to the bench, and Finn conceded.

"I overheard him telling Farraday's mother that he almost sacrificed his best prosecutor to keep Farraday out of prison."

"At least that's a partial confession about him being behind the attempt to discredit you, but what was Farraday's mother doing in Carlton's office?"

"Let's just say they have a shared interest. A son called Frank."

"Wow," Tommy uttered. "Carlton fathered a bastard?"

"Apparently."

"No wonder he went to such lengths to cover for him."

"He'll have to resign his post," Finn mused. "He's the bloody Chief Prosecutor. And I thought going after a corrupt police inspector was a high profile case."

"Let's let it sink in over the weekend," Tommy suggested. "With Farraday off the streets, he's not likely to do any further damage, is he?"

Finn shook his head and squeezed Tommy's hand, only then realizing they were sitting on the bench like an old married couple, hand in hand.

"We're visiting Ayse's little princess tomorrow," Tommy reminded him.

Finn smiled. "At least there's one thing to look forward to, then."

Tommy nudged Finn with his elbow. "You got a serial rapist off the streets today. I wouldn't exactly call that a downer."

"True, even if he's only convicted of an abuse of public trust."

"Like we agreed, it buys us time. And if we get Carlton out of the way, that's one less person who can work against us."

"I wonder who they'll find to fill his shoes?"

"You, of course."

Finn chuckled. "Carlton was the first Chief Prosecutor who rose through the ranks. It's not likely they'll make that mistake again."

"Let's sign out early and go buy Little Miss Jasmine a present."

Finn looked at Tommy sideways. "I have filing to do, but I'll pick you up at five."

"Spoilsport."

Finn was smiling as he said good-bye to Tommy. He didn't dare kiss him, but he squeezed his hand once more before he let go and walked away. Like Tommy liked to say, everything would work out for the best.

TOMMY

HE WAS just about to leave to meet Finn when Stevie walked up to his desk. "Look who's here."

"Hi, Kase. What's going on?"

"They're fighting again. Can I sleep at your place?"

He put his arm around his daughter. "I'm staying at Finn's tonight, but I'm sure he won't mind if you tag along."

Tommy took out his mobile and speed-dialed Finn. "You about ready to go shopping?" Out of the corner of his eye he saw Kasey's face light up. She was frantically nodding "Yes."

"There's three of us. Kasey's staying over."

He ended the call and slipped the phone back into his pocket. "Finn says 'fine,' but you need to come with us to visit Ayse's baby tomorrow. And we still need to buy her a present."

"This is the best visit ever."

THE NEXT morning they walked up to Ayse and Charlie's house with two presents. Kasey wanted to give Jasmine a cuddly teddy bear, and Tommy bowed to Finn's sense of usefulness, carrying a baby bath with a large pink bow around it.

At the door they were greeted by Charlie, who'd been given leave from duty to be there for the birth of his daughter. Once inside, Ayse walked toward them carrying her little princess, and she looked absolutely exhausted.

Finn kissed Ayse on the cheek. "We won't be here long. I promise. You look like you need your rest." He caressed Jasmine's pitch-black hair with his finger. "You did a good job. She's gorgeous, Dr. Kartal."

"Thank you. And yes, more sleep would be nice, but it's not like I wasn't prepared for this."

"Nobody is prepared for the sleepless nights, Ayse," Tommy interrupted. "But that too ends, and soon she'll be smiling at you, and then she has you wrapped around her little finger."

"Looks like your princess is here too," Ayse said with a wink as they watched Kasey help Charlie unwrap the presents.

Tommy smiled. "She'd never forgive me if we visited a baby without her."

"And gone is the sulking teenager," Ayse added. "She's always welcome to come along and admire this little one."

"I thought so."

"Speaking of which, Tommy, can I hand her over to you for a moment?"

She didn't wait for an answer, and Tommy was surprised how easily he fell back into supporting a newborn infant.

"Finn needs to talk to me for a moment about his boss." She whispered that last word. "You can let Kasey hold her, but supervise her, okay?"

FINN

THEY MOVED to the kitchen, out of earshot of anyone not involved in the case.

"So shoot. Tell me what's going on with Carlton."

Finn inhaled deeply to gather his thoughts.

"I overheard Carlton dealing with a screaming woman who is apparently Frank Farraday's mother. She accused Bill Carlton of being Farraday's father, and this clearly wasn't news to him."

"Christ, Finn."

"That makes it very likely that Carlton is Farraday's inside man high up."

"He can't have done this alone, Finn."

"No, but he did lead me on some of the cases that were dismissed. I recall a few that I would have wanted to take to court, and he overruled me."

"You and your amazing memory."

"I spent most of this morning at the office going over my notes. Tommy is barely speaking to me."

She laughed out loud. "You're at that stage of your relationship, then?" She punched him in the chest. "Congratulations."

"I couldn't let it go, Ayse. I need to build a case against my own boss. I can't tell you how low on my favorite to-do list that is."

"You always do what is right, Finn. You'll be able to do this as well. In fact you're probably the right man for it." She gave him her most compassionate look. "Don't forget you kept him outside of this investigation, and now you know the reason."

"It was gut instinct."

"And that has come in handy ever since you were reading law at Oxford, right?"

Finn nodded, smiling at how she could always make him feel better. In that respect Tommy had pretty much the same effect on him. He looked in the direction of the sitting room and saw Tommy getting up from his crouched position. He looked worried as he walked into the kitchen.

"I just got a call from the warden at Wandsworth. Farraday was beaten up and taken to hospital. He escaped his guards. He's out."

"Veronica Shaw," Finn said, knowing Tommy was thinking the same thing. "We need to warn her."

Chapter Twenty-Eight

TOMMY

"YOU SHOULD call for backup," Finn suggested to Tommy as they left Ayse's house through the back gate where Tommy had parked his car.

Tommy shook his head. "Ronnie's not in any documented danger, since you didn't use her to convict Farraday. But we know he's smart enough to realize we connected the dots and she was a part of our investigation. And Stevie's in Brighton with Natalie. We just have to ask Ronnie to get to safety until we find Farraday and bring him back to prison."

"I hope you're not going to do that on your own too?"

Tommy could hear the anxiety in Finn's voice. He had to admit that he was a little scared as well, but he wasn't going to show it to Finn, because he didn't want to do this alone. He'd have rather had Stevie along, since she'd formed a connection with Ronnie, but they didn't have the time to wait for Stevie to return from Brighton.

"For all we know Farraday made a beeline for Ronnie's house to threaten her as soon as he got out. We owe it to her to protect her."

"I know," Finn whispered.

When they arrived at the rundown house that was Ronnie's home, all seemed quiet. A few youths were hanging around the corner, but there was a light on in the kitchen, and they could see Ronnie doing dishes.

Tommy rang the doorbell, and a few moments later, Ronnie opened the door just a little. When she recognized Tommy, she opened the door the rest of the way.

"What's wrong?"

Tommy looked at Finn before answering. "Do you have family up north you can stay with for a while? Someone Frank Farraday doesn't know about?"

"I have an aunt in Edinburgh. I suppose…. What's this about?"

"Farraday escaped from custody. We're worried he might look you up."

"Fuck," she cursed before turning around, leaving the door open.

Tommy and Finn followed her inside, but only so far as the corridor. They watched her walk upstairs.

"She clearly knows how much danger she's in. We didn't even have to explain it to her."

"Farraday's a manipulator," Finn agreed. "She was afraid of him to the point where she let him rape her to protect her sister."

"And once he was behind bars, she felt safe again for the first time in a long time," Tommy added. "Now that safety is gone."

"Think he'll find her in Edinburgh?"

"On the one hand I'm tempted to tell the Met that we should check trains to the north, but if that information got in the wrong hands, we'd be giving away her location." Tommy looked up the stairs to see whether Ronnie was coming yet, but all he heard was stumbling and rummaging.

"They would be aware that he's a flight risk, right? That he'll try to get on a plane to a country without extradition treaties with the UK."

Tommy nodded. "First thing they do is alert airport security and border patrol, but I wouldn't put it past him to find some way to get on a ferry to Calais."

"Let's hope he stays closer to home," Finn said with a sigh.

"In that respect, don't go anywhere without an escort, Finn. You're his prime target."

Finn raised an eyebrow. "If I had to be protected against every criminal I put in prison, you'd need to lock me into Central Archive."

"Don't tempt me." Tommy winked at Finn as Veronica walked down the stairs with a large suitcase. By the time she'd reached the bottom step, he was all business again.

"We'll drive you to the train station. Will you be okay to go from there?"

She nodded, and Tommy hoped she would be.

IT FELT like an anticlimax, dropping Ronnie Shaw off at King's Cross Station for her train.

"So now what?" Finn asked.

"Let's pick up Kasey from Ayse's before she outstays her welcome, and go home, I suppose," Tommy replied. "There isn't much we can do."

"Except stay safe ourselves."

"Exactly." Tommy showed Finn the keys to his car. "You want to drive?"

"No, thanks. I… I don't drive."

How could he not know that? "You never drive, or you don't have a license?"

"I don't have a license." Finn didn't seem too proud of that fact. "Never really needed it, I suppose."

Tommy smiled and tried not to joke about it. He had to go and pick a rich guy, right?

"So what are we having for dinner?" Tommy asked on the way to Ayse's house.

"We could ask Kasey," Finn suggested.

"We'll end up having Burger King."

Finn pulled a disgusted face.

"Hence my question."

"Well, what does she like to eat?"

"Pretty much anything I cook," Tommy replied, not hiding his pride.

"I forgot her mum's not a great cook."

"Which tells you why she has a taste for greasy American burgers."

Finn laughed, and Tommy felt himself relax as well. The streets around Ayse's house were busy, and it took them a while to find a parking space. As they walked toward the house, Finn took Tommy's hand. Tommy gave Finn a curious look but didn't pull back his hand when Finn smiled at him. It felt strangely relaxing to walk this close.

Rounding the corner to the house, Tommy spotted that most of the downstairs lights were on. He saw Ayse standing in the sitting room, and her composure made warning bells go off in his head. She looked overly tense, stock still, with her arms next to her body and her hands clenched, looking straight ahead. He couldn't see her expression, but the whole picture made him squeeze Finn's hand.

"There's something wrong, Finn."

"Where's Charlie?"

"I can't see him. Only Ayse."

There was no sound coming from the house and very little from the quiet streets, but then Tommy heard it. The faint crying of an infant.

Finn heard it too, because he turned his head toward the sound.

While also trying to keep visual contact with Ayse inside, they walked toward some bushes by the gate that led to the small city garden in front of the house. As soon as they approached, Tommy heard, "Daddy?"

Tommy crouched down to find Kasey sitting in the dirt, holding a bundle. "She won't stop crying, and Ayse told me to keep her quiet."

"What happened inside?" Tommy asked, trying not to let his fear bleed over into Kasey.

"A man entered the house and knocked Charlie down. He was bleeding and didn't move. Ayse gave me the baby and told me to get as far away as possible, but I was worried about what the man would do to her. I'm sorry I didn't do what she asked, but Jasmine kept crying, and I didn't know what to do."

Tommy took the baby from Kasey and tried to soothe her. He then handed her to Finn so he could get his phone out and ask for backup. Finn looked helpless holding the baby. "Just hold her against your chest, and your heartbeat will calm her down," he instructed Finn. "I need to call this in."

FINN

TOMMY DIALED. "This is Detective Sergeant Thomas Drummond of Serious Crime Command. Please send armed backup to Kensington." He gave them the address of Ayse's house. "We have located Frank Farraday, who escaped from HMP Wandsworth this afternoon. He is holding two people hostage at this address."

When Tommy closed the call, he looked at Finn.

"Are they coming?"

"No, they're letting us settle this ourselves." He sighed. "Of course they're coming. But I'm going in. I need to know Ayse's okay. And to check up on Charlie. I should have called an ambulance as well, just in case."

Finn's heart rate reached an all-time high, and it had nothing to do with holding a newborn and everything with Tommy getting himself in harm's way. "For fuck's sake, don't go in there, Tom."

"No, don't go, Daddy."

Finn moved close to Kasey, forming a united front. Despite his worry for Ayse, he hoped it would make Tommy see they were more important than what was going on inside. Finn knew it was a futile attempt, but he needed to try anyway.

"Walk to the corner. Direct the police coming in," Tommy instructed.

Finn shook his head. "This place isn't hard to find."

"Finn, go. I need you to keep Jasmine and Kasey safe for me."

"And what about you?"

"I'll be fine. I'm not going to do anything heroic."

"So stay out here, then."

"I can't, Finn. If he hurts Ayse, I'll never forgive myself."

Finn had one last chance. "Wait for the Specialist Firearms Command to arrive, Tommy. If you get shot, *I'll* never forgive myself."

"You'll know you saved the kids," Tommy said before turning around and making his way around the back of the house.

Chapter Twenty-Nine

TOMMY

OF COURSE he knew it made sense for him to wait, but he had to be sure Ayse and Charlie were okay. It wasn't like he was going to throw himself in front of Farraday to prevent him from hurting Ayse. In fact, for all he knew, Farraday was unarmed. Just like him, Farraday didn't carry a gun for work.

The house was quiet, and he managed to find his way inside through the back door they'd used to leave about an hour earlier. He knew he had to tread carefully. He didn't want Farraday to be aware of his presence because he didn't want to provoke him. At the same time, he wanted to get Ayse and Charlie out of harm's way. If he could do that, he'd let the firearm team do the actual arrest.

The house didn't cooperate, though. It was an old house—nicely refurbished but still creaky and noisy—and the fact you could hear a pin drop when nobody moved around didn't make his search any easier. After moving halfway through the kitchen Tommy decided to take his shoes off and walk around in his socks. This helped somewhat, but he managed to hit all the squeaky floorboards between the back door and the landing. He stopped to listen for sounds but didn't hear any, so he stuck his head out.

At the other end of the landing, Ayse was sitting by a supine male form, most likely her husband, Charlie.

"Ayse," Tommy whispered. When she looked up he held his finger in front of his mouth. "Is Charlie okay?"

Tears welled up in her eyes. She shook her head.

Tommy swallowed, but he had to know. "Is he alive?"

"Yes, but he's bleeding," she whispered back.

"An ambulance is coming," he lied.

She gestured upstairs.

"Is he upstairs?"

She nodded.

"Is it Farraday?"

Another nod.

"Is he armed?"

"He has a gun," she mouthed.

That wasn't good.

"Everything will work out," Tommy told her, not entirely sure how truthful he was, but he knew from similar situations it helped to be positive. "Just stay calm."

"Jasmine?"

"Jasmine and Kasey are with Finn."

As some of the tension left her body, he knew that news was worth more to her than anything.

"She needs her mum, though." He gestured for her to move toward him, but she shook her head determinedly.

"I need to stay with Charlie."

"You need to get out. Now!" Tommy tried to keep his voice down but needed to persuade her to walk out with him now Farraday wasn't anywhere near.

Commotion outside the house made him look up. He could just see into the sitting room through the opened door and noticed the firearm squad getting into position. He gestured up, in the hope they would realize this meant the assailant was upstairs, but they didn't acknowledge him.

"Ayse. Backup is here. Keep your head down."

She nodded and then dived down, covering her husband with her own body. At that moment Tommy heard the pop of a bullet being fired. It came from upstairs. He pushed himself against the wall in an attempt to make himself as small as possible. Heavy boots came thundering down the stairs. Tommy didn't scare easily, but right now all he could think of was how he was going to explain it to Finn if anything happened to him. If he was in any position to do the explaining, of course. God, he hoped so.

The boots stopped, and Tommy had to curb his curiosity, knowing that if he looked past the doorjamb, he'd be discovered.

"How did you call them?" a rough voice spit out. "Show me the mobile."

"I don't have a mobile. You took it from me."

A thump and a gasp. Oh God, it came from Ayse. He looked quickly, then pressed himself against the wall again. Farraday was standing with his side to the kitchen. All he had to do was look to his right and he would see Tommy if Tommy dared to sneak another look. Although the moment had been brief, Tommy hadn't seen any blood on Ayse that hadn't been there before. He kicked himself for not being braver, but it wasn't just him anymore now. He had a family. Finn, and more and more Kasey too. If anything happened to him, Kasey would have nowhere to run to if it went sour with her mum. Finn probably wouldn't see Kasey either, and he knew they got along even better than he and Kasey did.

Tommy made a promise to himself. It he came out of this alive, he was going to commit himself to Finn and make it absolutely clear to him he was making a conscious choice. Despite all of Finn's hang-ups and fears and despite having told Finn he needed the sex in a relationship too, he was going to take that leap. They'd get there eventually. Right now he just wanted to hug the stuffing out of Finn and never let him go.

"So if it's not you, then it's that copper who thinks he can save the world."

There was a short silence, but Tommy knew Farraday was talking about him.

"He mislaid evidence once. He was exonerated. Does he think he's perfect now? I bet if I go through that poof's files even that Crown Prosecutor he's shagging will find something not quite picture perfect about what he writes down every day. Every copper cuts corners, only Drummond had his eye on me. If you see him, tell him I'm not going back to prison for something everyone does."

Tommy felt kind of sorry for Farraday. It wasn't good to feel sympathy for an assailant, especially not one with a severe lack of conscience and an even bigger absence of remorse. He was sure Ayse would find a classification for this guy without opening any of her fancy books.

Stretching his neck to see what the firearms squad was doing outside, Tommy heard the plank under his feet crack. He held his breath and closed his eyes just for a moment, praying Farraday hadn't heard him. When he opened them again he was staring into the face of a guy who looked like every street thug he'd ever grown up with.

"Can't resist getting into trouble, can ya?"

"I'm here for Dr. Kartal. Let her go and I'll call off the troops." Tommy sounded a lot calmer than he felt.

"As if you've got anything to say about what they do." He pressed his bulky frame against Tommy, pushing him against the wall.

"I called them, just like you deduced."

Farraday pushed himself against Tommy and then started grinding. Tommy felt the bile rise.

"What? I thought you liked this. Does your prosecutor know you like going to gay bars?"

"That's none of your business," Tommy said through locked teeth.

He poked Tommy just below the ribs, and Tommy jumped.

"That's right. I stabbed you from behind. So it was… on this side."

Tommy's stomach muscles contracted as the memory of the attack came back to life. The space around the puncture hole was still sensitive, and Farraday poking it repeatedly—even though Tommy knew it wasn't with an ice pick—brought back the pain. He needed to get away from him. He tried pushing, but Farraday was a big guy, taller than him and quite a bit broader too. He tried a knee jerk, but that didn't get very far. And with Farraday pinning him to the wall, ducking down wasn't on the books either.

"I like it when they struggle," Farraday said with smile as if he'd just confessed to Tommy to liking ice cream. "It's so much better when they fight me a little. That homeless guy just lay there and let it happen. That was a letdown. That law student was more fun. 'Can I ask you some questions about police procedure, sir?'" Farraday's tone was mocking and childish at the same time. "He didn't see it coming, and he fought hard. That was good. What was even better was that couple who wanted to be hurt. They asked for it in a contact ad. 'We both want to be tied up and made to suffer while we watch each other go through torture.' I gave them exactly what they wanted, and then some. Wore me out. I couldn't even get out of bed in the morning. And too bad you came back here so early. I would have loved to have seen your prosecutor's face as he walked into a crime scene belonging to two people he knew so well."

Tommy tried to commit everything Farraday was telling him to memory, but it wasn't easy because Farraday had his hand kneading Tommy's crotch, and Tommy's body was betraying him by responding.

"Come on, struggle just a little," he invited Tommy.

Tommy didn't. He couldn't because every movement from him upped the friction, and he didn't want to give Farraday the satisfaction of coming into his hand.

"No struggle. Damn, I hate guys who play hard to get."

Before Tommy could react, he felt Farraday's lips on his mouth. He tried not to let him in, but Farraday's tongue insisted. He tasted vile, and Tommy tried not to gag.

"Step back and drop your weapon!"

Farraday did no such thing and kept Tommy pinned to the wall while he looked in the direction of the voice. "Come on, guys, I wasn't done yet. And my only weapon was my hand." He smiled. "Was all this guy needed."

The firearms unit stood with their semiautomatics pointed at Farraday.

"DS Drummond? Are you okay?" the unit leader asked.

Tommy nodded. He felt in dire need of a shower, but that could wait.

Even now Farraday was mocking the men as he slowly released some of his hold on Tommy and turned to face them.

Tommy had only just caught a glimpse of something shiny hiking up Farraday's jacket when Farraday reached behind himself and pulled a handgun out. All the men shouted at once, but Farraday, frostily calm, took a step back and pointed the gun at Tommy's head.

"I already told the poof sergeant I wasn't going back to prison. But where I'm going, I'd love to take him with me."

Tommy felt nauseous and light-headed at the same time. He also felt like he might wet himself. This man was a psycho. Crazy. Cuckoo. He'd proven more than once that he didn't care what other people thought or cared about. He'd shoot him just for kicks, and the thought of someone having to explain to Finn that Tommy was dead came back to mind.

The unit commander's hand was still in the air, signaling they had to hold fire.

Tommy had to take a chance. He whipped his arm up, hoping he could get the gun away from his temple before Farraday pulled the trigger. He heard shots being fired but had no idea who they were aimed at or whether he'd got shot. He felt numb as Farraday slumped down next to him, a small puncture wound in his forehead and his eyes dead.

It was as if he was moving through goo. He turned a little to look into Ayse's shocked face.

Men in combat uniforms were asking him questions, but he couldn't understand them, let alone give them a coherent answer.

Ambulance men walked in and took care of Ayse and Charlie, and then one of the firearm unit men walked him outside. When the crisp air hit him, it brought back the use of his brain.

"Am I okay?"

The guy nodded. "He shot into the ceiling. You were quick."

"So were you."

"Just doing our job. Well, we weren't supposed to shoot him in the head, so there will be an inquiry, but that's not something you should think about, Sergeant. Go get checked out to make sure we didn't miss anything."

Still feeling a little dazed, he walked toward an ambulance with the back end open.

"Daddy!" Kasey cried out. Instinctively he pulled her into his arms, but it was the sight of Finn, sitting inside holding Jasmine, that made him smile.

"You look good there, Mister Crown Prosecutor."

For once Finn didn't protest. "She fell asleep as soon as I sat down. She smells lovely." He looked at Tommy while he kissed her head. "Is it over? Did they arrest him?"

"Yeah," Tommy said, not wanting to elaborate in front of Kasey. "Can we go home now?"

"As soon as I hand this one back to her mum."

Chapter Thirty

FINN

HE HAD no idea what had happened inside Ayse's house. Nobody was telling him anything, least of all Tommy. Ayse had seemed elated, almost too cheerful when she picked up Jasmine. She'd rattled on about Charlie being knocked unconscious by Farraday, but that he'd woken up and would be fine after a night of observation. After taking Jasmine from him, she'd put something warm and metallic in his hand. When he'd looked at it, he'd recognized it to be a digital voice recorder.

"I'll testify to taping it, if you need me," Ayse had said.

Finn hadn't had time to listen to it, but he was sure it would be interesting.

While he was sitting in the ambulance soothing Jasmine, Finn'd heard gunshots, but he'd been too preoccupied with the baby and keeping Kasey distracted. It hadn't been easy, but he'd learned a long time ago to keep his emotions in check when it was necessary. His heart hadn't started racing until he'd noticed the blood spatter on Tommy's clothes, but at that time he'd seen with his own eyes that Tommy was okay—at least physically—and then too, he'd been able to keep the emotional outburst to a minimum.

But now they were home, and Tommy still wasn't telling him anything.

Finn had let him drive his car home and hadn't pushed for Tommy to tell his story. He'd let him step into the shower and had taken Tommy's clothes to the washer. He'd stayed at Tommy's flat, hoping his presence would somehow help Tommy feel safe. But instead of talking to him about what had happened, Tommy ignored him in favor of Kasey, who was busy and overly talkative to the point where Finn wanted to raise his voice above the two of them to make them shut up. He couldn't, though. Kasey had also been through an ordeal, having been witness to a home invasion, and she came first, without question. Then to add to the whole drama, Tommy had received a frantic phone call from Kasey's mother, and he was left to soothe her as well. Once Tommy had dealt with his ex, Kasey told him her story, over and over again. Finn was a silent witness, trying to stay occupied with making sandwiches and checking on the laundry. He was happy she never questioned Tommy about what happened inside the house once she'd left it and understood that Tommy wouldn't volunteer the information as long as she was within earshot, but it left him without answers too.

He wasn't stupid. If Tommy wasn't telling him anything, that meant he'd been close to Farraday when he got shot. The blood that had been on his clothes was either Farraday's or Charlie's, if Tommy had checked on Ayse's husband somewhere during his investigation of their house. Although Finn silently hoped Farraday was the casualty, he also preferred it if Tommy wasn't anywhere near him when the firearms squad shot him.

"That smells good," Tommy said as he suddenly appeared next to Finn as Finn was making tea.

"I thought you could use a cup. Is Kasey asleep?"

Tommy sighed. "Finally. She wouldn't stop talking, but she wore herself out before she wore me out. But not by much."

Tommy's curls were damp again and flattened, and he smelled of shower gel and soap. His skin was a little flushed, and Finn could so understand if he'd scrubbed his skin after being covered by someone else's bodily fluids.

"You took another shower?"

Tommy nodded. "I still feel dirty."

What Finn wanted to do more than anything else was pull Tommy into his arms and hug the breath out of him, but when he tried to test the waters by putting his hand over Tommy's, Tommy pulled away. A little confused, Finn followed Tommy into the sitting room with their two cups of tea.

"We need to talk, Finn."

Finn sat down, putting the cups on the table, and swallowed away his nerves.

"You were right about asking me not to go in there, and I'm sorry I ignored your advice."

"That's okay. It's done now." When Tommy didn't immediately continue, Finn decided to take the plunge. "What happened in there, Tom?"

"He put a gun to my head."

The impact of Tommy's statement hit him hard, but at the same time the implications trickled into him slowly. He'd worried when he was waiting outside with the two kids, but he'd never imagined that Tommy would have come so close to being lost forever. Again. He closed his eyes and tried to do what he'd been doing all evening, and that was letting the emotions wash over him without being overwhelmed. It wasn't working. He was mad. Mad at Farraday for doing what he did and mad at Tommy for being so reckless and going inside the house before backup had arrived. At the same time he was immensely grateful for having Tommy here, alive and well.

When he opened his eyes, his vision was blurry. He was also shaking on the inside and hoped it wasn't too apparent to Tommy. He wanted to touch Tommy, but after being turned away earlier, he found he didn't have the nerve. He couldn't stay seated, though.

"Finn."

Finn knew tears were streaming down his face, so he couldn't turn around. He put his outstretched arms against the mantelpiece of the nonworking fireplace.

"I'm sorry, Finn."

"You could have died."

"I realize that now. At the time all I could think about was that Ayse was inside and we had no idea what he was capable of."

"I could have lost you, you stupid bugger."

The arms around his chest had never felt so good. He tried to turn around, but it took Tommy a few moments to realize Finn's plans before he loosened his hold. When Finn looked him in the eye, he saw Tommy was fighting tears as well.

"I'll never do that again."

Finn chuckled. "Yes, you will. You're a copper. Just don't tell me you're doing it, okay? Tell me afterwards and let me be mad at you then, but don't make me a part of it like today. I'm a paper pusher. I don't have your nerve."

Tommy squeezed him so hard Finn could hardly breathe, but he didn't have the heart to stop him. He simply didn't want to let go of his man.

TOMMY

TOMMY WOKE with a start. His hand automatically reached for his temple, but the blood he'd felt trickling down just a moment earlier wasn't there. It was all just a dream.

"You okay?" Finn asked in a voice that sounded like he was still asleep.

"Fine," Tommy whispered. "Go back to sleep."

Finn pulled Tommy's arm tighter around his chest to make him come closer before relinquishing his hold as he fell asleep.

Tommy kissed Finn's neck and realized he was sick and tired of his life being on hold. He wanted to move back into Finn's apartment, ace his inspector's exam, and get permanently assigned to the Central Criminal Court Trials Unit so he would no longer need excuses to work with Finn during the day. To hell with the fact their relationship was far from picture perfect. It wasn't like loving Finn was a conscious choice. If it had been, he'd have chosen a guy with a lot less baggage.

He was a little surprised when Finn turned around and lifted his arm over Tommy's head so he could pull him against his chest. He entwined his fingers into Tommy's curls and gently rubbed his scalp.

"I know I'm not the best example to tell you this, but talk to me, Tom. I let nightmares torment too many of my nights. They pretty much disappeared when I shared what was bothering me with a few people and I didn't need to carry the load all by my lonesome."

Tommy didn't want to bother Finn with his existentialist angst. "I love you."

"Boy, that must have been some nightmare," Finn quipped.

"Well, I do."

Finn smiled at him. It was dark in the room, but not dark enough to miss that. Besides, Finn was so lily white he almost glowed.

"When he had that gun against my head I heard a shot, and I could have sworn I felt blood trickling down the side of my head. I reached up to feel it, and there was nothing there, but for a split second, I thought those were going to be my last conscious thoughts before I bit the dust."

"And that's what you relived in your dream?"

Tommy looked up at Finn and saw the compassion in his eyes. He nodded.

"He's gone, Tommy. He can't hurt you anymore."

Tommy smiled. Finn was making him feel like a little boy who'd cried because there were monsters under his bed, but he knew Finn meant well. And he did feel safe with Finn here. He rested his head over Finn's heart.

"You still have some bad guys to catch."

Finn sighed, making Tommy's head bob up and down. "And for the one I'm dreading most I need to go talk to our Attorney General. I hate going over Carlton's head."

"It's not like you have a choice, since it's Carlton's head that might be rolling."

Another sigh. "I still can't believe Carlton was involved, but all the evidence points at him. And he has motive."

"His family connection." Tommy inserted his hand under Finn's cotton T-shirt. The feel of Finn's warm, dry skin comforted him.

"Misguided loyalty for an illegitimate son. I can sell that to a jury."

"Yes, Mister Crown Prosecutor."

"Doesn't change the fact he's just as culpable as Farraday was of misleading the public he swore to serve."

Tommy snuggled closer and kissed Finn's shoulder before nestling on his chest again. "Nothing you can do in the middle of the night, Finn. Go to sleep."

Chapter Thirty-One

FINN

"MISS CARSTAIRS, can you find me an urgent slot in Carlton's calendar, please? Preferably today?"

The well-preserved, middle-aged secretary, who the rest of the office lovingly referred to as Carlton's bulldog, looked over her rimless glasses at Finn. "Mr. Carlton has called in sick, Mr. DeHavilland. He hasn't given us notice of how long he will be indisposed, but I'll make a note you wish to see him."

Finn knew arguing with her was futile. "Thank you." He was also well aware of how urgent his talk with Carlton was, so he walked back to his own office to get his coat. If the grieving father wasn't coming to the office, the office was going to have to come to the father.

HE'D HAD almost an hour on the train toward Carlton's house to contemplate what he was going to tell him, but he still dreaded any possible outcome. He didn't know whether he preferred a Carlton throwing out any possible explanation or one that succumbed to his senior prosecutor's accusations without recourse. Either way he was going to have to stand his ground as if it wasn't his mentor and career-long friend he was accusing of fraud.

Even near midday, there was a sharp northerly wind in the affluent neighborhood making the air chilly, and Finn was happy to be wearing his scarf during his brisk walk from the train station to Carlton's house. Luckily it wasn't the first time he'd visited, but it was the first time without an invitation. He doubted he'd be welcome this time.

The house was surrounded by a garden that clearly benefitted from a wife with green thumbs and no other hobby than to putter in that garden. Finn doubted Carlton gave it any thought. Finn, on the other hand, studied the flowers and borders as he slowly walked up to the door, realizing all too soon he was stalling the inevitable. He straightened his back and took one last breath in before ringing the doorbell.

"Finn, so nice to see you!" Mrs. Carlton greeted him. She was clearly surprised, but, as a wife of a well-to-do man befitted, she was all smiles and welcoming gestures. "Come on inside. Carlton is in the back garden. I'll make you some tea."

From the quick succession of sentences coming from Mrs. Carlton, Finn deduced she knew something was wrong, and Finn's arrival had only added to that certainty. Looking at the coatrack in the hallway, Finn hesitated but eventually decided he wasn't going to take his coat off just yet. He only took his cap off and walked toward the back garden still holding it in his hand.

As he walked up to Carlton, who was sitting in the shade of a huge magnolia tree, Bill Carlton looked up at him as if he was expecting him. "Finn. Pull up a chair. Sit. It's lovely out here."

Before Finn could respond, Mrs. Carlton was there with a tray. "I'll bring out the tea in a minute, dear, but I thought you'd like a biscuit since it's almost time for lunch." She turned to Finn. "You've been on the train. I'll make both of you sandwiches, then. What do you think?"

Just as Finn wanted to tell her that was not necessary, she turned around and walked back to the kitchen.

Carlton sighed. He looked up momentarily and then talked in a subdued voice. "Grace isn't aware of anything that goes on at the office, so I'd like you to be discreet."

Finn nodded. He'd rehearsed what he was going to say a hundred times by now but knew he would never be able to get everything out there before Carlton derailed him. He was going to give it his best effort, though. "I know why you're home and not at the office. I also know what happened to Frank Farraday last night. In fact I was there."

Carlton smiled. "What does Frank Farraday have to do with me not coming to the office? I was simply feeling a bit under the weather and decided I could work from home."

"I know—" Finn stopped speaking as Grace Carlton walked toward him with a pot of tea.

"Sandwiches will be ready in a moment." She put the pot down and was gone even before Finn could finish saying thank you.

"I overheard your fight with the woman who claims—"

Again Grace appeared with another tray, this time with small plates and cutlery and paper napkins adorned with bright sunflowers. In the middle was a stack of small, neatly decrusted and cut white bread sandwiches. Finn had no idea how she could have made them in the short time he'd been in the garden.

"I'll leave you alone now," she said. "The tea needs another five minutes, darling."

Carlton's stern nod at his wife made it clear to Finn that Carlton was well aware of the end of Finn's sentence, so Finn didn't start talking as soon as Grace was out of earshot.

Instead, after a long, tense silence, it was Carlton who started. "You have no context for what you heard."

"I know," Finn admitted calmly, "but it was fairly clear. You have a son, and that son is… was Frank Farraday."

To Finn's relief and Carlton's defense, he didn't argue. Finn took that to mean he was right.

"I'm sorry for your loss."

Carlton shook his head. "I didn't know about him until he was already in the Metropolitan Police Force. His mother kept it a secret from me." He looked toward the house for a moment. "Needless to say, Grace still doesn't know."

"I think you should tell her, Bill."

"Why? I can't possibly do that to her."

Finn took a deep breath in to muster courage. "This is a courtesy visit. I have an appointment with the Attorney General this evening to suggest he relieve you of your appointment."

"Wha…?" Carlton looked at Finn with his mouth half open and the word unfinished.

Then it seemed to dawn on him, and Finn wanted to put him out of his misery.

"Frank Farraday had several people high up the ranks protecting him. These people are the reason why he could continue to do the things he did and remain unpunished. I have evidence strongly suggesting you were one of those people."

"He was lazy and nonchalant. He made mistakes. Do you know a copper who's never made a mistake? Even your Tommy has been the suspect in an inquiry."

"Leave DS Drummond out of it, please," Finn interrupted.

"I'm just saying nobody's perfect. And yes, Frank made mistakes, for which he lost his job. They didn't have to shoot him for it!"

Finn could see the pain in Carlton's otherwise always stoic features. He knew he was only going to make it worse, but a large part of why he wanted to talk to Carlton before everything was exposed was that he wanted to prepare him for the things Carlton hopefully didn't know about.

"He was shot because he threatened Ayse Kartal and DS Drummond with a handgun."

"Why would he do that? He wasn't a violent man."

Finn was wavering between wondering if Carlton was really so blind and remembering what a great actor he'd been as a prosecutor. He decided to give him the benefit of the doubt.

"We have evidence linking him to several of the rapes he investigated and four unsolved murders, Bill."

"No."

Finn felt sorry for his boss. Carlton's eyes spoke of disbelief and regret, or maybe Finn was just reading that last emotion because he hoped for it.

"You are on record regarding the decision not to prosecute on several of the rape cases, sir."

"And lucky for you, in most of those cases your objection to my decision was noted as well." Carlton got up from his seat. "I think it best you leave now."

"I simply wanted to give you a heads-up before I saw the Attorney General."

Carlton turned around. "In light of that, your presence here can be construed as a conflict of interest, just like my decision regarding Frank's cases will be. So leave and don't come back."

Finn looked at the beautiful sandwiches and cold tea. His watch told him it was past his lunchtime and he should be hungry, but he wasn't. He started to leave.

"Ask your sergeant why he had a standing appointment with his DSI every Tuesday. And why he used you as an excuse with his partner to go there alone."

Finn stood rigid, not turning to face Carlton. He dismissed the statements as those uttered by a desperate man who knew where he could hurt him the most, closest to home. He said nothing more as he walked out through the corridor, tipping his cap at Grace Carlton, who clearly had no idea what was going on.

On the train, he kept hearing Carlton's words. Even if Carlton had said them to drive a wedge between him and Tommy... *especially* if that's why Carlton had told him, he had to confront Tommy about it. He had to know if it was true and whether Tommy had betrayed him. He had to know what other lies Tommy had told him.

Finn shook his head. He couldn't think about Tommy that way, not until he'd heard his side of the story. Besides, he had other fish to fry first.

After this morning, his appointment with the Attorney General was going to be a walk in the park.

Chapter Thirty-Two

TOMMY

AROUND 7:00 p.m., Tommy got a text message from Finn asking him to come to St Dunstan's in the East, a church garden that had been bombed during World War II and that was now open to the public. Finn had taken him there before, showing off his penchant for finding romantic, secluded spaces to talk in the otherwise busy city.

He knew Finn had an appointment to see the Attorney General, so the message worried him that it hadn't gone well.

At that time of night, it wasn't too hard to find a parking space in that area of the City, and Tommy walked the rest of the way there. When he passed the vine-covered ruins, he saw Finn sitting on the bench near the fountain in the fading light.

"Did your meeting not go well?"

Finn looked up, his forehead beset by deep lines. He also appeared utterly exhausted.

"He found my evidence warranted a thorough investigation, and he's going to officially suspend Carlton from tomorrow."

Tommy sat next to Finn on the bench, resting his back against it. Finn remained sitting upright.

"Why did you see DSI Stanton every Thursday without Stevie?"

Fuck!

Tommy knew if he lied to Finn, he'd see right through it. Besides, his appointment with Stanton was every Tuesday. He had no doubt his too-smart-for-his-own-good prosecutor had intentionally made the mistake to lure him out.

"It was every Tuesday."

"So you're not denying it?"

Tommy sat up and leaned his elbows on his knees. "Right after we were transferred to Stanton, he accosted me in the loos and told me to come see him on Tuesday. Alone. When he asked me to make some excuse to Stevie so she wouldn't be with me, I knew it wasn't for anything good."

"And you used me as an excuse."

It wasn't a question, and Tommy noticed. He was going to have to stick to only the truth.

"You know Stevie. She thinks you're the bee's knees. Telling her I had a standing lunch date with you on Tuesday was the only thing not met with a questioning look. I also knew she wouldn't check up on me for that."

"So what did you and Stanton discuss on *your* lunch dates?"

"They weren't lunch dates," Tommy was quick to rebut. Then he realized that wasn't the real question. "He wanted me to keep him up to date on our progress."

Finn got up from the bench and walked over to the fountain, which was a large, flat boulder where the water bubbled up in the center and flowed smoothly over the rock.

Despite the fact it was rapidly growing darker, Tommy resisted the urge to get up to stand next to the man he loved. He knew by now that Finn's legendary self-control was not as infallible as he liked, and distance helped.

"Did it occur to you even once that he might be one of the inside people helping Farraday?"

"He said he needed to protect you, but he could only do it if he knew what danger you were getting yourself into."

Finn shook his head. "I never expected you to fall for such a lame excuse."

"Finn, he told me Frank Farraday's name before you even briefed us on the cases. He warned me about how dangerous that man was. And let's not forget he was on my side when Marchand tried to get me thrown out of the Met."

"I remember," Finn replied flatly. "But that fact makes him an easy target for Farraday."

"I only gave him the information he requested, and even then I tried to stay as vague as possible."

"And he bought that?"

"Yes."

"Then you're an even bigger fool than I thought."

Tommy sighed, letting his head fall forward. "What if he was right? What if he was playing both sides? In on what Farraday was doing but feeling loyal toward his job and you, a senior Crown Prosecutor. What if he wasn't lying and was actually trying to protect us? When we were assigned to him he told us we weren't reporting to him, but that he'd look out for us to alert us if we came too close to the truth and were setting off red flags. What if he was as afraid of tipping off insiders as we were? I believe his weekly meeting with me was his way to keep this as close to his vest as he could."

"What if he was playing you, Tom?"

"I can't win with you, can I? You can confide in Ayse all you want, tell her all about the case, but if I have a sounding board as well, I'm blasted for it."

"I told you about confiding in Ayse. You didn't tell me anything about Stanton."

"And what? You're jealous?"

"Don't go there," Finn hissed. He turned around and pointed his finger at Tommy. "You lied to me."

If looks could kill, Tommy would be dead now.

Tommy knew he had to go for broke. "It was a lie of omission. You always say that is the one lie you can get a jury to forgive."

"If the reason is solid enough."

"I trusted Stanton. I *trust* Stanton. Don't ask me why. Just like you, I have a gut instinct I tend to follow. That doesn't mean I wasn't cautious. If this case has taught me anything, it's that everyone has an agenda and even the people closest to us can betray us."

Finn didn't say anything, but the mean look on his face was gone.

"We were all alone in this, Finn. Trust no one? That's easier said than done. He coerced me into giving him information, but only because he knew that being my supervisor wouldn't be enough of a reason for me to give it up. He knew my loyalty would lie with you."

"And now?" Finn looked to be mellowing. He was standing less upright, and his face was softer. Also, he was actually looking at Tommy.

"Still the same."

"You still should have told me."

"And what would have happened then? You would have excluded me from your investigation."

"No."

"It wasn't like I could go to the DPS and tell on Stanton."

"I know."

Tommy exhaled as if he'd been holding his breath for the last ten minutes. Maybe he had.

"I still would have liked it if you'd told me."

"Why?"

"So I would have known that there was someone else listening in."

"Noted."

Finn wasn't smiling, but the muscles around his mouth were twitching, so Tommy knew he'd won this small victory.

"Now will you come home with me? I made fried rice with chicken because I knew I'd need to heat it up for you and it heats up pretty well."

"Okay."

By now it was so dark they could barely see each other.

"The car is parked over there."

"Let's go home."

Chapter Thirty-Three

FINN

HE FELT totally depleted by the time he arrived at his apartment. This had been one day to forget as quickly as possible.

Tommy pushed him in the direction of the sitting room. "Go. Drop into the couch and try not to fall asleep before I heat up supper."

He sank into his old leather sofa, but as soon as he felt himself drift away, Tommy walked in with two flutes of something bubbly.

"Alcohol?" Finn asked.

"Cava."

"What are we celebrating?"

Tommy shrugged. "I thought I'd either need to console you or congratulate you." He handed one glass to Finn and took a sip of his before sitting down next to him.

"Getting Carlton suspended is nothing to celebrate."

"I know, but it's the right thing to do."

Finn took a sip as well. It went down so smoothly he wondered why he didn't drink this more often. He raised his glass. "To doing the right thing, whether it feels good or not." He drank again, this time a bigger gulp. Tommy was smiling at him.

The microwave pinged, and he watched Tommy get up to go to the kitchen. He knew it made sense to follow him, since he didn't like to eat in his sitting room and the kitchen table was better equipped for that.

He was surprised at how much half a glass of bubbly affected his legs, but he made it to the kitchen without knocking anything over. "You want to eat in here? Okay," Tommy said, sipping from his glass as he set the table with only the most necessary utensils.

To Finn's surprise, he only set one place.

"You're not eating?"

"I ate about two hours ago."

"Mmmh." What a disappointment.

Tommy sat down where he always sat and dished out the rice and chicken. It smelled delicious.

Finn eyed his glass of bubbly suspiciously. He hardly ever drank. Was he really such a cheap date? Then he realized he hadn't eaten anything since breakfast.

"You're drunk already." Tommy giggled. "I remember that pint of lager just before you kissed me."

When Tommy topped up his glass, Finn saw the bottle was almost empty. Had Tommy drunk the rest? No wonder he was giggling.

Finn wasn't terribly hungry, but he did eat some since Tommy's cooking was always too good to leave. He even insisted they do the dishes afterward.

Tommy didn't seem to feel as much influence as Finn, or at least it manifested itself differently. Tommy became very touchy-feely, grabby almost. And although Finn was playing hard to get, he found himself enjoying it.

"The bubbly is making you look good tonight, Mister Prosecutor," Tommy said as he handed the last bowl to Finn to dry. He reached up to put the wok away and rubbed against Finn. "And it's making me randy," he purred.

"We can't leave that unanswered, now can we?" Finn said with more confidence than usual.

Tommy grew serious. "Don't promise me what you can't deliver."

Instead of answering the taunt, he kissed Tommy passionately, leaving both of them out of breath. As Tommy rubbed his groin against him, Finn could feel his words rang true.

In the back of his mind, Finn felt a niggling doubt about whether he could do what Tommy expected of him, but there was only one way to find out. He knew by now that if he couldn't go all the way, he could still stay in bed with Tommy and more or less finish what they started without running off to the bathroom. It was a hard-fought trust between them, but it was certainly there.

"Let's go, then, before I burst right here in the kitchen."

Tommy trailed off in the direction of the hallway, and Finn surveyed the kitchen one more time before turning the lights off and following. In the sitting room he finished the last of the cava.

When he entered the bedroom, Tommy was sitting on the bed in his briefs and T-shirt.

"Leaving some for me to take off?" Finn suggested.

Tommy opened his arms in a welcoming gesture, and as Finn came closer, pulled at Finn's clothes. Tommy's hands seemed to be everywhere at once, and although Finn felt his flight reaction kick in, he stayed put. This was Tommy. Tommy, who would stop at the first sign of discomfort from Finn's side. Tommy, who knew they'd agreed that Finn could stop their actions with a single word. It wasn't a moot agreement. Finn had actually asked Tommy to stop on several occasions, and Tommy had pulled away, despite being left hanging every single time. Finn felt infinitely guilty about all those instances and had purposely had that second glass of cava so he'd be able to continue this time.

"Will you trust me?" Tommy whispered against Finn's mouth as he broke their kiss.

Finn pulled away just enough so he could look Tommy in the eye.

"Trust me enough to leave everyone else out of this," Tommy continued in his velveteen voice. "This is just you and me. And everything we do will be good."

Finn nodded so faintly he doubted Tommy had actually seen it. Tommy's skin felt good under his hands. He'd grown accustomed to it and the tight muscles underneath. Without lifting his hands he pushed up the gray T-shirt Tommy was still wearing, and Tommy helped him by pulling it over his head. As soon as Tommy relaxed against the headboard, his near-washboard stomach disappeared, but it reappeared as Tommy straightened his back to come closer to Finn again.

"Your turn."

"My…?"

"You're still dressed."

Finn looked down between their bodies. He was still wearing his work trousers and shirt, of which the shirttails were pulled out of the trousers, but other than that, Tommy was right. He pulled back, but Tommy was quick to grab him.

"Uh-uh." He shook his head. "I'm not letting you move off the bed."

"But I need to—"

"Your clothes will be just fine lying on top of mine. On the floor." Tommy was smiling, and Finn knew part of that was a little mockery about how Finn always needed to neatly fold his clothes otherwise he couldn't sleep.

"I suppose I could—"

"I know you can," Tommy interrupted while he started unbuttoning Finn's shirt.

At least the buttons weren't flying. Finn could live with his clothes on the floor, since they needed washing anyway, but he liked this shirt, and he was rubbish at sewing buttons on again.

As soon as Finn's shirt was open, Tommy pulled him flush against his chest, and Finn reveled in feeling their bare skin touch. By now this was one of the things he could stay relaxed with while they were kissing, and even as Tommy pulled Finn's shirt over his shoulders, they weren't leaving his comfort zone yet. That changed when Tommy flipped them over until he was lying on top of Finn. The evidence of Tommy's arousal dug into his hip, and it brought back memories he didn't want while he was alone with Tommy. Tommy by now was an old hand at this, and he waited, giving Finn ample time to call it to a stop before slowly moving his hand toward the button and zipper on Finn's trousers.

Finn was breathing hard, hovering between asking Tommy to end it altogether and pulling him closer so he could devour him. He fervently hoped he wouldn't panic this time. As long as he could keep himself convinced that what he was feeling was arousal and need, not his dreaded flight reaction, he was going to be fine.

Tommy managed to open up Finn's trousers and started peeling them off him while Finn wiggled around to facilitate him.

Finn let out a nervous giggle as he kicked most of the clothes off the bed until they were lying on the bed in just their briefs.

Tommy was still holding him close. "Just you and me, Finn. And anything goes as long as we let the other know we're both okay with it. Or not."

Finn nodded, feeling both very self-conscious and strangely comforted by the fact they were practically naked together in a fully lit room. There was none of the sneaking around, huddled under a blanket, listening for noises from the rest of the house or from people who could overhear what they were doing. All of that didn't matter. There was just him and Tommy, like Tommy had asked.

"Just you and me," Finn repeated as he dared to lead Tommy's hand to the bulge tenting his underpants. His breathing became even more pronounced when he felt the warmth of Tommy's hand seep through the cotton of his briefs, and his body reacted to it. He could blame the alcohol for the reaction being more relaxed than he expected.

"Feel good?"

Finn was surprised to see Tommy panting as well.

"Tell me if it becomes too much."

"I will." *Just not right now*. Finn didn't care that this was the alcohol talking. He wanted to see more of Tommy. He wanted to see all of him. Almost without permission from his brain, Finn inserted his hand into Tommy's briefs and enveloped Tommy's erection. Tommy inhaled sharply and pulled his head back with a smile.

"This okay?"

"Fuck, yes."

Tommy raised himself on his arms until he was hovering over Finn, their groins still close together. By slowly moving back and forth, he slipped his cock in and out of Finn's fist while they both watched.

A small wet patch was forming on Finn's gray cotton briefs.

"Take it out," Tommy demanded.

Finn used his other hand to pull the elastic on Tommy's briefs down to expose Tommy's ample erection.

"I meant yours," Tommy said, his voice strained by the effort of maintaining his position.

Finn looked up into Tommy's eyes, momentarily hesitating until Tommy dived down and kissed him.

"Your hand, touching both of us." Tommy continued the slow rocking, creating friction that felt so glorious Finn opened his legs so Tommy could lie between them and add to the sensation by grinding even closer. "Your cock and mine, together in your hand." Finn pulled his briefs down, and Tommy lined up his cock with Finn's, which by now was at full mast as well. "Fuck yes, feels as good as it looks."

"I can't look," Finn whispered against Tommy's mouth.

"You should."

Tommy raised himself to give Finn the chance, but Finn pulled him closer again. "I want to be on top."

"Ooh, Mister Crown Prosecutor," Tommy mocked.

"Stop it."

Tommy let himself fall to the bed, so Finn rolled on top of him. "I didn't mean stop doing… what we're doing. I meant stop calling me that. I'm not him here in bed."

"I know."

Finn barely dared to grind himself against Tommy because every movement, no matter how minute, made sensations shoot from his groin to the rest of his body. He was so close to coming even the kissing was too much, and he dived down against Tommy's neck. He wanted to make it good for Tommy first but feared he wouldn't last long enough.

Tommy grabbed the back of his head with one hand and his arsecheek with the other. He turned toward Finn and groaned loudly in his ear.

The hot, sticky jizz that coated his hand was enough for Finn to give up holding back, and he thrust into his hand, adding his own release to the mixture.

Tommy's grip on him was tight, but instead of feeling caught with nowhere to go, Finn savored the closeness and the love he felt coming off Tommy in waves. Part of him wanted to clean up the mess they made, but this wasn't just about him. He knew Tommy didn't mind, and he wanted to show him he was more important than his hang-ups. He rolled off Tommy but kept him close so they ended up on their sides, still touching head to knees.

"You okay?" he asked Tommy as soon as he had enough breath to talk.

"Perfect," Tommy whispered. "Don't move yet."

"The lights are still on."

"I don't care."

Finn waited, but Tommy rolled his eyes. "Fine. Get up, get a washcloth, and turn down the lights."

"I can do it the way you want it."

Tommy laughed. "No, you can't." He pushed Finn out of bed.

As Finn walked to the bathroom he could hear Tommy say, "But that's okay. It's you, and I happen to like you."

In the bathroom he threw his soiled briefs in the wash basket and looked at himself in the mirror. He hadn't run away.

Chapter Thirty-Four

TOMMY

HE STOOD leaning against one of the marble columns, looking at the door to the robing room, which remained closed for now.

He'd stayed inside the courtroom just long enough to hear the jury foreman announce that the suspect was guilty of the major charge and had then popped out into the elaborate Old Bailey hallway. In the past, he'd passed the time reading the inscriptions on the wall and near the ceiling, all important sayings about the justice system and how it was supposed to work, but by now he'd stood here so many times he knew them by heart. His own warden of justice was about to emerge, and that was who he was waiting for.

Still dressed in his robes, his collar undone and his wig safely tucked away inside a shiny black box with his name written on it in gold letters, Finn DeHavilland walked out of the robing room with a spring in his step, a smirk on his face, and heavy-looking file folders under his arm.

"I know you won, but usually you hide your glee a bit better," Tommy remarked as Finn came close enough to hear him. He took some of the folders from Finn without asking for them.

"Then I'm not smiling about winning. It's Friday. We have a whole weekend ahead of us. What's for dinner?"

"Shrimp pad Thai. From scratch."

"Naturally," Finn replied with a sparkle in his eye.

Tommy soaked up the attention he got from Finn, but it sometimes bordered on making him uncomfortable, because he never knew what the Crown Prosecutor was thinking. Unless he asked.

"I meet you here most Fridays after work. So what is making you so happy today?"

Finn kept smiling as they walked to one of the side doors and emerged in the street.

"It never ceases to amaze me how happy the idea of going home together makes me. A year ago I was settled in to live the rest of my life alone, and I wasn't even that miserable about it. Now I have a lovely man to go home with."

"Just lovely?"

Finn looked at him sideways. "You're fishing."

"Getting a compliment out of you is like pulling teeth sometimes," Tommy joked. He had a hard time preventing a smile from forming, though. "You're such a tough nut." He frowned to stress the point.

And then something totally out of the blue happened.

Finn grabbed him, pulled him close, and planted a kiss on his mouth, right there in the street. Tommy had a hard time keeping hold of the folders.

"Why, Mister Prosecutor," Tommy said, panting, after they broke apart and Finn took a few steps in the direction they had been walking. "You *are* happy, aren't you?"

Finn returned to where Tommy was standing. "Ecstatic, Detective Inspector Drummond."

He sounded calm and collected, but Tommy recognized the sparkle in his eyes and knew he was telling the truth.

"So shall we go home, then?" Tommy suggested.

"Let's drop these at the office, and then I'm all yours."

mmy eyed Finn as they walked along the street. "What? Not bringing work home?"

"I'm the chief now. I delegate."

Tommy snorted. "That'll be the day."

"I do," Finn said, defending himself.

"But you still want to know what everyone is doing and how they're doing it."

"That's my job."

"Most Chief Prosecutors take on very few court appearances themselves." Tommy was teasing, and he knew how Finn felt about prosecuting certain cases himself.

Finn smiled. "You'd hate me if I stopped doing what I like best."

Tommy nodded. "But you're serious about not working this weekend?"

"I didn't say I wasn't going to work. I'll go to the office tomorrow morning. But I thought I wouldn't take any work home for a change."

Tommy didn't know what to make of it, but he decided not to look for reasons. He was just going to enjoy having Finn's full attention when they were together.

Finn pushed open the door to the Crown Prosecutor's offices. "And let's get married."

This time Tommy did drop what he was holding.

ZAHRA OWENS is a multilingual globetrotter who loves big cities but also has a weak spot for the wide-open spaces that are so rare where she lives.

She likes her men every which way they come and never tries to change them. Men who are tough on the outside but have a huge soft center get extra credit, though, as do the strong, silent types who think they hide their damage well… but don't. She makes it her personal goal to find them their happily ever after, even if the road toward this leads via hospital beds, villas with gorgeous vistas, or ranges full of horses.

Zahra is a proud member of the Rainbow Romance Writers, a special interest chapter of the Romance Writers of America, and won't quit until M/M romances are treated like every other romance story. RWA allowed her into its Professional Authors Network, but she hasn't quit her day job yet since it allows her to work in a man's world. And what girl can resist that?

If Zahra had her wish, a day would have at least thirty-six hours, because how else would she find the time to finish all the novels still inside her head?

Website: http://zahraowens.com

Balance

By Zahra Owens

By day Cooper Miller is a bland paper pusher, a health and safety inspector who does everything by the book. Deciding he needs some excitement in his life, he sheds his off-the-rack suit and tan raincoat and signs up for an introductory session at a BDSM club. His welcome mat turns out to be Nando Arenas, the man who owns the new tattoo shop Cooper inspected just that morning. At first glance, Nando seems like forbidden territory, but when Cooper discovers a taste for being tied up and dominated, the enterprising tattoo artist delivers all the excitement Cooper could want.

http://www.dreamspinnerpress.com

Charity Starts at Home

By Zahra Owens

During the Christmas holidays, the affluent Haden knocks on the door of Quinn's homeless shelter with a proposition: he wants to help make Christmas a little brighter for the shelter's residents. But Quinn is suspicious of Haden's motives and money. The fact that their worlds are miles apart is painfully clear, and although Quinn finds he just might be able to love Haden, his own prejudices might block the way to a future together.

http://www.dreamspinnerpress.com

Cleary Palit

By Zahra Owens

Edward "Ted" Cleary and Cazimir Palit have shared everything for eight years. Well, almost everything. They own a successful business together, share a house in West Hollywood, and never travel anywhere without each other, but they've never slept in the same bed.

There's one more thing Ted hasn't shared with Caz. Ted has a mother, sister, and brother in Atlanta Caz has never met. With good reason. They threw Ted out when he wouldn't "change his ways," and he's never looked back. When Ted is rejected all over again, Caz steps up and proves he isn't the superficial man Ted always took him for, and Ted's long-hidden feelings might finally be returned.

http://www.dreamspinnerpress.com

Diplomacy

By Zahra Owens

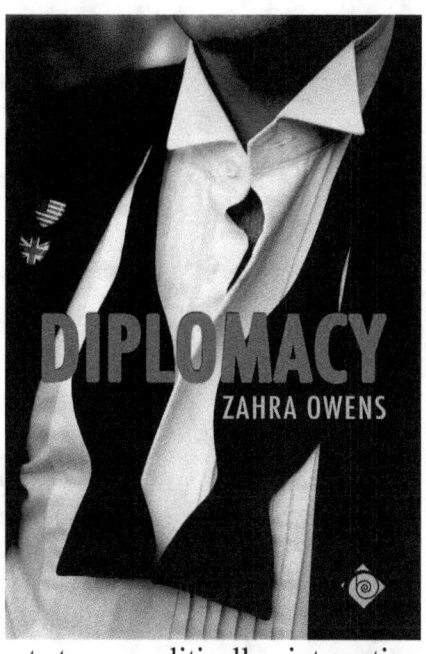

Jack Christensen has everything he ever wanted. He's a rising star in US Diplomacy, the youngest man to have been appointed as an Ambassador of the United States. A career diplomat who's just been sent to a politically interesting Embassy in Europe, he has the perfect wife, speaks five languages and has all the right credentials, yet there's something missing and he doesn't quite know what.

Then Lucas Carlton walks into an Embassy reception and introduces himself and his American fiancée. From the first handshake, the young Englishman makes an impression on Jack that leaves him confused and uncharacteristically insecure. Lucas' position as the British liaison to the American Embassy means they are forced to work together closely and they have a hard time denying the attraction between them, despite their current relationships.

When their women decide to go on a weekend trip together, Jack and Lucas start a passionate relationship, which continues long after their partners return. Diplomatic circles are notoriously conservative though, and they each know that the right woman by their side makes a very significant contribution to their success. Will they be able to make the right choices in their professional and personal lives? Or will they need to sacrifice one for the other?

http://www.dreamspinnerpress.com

Façade

By Zahra Owens

Jonas Hunter is a high-class body for hire with a small, exclusive, mostly male clientèle who pay big bucks for his undivided time and attention. Discretion is Jonas's middle name— he can play his role to the hilt for the client's benefit and at the same time disappear seamlessly into a crowd, safely anonymous.

He's persuaded to take on a new client who is everything he despises in a man: the effeminate, tantrum-throwing, attention-seeking bad boy of Paris haute couture named Nicky Bryant. Nicky's shows are outrageous and always good for a front cover, and his appearance never fails to turn heads. But Jonas soon learns Nicky is a carefully maintained façade himself.

As a fiery attraction grows, Jonas and Nicky have to find a way to walk the tightrope between their public and private personas. They'll need to learn to love and trust each other around the other people in their lives if they're going to share their hearts.

http://www.dreamspinnerpress.com

The Hand-me-down

By Zahra Owens

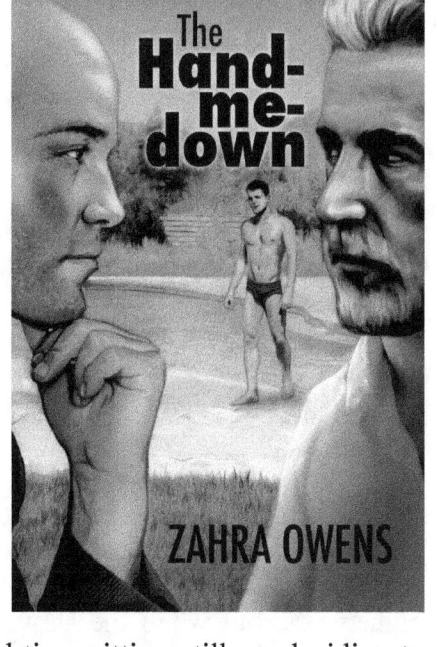

When a volcano erupts in Iceland and leaves globetrotting headhunter Jez Robinson stranded in Barcelona, he isn't sure what to do. He has a hard time sitting still, so deciding to make the best of his situation, he pays a visit to his old friend Nick Stone, a retired porn star he shares a history with. Only the visit doesn't go anything like Jez expected.

First Nick introduces Jamie, his much younger lover, a man so painfully shy he can't even bring himself to talk to strangers. The love he and Nick share is plain to Jez, but also puzzling, because Nick was never the monogamous type. Then Nick tells Jez he's dying and wants Jez to look after Jamie.

In his whole life, Jez has never committed to so much as a house plant, so at first he refuses. But Nick and Jamie are insistent, and soon Jamie worms his way into Jez's graces and his bed, determined to do the convincing Jez's heart needs.

http://www.dreamspinnerpress.com

Happiness for Beginners

By Zahra Owens

Jesse harbored a crush on his TV series costar, Kaye, for more than eight years, but when the show was canceled and he realized those years of playing gay hadn't convinced Kaye to leave the straight and narrow, Jesse turned his back on acting for good. Ten years later, Kaye is back in Jesse's life, on Christmas Eve—and the eve of his third divorce. Jesse's not sure his heart can take another beating, but Kaye has a few tricks up his sleeve—and a few truths from his own heart—that might just convince Jesse that the gifts of love and happiness are not just for Christmas.

http://www.dreamspinnerpress.com

I Can See Right Through You

By Zahra Owens

When Lander's Great Aunt Angie is shipped off to a convalescent home, she asks him to house-sit. Soon enough he finds out why: she wants him to keep James, a rather attractive and benevolent Victorian ghost, company. Their new friendship is threatened when a not-so-benevolent and very menacing burglar breaks into the house, threatening Lander—and the last thing he expects is for James to come to the rescue.

http://www.dreamspinnerpress.com

Isali Dreams

By Zahra Owens and
Stuart Wakefield

Diplomat and linguist Everett leads a quiet life on an Earth colony outpost until he's called on to translate for a strange creature discovered on a crashed ship. Despite the magnetic attraction he feels to it, Everett can't communicate well enough to resolve the apparent murder of the ship's pilot. At least not until Isali, the survivor, shows up in Everett's dreams.

Isali is on the run from a supreme being hellbent on destroying him, and Everett soon finds himself caught up in a fight for their lives. The increased intimacy between them triggers memories for Everett, but can he put the pieces together before Isali's nemesis destroys them both?

http://www.dreamspinnerpress.com

You Can't Choose Your Family

By Zahra Owens

Jay and Fran have been a couple for twenty years. They have a great relationship with only one minor bone of contention: while Fran is very much a member of Jay's extended family, to Fran's family, Jay is just "his business partner." It's not that Fran doesn't want to come out to his family; it's more that they don't want to hear it.

When Fran's father, an evangelical minister, dies, Fran hopes the rest of his family will be more accepting. This hope is nipped in the bud by his very conservative older brother, so Jay's mother steps in and invites Fran's mother over for Christmas... but will joining Fran's happy-go-lucky in-laws be too much for Fran's mother, or will they help her see the truth of just how much Jay means to Fran?

You Can Choose Your Friends

By Zahra Owens

Franklyn Galloway is the youngest son of a conservative Evangelical minister, and it goes without saying that he is stuck in the closet. He dreams of being an architect, but his father puts a stop to that faster than Fran can say "Frank Lloyd Wright." So when Fran meets popular, laid-back Jay Molenski, he does everything he can to deny the sparks flying all around them. It only works for so long.

After a brutal trip home, Fran finds himself staring down a fifth of vodka and a bottle of sleeping pills. How can Jay and his family make Fran see that he deserves not just love, but the freedom to be himself?

Clouds and Rain

A Clouds and Rain Story

By Zahra Owens

Flynn Tomlinson has drifted for several years, working odd jobs when he needs the money and moving on when he doesn't. He's content with his freestyle life, not tied down, not responsible for anyone but himself. Then he comes across a Help Wanted ad in a post office in Idaho and meets Gable Sutton. Gable can't pay Flynn until he sells his horses, but a serious accident has left him unable to work his ranch alone.

Working with horses beats stacking shelves at the supermarket, and so Flynn agrees to Gable's terms. What Flynn doesn't bargain for is being captivated by this gentle, lonely man who captures his heart and moves Flynn to take on an incredible burden: saving Gable's ranch.

http://www.dreamspinnerpress.com

Earth and Sky

A Clouds and Rain Story

By Zahra Owens

Hunter Krause knows better than anyone that running a ranch is hard work. Wranglers are hard to find, and even with Hunter's foreman and entire extended family on hand, the busy ranch is constantly short-handed. So when horses go missing, Hunter's brother-in-law hires a man Hunter would never have considered: Grant Jarreau, a man Hunter can't forgive for leaving Hunter's best friend Gable after an incapacitating accident.

Grant quickly fits in, befriending Hunter's sister and making himself invaluable. Despite Hunter's misgivings, he can't quite control his body's reactions to Grant, and he isn't sure what to do about it. Then Grant saves Hunter's young nephew from drowning and one thankful kiss opens doors Hunter never knew existed.

While Hunter and Grant tentatively move toward a relationship, the family's in an uproar, the ranch is struggling, they can't figure out what happened to the horses, and to top it all off, Grant is hiding something. Can Hunter learn to trust Grant, or will the turmoil already tearing up his family claim another victim?

http://www.dreamspinnerpress.com

Floods and Drought

A Clouds and Rain Story

By Zahra Owens

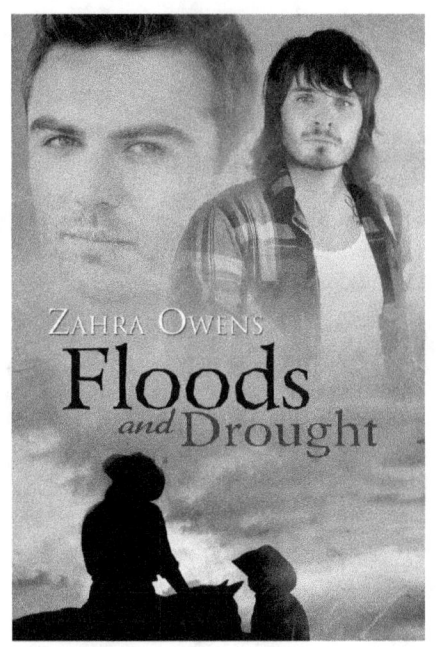

Tim Conroy knows all about patience. He's waited three years for Rory McCown to get out of jail after doing time for stealing horses from the Blue River Ranch. Now that Rory is eligible for parole, Tim makes it his goal to persuade his boss, Hunter Krause, to give Rory a second chance.

He almost regrets it when Hunter agrees. Rory is a morose loner one moment, then arrogant and overconfident the next. The attraction between them is still there, but as soon as they start to get close, an old enemy throws a wrench in the works… and their fledgling relationship may not be strong enough to weather the coming storm.

http://www.dreamspinnerpress.com

Moon and Stars

A Clouds and Rain Story

By Zahra Owens

After an affair with a married DA led to scandal and disbarment, Cooper Nelson left his legal career in shambles and found solace working as a hand at the Blue River Ranch. Eight years later, during a rare visit into town, Cooper bumps into Kelly Freed, a man he left behind fifteen years earlier when he started out as an attorney. Unfortunately, Kelly is running for sheriff and his wife is terminally ill, so Kelly can't even consider rekindling their relationship. Cooper knows from sad experience that hiding the truth leads to lives being ruined, so for his part, he refuses to be anybody's dirty secret.

In the meantime circumstances at neighboring Blackwater Ranch have taken a desperate turn. Gable's friend Calley has breast cancer, and when Gable and Flynn take in Calley's kids, they need help from their friends. Cooper and Kelly's combined talents are put to work to ensure Gable can make a bid to become the legal father of his children, and that Calley's affairs are in order if worse comes to worst. For Cooper, staying away from Kelly was never easy, and now with a common cause, Cooper finds he can't stop himself from seeking the man out.

http://www.dreamspinnerpress.com

ILLUSIONS

S. A. Ozment

http://www.dreamspinnerpress.com